The MAGE CROWN

The
Immortal Coil Saga
Book 2

For my family.
And especially for Dax.

THE LANDS OF THE

IMMORTAL COIL

SAGA

Reaches Outpost

Seahome

HOUSE ELIDAHL

HOUSE ORTAK

HOUSE LORCE

HOUSE KORR

Reaches Outpost

HOUSE MUNNE

HOUSE SUHONNE

VHALEESE

STONE GIANT MOUNTAINS

OLD ARDWYN

ATHTULL KEEP

DARK MOUNTAINS

Arad River

NORTHERN TERRITORY

MORNING HILL

KARTH

Legion Outpost

CALLIWAY

THE HANDAALS

Arad River

BANMORROW

THE PEARL CITY

Cliff's Edge

The Lakrim Sea

PROLOGUE

The dust had settled days ago.

Athtull Keep lay in ruins at the foot of the Dark Mountains. Most of the fires had dwindled to a smolder beneath the slabs of stone that lay haphazardly across the small valley where the Keep once stood. Animals were returning, nosing through the wreckage, and any survivors were well on their way south into Karth.

A doe set one delicate hoof in front of the other, interested in the greenery that protruded from a patchy section of the ruins. Shards of broken glass, scattered among the stones, sparkled in the late afternoon sun. Though bruised and tattered, bright blossoms caught the doe's attention, and she picked her way toward them. As her soft nose touched the blooms, a groan wafted from beneath the rubble. She lifted her head and froze, eyes scanning the area for danger. The sound faded away, and she hesitated, then lowered her head again until a stone shifted. She bolted into the forest.

Rock groaned and gravel sifted through spaces between the slabs, while sharp cracks echoed throughout the wreckage. The low, rumbling moans ebbed and flowed, then were joined by a different type of sound. Heavy panting grew louder until a dust-covered hand emerged from the small space beneath one of the slabs. More scrabbling revealed another hand, this one wrapped in a thick metal cuff. Before long, it was followed by a head, its tight curls a multitude of swirling colors barely visible through the dust, pushing through until a body emerged from the rubble.

The man lay still for several minutes, his breath coming hard and fast. His hands gripped the ground, fingers taking their time to savor the freedom to move. Around him, the forest was still busy with rustling leaves, soft grunts, and chirps from creatures flitting and moving about. A gentle breeze blew, so soft and delicate it seemed to mock the devastation at the forest's feet. After a few deep breaths, the man heaved himself to all fours, tucking his knees beneath him. Leaning forward, he cradled the cuffed arm with the other, staring at it in surprise.

"Of all the things to save me." His voice was a ragged whisper. Sitting back on his heels, the Handaalian man surveyed the surrounding wreckage. His brows furrowed over his golden eyes — bright, even through the layer of dust clinging to his mahogany skin — and he took in the scene surrounding him. The magnitude of the collapse stole his breath, and he shook his head, unsure of how he could still be breathing. Athtull Keep had nearly brought down the entire mountain when it fell, collapsing from within. He had felt the magical surge just before tremors rocked the fortress. He was certain the mage Venalise was to blame, but entangled in the dark, earthy chaos there was another energy unfamiliar to his own fire-wielding senses.

A cry rang out from the cliffs above the Keep, followed by the emergence of an atranoch. The great creature, larger than a horse, launched from its perch, unfurling its broad wings and banking to the north. Plinus shielded his eyes from the daylight and followed the creature's path until it disappeared from sight. He listened intently, but only heard the occasional creak and groan from branches swaying in the breeze. The forest had gone quiet.

He rose, legs unsteady as cramped muscles stretched, and scanned the ruins. A handful of days ago, there stood a fortress he feared he would never escape; Athtull Keep had been reduced to piles of rubble and ruin, a frail shadow of what it had been. He swallowed, but dust caught in his parched throat, and he fell into a coughing fit. Plinus swayed as he caught his breath, scanning about for anything to help him in his weakened state.

There.

Many ironwood timbers from the bailey yard still stood, but the wooden wall closest to the Keep had fallen and burned. Plinus took a faltering step in that direction, hoping to find some embers still smoldering. He hoped... as he neared, he sensed them even before the glow of coals became evident. He quickened his pace. The little man fell to his knees, paying no mind to any danger to his flesh, landing among the glowing embers.

Plinus held his hands over the coals, letting the heat sift through his fingers as easily as one might run their fingers beneath a stream of water. Warm energy crept through his arms and into his body; as it did, he felt strength building within. While he watched the fire, colors deepened and embers brightened, tiny licks of flame darting and dancing along the charred wood. He steadied his breathing and stood with his arms still outstretched. His small frame trembled but the wiry muscles in his limbs remained taut and steady. The flames rose with him.

With considerable effort, he resisted the urge to draw the fire into an unfelled timber beside him. He had no desire to destroy. Restoring his elemental energy had been his first aim — now that he was coherent and able, he switched his focus to finding nourishment.

He took another look around. There were no dead. Baskets and carts lay scattered, tossed about haphazardly, but there were no bodies, neither of people nor animals anywhere. Odd, he thought, considering the devastation before him. But then he caught the odor that emanated from beneath the rubble, wondering how many did not make it out of the fall. He glanced at the cuff around his forearm again. If he had not had that on when the Keep fell, the stone that pinned his arm would have crushed it, trapping him along with all the other unfortunate souls that must lay beneath the Keep. Twisting and grinding the cuff between the ground and the stone had taken time, almost more than he had had, but he had finally freed himself.

Heaviness pressed down on him, the weight of so much death finally registering. He returned his attention to the fire. Watching the light for a time, Plinus knew what he had to do. Most of the people who had lived and worked here had no choice. They were prisoners, as he was. Everyone who was able had fled, and now, the abandoned dead had no one to invoke Lakron. No one to say the words that would send them into the After. He could not let Lors and Venalise's cruelty be their end. They deserved better; his sustenance would have to wait.

However, words weren't enough. Most of the folk in the Keep were from the Handaals. After King Lasten of Karth had invaded and established himself as the sovereign ruler, Venalise managed to lure many to follow her north. Most of them would be of the Lakrimini faith, but even if they weren't, Plinus knew his god wouldn't hesitate to usher them into the After.

Plinus pulled a little harder on the flames; this time, he allowed them to overtake another fallen timber nearby. As the fire grew, he spread his arms wide to take in its energy. When he felt he could hold no more in his weakened state, he released his control, and the flames retreated into the embers. He took care as he picked his way to a part of the rubble that allowed him to get as close to the center of the fallen Keep as possible.

He stood for a time, the weighty sadness threatening to consume him. Then he took a seat and removed his thin leather boots. Typically, the invocation was done over several quiet hours before it was time for the words, but he did not have time for that. Plinus had pleaded with his gods for the last few hours as he worked to pry himself from the Keep's grasp. Surely, they were still listening to him now.

He rose, taking a step onto one of the slabs of stone, now warmed with the power he exuded. Plinus crossed his arms over his heart and inhaled deeply. The diminutive priest started to hum, low at first, then changing pitches as a melody formed. The surrounding air dried and warmed around his still form. Then, the humming stopped, and he began to speak.

"uqal kwa xudnt
uqal kwa gnuba
paa luk adh cuync
elku kwa waudk ug unn NEGAL!"

Plinus flung his arms wide. In front of him, a faint orange glow surged from the wreckage. He kept his arms wide and began a slow rotation, turning to face each part of the fallen Keep; as he did, the warm glow followed. He drew his arms back into his body when the circle was completed, muttering a whispered prayer. The glow emanating from the ruins faded away and the spaces went dark. In the following silence, Plinus whispered a prayer as he raised his hands to cover his face, fine grains of sand and dust falling from his fingers. His shoulders sagged as his hands dropped back to his sides, but he smiled. He had brought peace to the poor souls beneath the stone.

The sun was in its descent when he finally made his way out of the ruins of the Keep. The ritual had taken its toll — he was a husk of his former self. So many days without food or water had taken its toll, and now that he was free, he needed more sustenance than the embers could provide. He was exhausted, but he had no time to sleep. The priest scavenged what he could — a blanket and some over-ripe fruit — then looked to the south and the road that led to the lower pass. There was an urgent message he must deliver to Prince Jael and Regealth.

When Athtull Keep had crumbled days ago, Plinus witnessed Venalise's escape. His good fortune had put him in the terrarium, where he watched through the glass as the wicked mage Venalise ushered Sia and a handful of soldiers out of the Keep. He was certain that Venalise was still in possession of the Gate stone, the magical crystal capable of pulling beings across dimensions, and she had found something exceptional about the child. Their heavy cloaks and the large bundles they lashed to their horses could only mean one thing: Venalise was heading for the Stone Reaches, and the consequences would be dire if she made it.

PART ONE

CHAPTER 1

Sweat trickled down the sides of Amarynn's face, plastering her auburn curls to her cheeks. She grimaced and raised Frost in heaven's guard position, stepping back with her right leg to brace herself.

"Y'know, it's not entirely fair that you are using that big bastard to fight me." Aron changed his tactic and spun, swinging his short sword upwards. The two blades connected, the sound of metal on metal reverberating off the palace walls. Amarynn used Aron's momentum to twist around, bringing the flat side of her broadsword into her opponent's armored side. This unexpected move from the five-and-a-half-foot woman, and the shock of the impact, forced him to drop his weapon. She leaned down and retrieved it, twirling it in her right hand.

"Who said we were fighting fair?" Though her expression was serious, her hazel eyes glinted with amusement.

Aron sighed heavily, wiping his sweaty palms on his breeches before pulling out his dagger. Amarynn chuckled and tossed the swords to the ground. She winked and retrieved her own two daggers, brandishing them melodramatically.

"Are you serious?" His brow furrowed as he set his feet in a defensive stance.

"Oh, very serious," she countered, then charged.

He braced and blocked her right hand, sending one of her twin daggers flying. Amarynn grunted, then used her free hand to grab his wrist, pulling him off-balance. A tall man, Aron hit the ground hard, and she was on him before he could recover. Straddling his broad chest, her knees pinned his arms to his sides, and her remaining dagger pressed against his throat, the metal scraping against the stubble on his neck.

Amarynn leaned in close, a wicked grin on her face, Aron's heady scent filling her nostrils. He narrowed his icy blue eyes when she grinned mischievously. "You need to work on your balance, you big oaf."

He grimaced and braced himself against the floor. "And you need to work on your manners, girl," he hissed.

"What did you call me?"

In one swift move, Aron arched his back and threw her off. Before she hit the ground, she twisted and rolled, but not before Aron's knee connected with her shoulder blade, grinding her into the rocky ground at an angle while her dagger skittered across the yard. A sharp snap reverberated off the walls of the practice yard.

"Gah!" Her response was sharp and guttural. Amarynn pushed herself to one knee, her chest rising and falling in heavy breaths.

"Em..." Aron winced as his eyes drifted to her shoulder. She hissed through her teeth as she stood, following his gaze to her collarbone. One end protruded in an unnatural lump beneath her shirt, her dark blood beginning to seep across the fabric. Turning her head away, she placed one hand over the wound. After one deep breath, she shoved, forcing the bone back under her skin. She cried out, then bent forward and vomited. After a moment, she sucked her breath between her teeth, then spat the taste of blood and bile from her mouth.

Aron bent forward. "Aye, I know," he consoled her. "Collarbones may be small, but they hurt the worst."

Amarynn wiped her mouth on her sleeve and turned to face him. She winced as her magic began to knit bone and flesh together. Her Traveler immortality aside, the process was typically slow and torturous, but since her return to Calliway, her wounds had healed more quickly than before.

She had not mentioned this phenomenon to anyone, so she feigned the pain a little longer. "You're going to pay for that, you know," she growled.

"Aye, to be sure!" Aron agreed, ignoring the dangerous glint in her eyes. "I'll be sleeping with a pillow 'tween my legs tonight. Wouldn't want to find out if my balls would grow back!"

Despite her irritation, she couldn't stop the corners of her mouth from turning up. As Aron joined in her amusement, Amarynn swiped out with her left foot, knocking Aron to the ground for a second time. She dropped to her knees — one on the ground and the other between Aron's legs.

"Am I interrupting something?"

Amarynn and Aron's eyes were locked on each other in a test of will, their breath coming hard and fast. Neither moved in response to the new voice.

"I said—"

"Not now, Jael," Amarynn snarled, her eyes still fixed on Aron's. She challenged the blue-eyed fellow Traveler with her stare, but he only chuckled. Her leg tensed, ready to use her knee to strike in a most unpleasant location.

"Oh now," Aron breathed, sensing her move, "you don't want to do something so low and petty in front of our Lord Prince, do you?"

Seconds passed. A bead of sweat trickled down Amarynn's nose and clung to the end, threatening to fall. Aron lifted his chin defiantly and smirked, an obvious dare. Her knee struck the precise location she aimed for, and Aron moaned, rolling away from her. She jumped up, dusting her hands on her breeches.

"Like I told you, who said we were fighting fair?"

Amarynn retrieved her daggers, Frost, and her short sword, still in its scabbard. As she stalked past Aron, who still lay on the ground, breathing heavily, she dropped his blade beside him with a sweet smile.

"I'll see you again tomorrow?"

"Aye," Aron grunted, rolling to his side before standing. He avoided looking toward the Prince as Amarynn crossed the training yard towards him, then tugged his elbow and pulled him to the benches that lined its perimeter.

Amarynn handed Frost to Jael while she sheathed her daggers and looped her short sword in its leather scabbard around her waist. She tightened its buckle without looking up. "Why are you down here?"

It had only been two weeks since their return from Athtull Keep, and since the surprise announcement of Jael's betrothal to Lady Caeda, and she preferred to keep her distance from him now — as much as that was possible.

She had regained her strength more quickly than anyone expected. Regealth believed it could be attributed to Jael's magic and their shared bond. If only her mind could experience the same miraculous recovery. Nightmares ceaselessly plagued her with unsettling details of her former life. Most of it made no sense, but there was enough information for her to understand she came from extraordinary pain and sadness.

"I thought you might have forgotten about our meeting." Jael's tone hinted at irritation, but she shook her head.

"I hadn't forgotten," she shrugged and finally looked up, making eye contact with the Prince. "I'm not going."

Jael chuckled. "Do I have to order you, Amarynn?"

She knew he said it in jest but planted her feet, lifting her chin in defiance. "Order me?"

Jael stopped and sighed. "I would never order you to do anything. But you can't ignore responsibility. It has been two weeks, and there is much to do now that we've lost the Gate."

Amarynn closed her eyes as she sighed. It was hard to think about the magical stone called the Gate, the very thing that bore her across dimensions. Not long ago, she had been desperate to see its return, so she could end her Traveler existence. However, because of the newly discovered magical bond with Jael, her perspective had changed, and she was no longer interested in release, at least not the kind the Gate could offer.

"What responsibilities? We aren't at war."

"Not yet." Jael grimaced. "But you know Venalise — how she thinks."

"Yes, I do." Amarynn rested her hand on her short sword's hilt. Amarynn knew more than just how Venalise thought. She experienced her treachery first-hand. The mage was a liar, a master manipulator, and she was singularly focused on discovering how to call her own army of Travelers, no matter the cost. "It's quite simple. She hates, and she likes to inflict pain. I can verify that personally. Her cruelty and her need to hurt absolutely anyone to get what she wants is a fact. There. Now you know what I know."

"You are being ridiculous. We need you." His voice lowered, Jael leaned closer, the intensity of his storm-grey eyes accentuated by traces of blue energy. She could feel his breath on her cheek. "I need you." The resonance of his quiet whisper raised the hair on the back of her neck.

"Jael, we both have very different roles to play. The further I am away from you right now, the better." She softened her tone when the Prince's eyes dropped to the ground. "For both of us. We have a bond, you and I, and I will uphold my duties fiercely. But I am just an instrument, not a leader."

She glanced over Jael's shoulder. No longer on the ground, Aron now stood with his hands on his hips, watching her. When Amarynn met his stare, he cast his gaze elsewhere and busied himself with retrieving his own weapons. Her eyes lingered on the other Traveler until Jael's movement drew her attention back to him.

With her scabbard buckled and knives stowed, she held out her hands for Frost. Jael handed her the ice-forged blade, noting the dirt that had worked its way into the runic markings along either side of the fuller. She'd need to clean her blades before Bent took notice and chided her for being lazy. Amarynn dismissed the thought and refocused her attention on Jael as she turned to leave the practice yard. The truth hurt her as much as she knew it hurt him. She had allowed herself a brief moment of hope that maybe there would be a way, but Jael was the Crown Prince of Karth, and she was an immortal Traveler: a soldier. She had no business pursuing an attachment to him. Her thoughts strayed back to Aron. She had other distractions to keep her busy for a while.

She could feel the Prince behind her as she exited the yard and turned toward the castle kitchen. It had been hours since she last ate, and she was hungry. But as soon as she stepped into the dimness, his hand slid into hers. She turned as Jael ducked through the low doorframe and lifted her hand to his lips, pulled her close. She breathed in, his scent making her heart beat faster.

Amarynn pulled her arm free, and Jael left the kitchen, entering the palace through a servants' corridor, where he turned down one of the side passages. She hesitated, then followed him. He drew her to him as soon as they were out of sight.

"I don't like seeing you with Aron," he growled. "Not like that."

She breathed in, hating that she relished his possessiveness. No matter how much she pushed him away, she couldn't fight how her body reacted to being so close. She leaned into him and rested her forehead on his chest.

Jael took her face in his hands and lifted it. He brought his lips to hers in a feverish kiss, insistent and demanding. At first, Amarynn responded, opening her mouth to his, tasting his lips, his tongue. Her body warmed, and she pressed into him, the bond created by the Gate trying to claim both of them, but then she pulled away. The attraction wasn't real. It was created by the magic of her crossing and the part Jael played in it.

"Jael, we must stop this," she mumbled.

The Prince's stormy grey eyes flashed with determination, and she could have predicted his next words.

"I will not marry Caeda."

Amarynn pushed further away from him, held him at arms' length, her cheeks flushed.

"And how, exactly, are you going to avoid that?

He put his hands on his hips and refused to meet her gaze.

"Jael." She reached out and laid her hand over his heart. He covered it with his own, gripping her fingers tightly.

"How can you ignore this?" he whispered, looking at their hands, entwined. He looked into her hazel eyes, reaching up to tuck a loose strand of her auburn hair behind her ear. "Everything you went through? We went through?"

"I do what I must," Amarynn said, "as should you."

Jael looked back down the corridor. "Is Aron a part of that?"

"Aron is one of the men I hand-picked to protect you. We train together because we must fight together," she said, her eyes narrowing.

She freed her hand and adjusted her sword belt, then reached for Jael's arm, pulling him off the wall. Stepping back into the kitchen, she leaned over a long table and snatched a roll and a wedge of cheese.

"I'm going to the barracks."

Jael frowned.

"I still don't understand why you left your rooms in the castle."

"I know you don't," she mumbled as she brushed past him. He would never understand if she didn't end this now. Amarynn resisted the urge to look back toward the doorway, but she knew he was still there, watching her walk away.

The little boy threw his head back and laughed, his squeals and giggles like a million tiny bells. Late afternoon sunlight streamed through the trees as he turned his head toward her and gasped, his ice-blue eyes wide

with surprise. Then, he was clumsily making his way through the tall grass toward her.

Rumbling sounds drifted past her on the wind. She pressed up to her knees and stuck her head up over the tall grass so she could look toward the road. Her heart thundered in her chest. She immediately dropped back onto her belly, pulling the child with her, calculating how to get back inside without being seen.

"Let's play a game, Sam!" she whispered to the boy.

"Oooh!" he patted his hands on his mouth. He grinned. "A game, mama!"

"You're gonna be a baby mouse," she started.

"And you're my mama," he whispered, still grinning.

She nodded. "That's right, baby."

She got to her feet but stayed in a low crouch. "There's a big ol' mean tomcat coming, and we gotta get inside before he sees us, okay?"

Sam nodded and grabbed her hand.

They slipped through the tall grass all the way to the back door of their little house. As she straightened up, a shadow appeared in the doorway. Anxiety knotted in her gut and began to wind and twist up her belly as the screen door opened. The man behind it leveled his dark eyes on them and stepped forward. She felt his rage all the way from the bottom of the back steps and as he reached for the boy with his mangled, meaty hands, a strangled cry escaped her throat.

"Shhh..."

Arms were holding her tightly. A man's scent filled her nostrils, and she panicked, pushing away violently in the blackness. It was too dark for her to see his face.

"I've got you," the voice soothed, pulling her close.

She relaxed as the room came into focus. She was in Calliway, in Bent's old quarters. At the announcement of Jael's betrothal, King Lasten had granted her request to return to regular Legion service and have Bent take her place as Jael's personal guard. After the unfamiliar entitlement of palace duty, the daily drills and patrols she had been so used to before gave her some solace. Jael had protested the switch, of course, but she had held firm and made the move that night. It had been a wise decision, Amarynn thought, now that her nightmares had worsened. Jael had come to her once... the night before she switched places with her aging mentor, Bent. His presence that night was the only thing that kept her from running to the stables and fleeing Calliway all over again. "You're alright." The voice was tender, familiar.

Aron.

She curled up for a moment and buried herself in his chest like a child, then quickly collected herself and rolled over on her side, pulling the blanket to her ear. She couldn't look at him; her vulnerability was humiliating, and she wouldn't allow him to see her cry.

The first few nightmares had made little sense and only left her shaken. Now, the memories that Venalise unleashed were coalescing, putting the puzzle of her former life back together. The past week, the barrage had been relentless, and her only respite was that these flashes of her past lay dormant during the day. She did her best to stay awake, but as soon as sleep claimed her, so did her past.

The bulk of her memories held nothing but fear and pain, and until this evening, there had been little else she could discover about herself. Tonight, she realized with sickening horror that she had been a mother — this brought the kind of agony she was not equipped to manage, let alone share.

"I'm fine," she mumbled into the pillows. "You can go."

Her belly twisted and writhed with sorrow, but she squeezed her eyes shut and shoved the pain as far down as she could bury it. She gritted her teeth, stilling the cries that threatened to erupt from her throat. Aron sat for a few moments, as if waiting to see if she had changed her mind. When she didn't move, he sighed and rose. Amarynn's trembling hand shot out and grabbed his arm.

"Thank you," she whispered. In the darkness, she felt Aron cover her hand with his own, before slipping out the door.

CHAPTER 2

Morning light filtered through the tall stained-glass windows in Regealth's study. He was hunched over a hefty tome, quietly mumbling to himself while he read. The heavy door was slightly ajar, and Amarynn paused for a moment before stepping inside. Incense wafted through the air, smoky tendrils drifting in the multi-colored rays of sunlight. The ever-present crystalline bowl of water sat at his elbow reflecting violet and sea-green window glass.

Regealth had been asking her to visit since their return to Calliway. She knew he was anxious about her well-being, but he also wanted to learn more about how Venalise had tampered with Amarynn's memories. His assurance that he wanted to help unravel the meaning of those memories was honest, she knew, but she suspected he had more than one reason to help her. Until their captivity at Athtull Keep, Regealth only existed to her as a mentor and her only resource to try and escape her life as a Traveler. But after her connection to Jael was revealed, it seemed there was much more at play; she now questioned everyone's loyalties, except for Jael's. His was certain. Until this morning, she had refused Regealth's help; she didn't want to be anyone's pawn. She wanted to be left alone to forget the bond with Jael, to forget the memories that haunted her nightly, but that the nightmares had become unbearable, however, she had no choice but to accept his offer. She pushed the door the rest of the way open and stepped inside.

He looked up, surprised.

"Are you finally ready to get some sleep?" he asked, gruffly.

Amarynn cast a scowl in his direction. She wandered along the book-lined walls of the chamber, letting her fingers trail along the old leather spines that filled the shelves.

"They've gotten worse, Regealth. Much worse." She stopped at the end of a bookcase.

Regealth returned his attention to the book before him and marked his place with a flat wooden marker. Dust motes flew as he closed the book and set it aside. "What did you see?"

She pivoted and leaned back against the bookcase, her hands in tight fists. Eyes closed, she let her head rest against the soft fabric spines of the books behind her. The smells in this chamber reminded her of Regealth's quarters: old books and damp stone. If she weren't so distraught, it would be comforting.

"I—" Her pain was so great it threatened to overtake her, and she couldn't speak. Her chest heaved, and her emotions finally gained control, her clenched hands quivering as her rage broke through her defenses.

"I had a s-son!" Her voice cut off, strangled with grief as she slid down the bookcase and slumped to the floor. Clutching the sides of her head, she wept, her face buried in her knees.

The old mage pushed back from his table, as a steward walked past the open doors and glanced in Amarynn's direction. Regealth shuffled to the door and closed it, turning the latch. He pulled a stool over and settled himself next to the distraught Traveler. He touched her head, stroking her hair as if she were his child.

"My shining star. This was never supposed to happen. You should never have regained your memories. I am so sorry we are in this place now." She kept her face down, her sobs quieting to whimpers. He continued. "I chose you for a reason, you know."

Amarynn turned her tear-stained face to look at the old man.

"What *reason*?" she growled.

Regealth's brow furrowed. "You are not ready to hear that."

"You did not have the right to decide for me." Amarynn pushed herself to her feet, swiping her wet cheek with the back of her hand. Her voice shook, but anger had now overtaken her sadness. "My entire life here was not my choice. Serving this King was not my choice, nor was my bond with Jael. I have had precious few choices in the last twenty years, and I'll be damned if *you* will choose what I know about myself!"

Regealth dropped his chin and frowned as she started to pace the study floor like a wolf trapped in a cage. He let her go by him, once, twice, then stood and caught her hand as she passed.

"Sit with me." It was not a demand. He released her hand, returned to his worktable, and opened the book he had been perusing before.

Amarynn continued to pace but slowed her cadence. Nothing made sense anymore. She had thought she wanted her old life, but now she had seen things that made that wish frightening. She had thought she wanted to be free of Karth, but her bond with Jael had tethered her to this world in a way she had never expected. Her eyes darted to Regealth, who was making a show of looking busy at his table. He knew things, possibly everything, and he was the only person who did. She needed him on her side now, more than ever.

She finally took a seat across from him at his worktable, her shoulders drooping from the exhaustion she had been trying to hide for days.

"You want the memories to quiet?" Regealth studied her, his watery blue eyes scanning her face. His voice was kind.

"I do. For now." Amarynn looked away. "You are right. I'm not ready."

Out of the corner of her eye, she watched him close the book, set it aside, and extend his hands across the table. His fingers, long and slender, tapped on the tabletop before he turned his palms to face up.

"Let's begin, then."

She returned her attention to the mage and reluctantly rested her elbows on the table.

"Dip your hands in the water bowl and put them in mine," he prompted.

Amarynn dipped her fingers into the cool salt water, and the moment her wet hands touched his, she felt his cool presence slide beneath her skin. Instinctually, she resisted, but Regealth gave her hands a light, reassuring squeeze. *Close your eyes and try to still yourself, as if you were going to sleep.*

His voice was the faintest whisper in her mind, but she recoiled. This was no different than when Venalise whispered her sinister intentions while Amarynn had been chained in the aethertorium, at Athtull Keep. The Traveler could not will herself to relax, instinctively fearing the same onslaught of memories and pain. Still, she rallied her determination; this torment had to end. Her breathing slowed while she tried to soften her tense muscles.

Good. Now, relax your whole body. You are safe with me.

Unlike Venalise, however, Regealth was waiting for her to accept his presence. He did not force his way in, as Venalise had while she tried to pry secrets from her. Where the dark mage's onslaught had been a cataclysmic typhoon, Regealth approached her mind like a gentle breeze. Yet, the sensation of someone rummaging around in her head, however carefully, still unnerved her.

"Your name is from the old Vhaleesian tongue. It is Amarynn. Try to say it."

Her knees were tucked up beneath her chin in an overstuffed chair. A fire flickered in the wide hearth in front of her. She rubbed the coarse fabric on the chair. All of these things she knew: the fire was hot, and the stone of the walls was cold. She understood what these things were, just not what to call them.

"*Am-ah-rin.*" She let the syllables form slowly on her tongue. "*Amarynn.*"

"*Yes, that's it.*" The old man, who she recognized as a slightly younger Regealth, smiled. His watery blue eyes gleamed in the firelight. "*It means 'shining star,' roughly translated. And you are just that. My shining star.*"

His words meant little then; she barely understood his language. But there was something about him that made her feel safe.

Amarynn relaxed even more. The memory Regealth pulled to the surface reminded her that he would not harm her. She allowed herself to drift further from consciousness, inviting him deeper into her mind. She felt nothing much for a while, until the mage touched on her most recent memory — the nightmare from last night.

She could hear the little boy's voice, and her heart broke all over again. Then there was the pain. Not like a battle wound — that was nothing new. This was pain from the deepest parts of her soul, and it was shrouded in fear, an emotion she was not accustomed to.

Do not be afraid. I have found them.

Her heart raced. Amarynn clenched her jaw, bracing herself. But when she felt Regealth's hands tighten on hers, her resolve returned. With each of the mage's small movements, her fear faded, as did the images that plagued her every night. The pain, however, remained. What was already seen could not be unseen; no magic could take that kind of fear and loss away.

Amarynn let her shoulders relax when she felt Regealth retreat from her consciousness. He still held her hands, but now they felt more like the comfort of an old friend, a comfort she clung to. A few moments passed, and he slid them from her grasp. She opened her eyes.

His were closed, but confusion and surprise were etched in the lines of his face. The room was quiet, the sounds from the practice yard below a low murmur in the background. Regealth's head was still bowed, and he was speaking under his breath to himself. Several long seconds passed before his mumbling ceased, he sighed, and looked up.

"I have closed them off for now," he told her. "I don't know for how long, but you should be able to rest. Do not waste the opportunity."

The old mage pressed his palms into the arms of his chair to help him rise, more unsteady than usual. Amarynn noticed that his steps faltered as he made his way around the table. Before reaching her side, he retrieved a vial from a narrow workbench set beneath the stained-glass windows.

"I made this for you when we returned. It is an elixir that will help you sleep. Now that you won't be interrupted by memories for a while, I suggest you try it." Regealth handed her the small glass bottle, but before he released it into her grasp, he looked at her, narrowing his eyes. "Two drops under your tongue." He gripped the bottle to emphasize his point, repeating, "Only two."

"Why? Could it kill me?" Her smile was a clear contrast to her earlier demeanor.

Regealth grunted and released the vial into her hand.

"I can take comfort that you seem to feel a bit more like yourself."

She offered him a half-hearted smirk.

The chamber door unlatched, breaking the silence, and Jael's head appeared. Amarynn rose quickly and slid past the Prince, dropping her eyes to avoid his as he opened the door. She strode down the hall before Jael could say a word, and Regealth sighed, his brow furrowed with worry as he watched her leave.

"What was that about?" Jael muttered, still turned toward the space where Amarynn had stood only moments before. Regealth shuffled past him.

"She finally let me inside her mind to quiet those nasty memories," Regealth said, pushing the door to with a soft click.

Jael dropped his head. Amarynn was a woman who had endured the worst kind of torture — the darkest of situations trapped in Venalise's aethertorium — all without asking for help. He winced as he considered how terrible things must have gotten for her to seek the mage's assistance.

"What did you find?" he asked as he crossed his arms across his chest, still looking down. "Or do I really want to know?"

"Oh, yes," Regealth exhaled. "I believe you will find this most interesting, as did I." The mage moved to his writing desk and slowly lowered his aged body back into the chair. Absently toying with a feather quill on top of a stack of parchments, he seemed to be considering his next words.

"While I was searching for her memories, I noticed something," he began, folding his hands on his lap. "You do realize Amarynn's energies differ from any other Traveler I have ever worked with, don't you?"

"What do you mean, 'her energies'?" Jael approached and leaned back on the edge of the table nearest Regealth's desk.

"All Travelers possess latent magical energy. That should come as no surprise; it's a condition acquired through their crossing. That kernel of magic is at the very essence of why they remain immortal. It is their very life force."

Regealth smiled to himself.

"Because Amarynn was brought across using your magic. You are not just a source but a wielder of sky magic; therefore, she has retained a greater portion of that magic. When your father helped Travel the others, they only retained enough to maintain their immortality and their superior battle skills, because he is only a source. The difference between Amarynn's energy and the others is quite remarkable, actually."

Jael cocked his head to the side.

"That's what you and my father wanted, was it not? An even better warrior. And because you knew I would eventually wield, you played with both of our fates to yield an undefeatable army and a future Mage King — all inside your sphere of influence. Immortality wasn't enough, was it?"

In truth, Jael couldn't blame Regealth. If there weren't such an overwhelming bond between himself and Amarynn, securing Karth's future through the invincibility of the monarchy and the Travelers would make sense. More power meant more security. Jael pushed his six-foot frame off the table and paced the room.

Regealth's eyes narrowed, his voice lowering. "I wanted to make the most of the magic your aunt Dyaneth gave her life for that night on the cliffs when the Gate was created."

Jael's pulse quickened as Regealth's words registered. He stopped his pacing and faced the mage. "Whether you meant to or not, you exploited two unsuspecting people," Jael growled, gesturing to himself. "Amarynn and me."

"Yes," Regealth agreed, a hint of regret lacing his voice. "I did. And the trial continues even now."

Jael stared in disbelief at the man who was like a grandfather to him. The mage pushed himself to stand, taking a few unsteady steps in the Prince's direction, his mouth set in a firm line.

"You will be the first Wielder-King since your great-great-grandfather. Until Dyaneth, this kingdom was withering under the simplicity of sword and shield. All around us, magic lived and breathed." Regealth stopped, his hands in fists balled at his sides. "The Travelers were your family's last gasp at a show of magical strength, and Dyaneth gave her life for the power to pull them across time and space."

Moments passed; the silence punctuated by more distant sounds of sparring from the practice yard below. Jael could not get the heartbreaking images of a frightened and heartbroken Amarynn out of his head. The damage done to her was unjustifiable.

"Was it worth it?" Jael's voice was quiet.

"I'm beginning to think that it was." Regealth gestured to the window. "With your father, I was able to bring warriors to our ranks that cannot die — a never-ending well of strength we may draw upon to protect our kingdom."

He took a few more steps forward and reached for Jael's hand. "When you were born, I was gifted an opportunity to continue the work your aunt and I started so many years ago."

"At what cost?" Jael pulled his hand away and crossed the room to the window. Below, Jaren and Claas, two of the older Travelers, traded blows with morning stars and shields. Others, like Davet, Ehrinell, and Rell, were testing various dangerous-looking throwing knives while Legion men watched from along the low wooden wall that surrounded the yard.

The camaraderie below was a stark contrast to the alienation Amarynn suffered, the very reason she was seeking release. Her pain was a result of Regealth's lone gamble, his belief that he could hone a Traveler beyond the magnitude of immortality. And the fact that it was his magic that played a part was a shame he could not shake.

"So, she is a source now, like my father?" Jael leaned his forehead against the window, his breath fogging the glass.

"Don't you see?" Regealth's voice was barely a whisper.

Jael was silent, still staring down at the Travelers in the practice yard.

The door to Regealth's study groaned, and Jael turned as a page pushed it open. Regealth shooed the boy away with a stern look and a flick of his hand, then returned his focus to the Prince.

"What should I see, Regealth? That you used me when I was too small to know any better? That you used Amarynn when she had no voice to choose?" Jael flexed his hands.

"It is simple. You have a bond."

"We have more than a bond, and you know it," Jael growled through clenched teeth.

"Think, boy. What have I been teaching you about your power?"

"It is in the air around me, not only in me." Jael paused, ready to protest Regealth's obvious attempt at distraction.

"I also taught you that like..." Regealth prompted.

"—calls to like." Jael's breath caught as the words registered. He searched Regealth's face, seeking confirmation.

"Yes," Regealth nodded. "Your immortal warrior is a wielder, and her magic comes from you."

CHAPTER 3

Y ou keep leading with your left foot!" Amarynn used the end of her short sword to tap Jael's boot. He kicked it away in irritation.

"What if I *like* leading with my left foot?" he snapped.

"Then you must also like to leave your left side open to attack," Amarynn retorted, frustration lacing her voice. She tapped his side with the flat of her sword. "Vhaleesians are tall, and they have a long reach." Stepping back, she drew her dagger with her free hand and gestured to his unprotected flank. "And Handaalians are small and quick and will drive a dagger through your ribs faster than most."

Jael sighed and dropped his head, but Amarynn did not relent. He had been staring at her, studying her, the entire time they were in the training yard. She seemed steadfast in her determination to keep him at arm's length — something he was unable to do. He was certain she had noticed his extra attention, and she appeared irritated by it.

"If you keep doing that, you're just begging for someone to gut you." She stepped back and sheathed her sword. They had been sparring for over an hour, and Jael's sloppiness indicated he was ready for a break.

Amarynn sat on one of the long benches against the wall while Jael paced the practice yard. Two of the Prince's guardsmen, Legion men, leaned against the castle wall, not paying much attention; with Amarynn in close proximity, there was no need. The afternoon sun was high in the sky, and Jael's linen shirt was soaked with sweat; she'd been working him hard. He sheathed his own sword, then tugged his shirt over his head.

"Showing off for the kitchen maids again," Amarynn smirked. He smiled and turned away, wadding the shirt into a ball, then spun and hurled it in her direction. The shirt hit the wall behind her head and slid to the ground. She hadn't even tried to catch it.

As it fell to the ground, Amarynn stared at him, eyes narrowed.

"What are those?" she said softly, her gaze on his shoulder. He glanced down at his chest, then back at her.

"What?" he asked, but he knew what she meant even as the words left his lips. On his back, across his right shoulder blade, were two fresh tattoos: two small Legion swords with names written across them. Amarynn stood, leaving his shirt in its ball in the dirt, and closed the distance between them, then walked around to his exposed back.

"Aeric," she whispered, running her fingers along the raised skin. Her hand rested between his shoulder blades. "And Barrim. Who are they?"

Jael dropped his head. He had tried to bury the shame he had been carrying for his hand in the two soldiers' deaths. When Lors had put a dagger in his hand, he'd had no choice, and anyone in his place would have done the same. But then, on the night of his betrothal announcement, it had burst through. Taking his cue from Amarynn and the tiny, innumerable scars she bore from years on the battlefield, he found the person the Legion men called on to make their marks. He wanted to ensure he would never forget what he had done, what they had sacrificed.

"Old friends," he mumbled. Amarynn returned to face him. She shot him a look of suspicion, and Jael turned away. "Don't worry about it."

Amarynn said nothing, but her dark look was enough. She retreated to the bench and gathered her things.

"They were soldiers taken captive by Lors at the keep," Jael offered reluctantly.

"And," Amarynn prompted without looking back at him.

"And they died."

"Do you plan on commemorating all the fallen Legion men this way? Because if you do, I think you've left several thousand off your list." Amarynn turned, her arms crossed. She stared, refusing to break eye contact. Jael sighed heavily and lifted his face towards the sky to avoid her ire. He had been a fool to think he could keep that secret for long.

"I'd rather not talk about it," he said.

"I was in that keep with you, and I don't recall any Legion soldiers being held in the dungeon."

Jael, eyes closed, pursed his lips and cleared his throat.

"I will not have this discussion right now," he said, his voice soft and low but the finality of his words unmistakable. If he had any hope of convincing Amarynn they could be more than she saw them — as sovereign and soldier — he needed to carefully craft his words. But this moment, in the practice yard while her ire was up and he was off-guard, was less than ideal. He dropped his chin and opened his eyes, meeting her hard stare with his own.

Amarynn shook her head. "What are you hiding from me?"

"Rynn, you know things happened to *me* in that keep. Things I would very much like to forget." From the moment they escaped Athtull Keep, he had wanted to tell her everything, to empathize with her at a level only he could. But he refused to gamble that she would understand his dilemma. He tapped his temple. "Just like you want to forget."

Amarynn narrowed her eyes again, frowned, then strode away across the yard. Before she cleared the gate, she turned. "You need to keep practicing."

Jael watched her disappear into the castle, then walked to the bench to retrieve his damp, dirty shirt, tossing it across his shoulder as he looked up to the sky to gauge the time. How could he tell her what he had done? He had sworn the few who knew to secrecy, that night in the forest outside Athtull Keep. No. If Amarynn ever found out he had killed two Legion men to save her, she would never forgive him, and rightfully so. What he had done was despicable by any Legion standard. His gut twisted in knots as the memories of Lors' throne room flashed through his mind. Amarynn could never know.

Muttering to herself, Amarynn stalked the halls of the castle in search of Bent. She worked the names on Jael's shoulder over and over, trying to remember who they belonged to. Barrim was unfamiliar, but Aeric tugged at a memory she couldn't quite place. Looking for her Blademaster alongside members of court and serving staff still seemed wrong; he should be in the barracks or out in the training yard. She made her way to Bent's quarters, dodging busy castle staff as they bustled in and out of rooms, hefting large chests and ornate bags from corridors to rooms and back. The hustle and bustle was unusual for the castle, even on a busy day.

She stepped through the door to what had been her quarters, and found Bent standing over a chest, staring into it in disgust. At the sound of her footsteps, he turned and grimaced.

"I told them I don't need one of these," he muttered, gesturing to the dark wood-and-brass chest sitting on his bed. "A bedroll and pack'll suit me just fine."

Amarynn surveyed what used to be her room. The decor was as feminine as it had been the morning she first opened her eyes after her return from Athtull. The floral-patterned tapestries still hung beside the hearth, and it seemed Audra still insisted on fresh pastries and flowers on the table by the chair. She smiled at the thought of the no-nonsense chambermaid who had gone to great lengths to keep her happy in her short time there. But flowers and food were not nearly enough to keep her in her newly appointed position as Jael's personal guard. She had to get out of the

palace and away from Jael before it became too difficult. Though he tried
to conceal it, Bent had only taken her position to keep her from doing
something rash, and she knew he wasn't happy about it.

"You're sailing to Vhaleese on a ship, Bent. There are no campfires to
lay beside or horse to tie a pack to. You will need the chest."

Amarynn crossed the room and sat on the edge of the bed. She let one
hand rest on the small pile of neatly folded clothes that lay there, her
fingers playing along the shirt's seam on the top of the stack; only one sat
atop what looked to be a single pair of breeches and a thin cloak.

"Can I ask you something?"

Bent glanced up from the chest. "Aye, lass. I'm listening."

"Is Matteus going to Vhaleese?"

"Now, lass—" Bent sighed and shook his head.

"I need to know! Matteus is a snake, and I don't trust him." She
narrowed her eyes at Bent. "And neither do you after what he did to me."
Amarynn gestured to the knotty scar that crossed her neck. "Who else did
Lasten post?"

Bent cocked his head, squinting in thought. "Wake, Endric, and
Ehrinell, I believe."

A weight lifted the minute Bent said the other female Traveler's name.
Amarynn had no doubt that Ehrinell would make sure Matteus kept his
mouth shut. The only two female Travelers had an unspoken allegiance
to one another, especially since Matteus had jumped her. *This might all
work out, after all.* "You'll need something warmer," she murmured.

Bent's eyes were fixed on the wall behind her, his face stoic, the muscles
in his jaw working as he clenched his teeth. He was trying — and failing —
to hide his displeasure. "Aye, I know," he grunted, then faced her. Quiet
seconds passed before he spoke again. "I'm only doing this because you
asked, you know."

She nodded. Her mentor had suffered so many blows, both physical
and emotional, on her behalf, and it pained her to know how difficult

this new role was for him. Being the personal guard to the Prince paled in comparison to decades in the Legion as a Blademaster. Bent was not cut from lofty cloth — he was practical, utilitarian, and battle-tested. He was only doing this for her, and she was grateful. She lifted the clothing and settled it inside the chest. "See?" she smiled, "plenty of room for a sturdy cloak."

Bent was silent as he nodded his head. She hoped he understood how important it was to her that it be him, rather than her, with Jael on the journey to Vhaleese. The Prince needed to find some sort of bond with Caeda before their marriage; Jael needed to loosen his grip on the bond he shared with Amarynn so he could claim his birthright and the Kingship when the time was right. Even though her heart ached every moment she was with him, Amarynn knew this was the only way. The more distance between them, the greater the chance she had to sever their bond. Leaving was the only way to make sure their separation was unavoidable, and the best reason to leave was to search for Venalise. Laying that groundwork had been easy; Aron, Finn, and Stavin had volunteered immediately when she slipped it into their conversation three nights ago in the mess hall. It would be another unsanctioned mission but risking the King's wrath once again was worth it if it meant Jael finally accepted that she was not the right path for him.

"I suppose you'll be training some of the yearlings while I'm gone, eh?" Bent said, reaching over to pull a thicker cloak out of his wardrobe.

"Most likely," she nodded, looking away. Lying, especially to Bent, was not one of her strong suits. Her plans had nothing to do with the Legion, but if Bent found out, he'd be tempted to do something stupid that might earn him an early grave. Amarynn couldn't live with that.

Bent chuckled to himself, then sighed. He moved the chest further onto the bed and sat next to her. For a long moment, the two of them sat side by side, the quiet only broken by the sounds of porters and handmaids bustling down the hallway. Amarynn's hands rested on her knees, and Bent surprised her by resting one hand on hers.

"Don't tell me anything," he whispered. His hand tightened on hers, and she looked at him, but his gaze remained fixed on the floor. Even now, the old Blademaster still knew her best. "We'll say our goodbyes at the door, and that'll be it."

Amarynn cast a sideways glance at her mentor. The lines on his face had deepened over the last few years, and his grimace now only made them more obvious. She had trouble remembering that he was not immortal sometimes because he had been with her since the beginning. But his age was evident by the silvery streaks in his hair, not just the lines on his face. He was as much a father to her as he was a comrade and it pained her to know that most of his stress was because of her and her emotional, thoughtless mistakes.

Bent stood and went to the door, turning back to face Amarynn. His expression was almost tender as he flicked his head to the side. "Go on, now. I've got too much to do. No time to sit around running my mouth, even with the likes of you."

Amarynn nodded, a soft smile playing on her lips. She stood and crossed to the door, brushing past Bent. Their eyes locked for a brief moment, then she turned to leave. There was nothing else to say.

CHAPTER 4

Amarynn slammed the rough-hewn door to her quarters shut, making the sconces on the wall shudder. Since taking over Bent's old quarters, she hadn't bothered to change anything, not even the rickety fixtures that threatened to fall at the slightest knock. She unbuckled Frost's scabbard and tossed the broad sword on her cot. Next came her belt and daggers, depositing them on the small table by the door. Sitting on a stool by the small hearth, she rubbed her hands along the tops of her rapidly bouncing legs, then let her head fall into her hands. Not telling Bent where she was going had been like reliving her desertion all over again. The shame of running away under the cover of darkness felt no different than she did now. He knew, she was certain — his eyes had said as much — but not telling him outright kept him safer.

And then there was Jael. Her fingers curled in her hair and she pulled as if she could pluck him from her thoughts. Just when she had finally decided to suppress the memories Venalise had unlocked, Jael revealed hints that there were more dark pieces to the puzzle that was Athtull Keep, and that made her blood freeze. He was never supposed to take that kind of risk. She knew he had witnessed Lors, that monster of a self-proclaimed King, taking her down with a dagger to the throat, and she hoped that was the extent of it. Aside from that terrifying show of depravity in Lors' throne room, her most sincere wish was that he had otherwise remained unscathed, but after today in the practice yard, she was certain there was more to the story. She sat up and rubbed her face. How else could he have been so sure-footed and strong when he found her, shackled and bloody, in Venalise's aethertorium?

She dropped her hands to her lap. Light streaming through her small window highlighted the tiny scars covering her arms. She ran her fingers over the knotted scar at her throat softly, barely touching the raised skin. She had never thought to include any names, not even when it was someone she was familiar with. It was best to forget the details; otherwise, a person would drive themselves mad with remorse or, worse, regret.

Many men had been lost in battle. Goddess! They'd even lost men in training. So why would Jael have felt so compelled to mark those two in such a personal way? *Aeric and Barrim.* She worked their names over and over in her head. They sounded vaguely familiar, but with twenty years in the Legion and having been absent for some time, it was impossible to place those names with any faces she might recall.

The Prince was an enigma. In a matter of weeks, their relationship had changed from sovereign and subject to something much deeper and more undeniably connected. For the better part of twenty years, she had considered him an extension of his father. They had rarely spoken. But now, everything had changed. She knew him to be proud but loyal — strong but kind. He had managed to do what nothing else in this land could do, and that was to give her purpose as his protector, which was crumbling now that she had relinquished that role and returned to her old station as one of the Travelers.

Now, more than ever, she was determined to make peace with Karth. Jael had given her that much, no matter the distance she tried to put between them. She needed his eyes turned in a different direction, but she would always have hers on him. Her old life, a life of mindless battle and death was no longer an option. Making sure Jael stayed safe and continued to be part of this world — the world she had tried so hard to leave — was paramount now.

She opened and closed her fists and then shook out her hands, still conflicted between her desperation to ensure his safety on the trip and knowing that riding now in the opposite direction would not jeopardize his eventual ascension to the throne. He had to go through with the marriage to Caeda because defying the King could cost him his father's trust. Knowing that Bent was going with him made her breathe a little easier, but, while he would do his best, he was no Traveler — he was mortal. She was glad that he'd be among Travelers; however, hearing that Matteus would be going along in the Traveler ranks did not sit well with her, even if Ehrinell, and her calming influence, was there.

There was nothing she could do about it now. Hastily, she shoved supplies in her traveling pack — there was little she required — and re-belted her scabbard. Her provisions and weapons were secured; it was time for the more difficult task. If Jael was on a ship on the way to Vhaleese, he couldn't try to join her, or stop her. She had to get out of Calliway without him discovering her plan.

Moonrise cast a faint glow on the alley behind the stables. Ban, the larger of the two satellites, was a thick pearlescent crescent. Its silver-blue counterpart, Ahai, lagged behind. Torches cast an orange glow on the narrow space where Amarynn and the rest of her group were preparing to ride. She didn't hide her surprise when a young man, perhaps nineteen or twenty years old, approached from around the side of the building. She tensed; he wasn't part of the group.

"Who are you?"

"I am called Xan."

She appraised the young man. Short of stature, average build. and an evident hesitancy — not much unlike a young Legion recruit. The newcomer's eyes flitted over the team of Travelers preparing to leave.

"I don't think we need any more swords on this mission, Xan," Amarynn turned back to her horse, Dax, dismissively.

"I'm not a sword." Xan fidgeted with the straps on his pack. "Master Bent said you would say that," he mumbled.

Amarynn's hands went still. She pushed back away from the gelding and turned on her heel, approaching the young man. She looked him up and down as she circled him.

Aron, standing on the other side of Dax, shook his head. "Here we go," he chuckled to Stavin, who raised his eyebrows and turned away. Nioll, a Legion man who had traveled with Amarynn before, grimaced and shook his head as he slung a saddlebag over one of the horses. Aron ducked beneath Dax's head and stood behind Amarynn, arms akimbo.

"Short sword — so you are new," she said. Resting her hands on her hips, she continued. "No visible scars, except for that little one on your chin."

"A-a kitchen knife—" Xan started.

Amarynn cut him off with a laugh. She looked over her shoulder at Aron and gestured to Xan with both hands. "Travelers surround me, and Bent sends me *this*?" Her eyebrows raised in surprise.

Aron approached the young man, his eyes narrowing as he, too, studied him head to toe. Gesturing to Xan, he said "Not sure I understand this either, if I'm being honest. What good are you?"

"Bent said to tell you that Regealth is too old to accompany you on a trek into the mountains. He also said that because you are trying to track down mages, having one of your own might be a good idea."

"We have mages in the Legion now?" Amarynn shook her head. "Goddess! I was gone for three months, and everything has changed."

"Aye," Xan responded, his voice low. "I can swing a sword *and* wield fire." He waited for his words to register. He seemed unsure, casting his eyes from side to side before he dropped the pack from his shoulder. But he adjusted the cuffs of his sleeves, then held his hands out in front of him, palms up.

A flame, no bigger than a candle's, rose from his left palm. He covered the flame with his right hand, then drew it upward, pulling it like taffy. Aron's eyebrows raised, but the flame disappeared with a sudden clattering from the smithy nearby. Xan ducked his head, re-shouldered his pack, and shoved his hands deep in his pockets. "I am from the Handaals, and I wear a Legion sword because I *am* Legion. I train with all the other recruits — I am one of them," he said quietly, staring at the ground.

"Did anyone know you could wield when you joined? How did Regealth not know?"

"It was not intentional." Xan looked back up as he adjusted his grip on his pack. "My family migrated to Karth after the invasion. My parents—"

"Sold you off," Amarynn murmured. She took another look at the young man, setting her mouth in a firm line. She had to admit that having a mage with them would be wise, and she was glad Bent had thought of it — she certainly hadn't. While it appeared he was no match against Venalise, he could offer some knowledge of magic and how it worked. All that had been on her mind was getting away from Calliway and finding the Gate.

She eyed the young man with new respect.

"Get him better gear, then," she said to Aron. "And a horse. We leave in ten minutes."

CHAPTER 5

Amarynn and the others rode hard through the night. They understood the clock had already begun in their race to retrieve the Gate. They were swift, as only Travelers could be — no stops, no rest, no food. The new mage, Xan, was only one of two mortals among them, and Amarynn had to admit he impressed her with his ability to keep up.

As they passed through Morning Hill, she couldn't help but remember the night she and Jael had spoken in the stable. He had given clues about his involvement with her crossing and shared that she had never gone unnoticed by him — information that planted a kernel of purpose in her. So much had unfolded since that night — so many revelations about her past and future. She was not just another Traveler. She was the only Traveler without a bond to the King, and that inexorably changed her future.

The riders pressed on, using the road to Athtull instead of Amarynn's backwoods route. In the distance, the Stone Giant mountain range rose above the smaller Dark Mountains, their massive, impenetrable presence hinting at the enormity of the party's task. Venalise was somewhere on that daunting horizon, and with her were the Gate and the child, Sia, whom she had met in Venalise's aethertorium. Amarynn did not understand her significance, but Regealth mentioned her name with a strange reverence every time they spoke of how to bring the Gate back to Karth. One thing was certain, though. If Sia had not intervened when

Athtull began to fall, Amarynn and Jael would never have made it out of the Keep alive.

When Amarynn had returned from Athtull, the journey had taken three days — three slow and painful days filled with the agony of immortal healing and the anguish of her returning memory. Curled in the back of the infirmary wagon, she was a frenzied mess in her blood-stained clothes and hair. The entire journey, she refused food or drink, and she did not sleep for fear of the images and sounds that assaulted her every time she closed her eyes. By the time she was taken to the castle, she was almost feral — delirious and uncooperative. Now, she was purposefully returning to the center of that pain, her anxiety growing every minute they continued forward. What else could Venalise do to her? The mage had the power to unlock her memories. What if she could trap Amarynn in her own mind, caught in a loop of torment?

Dax tossed his head when she pulled back on the reins, asking him to slow his gallop. She allowed the others to pass one by one until the last rider, Xan, was cantering at her side.

"You holding up?" she called out over the thundering hooves.

He didn't respond verbally but nodded his head, his mouth set in a line of grim determination. Amarynn had to admire the young man. Very few untested Legion men would have kept up with the Travelers. Bent must have known he was a man of a different mettle than most; otherwise, he wouldn't have made the recommendation.

She relaxed her hold on Dax's reins, and he shook his head before increasing his speed. He wasn't the fastest horse she'd ever had, but his heart was a thousand times bigger than any she'd ever known. He would run until his heart stopped if she let him.

"My boy," she murmured, leaning close to his neck.

His pale golden mane whipped in the wind, the strands stinging her face, but she closed her eyes and smiled. A sure-footed friend who spirited her away in the night and a guard who had her back at every turn, he was her constant, her anchor in a world spun around and around.

They gained ground, slowly returning to the head of the pack, as the road narrowed as it wound through the forest. Great stone outcroppings soared overhead as the trees became denser and darker.

Amarynn scanned ahead. In the diminishing breaks of the tree line, she could make out the jagged peak that had been home to Athtull Keep. She lifted one arm high, signaling for the riders to come to a stop.

"Tired already?" Aron laughed as his horse pranced in circles around Amarynn and Dax.

She stole a glance at the back of the group. Xan's shoulders sagged, his exhaustion evident now.

"We'll make camp here tonight. The horses need to rest." She leaned down and gave Dax's shoulder a hearty pat.

"Another two or three hours, and we can camp up at the Keep," Aron reasoned.

"Better shelter there, y'think?" Nioll chimed in.

"No."

Amarynn's tone warned off any rebuttal. She needed Athtull Keep to stay out of her line of sight for one evening more. She knew the second it came into view, it would usher in memories she had no interest in reliving.

"Rynn." Finn approached. "I'll take a quick look around." He glanced back at his partner, Stavin. "Just make sure it stays quiet."

She turned and locked eyes with Stavin. He gave her a nod, and she relaxed. Something about both men always made her feel at ease. Each of them was fierce on the battlefield, but together, they had an underlying gentleness not possessed by most Travelers.

In fact, it had been Stavin who stayed with her most after Matteus attacked her in the practice yard. In the last year or two before that night, the Travelers had treated Amarynn more like a sister than a comrade. And since her return, their bond had only grown stronger.

"Suit yourselves," Aron groaned, swinging his leg over his saddle and dropping to the ground. He blew out an exasperated breath and placed his hands on his hips. "I'll gather some wood."

Aron led his mount to a nearby tree and tied her reins on a low limb. As he disappeared into the forest's shadows, Stavin dismounted and approached Amarynn.

"He's the newest," he started. "Full of piss, that one."

"Full of something," she muttered with a half-hearted chuckle.

Stavin grinned. "Let's go throw our blades around and get us some dinner. I'll wager I can bag twice as much as you." He gave her a quick wink.

"Ass," she chuckled. "I'll bag the game. If you come along, you're more likely to name it and make it your pet."

"Fair point," he laughed. "I'll set up camp off the road a bit, then. You go clear your head." He lifted his chin and surveyed the surrounding forest. "Nothing here but the living things that should be."

Stavin had been there when she and Jael emerged from the fallen keep. He was one of the few people, besides Bent and Regealth, that had witnessed her terror and pain that day. But Stavin knew her as only a fellow Traveler could, and he understood her need for solitude when taking on the demons she now faced.

She dropped to the ground, leaving Dax's reins around the pommel of her saddle. The great yellow gelding took a step towards Stavin's mare. Without a second glance, she stepped into the trees and ducked out of sight.

Ban and Ahai had risen, and their silvery radiance mingled with the orange glow of the campfires. Iridescent mixtures of light from the two moons gave the branches an ethereal hue. Beneath a grove of amberwood trees, Amarynn tossed a log onto the dampening blaze, sending a shower of sparks upward. The Travelers, along with Nioll and Xan, settled their packs and bedrolls in a circle around the campfire to absorb as much heat as possible. Fall would soon become winter, and the air had the bite of frost to it.

Amarynn fixed her stare on the ground, her hazel eyes locked on the heel of her right boot, which rapidly tapped as she bounced her leg. Impatience got the best of her, and she stood. "I'm going to Athtull now; before we head north. I want to look at the cave where the atranoch were kept."

"So, we can't camp there, but you can go exploring?" Aron shook his head, sucking the last meat off a bird bone and tossing it into the fire. He rose and tucked his dagger into its sheath. "All right then, let's get a move on."

"Stop."

He paused and turned to look at Amarynn, his hand still on the hilt of his dagger. She flashed a warning glance, then sucked in a breath. "I'm not going." She wrung her hands as the skin on her wrist ached and stung. The memory of the chains on Venalise's aethertorium floor surged. When she noticed Aron watching her warily, she dropped her hands and rubbed the tops of her thighs. "But I have an uneasy feeling, probably because we are so close—"

"Understandable," he said, his expression softening. "Time to turn in, then?" He gestured to the rest of the men around the fire.

Amarynn pushed to her feet and stepped over the log, then ducked into her tent, dropping her sword belt by the opening flap, next to the gear she had piled off to one side. A slight bulge in the front pocket of her pack reminded her she had brought along Regealth's sleeping draught. Sitting cross-legged, she reached over and plucked it from its compartment. The vial was small but heavy; the thick amber liquid barely allowed any light to pass through. The nights were becoming more challenging to overcome each following morning, despite the healing her immortality offered. Perhaps this was because her exhaustion wasn't physical. The precious few hours of sleep she had gotten the night before weren't as harrowing. The dreams had been more random nonsense rather than specific, but that kind of dream was a rarity, and she wasn't sure if she was willing to risk it again.

"Can't sleep?"

Amarynn turned at the sound of Aron's voice. He stuck his head through the tent's opening. She nodded, holding up the vial Regealth had given her. Her shoulders were slumped in evident fatigue, and the dark circles growing under her eyes the last several days were becoming more and more prominent.

"I am supposed to use this. It helps, but I don't think it's wise to dull my senses while we are out here." Her shoulders sagged and she frowned.

"That's fair, I suppose," he agreed, moving closer. "Here's a thought. I'll stay awake to keep watch over you while you sleep."

Amarynn grimaced in disagreement and sat back nonchalantly in an attempt to hide her intrigue. "I don't need to be 'watched,' thank you very much."

Aron stepped the rest of the way inside and settled himself next to her, leaning in. "Sure, you don't *need* to be watched, but I certainly wouldn't mind." He gave her a slow, lazy smile.

His deep voice caressed her ear, making her heartbeat race. The scent of campfire mixed with musk was heady and she raised her eyes to his, but she couldn't help but think of Jael. The Prince's voice didn't quicken her heartbeat; rather, Jael's was a soothing balm that calmed the raging storms roiling inside of her. But now, with Aron, that tempest threatened to rise unbridled. She welcomed it.

Her departure from Calliway was as much about putting distance between herself and Jael as it was finding the Gate, but it wasn't easy to get him out of her mind, which she needed to do if she was going to move on, if Jael was going to truly bond with Caeda. Aron seemed willing and here, and better yet, he was not complicated. Where Jael was kind and loyal, Aron was an arrogant ass, albeit an attractive one. But he had his own brand of loyalty; most recently, when she woke from nightmares, he held her until she stopped shaking, and never made her feel ashamed. She pushed aside the comparison between the two men and placed her hand on Aron's chest.

"You wouldn't *mind?*" she teased.

He turned his head from side to side, scanning the interior, then leveled his gaze back at her. "Well," he rubbed his chin in contemplation, "it'll be a complete bore, but I'm willing to do my part to make sure our fearless leader gets her sleep."

Their eyes locked and her breath caught. Where Jael's eyes were the hue of a stormy sky, Aron's were the startling crystalline color of sea ice.

"How very noble of you," Amarynn said as her fingers started to walk upward from his chest to his neck, one after the other, in cadence with each word. Her head and heart warred with one another as she rested her hand on Aron's bare skin, the steady beat of his pulse in the palm of her hand. Perhaps she needed to clear her head and distract herself from the thoughts of Jael... and Aron had been trying to entice her for days.

"Aye, that's me," he chuckled, "very noble, indeed."

Amarynn's hand slipped behind his head and pulled him down to her. As their lips met, he gave a little growl and pressed his body against hers. His scent, sweat and pine, lingered in her nose. He seemed hesitant at first, which surprised Amarynn. His lips teased hers, his tongue only tasting her lips gently, softly, the tenderness a stark contrast with his usual bold behavior.

Aron cupped her face with one hand, sliding his thumb along her cheek. His other arm wrapped around her, pulling her close.

"You are quite the contradiction, lady," he murmured, nuzzling the soft spot behind her ear.

Amarynn pulled back and eyed him warily. "How so?"

"Well, for starters, you've a tongue that's sharp as one of your daggers," Aron slid his hand from her back to the sheathed dagger strapped to her thigh and tugged on the straps. He moved his other hand from her cheek to her back and pulled her to him. As his lips brushed hers, he murmured, "But you taste sweeter than honey."

Amarynn's hand tangled in Aron's hair as their lips met again, this time with greater urgency. As she opened her mouth to his, he pushed her to the ground, sliding one hand beneath her shirt and brushing the soft skin of her torso.

Shivers raced along her back as Aron's hand settled on the bottom of her rib cage. She teased him, her tongue flicking his ever so lightly, then bit his lower lip.

"I'd hardly call this watching me," she whispered.

"Oh, I'm watching you," he breathed, capturing her lips again.

She could now taste a hint of sweet wine on Aron's tongue as he explored her mouth. Her hands drifted to the sides of his face, the stubble of his beard rough under her fingers.

Suddenly, a rustle of footsteps outside the tent startled them both and they jumped apart. Amarynn sat up and blinked from fatigue that didn't escape Aron's attention.

"Well, that does it!" he said, pushing her aside and unfastening her bedroll.

"What are you doing?"

"What someone should have done days ago," he answered gruffly, unceremoniously pushing her onto the makeshift bed. "Give me that vial," he directed.

"Are you telling me what to do?" she replied, a challenging glint in her eyes.

"Aye, I am." Aron hovered over her, unmoving.

They locked eyes for several seconds, Amarynn waiting for Aron to relent, but he stood firm. She raised her hand and slowly uncurled her fingers. Aron gave a half-smile as he took the vial.

"How much of this are you supposed to drink?" he asked, holding up the glass container to examine its contents.

Amarynn dropped her gaze to her lap. "Two drops."

"So, four then?" She looked up to see him grinning and she immediately scowled. "Relax, woman," he said, pulling the dropper from the vial. "Open up!"

She did, and he dropped the sweet-tasting elixir under her tongue. He leaned forward, nose to nose. "Now, take off your shirt, m'lady," he said with feigned politeness.

Amarynn's eyes widened momentarily, making Aron grin even wider. He leaned back and held out his hand. "I'm not looking for a peep show. Just do as I ask and trust me." Still hesitant, the look in his eyes made her feel safe and appeased her reservations.

She twisted to the side, turning to face away from him. She doubled over to grab the bottom hem with both hands and, before she pulled her shirt over her head to expose her back to him, she spat the liquid from her mouth.

Lean muscle rippled over her medium frame. Her skin was pale and soft, except where scar upon scar marred it. One in particular stretched from the bottom of her rib cage, across her lower back to the base of her spine. An intricate tattoo of a vine followed it, disappearing into the waistline of her breeches. Several other small tattoos swirled and wound around the other scars, each intertwining with the marks of wounds received in one battle or another. Aron sucked in his breath.

"Goddess, you are exquisite," he breathed out as he lifted his hand to touch her along her shoulder blades. Amarynn shivered at his touch. "Calm yourself, she-demon," he said softly, pushing her back down onto the bedroll face-first. Aron straddled her thighs, and without hesitation, his strong hands were on her back, massaging the tense muscles. The feel of his hands on her skin ignited her senses, and as much as she hated to admit it, she didn't want him to stop.

"If you are going to get rest, it needs to be real rest," he said softly. "And you canna get that with your muscles all in a twist."

He brushed her hair to the side and kneaded the muscles around her shoulders and neck with skillful precision. Her body leaned into his touch, and she couldn't help but groan when he found a particularly tight knot.

When Amarynn knew the elixir should be taking effect, she allowed her eyelids to sag and her breathing to slow. Aron pushed off the ground and pulled the wool blanket up to cover her back. He knelt beside her, tucking stray strands of hair away from her face.

"What are you doing?" she mumbled, turning her head away toward the back of the tent.

"Preparing for the most frustrating night of my life," he answered, his hand on her neck, fingers twining themselves in her hair.

"Frustrating?" Amarynn's voice was as quiet as a whisper, seeming to succumb to Regealth's sleeping draught.

"Aye, she-demon," he smiled. "Just this once, though."

He settled himself on the ground near her head and leaned forward, elbows on his knees. "You get your rest, because the next time you kiss me like you just did, there'll be no sleeping for either of us."

CHAPTER 6

Amarynn waited until the clouds passed before venturing out from the forest cover into the rubble field where Athtull once stood. She glanced over her shoulder to be sure she was alone, though she was certain she hadn't been followed. It hadn't been difficult to slip out from under Aron's watch. He had fallen asleep, his breathing slowing, becoming deep and regular, not long after she'd spit out the drop of sleeping medicine and feigned her repose.

Moonlight filtered through large, jagged cracks above her head and holes where missing pieces had fallen from the walls of the stone passageways. Once buried deep within Athtull Keep, they were now partially exposed, following the collapse of Lors' fallen fortress, and the extent of the destruction was even greater than she imagined. Amarynn stepped into what was left of the central chamber and surveyed the room where she and Jael had nearly been crushed only weeks before. She squeezed her eyes closed as the memory of rumbling tremors snuck up her legs, making her knees quiver. Her chest tightened with the involuntary recollection of the thick dust that remained when the giant slabs collapsed. Walls that had previously risen to meet in a high dome overhead had been sheared off, the fragments at the top of the stone now only rising slightly taller than her head. There was no clear path. Boulders and pieces of wood were scattered amongst the still-standing parts of the Keep's interior, peppered with the remnants of the Keep's décor. She could make out the center of the room where she had stood, trying to convince little Sia to leave with them before the Keep fell. Two large slabs lay partially on top of one another amongst the debris — the two slabs Sia had kept from crushing them when Venalise pulled the mountain down. Her left hand rested on an archway. Most likely, it was where she and Jael had rushed into the room while searching for a way to the ground floor.

Amarynn pushed herself away from the stone arch and climbed over the rubble. Her movements were sluggish; she hadn't managed to spit all the elixir out when she lay down for Aron. Still, she stepped lightly across the wreckage to the perfect circle in the center that was still clear of large debris, the safe space that had surrounded her and Jael when Sia—

A sick sensation in the pit of her stomach rose and strengthened as she stood there. Closing her eyes, she tried to quell her blossoming anxiety, but images of Sia flashed through her mind. The child clutched a grey-white bear cub, her eyes wide, confused, and filled with frantic indecision as Amarynn beckoned her to join them, to escape Venalise. Then, she could again feel the stone floor under her knees, Jael pushing her down to the ground to shield her, and she saw Sia reaching toward the slab of the stone ceiling, painful strain etched on her tiny face...

Amarynn breathed out, knelt down in the circle, and let her fingers play over the pebbles and dust that had found their way into the space. She picked up a stone and let it tumble around in the palm of her hand. Her breath was coming faster as her body became enveloped in the memory of that moment, reliving the unfamiliar sensation of fear — without a known origin — overtaking her like it never had before. She clutched the tiny, grey stone and held her breath, the memory feeling more real than she could bear. Sia, Jael, Regealth... she had not wanted to attach herself more tightly to this world. She had only wanted to escape the emptiness — the feeling of no purpose — but she had not bargained for this level of entanglement with so many elements of Karth and its protection. Her wish had backfired most spectacularly, and now she had no idea how she would navigate her newfound role. Even if she was no longer Jael's personal guard, there was no world now where she didn't have an elevated position in the Prince's eyes.

She looked to her left. Where there had once been a narrow passageway leading to the enclosure where the largest atranoch had protected her, there was only rubble beneath an open sky. Amarynn stood and scanned the mountainside looming above her. She could scale the rocky outcrops to try to reach the ledge or return to camp. The need to search for the big creature was the real reason she was here, and it was almost overwhelming. She was positive they were Travelers like her, and she needed to understand how and, more importantly, why. As much as she hated heights, she felt an inexorable pull deep in her belly.

An urgency took hold, encouraging her to pick her way through the fallen boulders and debris. Scattered among the crumbled stone and mortar of the man-made portion of Athtull were the remnants of so many lives that had fallen as the mountain did. A scrap of worn black and red tapestry fluttered to her left, while the stem of a metal goblet that protruded from beneath a mass of stone glinted in the moonlight. Her heartbeat quickened, her reaction much more visceral than she had anticipated. In fact, she hadn't known what to expect when she bolted from the campsite and made her way into the ruins; she hadn't been thinking.

Distracted, she stumbled as her foot connected with an iron bar. Part of one of the dungeon cells lay uncovered amongst the rubble. Amarynn's breath caught as another rush of emotion took hold. She could almost feel the heat of the dungeon, and she nearly choked as the sensation of drowning in her own blood threatened to overtake her. The wound given to her by Lors was only slightly less devastating than what Matteus did to her. She had done her best to mask the excruciating pain and fear she felt as Lors plunged the dagger into her throat in front of Jael, but terror was never easy to hide. Her legs gave way and she fell to one knee, catching herself with one hand. Amarynn coughed and fought the urge to vomit when a wave of energy sizzled across her scalp, the welcome, cold energy rinsing away the onslaught of painful memories.

Safe.

Relief washed over her while her fingers gripped the stone beneath her, grounding her and slowing her breathing.

A piercing scream rang out as a familiar electric ripple washed down her spine. Amarynn stood and whirled around. A pair of broad wings emerged from a cloud bank, the moonlight casting an eerie glow on the atranoch as it banked back into the clouds. In the distance, Amarynn heard a faint reply.

"You stayed," she whispered to herself in wonder. The pull of energy strengthened, and she knew she could not resist; so she plotted her course by surveying the rubble at the mountain's base.

The journey began as an effortless climb. Amarynn refused to look over her shoulder to gauge her progress. *Don't look down.* Eyes fixed on the ledge above, she continued upward. Focusing so intently on not falling, she hadn't heard the flap of wings as an atranoch swept past her, the wind from its wings buffeting her against the rocky face. She clung to the rock, pressing herself as flat as possible while her heartbeat raced faster than before, though whether it was from her fear of heights or the sudden appearance of the atranoch, she did not know.

To avoid any more surprises, she listened for any further sign that the beasts were near, but heard nothing. Hand over hand, she crept ever closer to the ledge, trying to calm her mind. As she clung to the rock, the sleeve of her shirt caught on a sharp edge, and she experienced a brief panic; it tore as she tugged it free, and she was able to continue her climb. Finally, she could hoist herself over the side. She lay flat on her belly, panting, looking out toward the horizon. The wind had picked up, and clouds had moved in, obscuring both crescent moons' light. Not steady enough to stand so close to the edge, Amarynn rolled inward. Expecting to see the cave that had housed so many atranoch, she was surprised to find only a shallow indention in the mountainside, a single iron door in its center.

This wasn't the atranoch enclosure. It was the cliff-side arena where Venalise had tried to pit her against the biggest of the flying creatures. The mountain was so disfigured from the destruction of the Keep, she had mistaken it for the one she and Jael scaled to get off the mountain — not surprising, given that she had no memory of this side of the exterior.

Her eyes darted from left to right, and then she raised herself on her forearms to look out over the edge. She scrambled to her feet, knees bent and braced, and stared at the rolling hills she had seen once before from this vantage point. This was different from the aerie. Instead, she found herself in the arena where she had been pitted against the largest of the creatures.

A quick jog back to the iron door confirmed what she already knew: it was locked. There was no way out other than the way she had just come, and the moonlight was fading quickly as more clouds moved in.

She would have to stay up here till morning. Going up was one thing, and a difficult one at that, but going down the face of the mountain required vision, and without the moons to guide her, she might as well swan dive off the edge. She strode to the ledge to confirm her suspicion and then sidled to the edge, peering over.

Suddenly, a blast of air slammed into her, and she was tumbling sideways as an enormous atranoch burst from the far side of the mountain. It hovered above her, batting its wings to stay in the air. Green eyes whirled, and Amarynn recognized the beast as the one that had saved her when the mountain fell, the one she encountered on this very ledge.

She struggled to keep her footing against the buffeting force of its wings, but one final blast sent her tumbling, and she rolled backward towards the edge, her head slamming into the rock as she fell over the side, knocking her mercifully unconscious.

"That kind of night, was it?"

Aron woke to Nioll's snorting laughter. He was on his side, one arm flung across Amarynn's bedroll.

"Why? What'd she tell you?" he groaned as he sat up and rubbed his eyes, but Nioll was already gone. He stretched; a quick survey of the tent revealed that Amarynn's scabbard belt was absent, but her pack remained. Yawning, he pushed himself to his feet and ducked out into the early morning light. The other Travelers were sitting by the fire, finishing breakfast as Aron joined them.

"Where's Rynn?" he asked. His question was met with blank stares.

"Was it that bad that you scared her off?" Nioll quipped after a long silence. He cackled at his own suggestion.

"She took a sleeping draught. She should still be asleep." His gaze fell on each of the men in turn. Finn nudged Stavin's boot with his own, but it did not go unnoticed by Aron.

"What? Do you know something?" A sinking feeling took hold in Aron's gut.

"No, but this is classic Rynn," Finn frowned. "Two gold says she spit it out."

Aron grimaced and rolled his eyes. She had played him, and he had fallen for it.

"She snuck off to Athtull on her own, didn't she?"

"Aye," Finn rubbed his face in frustration. "As always, she thinks she's ready to do whatever it is she plans to do, but I guarantee that's the revenge talking."

"You have no idea," Stavin sighed. "She won't stop until the score is settled. You can be sure of that."

"Do we follow her?" Aron looked between the two Travelers.

"I could keep an eye out," a tired voice called out from behind Amarynn's tent. A glow, warm and soft like a candle, came into view from the shadows. It was Xan. He held a ball of orange light in one hand and, in the other, one of Amarynn's throwing knives. He stepped closer to the fire.

"Oi, if she finds out you nicked one of her blades, yer done for," Nioll scoffed.

"It was stuck in one of the rabbits. She left it."

Finn and Stavin exchanged worried glances.

"But I can use it," Xan continued. "I can track her with my magic."

"That's not a good sign, is it?" Aron was eyeing Finn and Stavin. She would never leave a weapon behind.

Stavin cleared his throat. "She's been..." he started.

"Off." Finn finished Stavin's thought. "These dreams she's been having—"

"Her mind is scattered." Stavin cut in.

Back in Calliway, Aron had taken turns with the two other Travelers listening for her screams during the night. Each of them had comforted her, seeing the devastating pain etched on her face. But, of the three of them, only Finn and Stavin had known her for many years before, and it was clear that their concern ran deep.

Aron stood.

"I'll help you keep an eye on her," he called to Xan, stepping over the log he had been sitting on. "I have a feeling things are going to become much more difficult."

"As they usually do when that lass is involved," Nioll muttered to no one in particular.

"She's alive," Xan announced.

The apprentice mage and Aron had made the decision to take Dax along with them to try to locate her. They had made their way to the ruins of the Keep and were exploring what they could access, Xan tracking Amarynn using the blade, and Aron following more practical leads. He had easily identified her footprints and had moved on to identifying more subtle signs like bends in the foliage and displaced rocks.

"She's an immortal, wise one," Aron sneered. "Of course she's alive."

The young mage had lost his ability to sense her only a handful of hours after she'd left camp. Now, Aron had a nagging suspicion that they should try to find her, not trail her. Finn, Stavin, and Nioll had stayed behind on the off chance she might make her way back to camp on her own.

"What I meant," Xan rolled his eyes at Aron, "is that I've found her again, and she's on the move. I can feel her presence ebbing and receding."

Aron surveyed the wreckage of Athtull and the surrounding valley. The wind whistled through the soaring oldwood trees, pushing clouds through the blue-grey sky.

"Where are you, she-demon?" Aron murmured as his eyes flitted through the rubble. A piercing shriek sounded from somewhere aloft, the cry echoing off the great mountain peaks surrounding the two of them. Xan ducked, covering his head at the sound. Aron recognized the calls from when Athtull fell, and he scanned the skies to catch a glimpse of the flying creatures.

"Lost her again!" Xan threw his arms up in exasperation as he stood back up.

Aron shook his head, then began to pick his way through the debris to look for any trace of Amarynn.

"And you came so highly recommended," Aron mumbled, keeping his eyes on the ground before him.

"Even magic has limitations," Xan mumbled, following Aron over the broken stone blocks.

Aron paused, hands on his hips, and looked up toward a wide ledge, searching for anything to confirm she had been at the Keep. He had nearly given up when his eye caught a piece of fabric that whipped in the cold wind near the cliff's edge.

"She was here," Aron said, pointing toward his discovery.

"She climbed that?" Xan shielded his eyes to look up at the cliff. The whistling wind accentuated the staggering height.

"Well, she didn't fly."

Xan scowled at Aron. "But where do you think she's gone now?"

"Knowing her, she's gotten her fool self into trouble." Aron frowned and looked down at Xan. "Which is something she seems to do more often than most."

"What should we do?" Xan fidgeted with the throwing knife, wincing when he accidentally pricked the skin on his palm. He quickly tucked the injured hand into his pocket.

"Your magic is spotty, and your blade handling is lacking," Aron chuckled as he looked back up toward the cliff. "I'm really trying to understand why Bent sent you with us!"

Xan furrowed his brow, muttering to himself. He tucked the throwing knife into his belt and made a fist in Aron's direction, a faint glow of heat radiating from between his fingers.

Something nagged at Aron. He knew of Amarynn's fear of heights, so he couldn't fathom why part of her shirt would be so high near the cliff's edge. Fear or not, though, she might have attempted to climb it, but for what reason?

Another shriek reverberated off the surrounding mountains. The few times she spoke of her last moments in the Keep, she mentioned the scaled creature that had protected her from the falling rocks — the same beast that refused to attack her on the ledge. Would it be possible that one of them snatched her from the side of the cliff?

Aron dismissed his thought as quickly as it came to him. Why would the beast, who she says protected her, make off with her now? The pair picked their way back to Dax, who they had left at the edge of the ruins. He greeted them with an impatient stamp of his hoof.

"Maybe one of those flying things attacked her," Xan whispered as he gathered up Dax's reins, adding a new worry to his thoughts. "She could be injured."

"No," Aron breathed as he followed the sound of the beast's cry. Considering the mountains' differing heights and positions, he tried to decipher its location while he searched the sky for any sign. But it was empty, save for a sprinkling of wispy clouds and the bright sun. A few thicker and heavier clouds drifted across the pale grey blue. "Something tells me that they won't hurt her."

One more cry echoed, this one more distant than the others. Aron concentrated on the sound. Once certain of the general direction, he turned and ducked back into the forest's shadows. Xan followed without a word, trying not to stumble as they rushed back the way they came. Aron quickened his pace back toward the camp, casting a glance over his shoulder.

"How are your mountaineering skills?"

THE
STONE REACHES

CHAPTER 7

S unset came quickly after the Suhonne patrol found Venalise and her group of riders. The former Darkland guards — three men and one woman — who followed her into the mountain pass after Athtull Keep's fall, lagged behind them. No one spoke. The only sounds were the horses' breath and their hooves crunching the hard-packed snow.

Venalise scanned ahead at the backs of the Suhonne riders. The reality of being back in her homeland had not quite registered, but she felt the power in her former station stirring. She had left this place, well-established as the banished heir to her mother's power, but she felt no trepidation now with the Gate and Sia in her possession.

Ahead, the white ground gleamed with the rising moonlight. Venalise's breath caught as she looked up at the sky; she had forgotten how beautiful and dark the evening sky was up on the plateau. Stars were just beginning to twinkle where the violet and indigo faded into black, but a sharp order from Sashtra brought Venalise's attention back to the ground. The leader of the Suhonne patrol's words were low and guttural in the Eorath dialect of the Reaches, but their meaning was clear.

At Sashtra's directive, five of the Suhonne riders urged their horses to the front Another five slowed and fell from Venalise's periphery. The Suhonne were a people of the frozen steppes, and most likely the riders were breaking off to continue their patrol. The last four, including Sashtra, stayed close to Venalise and her men.

"We are near, *Emmina*." Sashtra said, pointing at the low lights of the Suhonne stronghold ahead.

Venalise tried to hide her surprise at the use of the title. It had been years since she had answered to *Emmina*. She had left her status as prime heir to the Stone Reaches long ago and honestly, she never wanted that title attached to her name again. It would be Empress, or it would be nothing.

She hadn't intended to announce her return so quickly, but she had not expected to encounter a patrol. In her rush to get to the scholar enclave of Lorce, she had forgotten how thorough the Suhonne were in their surveillance. So when she had been confronted by the leader of the Suhonne riders in Eorath, the common language in the Stone Reaches, she couldn't resist adding the feel of Ceadari to her tongue. Though all understood it, only the noble houses of the Reaches spoke it. The brief conversation in her native tongue had ignited an urgency in her belly to put her plan in motion.

"I'm tired," Sia murmured from beneath the wool wraps as warm breath and a cold nose snuffled free of the coverings. Thera, the stone bear cub, blinked innocently before taking a mouthful of Venalise's cloak. The little cub tugged and grumbled when the child pulled her back beneath the wraps.

"Stay quiet, child." Venalise whispered. "We are nearly there."

The lights grew brighter as they neared the wide, low stronghold. Venalise was aware of what awaited her behind those walls. She knew this would be the first test.

The stronghold loomed ahead, a dark silhouette against the starlit, indigo expanse of sky. It was time.

Her group of riders, flanked by the Suhonne patrol, approached the entrance of the stronghold when the sky had plunged into the inky black of night. The low wall that surrounded the collection of structures had only one entrance that was protected by the wide, thick gates. Two small sconces on either side flickered with torches that fought the cold, damp wind. The atranoch, most of whom had trailed then since they left Athtull Keep, were nowhere to be seen now. They were likely roosting in the craggy outcrops that surrounded the wide, low cluster of structures. It was curious, though, that they were all younger creatures. The older, larger beasts had not made an appearance.

Torches lined the inner walls, their flickering light casting eerie shadows on the stone. The Suhonne riders dismounted, sliding effortlessly off their mounts, and made their way to the stables, their horses following them without encouragement. One by one, each disappeared into the darkness of a wide door.

Sashtra remained behind while Venalise let Sia slide down onto the hard, snow-packed ground. Venalise swung her leg over and followed.

"*Emmina*, you will bring your horses this way." Sashtra's chin dipped in a quick nod, and she turned toward the stable. Venalise reached for Sia's hand, grabbing her horse's reins with the other. Together, they followed Sashtra.

The stables were warm, a welcome respite from the blistering cold, but she watched as Sia wrinkled her nose at the pungent odor of animal dung that hung heavy in the air. Wet, ripping sounds drew her eyes to the right, where a massive creature, suspended from the rafters, lay open for butchering. Two men worked at removing the shaggy white pelt, arguing in Eorath.

"A white elk," Venalise explained. Sia squirmed out from beneath the large blanket wrapped around her shoulders, letting it fall behind her.

"Sia," Venalise snapped, motioning for her to cover the bear cub she still clutched. The child scrambled to gather the blanket and cover herself so that Thera was invisible. As they made their way across the hay-strewn floor, Sia cast several long glances behind her, marveling at the size of the great elk. Its front hooves brushed the ground, even with its hind legs hoisted to the rafters. She glanced down at the tiny creature, still shoving its nose into the crook of her arm. Venalise placed a hand on Sia's shoulder, and the child looked up in awe.

Venalise stopped and crouched in front of Sia, offering her an apologetic smile. She had forgotten what a shock all of this must be to the child.

"Stone bears like yours are instruments of war — warriors of the Reaches must earn them, which can take decades. Being given a cub means you have proven yourself and are of the elite. They would view a small child keeping one as a pet to be irreverent," she whispered, tapping the blanket where Thera hid. "This outpost doesn't keep bears for the safety of the horses, so we are fortunate. Still, keep her quiet and hidden until we leave for Lorce." Sia tightened her grip on Thera and stepped behind Venalise as the mage straightened up.

Venalise turned to the riders from her party. "Take care of our horses. You can bed with them in here. I will send for you when I am ready."

"*Emmina*, I will see them taken care of," Sashtra said from behind her. "Come with me now."

Venalise nodded and she and Sia followed Sashtra through a squat, narrow doorway into a sprawling hall.

A blazing hearth roared at the end of the low, long room filled with Suhonne people. The atmosphere in the community hall was relaxed, the air drier and much warmer than the stables, almost stifling. Aromas of roasting meats and brews of strong jhea permeated the air while a smoky haze drifted in the low rafters. A table stretched before it, and seated around one side, their backs to the fire, were three women and one man. The women, elders by the wrinkles on their faces and rigid posture, sat silently observing the hall. They spoke in hushed tones to one another, their eyes never leaving the expanse of the room. Only the man, dressed in too many furs and a tight leather cap, seemed involved in the goings on around him. He laughed as he lifted his tankard and cheered at a pair of younger men engaged in a wrestling match at the side of the hall. In the middle of the room, Sashtra stopped Venalise and Sia with her outstretched hand, then continued to the table, where she whispered something to the four seated there.

The eldest of the three women rose from her seat and walked around the table to stand with Sashtra. A collective hush fell as she moved. While the two women talked, one or the other would glance in Venalise's direction. The older woman shook her head and sighed. Finally, they began to walk towards Venalise and Sia, the elder more agile in her gait than her age suggested. They reached the middle of the hall, where Venalise and Sia waited. The occupants of the hall remained quiet, all eyes trained on them.

The old woman approached, narrowing her nut-brown eyes, with the firelight making the wrinkles on her face even more pronounced. As they neared and slowed her pace, Venalise recognized her and met her stare, lifting her chin proudly. The last time she had stood in front of her, she was much younger, though no less defiant.

"T'Korr Vena." The older woman drew out each syllable of her name the way she had done when Venalise was a girl.

"*Aba* Steffa," Venalise replied, using her customary Eorath title in a reluctant show of respect.

The woman's eyebrows raised slightly, her leathery skin mottled with the varying colors of age and past rounds of frostbite. Her eyes were familiar, though, the same ice-flecked green of her mother's. "You remember your place here, in my house?"

"I remember the whippings I received every time I fell from my horse," Venalise replied, her tone guarded.

The old woman arched one eyebrow, "There *were* many," she said.

Steffa, her aunt, was correct. Horsemanship had never been one of Venalise's strong suits.

The old woman turned her gaze to Sia. Venalise followed the old woman's eyes and placed a possessive arm around the little girl's slight shoulders. Sia leaned into her embrace, clearly uncomfortable under scrutiny, and confused. She wouldn't understand the language being spoken between the two women.

"The child? She is *sama*?" Steffa leaned toward Sia as if to inspect her. As she reached for her, Venalise quickly shuffled the child behind her. Perhaps it was a reaction to her harsh childhood with the Suhonne, but she couldn't help but try to shield her. The less her aunt knew about her, the better.

"No, *Aba*," Venalise said. "She is not my child. She is my ward."

Steffa nodded, pursing her lips. "Follow me." Her curt directive did not surprise Venalise. There was no warm greeting for family, no welcome, just as it had been when her mother delivered her here when she was a child. Even her mother had not said goodbye when she'd left her; emotions weren't welcome in House Korr or Suhonne. Warriors lost battles because of emotions.

Steffa and Sashtra wound through the tables scattered throughout the hall at a clipped pace, Venalise and Sia trailing behind them. Venalise kept the girl behind her, but she still held her hand. At the back of the crowded tables, one woman, clad in a deep blue hooded cloak, rose from her seat as they passed. Venalise's gaze lingered on her and the man seated next to her; they seemed familiar. When the blue-cloaked woman gave his shoulder a tap, he rose, his eyes averted, and the pair hastily left the hall in the opposite direction.

Venalise and Sia followed the Suhonne women through the dim, narrow passageways into another wide, low chamber lit by firelight. Steffa clutched the arms of the chair nearest the hearth with gnarled fingers and eased down with a sigh. She lifted her hand and gestured for Venalise to take the seat closest to her. Sashtra ushered Sia to the far side of the room.

"A stone bear cub?" Steffa glared at her niece as the pair faded into the shadows. "That is forbidden."

Her aunt could smell a wild animal two miles away, Venalise mused. It was another reason she had not done well with the Suhonne as a child.

Her hunting skills and instincts were dismal compared to the people of the icy steppes.

"It is none of your concern. She is not from the Reaches. Our ways are not hers." Venalise did not try to hide the distance she was keeping between Steffa and Sia.

The old woman grunted and shifted in her chair. A gust of wind blew small flurries through a crack in the seam where the low roof met the building. Aside from the blustering gusts, and Sashtra and Sia's murmurs, the only other sound was the snapping and crackling of the fire.

"You were always stubborn, Vena." Steffa broke the quiet. "I told my sister so when I sent you back to Korr. You belonged in the Spire, not here." Steffa's admission shocked Venalise, but she hid the surprise she felt by staring straight ahead into the hearth. She leaned back on the utilitarian elk-hide chair, twisting her neck to relieve the tight muscles in her shoulders.

Steffa leaned forward, towards her niece. "Eleven years!" Shaking her head, she reached over to a side table and produced a short bone pipe. Once lit, she inhaled deeply and let the pungent white smoke escape her lips before continuing. "It has been eleven years since you left your house without a word, and now you return. Why?" Steffa leveled a hard look at Venalise.

"My mother wanted me to be a warrior." Venalise continued to stare into the low flames. "Me," she said, her quiet tone laced with disgust. "My weapon is my magic, but the almighty Uhll refused to see the truth of that."

"Uhll is my sister." Steffa rapped loudly on the arm of her chair with the pipe. Venalise flinched, turned her attention to the old woman. Satisfied, Steffa continued. "She had the interest of the Stone Reaches in mind. You would have inherited that had you not only been thinking about yourself."

"The warrior houses of the Stone Reaches are archaic, *Aba*. But the scholars of Lorce—"

"Those old fools in the Spire have no business in the defense of the Reaches!" Steffa sat up straighter and gripped the arms of her chair.

"No?" Venalise hissed, leaning forward. "You have no idea what I am capable of now." She cast her eyes around the room.

"Magic can make pretty lights and coax a flower to bloom." Steffa scoffed, puffing on her pipe. "It is no weapon!"

Venalise's eyes narrowed. If it would take a blade to speak the language of the warriors and show her power, since the old woman refused to listen to reason... With a flick of her wrist, a small serving knife flew across the room and embedded itself in the wood of Steffa's chair, the metal vibrating beside her head, escaped wisps of her hair fluttering with its sudden trajectory. The old woman did not flinch, but raised her eyebrows. Steffa studied Venalise for several seconds, then called for Sashtra.

"Take the *emmina* and the child and give them appropriate quarters. They will rest tonight." It wasn't a request.

Sashtra nodded and motioned for Venalise to follow. Sia, still wrapped in her blanket with Thera, shuffled over to Venalise as she stood. Sia yawned, adjusting her hold on the squirming bundle hidden at her chest.

"You will need to think about what you plan to tell your mother, Vena," Steffa said. "There have been many changes since you left. You will not find Korr the way you left it."

Venalise let her eyes linger on her aunt's back, still erect in her chair for a moment, and then she reached for Sia's hand. Together, they followed Sashtra into the dark hallway. The sooner they could be on their way to Lorce, the better. Time was precious, and if Venalise wanted an army strong enough to help her realize her plans, she didn't have a minute to spare.

CHAPTER 8

"Who was that lady you were talking to before?" Sia crawled into the mass of furs and woolen blankets that covered the low sleeping pallet. Venalise wandered around the small room. As a way to make sure she still knew her place in the Suhonne stronghold, her aunt had told Sashtra to put them in Venalise's old quarters. It had been years since she had even thought of her time here, and now it was all around her. The experience was becoming more than she wanted.

"That, my dear, was my mother's sister," Venalise said, her irritation obvious by her sharp tone and her frown.

"She's mean," Sia mumbled, snuggling beneath a fur of white and silver-grey. Now that they were in the room away from the Suhonne, Sia lifted the edge of the fur-lined blanket and released Thera from her hiding place. The cub rolled around on her back in the bountiful furs, her paws batting at the air.

"She is," Venalise nodded, opening a chest next to the pallet. She rifled through the contents, expecting to see some of her things, but only found more skins and furs for sleeping. Thera, now completely free of Sia's control, explored the room, appearing beside her. She shoved her nose beneath Venalise's arm to investigate the open chest and letting loose a playful growl. Sia peeked over the edge of the furs, her mouth turned up in a rare smile. Venalise was reminded of herself at that age.

She would have been sleeping exactly where Sia lay, though she was certain a smile never touched her lips while she was here. The memories of her warding with her mother's sister were only unhappy. It was the last place she ever wanted to be because it meant she would never receive the training she yearned for in Lorce. Thera nipped at her arm and rolled to her back, exposing her stomach. Ruffling Thera's fur, she noticed that the cub had already grown wider than her splayed fingers. Venalise tucked the blankets around Sia. "Now, you must sleep. We will ride deeper into the Reaches soon, and you will need your strength."

Sia closed her eyes for a moment, then opened them again, her silvery irises accentuating her furrowed brow. "Why did we come here?"

Venalise thought for a moment before she answered. It had taken weeks for Sia to trust her, and she did not want to say anything that might cause the child more worry than she already felt. If she wanted Sia to cooperate with her, she needed to solidify their growing bond.

"We needed to hide from the Prince, remember? And the scholars at a stronghold called Lorce can help us understand your gifts," she explained. "I want you to learn how to use them, sweetling. Now, sleep."

Sia closed her eyes again when Venalise stroked her hair. It was hard to comprehend how such a tiny slip of a girl could hold so much power. Venalise had fought long and hard to develop her own gift, but Sia held it as naturally as she breathed. *And she doesn't even know it.*

Now she must learn to refine it and channel it.

A quiet knock interrupted Venalise's thoughts. She pushed herself off the low, fur-lined bed and glided to the door. Sliding the wooden latch aside, she opened the door just enough to make out the face that waited in the dark hall. Expecting one of the Suhonne, she was taken aback by uncharacteristic green eyes flashing beneath a fur hood. The figure leaned further into the light.

"Oravae?" Venalise breathed. It *was* her that she saw in the hall when they arrived.

"Greetings, *isa,*" a lilting voice replied in Ceadari, a dangerous edge to her voice. You have returned to us. Welcome home."

Venalise pulled the door open. "Why are you here?" She reached for the woman's arm, pulling her into the room. Another figure materialized from the dark shadows in the hallway, sliding inside before Venalise closed the door. He pushed his hood back, letting long, dark brown braids fall around his broad shoulders. Venalise's eyes widened in surprise. With his ice-blue eyes and dark hair, he looked so much like her brother, it was startling.

"Tasar?"

"Cousin," he nodded curtly.

Venalise was speechless. Oravae was here. It had been nearly ten years since she'd seen either of them. Oravae should be in Lorce with her father at the Spire, not at the Reaches' edge with the Suhonne. And Tasar? How he was able to steal away from her uncle and the Korr forces, she had no idea.

"We've been waiting for you, Vena." Oravae raised her eyebrows. "It took you long enough!"

"Waiting? Why?" Venalise stole a quick glance behind her at Sia, who was sitting upright, wide-eyed, trying to conceal a rambunctious Thera — to no avail.

Oravae cast a quick look at the two on the fur-covered pallet. She didn't seem to try to hide her questioning look. Instead, she pulled the blue hood back and leaned against the wall, crossing her arms and arcing one eyebrow. Several red curls escaped their braids and fell around her face, just like they did when she was a girl. Oravae was the wild one, always countered by Venalise, who had tried her best to appear serious and well-kept. Even though they were inseparable as girls, they couldn't have been more opposite. "You've been busy, it seems. A child *and* a pet?"

"She's not mine," Venalise said, taking a side-step to block Oravae's view.

"*Isa*, sister, we must speak privately," Oravae whispered, her eyes fixed on the space past Venalise's shoulder where Sia and Thera sat.

"She doesn't speak Ceadari or Eorath," Venalise said quickly.

Tasar nodded in the child's direction. "She's not yours, then?"

"No!" she exclaimed, then her face softened a fraction. "But she's under my protection."

"Ha!" Oravae huffed. "You? *Protect* anything? She must be valuable, or you wouldn't bother." Venalise whirled back to face Oravae. Her childhood friend often pushed her boundaries, but she was stepping dangerously close to a line she shouldn't cross.

Tasar stepped between the two women and touched Oravae's shoulder, a gesture which made Venalise frown. Tasar's familiarity with Oravae seemed out of character, for both of them. He turned to Venalise. "*Emmina*, we need to get you to Lorce."

"What?" Venalise couldn't help but roll her eyes at the use of her title. Up until now, it hadn't bothered her, though her cousin's use of it was too much. Her brow furrowed. "You don't have to call me that."

Oravae remained quiet as she looked at Tasar, waiting for him to speak.

"Vena," he began again, "We know where you have come from and what you have been doing. Reaches people — *our* people — have been keeping to the shadows in the lowlands, following you. Even on the shores of the Handaals, through the years—"

"Reaches folk? In the shadows?" Venalise cocked her head.

"You know my father has wanted Lorce to control the Reaches since before we were born." Oravae dropped her voice to an urgent whisper. "He planned to bring you back when he discovered you harnessed the magic."

"Bring me back?" Venalise stepped back from Oravae. She had not planned for Reaches folk to know as much about her exploits in Karth as they apparently did. This would make her plan much more challenging and entangled than she had planned. Her eyes narrowed. "What magic do you—"

"We know you learned Traveler magic," Oravae cut in, her tone impatient. "He wants you so you can help him take control of the Reaches. But I need to know whether you plan to travel to Lorce or to Korr."

Venalise laughed out loud, at the idea of Rhymere thinking he had any control over her whatsoever, but quickly stifled her mirth. Before she could respond, the sound of voices from the hallway silenced her.

Tasar and Oravae hastily pulled their hoods up and backed to the wall beside the door. When the noise subsided, Tasar pulled the door open slowly, listening to the dark hall. He nodded to Oravae before he slipped out.

"Vena," she said, so quietly that Venalise needed to lean in to hear her, "leave this place in the morning. We will find you on the road." She followed Tasar, but before the shadows swallowed her, she glanced back at where Venalise stood in the low light of the doorway. "You picked an interesting time to return, *isa*," she shook her head. "Go in the morning. We will find you."

Venalise watched her childhood friend disappear down the low corridor, then pushed the door to with a click. None of this made sense. Oravae was a scholar's daughter, a scholar's child of the Spire. She looked different, too — hardened by more than the years. She had said there was more to tell, which was evident by how she now dressed and the Korr clan company she kept.

Venalise sighed and pinched the bridge of her nose. Her plans had suddenly become more complicated. Oravae's father, Rhymere, and the Lorce scholars were supposed to be a resource — nothing more. Now he wanted to take the Reaches from her mother? Never in a thousand years would she have considered Oravae's father an obstacle.

Venalise moved through the room, turning down the lantern to a low flame, then removing her overdress and draping it across the stool near the foot of the pallet. She kicked off her boots before she lay down next to Sia, tucking a loose curl behind the child's ear. Thera nosed her way between the two of them and sighed as she rolled to her side, paws posing on Venalise's chest. Sia smiled, then closed her eyes.

Venalise hated that she had no other option to understand Sia's abilities, without the knowledge contained in Rhymere's Library in Lorce. Oravae's mention of her father's ambition was an unexpected and unwelcome impediment. She closed her eyes and tried to rest in the dim room, the silence only broken by the grunts and whimpers of a dreaming bear cub, though sleep was a long time coming.

CHAPTER 9

D arkness was a blanket, shielding any light. It was oppressive. And cold.

Sia shivered, her crossed arms scrubbing up and down her bare skin. The scene unfolded around her — snow was falling, heavy in the dark nighttime air. An animal growled behind her.

She turned and gasped at the bear at her back. Her cub was no longer an inquisitive and headstrong youngling; she was a behemoth, taller than the young girl by twice her height, her baby teeth now transformed into a terrifying maw. Thera shook her white undercoat, and the snow fell away, revealing the scattered grey of her adult pelt. She prowled around something that huddled near the ground. The air quivered with the tension that she emanated.

"Thera, come!" Sia commanded, but her words did not affect the massive animal. Thera swung her head back and forth, asserting her dominance over whatever she was circling, only giving a quick huff to acknowledge Sia's directive.

"Vena." A man's trembling voice broke through the sounds of the stone bear's heavy breaths and giant paws crunching on the snow. His voice was high — he sounded young. "Help me."

In response, Thera quickened her pace, tightening the circle. Sia felt the bear's growl, deep and resonant, more than she heard it as her vision clouded and her body went numb. When her eyesight cleared, her surroundings came into sharp focus, though her perspective had shifted, as if she'd grown taller. She could see all around her as she swung her head about, but her focus kept snapping back to the man. He was pale, and smelled of fear and desolation. His dark hair starkly contrasted with the snow surrounding him, and while he wore well-appointed clothing, the fabric was dirty and torn. Scrapes and bruises peppered his face and arms and one long, bleeding gash was visible across his left shoulder.

She could smell his blood, and his fear. The scents overcrowded her senses; it was familiar. She wanted to taste it, to tear into the anxiety huddled in front of her. Sia shook her head and gasped, the intrusive feeling startling her.

No, Thera!

Sia's voice felt small — powerless to fight the bloodlust that threatened to overtake her.

The man's eyes widened at the sight of the massive bear. His mouth moved as if he were trying to speak, but no sound came out while he reached for a crude, long knife belted at his waist. His fingers could not find purchase, though, his trembling hands unable to close around the hilt.

The snowfall had thickened, nearly obscuring the hulking figure of the bear. Sia felt rage flood through her, and she lunged forward at Thera as the bear roared.

"Help m—"

Thera!

Sia stumbled and fell, face down. Her vision clouded and as hard as she tried, she couldn't will her voice to sound out. The only noise she could muster was a guttural, visceral growl. Then, the rush of the blowing wind relented as the heat of the bear's blood faded, leaving Sia small and limp. She lay dazed in the snow, her eyes closing...

"Sia!"

Light flickered behind her closed eyes.

"Sia!"

Not the man, but Venalise, though the sound of the figure's voice still echoed in her mind. *Help me!*

"Child! Get up. We need to prepare to leave."

The furs were pulled away from her and Sia scrambled to sit, her breaths coming in heaves. Venalise's hands grasped her shoulders, but just as quickly as the mage's hands touched Sia's skin, she hissed and pulled them away.

"You are freezing, child!" Concern replaced the impatience in Venalise's tone.

Sia felt the padding footsteps of Thera, scrambling over the pile of furs, huffing and nuzzling her nose beneath Sia's arm. Sia rolled over, relieved to see her cub still just a cub, and pulled the stone bear and her warmth to her chest. She tucked her chin and nuzzled her nose on top of Thera's head.

"I'm fine," she mumbled as the images of the wounded man played in her mind. She hugged Thera tighter.

"By what standards?" Venalise muttered. She placed one of her hands on Sia's back and began an incantation. Sia recoiled at the first hint of warmth from Venalise's hand, then sat up, pulling Thera onto her lap. She eyed Venalise warily, unable to forget the man calling out her name. *Vena*, he'd cried out. *Help me!* Who was he? She wasn't sure she wanted to know. Sia had seen the way Venalise treated Amarynn, the warrior she held prisoner in her aethertorium, but she had been kind to her. Mostly kind, especially when she wanted Sia to try something with her magic.

"I said, I'm fine," she repeated, brow furrowed. Thera squirmed out of her arms, and Sia watched as the cub lumbered to the opposite side of the pallet. She had been so big in her dream.

Venalise eyed her warily. "You were dreaming. What did you see?"

Sia looked away. She didn't want Venalise to ask more questions because she had no answers for her, and she wasn't sure she would share them if she did.

"Listen to me, girl," Venalise growled. "With your powers unchecked, you are a magical cataclysm waiting to happen. I am all that is standing between you and disaster. Now." She adjusted her speaking voice to sound concerned once more. "What did you see in your dream?"

"Thera," Sia mumbled, eyes still averted, wishing Venalise would leave her alone. The dream and the feelings it conjured were frightening enough. Sia licked her lips, the iron-sharp tang of blood lingering in her nose. Part of her wanted to tell Venalise, so that perhaps she could help her make some sense of it, but a nagging feeling made her hold back.

"That doesn't explain why you were so cold."

Sia hesitated. Maybe she could share a little about Thera's size and the man, but not what she felt and saw. That was something she needed to keep to herself.

"She was grown — massive. We were in the snow, and she was getting ready to kill someone." Sia turned back towards Venalise, meeting her gaze hesitantly. "She wouldn't listen to me."

"Who was she trying to kill?" Venalise couldn't hide the anticipation in her voice. Sia looked closely at the woman responsible for her care and safety, wondering why her eyes were suddenly glittering.

"I don't know. I couldn't see him." Sia looked away again.

"Him?"

"I think so. I didn't recognize the voice." She kept her eyes fixed on the wall across the room. The man had cried out *Vena*, but Sia felt she needed to keep that to herself, as well, especially considering Venalise's apparent eagerness to know.

Venalise studied Sia for a moment, then reached for her hand. This time, the child reciprocated, and the mage noticed the girl's hand was warmer now.

"Well done," Venalise nodded, lifting Sia's hand. "You didn't catch anything on fire. That's progress."

Sia looked away again. An uncomfortable energy writhed in her belly, dark and angry. She pulled her hand from Venalise's grasp and slid her feet beneath her to rise to her knees. The energy settled in her, less angry now, but it was still there, just out of reach.

She knew Venalise was eyeing her, so she feigned a smile. "Thank you. I'll get dressed and packed up."

She could feel the mage's gaze on her while she pulled a heavy wool tunic over her head. Thera batted at the fringe along the bottom, grunting and growling, but Sia pretended not to notice the cub as she stuffed a blanket and small pillow into her pack.

Venalise was behind her now.

"Are you sure you didn't recognize the man you saw?"

"I'm sure." Sia's tone was tinged with impatience. She closed her eyes and tried to quell the rising energy she had just suppressed.

"Nothing at all?

Sia whirled around, the blanket around her shoulders dropping to the floor. "No!" Her body was warming up even more. Like it had on the boat when Venalise caught her trying to steal the Gate stone for Regealth, fire raged in her belly and threatened to overtake her, but harnessing the lessons that Venalise had taught her, she controlled it, pushed it back down. Her breaths, quick and shallow, slowed as she calmed herself.

"Excellent," Venalise breathed, and Sia could see the mage's excitement at her progress. "Your control is improving. Now let's get moving. We need to get to Lorce as soon as we can."

Atranoch calls echoed and bounced around the frozen valley, the breadth of the sound diminishing further the small line of horses that trudged along the glacier's edge.

Sunlight cast crisp fractals of shimmering light across the frozen landscape. The five horses created a dark smudge on the pristine white background, interrupted only briefly by an occasional whirling shadow of one of the winged beasts as it circled in the morning sky.

Venalise tugged on the leather lead attached to the smaller pony that carried Sia.

"We need to move faster to get to the mountain lodge before nightfall." She looked over her shoulder at Sia, who was struggling to hold Thera. The bear was thrashing wildly, her claws nearly injuring Sia's face.

"Stop!" Venalise called out to the other Suhonne riders. Her own people from Athtull, unaccustomed to the prolonged cold, had stayed behind at the Suhonne compound. She dismounted, making her way back to the girl. "Give her to me." She held her arms out.

"What are you going to do with her?" Sia frowned.

"I'm going to let her walk," Venalise replied, lifting the wriggling Thera from Sia's arms. She crouched down to set the bear onto the hard-packed snow and then stood up, hands on her hips. She looked pointedly at Sia.

"She's a stone bear. This—" Venalise gestured to the barren landscape— "this is where she belongs. She needs to learn how to be a bear—and it won't kill her to run a little."

"But what if she gets lost?"

Venalise smirked.

"Child, she has bonded to you. Yours were the first eyes she saw when you Traveled her with your magic. Your arms were the first to hold her." Venalise swung herself back up into the saddle. "She'll never be far from you. Never."

Venalise pushed them to continue. As the morning wore on, snow gave way to smatterings of ice, then the sun broke through. Still, the harsh winds of Suhonne territory assaulted them mercilessly while Thera bounded along behind the horses. Delighting in her newfound freedom, she careened through the snowdrifts that lined the trail. Sia sat tall in the saddle, smiling at her antics now and then, but clearly uneasy about her bear cub being out of her protective grasp.

At midday, Venalise called a halt, and they let the horses rest and eat. If she had learned anything from her time here, it was that horses in this climate need to be meticulously cared for and respected. She had never mastered riding in the way of the Suhonne, so the only thing she truly excelled at was understanding their tough, hard-working horses. Not only the horses; she was intrigued by all the animals of the frozen steppes — the majestic white elk, the snow wolves, and the formidable stone bears. Bonding with a stone bear was a rare Stone Reaches privilege that even her aunt had never achieved, making Sia's bond with Thera a source of pride for Venalise.

Thera, still full of energy now that she had an outlet, playfully tumbled through the caravan, antagonizing the horses as she tried to bat at their tails. Sia chased her away each time she got too close, worried the cub might get under the hooves of the horses, or worse, get kicked. One of the riders suppressed her laughter.

"A kick will not hurt it; it will teach it. Stone bears hunt horses. Even the smallest bear is not afraid of a horse!"

Sia grimaced at the unsolicited advice and continued to try and redirect her towards the snowdrifts in front of the group.

Not quite refreshed, they pushed on anyway. Venalise was anxious to arrive at the mountain lodge before sundown, her pace relentless. This was snow wolf territory and after dark was when the packs emerged to hunt. As the sun dipped lower in the sky, she became more alert, constantly scanning the horizon. Their destination should not be much further.

The atranoch had disappeared, and now the sky was fading into brilliant hues of orange and purple as twilight flirted with the late afternoon

horizon. The mountain peaks changed into craggy hills dotted with
scrubby pines, shadows casting a premature darkness on the trail. Wide,
white plains slanted down and eventually disappeared into ravines filled
with an overgrowth of trees and scrub. Snow still covered the ground, but
the further south they traveled, the more patches of winter groundcover
peeked through the fresh white.

The group was just below the tree line, and even at their lower eleva-
tion, they could see that the landscape before them was vastly different
than the snowy plains the Suhonne called home.

As they rounded a low hill, the mountain lodge came into view. Nestled
in the low trees along a rocky outcrop, it was shielded from the harsh
winds that roared out of the Stone Giant range. The log structure had
been there as long as Venalise could remember. A low, spartan building
made to shelter travelers crossing into the interior of the Reaches, it was
large enough for a larger party, complete with simple stables built along
its side wall — a Reaches trick to help keep their horses warm. Venalise
spent many nights here as a girl, though her memories weren't fond as it
meant a trip to the Suhonne was imminent.

"What?" Venalise spoke without meaning to; this wasn't what she
expected. The lodge should be empty at this time of year because most
of the elk had already migrated to the lower climates.

"What's wrong?" Sia's horse ambled up to Venalise. Thera's cavorting
had slowed, and the little bear was trudging along beside her, snow and
ice clinging to her thick fur and ears.

"No one should be here." She pointed to the lodge, where smoke rose
from the chimney and a soft light glowed from the single window. There
was movement from the open-fronted stable, and as they drew closer, two
horses were visibly tethered inside.

"Who is it?" Sia looked back and forth from the lodge to Venalise,
picking up on the mage's concern.

As they approached to just a few tree lengths away, the rough-hewn wooden door opened, and a hooded figure stepped outside. One bare hand pushed the hood back, and, even in the dimming afternoon light, Venalise recognized the red curls that tumbled over the figure's shoulders. She let loose a breath and raised her hand in greeting. Venalise dismounted, gesturing for the others to do the same. Sia busied herself with chasing down Thera and scooping her up in her arms.

"How did you arrive here before us, Oravae?"

Oravae shrugged, then waved off Venalise's question. "We left last night. We didn't want anyone to see us go."

"Who would be watching?" Venalise narrowed her eyes. "What haven't you told me, Ora?"

"Here," her old friend indicated the open door. "Get your horses settled and come inside. I put a kettle of jhea on as soon as I saw you come over the ridge. You'll get warm and then we'll talk."

Venalise scowled and held the red-headed woman's gaze, not interested in following someone else's orders, especially Oravae's. Finally, she nodded to one of the men.

"Take the horses and bring our supplies inside. Leave the blankets on the horses, though. It's too cold, otherwise."

He reached out and took her horse's reins, dodging Sia as she struggled towards the door, Thera thrashing in her arms. As she stumbled past Oravae, the red-headed woman raised her eyebrows.

"A stone bear cub? When I saw it at the stronghold, I thought my eyes were playing tricks on me. Are you trying to get mauled, Vena?"

Venalise shook her head and ducked inside after Sia. "I'll explain," she mumbled as she, too, brushed past Oravae. Once inside, she turned to face her old friend, pink spreading across her cheeks and nose as the warmth of the room reached her. "But only after I hear what you have to say."

CHAPTER 10

"I always said my mother's exploits would come back to haunt her." Venalise leaned back in her chair and sipped from her cup. It had been years since she tasted the nutty spice of jhea, and she relished the warmth as it slipped down her throat. Having been out of the Reaches for so long, the cold was harder to take, though she refused to admit it. Fortunately, the lodge had had time to warm before they arrived; otherwise it would have been a long, chilly night. Designed for larger hunting parties, the great room occupied the center of the building, with bunk rooms branching off the central space. Because the large hearth in the center was the only one in the lodge, it took many long hours for those bunkrooms to warm.

Oravae took a sip from her mug and cleared her throat. "No one could have predicted that her power would control her the way it has."

"I did," Venalise murmured to herself before glancing at Sia and Thera as they played near the fire. Thera had worn herself out, only idly batting at Sia as she lay on her back. Sia seemed tired, as well. She stifled a yawn and rubbed her eyes. "But no one listened." She leveled her gaze at her childhood friend. "Not even you."

Oravae met Venalise's dark look with one of her own. "You're right. I didn't, but I—" she nodded toward where Tasar sat at the table, his eyes on both the women "—we do now. For what it's worth, my father always listened to what you had to say."

Venalise nodded. She recalled their first meeting and the conspiratorial wink he gave her when her mother decreed he would train her in the way of battle magic. He never did.

"Your father is the only reason I made it out of the Reaches."

"This is truth," Tasar said, rising from the bench near the door to move a few of the supply bundles stacked on the table. "And Rhymere is also why we knew when you would return."

Venalise turned toward the Korr warrior, one eyebrow arched. He joined them at the table, easing into an empty chair as she sat back and leveled her gaze at Oravae.

"How would your father know I would return?"

"He speaks with the mountains, just like you," Tasar shrugged. Oravae pursed her lips and scowled at him.

"Oh." Venalise ran her fingers over the iron nails at the edge of the table. She smirked. Pulling half a mountain down at Athtull would most certainly have gotten his attention. She smiled as a needle-fine tendril of energy wound along her hand, remembering the first time her magic greeted her.

So many years ago, the moment her hand had closed around the ceremonial dagger, she had felt it — a cold, sharp energy that stung like a brittlebug bite laced with ice. Only seven winters old, she had yelped and dropped the blade, the sound as it clattered to the floor both painful and energizing. Echoes of metal on stone had spoken to her, though she didn't understand the language.

Venalise's manifestation of elemental magic could not have appeared at a more inopportune time. Standing in front of the Korr war leaders, she was supposed to claim her destiny as the future of their house. Yet, simultaneously, this power of stone and ore had claimed her as well. Her mother, T'Korr Uhll, the iron-fisted ruler of the entire Stone Reaches, denied the occurrence, though everyone in the room felt the connection.

"I will root out the cowardly and weak-bodied wielder playing tricks at my daughter's claiming ceremony," the Empress had proclaimed. No less than seven bodies lost their heads that day.

In the following years, the Empress immersed her daughter in the art of war and ruthless leadership: horsemanship with Uhll's sister Steffa of the Suhonne house; navigation on land with House Ortak and on the water with the sea-faring Grunn; and, of course, battle practice with the Korr. She had wanted Rhymere to help Venalise learn to use her magic as a weapon, and while he told the Empress he would comply, he didn't. Uhll was determined to exploit her daughter's magic and force Venalise into the role she was born to fulfill. Fortunately for Venalise, her mother's duties as Empress always took her elsewhere and she was left on her own in Lorce, free to learn whatever Rhymere would teach her.

"Vena?"

Oravae stilled Venalise's hand with her own.

"Your mother will destroy the unity of the Reaches. My father believes she will be its destruction."

Venalise closed her eyes and sighed. She could not let Oravae know the real reason she was back home. If her friend's father wanted control of the Reaches, that control was something Venalise would not give away. She had always suspected that Rhymere had grander designs on the Reaches, but it surprised her that he would be so bold as to think he could wrest control away from her mother and House Korr. Knowing that he wanted that power for himself meant Venalise had to keep her intentions secret.

"Why does no one understand? I left this place. I—" She opened her eyes and leveled her gaze at Oravae. "Don't." She swiveled her head to look at Tasar. "Want it."

If only she meant those words.

"What, then? We let it all fall apart?" Oravae shook her head, her jaw clenching. She looked away from the table, her knee bouncing angrily.

"I just need to go to the Spire. I'll be gone in a few days." This new revelation about Rhymere was an entanglement she had not bargained for, and the faster she could be free of it, the better.

"What good is that for us? You get what you came for and then leave us to the mercy of whatever war your mother begins. The Reaches will consume itself and all of us with it." Oravae leaned forward, hands on her legs as if she were ready to spring out of her chair. Venalise marveled at how much her friend had changed. She had always been confident, but there was an edge to her voice, her actions, that was completely new.

As girls, Oravae and Venalise could not have been more opposite. While Venalise grew up in the harsh shadows of the Korr warrior caste, surrounded by blades and battle, Oravae was born into the elegance and culture of Lorce, immersed in learning and lore — a life Venalise envied.

"I'm just here for information."

"So that's the only reason you're back?" Oravae's voice was low.

Venalise turned away to watch where Sia and Thera still played by the fireplace. Oravae and Tasar would never understand. They were blinded by whatever rhetoric Rhymere had filled their heads with. The conversation was over.

For several minutes, the only sounds were of the crackling fire and the wind, gusting outside. Finally, Tasar broke the quiet.

"Who is the child?"

Sia sat cross-legged near the hearth while Thera lumbered around her, batting at a dried ball of tree moss before crawling over the child's legs and rolling to her back. Sia nuzzled Thera's belly and giggled when the cub emitted a playful growl. In any other world, she would just be a child and her pet, but this small thing would have such a role to play, Venalise couldn't help but feel a pang of regret. The coming days might break her, but if she didn't make her move now, what had all the years in Karth been for?

Oravae leaned forward on her elbows. "I know you, Vena. Toting a child around is not in your nature. It's not about who, Tasar." She peered across the table. "But *what* is she?"

"That's the real question, isn't it?" Venalise murmured as Oravae stood. In three strides, Venalise's friend was across the room, rummaging through her bag by the door. Even Venalise was still unsure what the girl was. Powerful, certainly, but Sia's magic was undefined — unheard of. As much as she had studied, there was no precedent for a wielder that could touch multiple elements. Strength with just one could be dangerous to the wielder if not properly understood. That was the unfortunate reason she needed Rhymere. If anyone knew of another occurrence of this or how to proceed unraveling all that Sia could do, it would be him. This child could be the key to unlocking the power of the Gate and summoning her own army of immortals to rival the Travelers of Karth, and it was the only way she could topple Lasten's reign and take control.

"We need to sleep," Oravae growled over her shoulder. "We ride at sunrise."

Venalise rose from her chair and lifted a heavy blanket from the supplies stacked at the end of the table. She knelt by the hearth, near Sia, and folded it over to form a thick pallet.

"Lay here, Sia. You and Thera need to sleep." Venalise patted the blanket. "We've an early morning."

Sia groaned, but scooped Thera into her arms and waddled onto the blanket on her knees, depositing the cub as she lay down beside it. Thera rolled onto her back, waving her paws in the air. Venalise ran her hand along the cub's belly, garnering a contented growl. Venalise tucked a blanket over the two of them and settled herself beside them. While there were more comfortable bunks in the other rooms, she had no intention of leaving Sia unattended. Before she had even settled the edge of the blanket over her own shoulders, Sia's slow breathing told her she was already asleep. She tucked one arm beneath her head, thoughts about Rhymere and her mother tumbling around in her mind. But her body was tired. The crackling fire and flickering light lulled her into a fitful sleep.

CHAPTER 11

I t was exactly as Venalise remembered.

The spires of Lorce loomed above the snow-crusted hills ahead, each radiating a faint, iridescent hue in the late afternoon light. The city, nestled in a miles-wide valley, stood tall and stark against the craggy mountains of the continent's northern coast. Snow gave way to golden winter grass while the gusty wind lessened. The group of riders, led by Oravae, descended into the lower part of the valley.

Venalise surveyed ahead, the sight before her stirring hollow feelings that she wasn't prepared for. The sense of comfort she used to feel on approaching the beautiful spires was overshadowed by the knowledge that her mentor had a new agenda. Still, surrounded by formidable stone walls, Lorce was a monument to all the knowledge of the Stone Reaches. Multitudes of vault-like libraries housed histories, bound in skins of animals long-extinct. These collections sat side-by-side on shelves stuffed with well-worn tomes detailing magical practices and all the elemental disciplines contained within.

The city was home to the true knowledge of the world. While the lowlands of Karth and the surrounding nations were oblivious to the centuries of research contained within the stone fortress's walls, lore-keepers, scholars, and wielders occupied this space. Warriors were not openly welcome, unless you were the daughter of the Empress, as Venalise was. While she enjoyed her time in the Spire with Rhymere, Oravae, and the other scholars, her reception by the folk outside of the scholars' domain had never been warm.

Lorce spread out before them like a sleeping giant at the foot of the jagged mountain range. No such place existed south of the Stone Giant's great peaks. Along the walls of the city, the dormant stems and runners of summer vines twisted and climbed all the way to the tops of the stone, some even visible along the towers within. Venalise chuckled to herself. Lasten placed such faith in mages like his sister, Dyaneth, and Regealth. But southern magic-users relied on knowledge passed from wielder to apprentice, rather than research and history. One exception existed in the island conclaves of Lakrim priests, but they were secretive and scarce.

Plinus.

Her mind wandered to the diminutive priest who had been in her service only weeks before. The Handaalian order he served followed the fire element and maintained a healthy reserve of knowledge and study. Plinus had brought her the closest to summoning Travelers like Amarynn from across all the dimensions. But while he gave her so much of the information she sought, his power was not enough to aid her in bringing humans across the void. Atranoch were the best they could conjure, and the beasts were no better than reptilian dogs. Attempt after failed attempt yielded smaller and smaller creatures until, finally, Venalise had given up and turned her attention to taking control of the Gate.

She had thought Plinus would be her key. Instead, the little priest had been only a map leading to a locked door — the door between Venalise and her aspirations.

She pulled the silver acorn locket from underneath her cloak and held it in the late afternoon sun. She couldn't see it, but the Gate lay safely inside, nestled in rowan bark lining; even through the heavy silver, she could still feel its radiating magic like a faint scent of perfume left in a room after its wearer was gone.

"Soon," she whispered, then tucked the locket back under the neckline of her dress.

As the group descended from the chilly heights of the frozen plains, the trees grew taller, and the air held more warmth. The midday sun was well above the peaks of the North Coast mountains, but the city was the centerpiece of the view; the walls of Lorce appeared to have been carved from the mountains themselves. Inside, the spires soared while slender flags fluttered in the breeze, adorning each pointed rooftop.

"Ooooh," Sia cooed from the middle of the pack. She urged her pony forward until she was beside Venalise. "That's where we are going?"

A smile tugged at the corners of Venalise's mouth. "You like it?" she asked.

"It's amazing," Sia breathed. Even Thera, who had run freely for several hours today, settled down as the city's grandeur unfolded before them.

"It is," Venalise agreed.

"It won't be so amazing when my father finds out you aren't staying," Oravae quipped over her shoulder. She pulled her horse back to a slow walk, allowing Venalise's mount to catch up. As Sia drew near, Oravae nodded in her direction. "He won't let you leave, you know."

Venalise frowned. She needed Rhymere to help her, but Oravae was right. She knew the guardian of Lorce was shrewd. He wouldn't be willing to help if he thought his efforts were for nothing. And once he understood what Sia was, he would never willingly let the child fall from his grasp — not with the power she held. Rhymere's quest to usurp her mother was a complication she didn't need. Not now.

Sia squealed as Thera wriggled in her lap. Venalise, startled, returned her attention to the child. If Venalise was going to attempt to learn how to harness the little girl's power, she would need Rhymere to play his part. Venalise furrowed her brow as she sorted through scenarios.

"I know that look."

"What look?" Venalise didn't bother to try to hide her aggravation.

"Really?" Oravae snorted. "You do remember that I grew up with you, don't you? And that you wear your mood like your mother wears her weapons — from head to toe."

Venalise shook her head. Perhaps she was making a mistake bringing Sia to Lorce; with Rhymere's eyes set on control of the Reaches, there was a chance this undertaking would work against her, not in her favor. An uncharacteristic dread rooted in her belly as she considered that the next few days could ultimately undermine her bid to unlock Sia's secrets. Sia had been an unexpected windfall, but losing access to her would be disastrous.

"I don't want to stay at the Spire," Venalise said, sitting straighter in her saddle.

"That's not going to go well," Oravae muttered.

"Nothing I want ever goes well," Venalise said as Sia squealed and giggled. Turning again to watch them, Venalise marveled at how unaware the girl was of her potential. How could a child, sold to a ship's captain, be poised to be the most potent magic wielder ever known? She eyed Oravae now. There was something about the look in her friend's icy-green eyes, the way her brow furrowed barely enough that few would notice. But Venalise could see it.

Oravae was hiding something.

"Remember that inn inside the gates? Where you and I would meet whenever I was able to come and visit?" Venalise watched her friend's expression.

Oravae kept her eyes fixed on the road ahead and nodded.

"I do. But it's a distillery now. The alchemists took it over after part of the scullery burned. And before you ask, the guesthouse near the war library has been turned into an extra stable. You'll stay at the Spire like all other visitors unless you want to pitch a tent on the terrace."

Venalise tilted her head and narrowed her eyes at her friend. Oravae was brash, but not stupid. She seemed not to fully trust Venalise, and wanted to keep a measure of distance between the mage and her father. *No, she was most definitely not stupid.*

"I'll turn these horses around and return to Karth before you, of all people, tell me where I will sleep," Venalise hissed through clenched teeth. "I don't care what your father has told you to do. You do not control me."

"Giving orders now, are we?" Oravae snapped back. "I thought you wanted nothing to do with ruling the Reaches. But you sounded quite like your mother just now." She met Venalise's glare with one of her own. "My father is concerned for the future of the Reaches. He is the reason you came, is he not? Besides," she nodded toward the looming walls of the city as the faint sound of a trumpet echoed off the mountainside. "He already knows we are here."

Venalise gripped the reins and scowled at Oravae's reminder. Of course he did! She needed to keep her thoughts from running away with her and focus.

"Sia!" Oravae called over her shoulder, smirking as she threw a glance at Venalise. "Come with me! We'll be the first to the gates!" She kicked her horse into a gallop, her laugh trailing behind her. Sia looked to Venalise, her eyes sparkling with anticipation.

"Can I?"

Venalise sighed and nodded. Her mind whirled, addled with all the complications that lay before her, but for the moment, there was little she could do about it. Had she thought more about it, she might have anticipated complications like this, but the windfall that was Sia had distracted her. She kicked her horse into a canter and followed Sia and her friend towards the ornate wooden gates that were already beginning to swing open.

KARTH

CHAPTER 12

Plinus hadn't stopped walking for days. He'd lost count of exactly how many it had been.

The first week, he'd been deliberate about food and water, taking time to forage and drinking from whatever stream he passed. The few carts and riders that passed him on the road ignored him or, worse, called out insults directed toward his Handaalian heritage or rough appearance. He tried to ask for help, to no avail. In the last few days, his sense of urgency overcame his need for sustenance, so he pressed on, hungry and thirsty.

By the time he reached the gates of Calliway, the moon was high. The priest's feet were cracked and bleeding, and dust from the fall of Athtull still clung to his clothes and hair, making him cough, a throaty, bark that brought up bloodied spittle onto his sleeve. As the gate opened, he stood, huddled in his tattered cloak. Thundering hooves signaled him to stumble off the road as a small group of riders galloped past him.

Plinus summoned the last of his strength and scurried through the open gate.

"Oi there!" a guard called from atop the portcullis.

He didn't know if the guard was speaking to him, but he didn't stop to find out. Shadows inside the city walls provided enough cover to keep him from being noticed, and stumbling, he stretched his arms toward the wall but fell before reaching it. His head struck the stone, a wayward corner landing a perfect blow to his temple.

Plinus struggled to maintain consciousness, but stars exploded behind his eyes, and darkness nearly claimed him just as footsteps approached.

"Are you alright?" A boy's voice was by his ear.

"Pl-please," Plinus's voice was nothing but a croak. "I-I ca..."

"Don't talk, sir! You don't sound so good."

Plinus reached for the shadowy outline of the boy, who grasped his forearms and pulled him to unsteady feet.

"Let me take you to my father's house. You need food and drink, and rest."

Plinus nodded, as words were impossible. The boy wrapped an arm around his waist, and they shuffled forward, him helping Plinus one step at a time. So focused on staying upright, he had no time to question the wisdom of blindly trusting a random boy in the streets. He could only hope his instincts would warn him if he was in any danger.

"It's not too far, sir. Right around the corner, it is."

Plinus gripped the arm at his waist. His toes kept catching on the uneven cobblestones, each stumble amplifying the screaming headache radiating from the top of his forehead. Only a few minutes more and the boy pushed a door open, revealing a small room that Plinus could see was warmed by a healthy fire in the hearth.

"Da!" the boy called out. A short, burly man appeared from around the corner, wiping his hands on a cloth. He stopped near the hearth when he saw the two in the doorway.

"Lucas! What's this?"

Plinus recognized the pungent smells of tree extracts and smoke — his father had been a tanner in his childhood home on the Handaalian mainland, and years of helping collect tree bark and rowan root left an indelible mark on his memory.

"I found him near the gates, Father. He's hurt his head, I think." Plinus felt himself being eased into one of the two roughly made chairs by a simple wooden table. Once the boy pulled his arm away, he carefully prodded Plinus' temple and scalp, examining the injury. When his fingers found the growing lump, Plinus winced and sucked in a breath, but offered a weak smile at Lucas to try to show appreciation for his help.

"Yep," Lucas grimaced. "Nasty bump y'got, sir."

Lucas's father had not moved from his place near the hearth, his gaze fixed on the pendant hanging from Plinus's neck.

Lucas's father took a slow step forward, his eyes never leaving Plinus. "Lakrim priest, are ya?" His question was hushed with undertones of reverence.

Plinus nodded and tried to sit straighter in his seat, but his head was throbbing, and darkness still threatened to consume him.

"Do the fires still burn?" The man was clutching his cloth in both hands, his jaw clenching. "I-in the temple, I mean. I have," he paused. He dropped his eyes. "Well, I suppose I *had* a brother who served the Lakrimini. When the Handaals fell, I never heard from him again."

Plinus laid his head down on the table atop his folded arms. He wished he had more to tell the man, but he, too had no idea what the state of the Lakrimini temples. "Perhaps," he whispered, his eyes slowly closing, his words starting to slur together, the pauses between phrases lengthening. "There are many islands. Many temples. Though I do not know which of them were razed... I was taken before the end of the siege..."

"Who took you?" He barely heard Lucas, did not see him lean in closer, his eyes wide, but Plinus was still except for the shallow rise and fall of his chest.

"Lucas," his father placed one hand on the boy's shoulder. "Do you know how to find King Lasten's mage? I know you talk to that Traveler the old man favors."

"Amarynn." Lucas nodded. "Yes. I think there's a door near the kitchen. She had me come with her to deliver something to him once."

"Go. Find him. Bring him here.

Lucas took one last look at Plinus before bursting out the door into the night.

"My friend," an unsteady voice drifted into Plinus' awareness. His head no longer throbbed, and he was lying comfortably without pain.

The small-statured priest pried his eyes open to find a familiar face peering over him. At the sight of the water mage, Plinus let out a quiet gasp. He felt another pair of hands tenderly attending to his feet, but he could not tear his eyes off Regealth.

"Regealth? How did you find me?"

"Your magic is irritatingly noisy," Regealth chuckled. "I would know. It rattled all over Athtull, even with the suppression cuff Venalise placed on your wrist. To answer your question though, I sensed you near the gates. But Lucas," he nodded in the boy's direction, "thought it a good idea to alert me to your precise whereabouts."

Plinus closed his eyes again, soothing relief replacing the frantic urgency that had consumed him on his slow, painful journey to Calliway. But he had to tell him—

"She's gone," Plinus whispered, his tongue flicking out to lick his cracked lips. "The little one. Venalise took her to the mountains. You needed to know." He had more to say, but Plinus' voice trailed off.

"Leave us."

The tender hands left his feet; Regealth had shooed the healer away. As the door closed behind her, he returned his attention to the injured priest.

"Shh, friend," Regealth soothed his friend. "You are to be commended. That was no small feat, getting from Athtull Keep to Calliway in your condition."

Plinus' breathing slowed until the cadence was more like the ebb and flow of the tide on the shores at Banmorrow. He smiled, his eyes still closed. "It was... a challenging journey, indeed."

Regealth patted the priest's hand. "Something tells me your survival alone was no small feat, as well." He rose, tucking Plinus' hand under the quilt. "But that will be a story for another day. Amarynn has already set out to find Venalise, and she is aware of the child's importance."

"But how will your Traveler combat Venalise's magic? She could not manage the last time they encountered one another." The lines on his face deepened with concern as he recalled Amarynn's tortured state under Venalise's captivity.

"I have taken that into account." Regealth pulled a stool up to the side of Plinus's bed. "She has a mage with her this time. One that I believe you might know."

Plinus's brow furrowed. "Who?"

"Your brother had two sons, correct?"

Plinus's expression darkened. "He did, yes: Hoda and Xanus. But they were lost in the siege."

"*You* lost them, but they were not lost, my friend."

The priest's eyebrows shot up as Regealth continued.

"Your brother and the boys made their way here, to Karth. Sadly, there was no word from his wife."

"They are here?" Plinus pushed himself up to a sitting position.

"Yes, my friend. You will see your brother shortly."

Plinus reeled. He had no idea that his family had survived the siege on the capital city. He had already left them at the docks and gone to the palace when the attack began. And before he could return to look for them, Venalise had already whisked him away towards the Darklands.

"You never told me." Plinus's hands trembled as he reached for Regealth's arm. "Who did you send with the Traveler?"

"Xanus."

At the mention of his youngest nephew's name, Plinus's face softened. He had already tutored the boy in basic control, so it was good to know he had been in Regealth's capable hands. Plinus could sense he had an even temper, even when he was young. He would be a smart addition to the Traveler's party. "Good, good," he nodded. "He's got talent, then?"

"He does, most assuredly. And with Amarynn, he is in the best of hands. Now," Regealth leaned in. "Let talk more about Venalise and the child. I need to know what we are up against."

"Good morning, My Lord."

Bent stepped down from the grand staircase landing just before the main castle hall. Jael was seated on a bench, his arms crossed, one knee rapidly bouncing. At Bent's greeting, The Prince stood and cast a dark glance at his new protector. Bent's expression still hinted sourness, but it was less than when he'd first been ordered to take Amarynn's position. Regardless, Bent was the only other person Jael felt he could trust after their return from Athtull. His allegiance to Amarynn and his honorable service to the Legion was a formidable combination.

"Good morning, Bent," Jael replied. "I'm looking for Amarynn. Have you seen her?"

Bent grimaced, but Jael continued. "We were supposed to spar this morning. We leave for Vhaleese soon."

"My Lord," Bent started. "You'll not find her." The aging Blademaster dropped his eyes, placing his hands on his hips.

"What's wrong? What do you mean?"

Bent was clearly hesitant to respond.

"Where is she, Bent?" Jael's tone contained a warning edge.

Bent cleared his throat. "They left last night."

"They?" Jael's attention snapped to Bent's face. "What are you talking about? She's coming with me to Vhaleese."

"She had... other plans, My Lord."

"I thought I'd made it clear she was going with me." Jael's voice had a dangerous tone. Amarynn's reckless behavior, the behavior that had gotten her in trouble time and time again, had struck again. He was worried he would not be able to control his rising anger.

Bent frowned. "Aye, you did. But you know as well as I that she'll do as she pleases, no matter who tells her what to do." He shrugged, resigned.

Jael closed his eyes, struggling to control his rage. "Athtull Keep?" he whispered.

"My Lord?"

The Prince's eyes snapped open, glittering with a hint of his new-found magic. "She is starting at Athtull, yes?"

"I do not know, My Lord. She told me nothing of her plans."

"Very well," Jael muttered before he spun on his heel and strode away.

CHAPTER 13

H er head was pounding. Reverberating noises of metal striking on stone, in a regular cadence, made her jaw clench, which only made her head hurt more. She lifted a shaking hand to touch her right temple and found a cloth wrapping and poultice. Amarynn winced as much from the pain as the humiliation she knew she would face from Bent and the others when they discovered she had taken such a stupid risk.

She opened her eyes and sat up on her elbows. Whirling snowflakes, whistling past a narrow cave entrance indicated she was not in camp at the base of Athtull. Pushing herself gingerly to sit upright, her head spun, and nausea nearly caused her to retch. The clanging noise continued as the scenery swirled, her mind retreating into the darkness that kept spiraling into chaos.

Her fingers were covered in blood. The suitcase had struck her just above her ear, and when she reflexively covered it, her hand came away dripping with red.

"Oh, so you think you were gonna leave?"

Her breathing was ragged, and she kept her eyes on the floor.

"You think you'd have it better somewhere else?" His laughter was a razor blade. You couldn't even keep our son alive! You are useless!"

Her boy.

Her sweet little boy.

Grief gripped her heart and squeezed with an unrelenting fist.

She felt the bile rising in her throat. Not here. She couldn't vomit in front of him. That would make everything worse. Instead, she curled into her knees on the floor and waited for him to go away. She focused on the nothing behind her eyes.

Runners

Jumpers

Racers

"Are you listening to me?" Her eyes stayed fixed on the floor while she focused on a passage from her favorite book.

Tinkerers

Grabbers

Snatchers

He reached down and gripped her arm. The stink of bourbon and smoke only made her stomach turn more.

Sna—

She caught herself and moved to the next.

Fliers

Fly... She squeezed her eyes hard and tried to fly into the explosions of color behind them. Orange and blue danced in sparkly bursts with a bright blue background. Another blow fell on the back of her head.

"DO YOU HEAR ME?"

She cowered and pulled herself into a tighter ball, trying to disappear.

"Rynn, lass? Can ye hear me?"

She gasped, sucking in the air as if she had been drowning only moments before. Her hand was still clamped on the side of her head.

"Eh, lassie. Not healin' quite so lickety-split as yer used to, hmm?"

The deep voice was familiar. A steaming bowl was placed beside her. The familiar aroma of mess hall stew comforted her while she tried to focus on her surroundings.

"I wonder why the healin's takin' more time than it should?"

She recognized the gravelly tone but still couldn't place the voice. She rifled through her past, trying to remember, and her memory seized on another, less painful moment.

"What'er ya doing, lassie!"

Amarynn adjusted her grip on the short sword and bent her knees, keeping her eyes fixed on the greall that was barreling in her direction. The size of a bull, the winged creature's mouth was open in a gurgling snarl exposing jagged, pointed teeth.

"You'll be gutted! Yer too close!" The same deep voice called out to her urgently. Other voices shouted encouragement, while a few laughed.

"Rynn!"

She looked over her shoulder toward the group of men. The largest, a solid six-foot-eight behemoth, stepped forward and unsheathed the broadsword from his back. He tossed it at her, handle first, "Here! Frost'll do the trick!" She felt the weight of it land in her outstretched palm...

Another clang shattered her head. It was impossible.

"Essik?" She pushed herself around.

A giant man, sitting on a stone outcrop behind an anvil, with a hammer in one hand and a crude knife in the other, opened his arms wide and laughed. "In the flesh!" He brought the hammer down swiftly, and continued to shape the blade, still chuckling to himself.

Amarynn winced every time the stone and metal connected; it became too much to bear, and she gripped both sides of her head in pain.

Essik, noticing her discomfort, set the hammer down and wrapped one large hand around a cracked wooden tankard beside him. When the hammering stopped, Amarynn dropped her hands and stared. The first Traveler, the infamous madman that deserted the Legion, sat in front of her as if it were any other normal day. Other than a longer beard and different clothing, he didn't look any different than he had the day he left. Even the mischievous glint still shone in his eyes. He took a long pull from the cup, then wiped his mouth on his sleeve, his wide grin exposing a stone wedged between two teeth. "Sorry 'bout that."

"How—" Amarynn cast her eyes around the room, then let them return to Essik. "But... the Madness?" Her voice was a whisper.

"Ha!" He stood and moved toward the opening of the cave. One massive hand gripped the edge of the entrance, and he leaned out into the flurry. The wind whistled, whipping his red-brown hair violently, and snowflakes swirled for several seconds before he turned back to face her. He tapped his shaggy head, now covered in snowflakes. "I was ne'er the brightest of the bunch, was I?"

Essik scrubbed his face with both hands and walked back to the fire, grunting as he lowered himself to sit beside her. She had forgotten how big the man was until his massive frame was beside her.

Amarynn, still shocked at seeing Essik alive, couldn't speak. She stared at the legendary first Traveler in disbelief. "We... thought your mind was gone."

"The Madness," he waved his giant hands dramatically before picking up her bowl, "was a last-ditch effort to get them to leave me be. If I was uncontrollable, I was of no use." He chuckled and put the stew in Amarynn's hands. "I stayed piss-drunk e'ry hour of the day and night to look the way I did." A wistful look came over him. "Best damn time of my life."

He took a moment, then snapped out of his reverie. "Bah! Doesn't matter now." He nodded toward the fire. "I'm the King of my own kingdom now." He looked over his shoulder at the cave entrance, then back at Amarynn. "Even got my own army!" He grinned and winked.

"You were drunk?" Amarynn muttered, shaking her head. She tried to suppress a smile. "That's it? You were drunk, and all this time, the rest of us were always looking over our shoulders, worried the Madness would take us, too." She couldn't decide if she was relieved the Madness was a myth, or disappointed that Essik had left them to worry over that possibility for so long.

He laughed out loud. "I played my cards well, then. I figured the King wouldn't come looking for me if I was stark-raving mad." He leveled his twinkling gaze at Amarynn. "I made myself a liability."

Still dumbfounded, Amarynn surveyed the cave with a careful eye. Her head still ached, but the pain had lessened to a dull ache. Based on what she could see, he had been here a very long time. The cave was as comfortably set up as any hunting cabin might be, if the occupant was a surly single man. Its rough furnishings seemed well-used and darkened with age. She noticed a Legion short sword leaning against the wall. The blade, still sharp, glinted in the flickering light from the fire, its grip dark and worn. She glanced up and caught Essik eyeing her exposed arm.

"Ye took my words to heart, I see." His eyes seemed to soften as he looked at her other arm.

She lifted her arm, turning it so that her silvery scars glinted in the firelight. Several of her more prominent scars sported fine-lined tattoos that intertwined with the raised flesh. "I did," she murmured. "Though I think I might have quite a few more than you, now."

Essik tapped his neck. "That one's a wee bit shocking." He couldn't hide his grimace because she knew the pain was familiar to him. All Travelers suffered their share of mortal wounds, the earning and recovery of which were never easy to endure. "Surprised someone got the jump on you like that in battle." He chuckled. "You've always been a slippery thing when yer angry!"

A frown formed on her lips. No matter how hard she tried, there was no ridding herself of Matteus's sinister voice in her ear and the stench of his breath in her face. The pain she had blocked — that was something she was accustomed to — but even the gravest battle wounds weren't personal. War was war. What Matteus had done to her had no explanation other than pure hatred. She pushed the memory of Matteus away and sat the bowl down, untouched. "Not a battle scar, I'm afraid." Essik's eyebrows raised. She shook her head. "You may not have been the brightest, but I was certainly not the most popular."

The burly man snatched a rough-hewn cup from a ledge nearby, dunked it in the bucket next to him, and held it out to her. "It's my own brew. No worse than the piss yer used to!" She took the cup and took a long pull, wrinkling her nose as the cool, sour concoction slithered down her throat. Essik stood and pointed to the bowl still steaming beside her. "Eat, lass. You're not healing from a knock on the head fast enough; truthfully, I don't like it."

Essik's words sank in. Head wounds were always traumatic, but she should not be so affected. She took another drink of ale and glanced out into the snowy darkness. "How far are we from Athtull Keep?"

"Oooh," he wrinkled his brow, "A hun'erd miles, I'd say."

She began the calculations. One hundred miles to Athtull Keep and another sixty to Calliway. The wound she had suffered when she fell from the ledge at the Keep had been nasty, and her healing a bit prolonged, but she should already be back on her feet. Sore and slow, maybe, but functional. Conversely, her recovery in Calliway had been unexpectedly fast, as had her ability to function just immediately after Jael had found her in Venalise's aethertorium. The thread that ran between the flagging strength of her immortal magic and her distance from Calliway could be attributed to Jael's distance from here. It was far-fetched, but also the most likely explanation.

Essik eyed her cautiously. "What'er ye thinking, lass?"

"It's probably nothing," she murmured, though her gut had found conviction. Her connection with Jael must span more than just her loyalty. Perhaps he had become the key to her survival when he came into his power. Yes, she would heal, but the process would take much longer and be more painful than she was used to, without him. Her next move was clear. "I need to go."

She began to rise hastily, but dizziness got the best of her, and she staggered.

"Yer not going anywhere just yet, lass." Essik was by her side, guiding her to a sitting position like she weighed no more than a feather. "Let's get that head back in one piece, and then we'll talk about gettin' ye home."

There was no use fighting him — he was massive, healthy, and right. With a surprisingly gentle touch, he unwrapped the bandage on her head and started to mold a new poultice from a rough-hewn wooden bowl near the fire. He held another tankard of his home brew and watched to be sure she drank it all. Finally, she lay back onto the fur-covered boughs and uncharacteristically gave in to his ministrations, but all the while, her mind whirled. There were more twists and turns than she bargained for in this quest for the Gate stone. Regealth and Dyaneth's magic had produced a much more complicated outcome with her crossing, linking the magical source with the Traveler.

What if her bond was rooted in the *kind* of magic that was used? Jael's family legacy was the rarest of all the elements, and all Travelers were bonded to the source of that magic. But why did it matter? Jael was not meant for her, at least not in the way either of them wanted. Amarynn focused her thoughts on finding Venalise and retrieving the Gate as she let Essik's brew lull her into sleep.

"Someone wants to meet you."

Amarynn pried her eyes open. The snow flurries of last night had stopped, and through the narrow entrance, she could see early morning sunlight glistening on the snow. Her nose was cold, so she pulled the fur up to her chin, burrowing into the warmth of the pallet, but couldn't help but flinch at the ruckus coming from outside.

A large shadow blocked the sun as Essik approached from deeper within the cave.

"Up and at 'em, lass. If he sticks his head in here again, he may take the whole front of my home with him."

"Him?" Amarynn pushed herself up, her arms more unsteady than she'd like, but her headache had nearly subsided. Essik brushed past, wiping his hands down the front of the thin, but supple greall-skin cloak cinched around his barrel chest.

The first Traveler jerked his head back toward the opening. "Yeah," he grunted, "him."

On cue, the sunlight disappeared again, and a massive head thrust towards her, filling the entrance to the cave. Adrenaline coursed through Amarynn's body as firelight broke through the shadows, revealing familiar ridged scars and the front part of an arrow-shaped head.

Instinct had her scrambling to stand and reach for her weapon — any weapon — but her hands grasped at nothing. She was unarmed.

"Not necessary, lass." Essik was behind her, his slow, calm voice coming from somewhere overhead. He laid a meaty paw on her shoulder and gave it a gentle squeeze. "He's the one that brought you to me when you fell. I reckon if he'd wanted to eat ya, you'd already be dead."

She knew — before Essik said a word, Amarynn knew it was the creature she had faced in the forest and then again on the cliff. The atranoch's eyes whirled, sending a faint electrical ripple down her spine, the not-unpleasant buzzing she had experienced before both in the forest and on the ledge at Athtull.

"The atranoch carried me here? To you?" she whispered, her eyes never leaving the beast's. It was almost familiar; many times, she had encountered it. Its scarred snout inhaled the air just inside the cave, then blew out, vertical nostril slits flaring.

Essik snorted. "Atranoch? Why do you call it that?"

"He—he's a Traveler. Venalise brought them through, and that's what she named them." Why wasn't Essik bothered by this murderous beast pressing into his cave? Amarynn still pawed at the air around her, looking for a weapon.

"Who the hell is Venalise?" Essik edged past Amarynn. He tossed a hindquarter of a mountain goat near the creature's head. "And I can't imagine why she'd call them dogs. Look at this beast." He tapped his temple. "Is she a wee bit daft?"

"What are you talking about?"

He gestured to the entrance of the cave. The beast had snaked its neck to the side to retrieve the goat. "'Atranoch' means 'dog' in the language of the Reaches."

"The Reaches?" She pulled her gaze away from the monster to look at Essik in surprise. "How would you know that language?"

The large man barked out a laugh.

"I'm closer to the Reaches than Karth up here. I trade with the Suhonne occasionally." He disappeared into the deep shadows at the back of the cave, then returned with a wooden bucket of ale. "I speak little Eorath, but atranoch is one word I know for sure."

The old Traveler grinned and chuckled. "Atranoch means dog. That's what they always call me when I show up."

CHAPTER 14

Amarynn pulled Essik's greall-skin cloak tighter around her shoulders. It smelled of sweat and sour ale, but it was surprisingly warm despite the thin leather. The wind at this altitude was mighty and blisteringly cold. Though the ledge outside Essik's cave was broad, she stayed pressed as close to the mountain as possible when she stepped out to look for the big atranoch. It had snatched the mountain goat in its double row of teeth and disappeared before she'd gotten a closer look.

No fan of heights, even the idea of being outside in the bluster unnerved her to no end, but she wanted a closer look at the atranoch — this time, under friendly circumstances. The ledge narrowed into a cart-sized path that wound down and around the bend in the mountain, disappearing from view. Amarynn steadied herself on the steep rock with one hand and picked her way forward, her eyes never leaving her feet.

When she felt steady enough, she leaned back against the rough mountain rock and lifted her eyes to the horizon. Orange, pink, and yellow spread from the world's edge to the sky above her; wispy clouds to the east reflected the stunning hues. She couldn't fathom how Essik had come upon this place. Desolation, let alone survival, made this a most unlikely outpost, but Essik was like no other Traveler. He seemed to have fed off the challenge and appreciated isolation, even in these harsh circumstances.

To have woken to find herself in his presence still stunned her, not to mention how she had apparently gotten there. While she was grateful to have been taken to him, everything was in question now. If there was no Madness, how had Essik shed his bond of loyalty to Lasten? He shouldn't have been able to will himself to turn traitor. There were so many more questions now that she didn't have time to address.

A sharp cry rang out above her. As the echoes dissipated, she glanced up, then ducked when a smaller atranoch, this one only the size of a full-grown horse, burst from over the ridge, its wings spread wide as it caught a thermal and rose. Several more calls created a chorus of shrieks and roars that reverberated off the surrounding peaks. Folding herself down to her knees, she leaned back on the rock and pushed back the dizzying fear that heights brought her. She watched as no less than twenty of the beasts poured over the ridge, banking and gliding in unison like a flock of giant birds. She shielded her eyes from the Sun's glare and followed the weyr as they rounded a nearby peak and vanished from sight. The big one wasn't with them.

"Come out, come out, wherever you are," she murmured as she pushed herself back to her feet and took a few more careful steps down the path. Crunching and cracking sounds piqued her interest, but all the rock faces made it nearly impossible to tell the direction they were coming from.

Just as she was about to turn around and follow the path back to Essik's dwelling, a throaty snort sounded from above, and a familiar dark head snaked down from the ridge overhead. Its unmistakable eyes whirled as the beast inched forward, its mesmerizing gaze fixed on her. Sniffing, its nostrils flared wide, then narrowed as it opened its mouth, parting the rows of teeth. The atranoch swung its head from side to side, breathing in quick, shallow breaths; like a cat, it was scenting the surrounding area. Amarynn held her breath as it lowered its head directly in front of her.

Bolder, now that she was sure this was the same atranoch that saved her, she knelt before the creature, the cold of the snowy path seeping into her knee, and lay one hand on its scarred snout. One of its eyelids closed, and the soft electric sensation rippled down her spine. He raised his head, nudging against her touch.

All the breath left her body as her eyes rolled back in her head, and she sank to the ground. The world disappeared completely. Then, with the force of a hurricane, she was plunged into an abyss of color and sound. Fragments of the nightmares she'd been battling for weeks assaulted her from all sides, intertwined with unfamiliar scenes of clouds and sky — deep purple and orange vistas. Her own terror — her cries and whimpers — blended with the shrieks of winged creatures as they banked and rose through the strange but beautiful sky.

On her hands and knees now, unfamiliar scents reminiscent of blood and metal filled her nostrils, mixing with the softness of soil and green things. Her hands gripped the mossy ground, droplets of liquid running down her face, dripping from the tip of her nose.

Sounds became awareness as shrieks and cries of the flying beasts registered a new meaning. She was experiencing the home world of the atranoch — the world Venalise had ripped them away from. Unlike her, they remembered their home from the minute they left. Their agony at the loss was apparent with every shriek that echoed off the Frost Giant's peaks. She wanted to cry with them, to share their grief. Just as the return of her own memories crippled her, their pain was now her pain, too.

Again, the vastness of nothing swept over her. Then she was on the ledge of Athtull, wind tearing across her body, intertwining with the electric ripples that still coursed through her like a raging river. She registered the atranoch barreling towards her, but in a dizzying twist, her perspective shifted and her vision sharpened. Her own face rushed towards her as the creature banked and landed, skidding to a stop. It was bizarre to watch her chest rise and fall, witnessing her stillness, her reaction as the beast did not engage.

And in an instant, it was over. Her breath rushed back into her lungs, the cold air shocking her system. She gripped the atranoch's snout, gulping in breaths as the beast released a low rumble in response. She wasn't frightened, though; the vibrations enveloped her, soothing her racing heartbeat.

Instinct led her on, and she leaned forward, embracing the creature's enormous head. She rested her cheek against the plated scales between its eyes, and her breath slowed. A calm she'd never felt washed over her when the atranoch's low rumble changed to a soft thrum.

We.

She knew he wanted to know her, to protect her. It was why he had shielded her in the keep. It was why he refused to attack her on the ledge. They were the same.

Know. He gave a gentle nudge and, with it, a vision of her and Jael on the outside of the keep as it fell.

Go?

Her head spun with a new vision. The open sky, clouds slipping past with the rush of wind in her ears. Then she was falling. She clutched the atranoch's head when the vision shifted but instead of falling, she was diving and banking. Treetops skimmed beneath her, then in a dizzying shift, the craggy walls of the Dark mountains slipped past as her muscled wings beat and lifted her high above the peaks.

The vision faded, and she sat back on her heels, overwhelmed by the enormity of all she had been shown.

Like the creatures described in folktales and legends, she knew there was nothing else like it in this world. Images of the drawings in Regealth's books sprang to life in her mind: fantastic beasts that were an impossibility now graced the sky. Amarynn smiled.

"You're no dog," she whispered. The animal butted its head against her chest, the warmth and the thrum building.

"You are a dragon."

CHAPTER 15

"My Lord, it's time to go."

Bent stood in the hallway outside the Prince's quarters, one hand resting on the hilt of his short sword. Jael stood near the window that overlooked the city, with his back to the door, pressing his palm against the glass.

"Why did she leave, Bent?"

Bent grimaced.

Jael dropped his hand and turned to face the Blademaster. There was no mistaking the pain in his eyes — and the blue filaments of magic.

"My Lord," Bent approached and lowered his voice. "You cannot lose control of yourself here. The Lady Caeda and her family left yesterday, headed overland toward the Ardwyn coast. Now, let's get you away and on the road towards Vhaleese."

"I don't wa—"

Bent raised his hand and tapped his ear. "Listen to me. I said we need to get you away and *towards* Vhaleese."

Jael eyed Bent suspiciously, unsure of his meaning.

"Trust me, My Lord." Bent gave Jael a nod and cleared his throat. He raised his voice enough so the guards in the hall could hear him. "It's best we go now. There have been talks of disturbances along the land route. We'll be sailing from Banmorrow before first light tomorrow."

Jael nodded. "Very well. Is my horse saddled and ready?" He shouldered past Bent. "I'm ready to get this over with."

Within the hour, Bent, Jael, and a small Legion contingency of soldiers and Travelers thundered out of the great gates of Calliway with Bent in the lead. Jael shifted uncomfortably in his saddle, his knees already beginning to ache from the girth of the grey gelding he rode. The stable master had informed him that his horse, Rhyssa, had been favoring her left front leg and needed to stay behind.

The midday sun warmed the chilly late-autumn air, which was crisp with the promise of an early frost. They rode hard, only stopping once to water the horses. As Jael took the opportunity to stretch his legs, Endric, a red-headed Traveler known for his serious nature and skill with horses, offered to trade mounts. Jael politely refused.

As the rosy sunset kissed the ocean horizon, they arrived at the keep on the cliffs of Banmorrow. As the stable hands led the horses away, the group of riders made for the kitchen, hungry after their long ride.

Bent grabbed Jael by the elbow and pulled him aside just before the Prince ducked through the door. Once in the shadows, the Blademaster spoke, his voice a low whisper.

"Swear to me." Bent squeezed Jael's arm tighter. "When you are King, you will reverse whatever punishment your father doles out."

"What do you mean?" Jael furrowed his brow.

Bent cast a glance at both sides before continuing. "What I am about to do is seditious. It's traitorous, and it will most likely earn me a swift death."

"What are you talking about, Bent?"

"Did you see the young fella riding with us? The new one?"

Jael hadn't given the traveling party much thought, but there was one soldier he did not recognize.

"I believe so," Jael raised one eyebrow quizzically.

"Well, he's going to be you." Bent lowered his voice even more, and Jael had to lean in to hear him. "We will board the ship tonight. We'll all get ourselves settled, then I'll tell the lad in front of the others that he's going to leave and relay our departure to your father."

"What are you doing, Bent?" Jael hissed.

"I'm giving you what you want, My Lord." Bent stepped closer. "What she wants, too."

"You mean—" Jael's brain worked furiously.

"Aye, My Lord. Go to her. Help her, but I swear on all the goddesses: if you get yourself killed, I'll most likely meet you in the after."

Jael had no words. Bent was right — Lasten would be furious, and Bent would pay a hefty price. Jael could only pray that his bond with the Traveler and her promise as an immortal magic wielder would be enough to sway the King toward leniency — if he could find her and if he could convince her to give their partnership a try.

A manservant approached from the kitchen.

"My Lord Prince," he bowed, "Blademaster. The carriages are waiting to take you to the docks. Your ship awaits."

Jael stood along the deck railing, looking across the bay from the ship's aft. The moonlight bathing the water cast a pearlescent glow across the gentle waves that lapped quietly against the ship's hull. He didn't turn when he heard the footsteps of Matteus's approach, nor when the burly Traveler cleared his throat.

"You have something to say, Matteus?" Jael kept his eyes fixed on the water.

"You know, it is good that your father sent Amarynn away, My Lord." Matteus eased up to the railing beside him.

Jael cast a sidelong glance at the stout Traveler. Matteus stood only slightly taller than the Prince, and ugly, knotted scars gleamed across his smug face as he twisted his head around, cracking his neck.

"Why is that?" Jael asked quietly. He turned to face the Traveler as another, Cam, sidled past. Jael paused as Matteus's crony took his time to turn the corner. Once he was sure they were alone again, he continued. "And why would you feel the need to mention it to me now?"

The challenge was there in the tone of Jael's voice. He had been keeping an eye on Matteus since the return from Athtull, hoping to catch a slip-up. He wanted a reason to hurt him.

Matteus chuckled to himself, shaking his head. He gripped the railing with his thick, calloused hands. Jael couldn't take his eyes off the man's fingers. He imagined them, as he had so many times, gripping the dagger that was drawn across Amarynn's neck so many months ago, and the hairs on the back of his neck stood up. A roiling anger took hold in his chest.

"No offense meant, My Lord," the Traveler said. "But that girl thinks far too much of herself — always has. I doubt she'd truly be willing to defend you unless there was something in it for her. She's a selfish one."

Images of Amarynn chained to the floor in Venalise's chamber flashed in Jael's mind. His heart lurched when he thought of her blood- and tear-streaked face. Jael knew she had been willing to sacrifice her eternity for him. He couldn't believe this poor excuse of a man dared to call her selfish in his presence.

"Good riddance, I say." Matteus pushed back off the railing and turned to lean against it.

Jael eyed him for a moment. "You really don't like her?"

"That demon? I'd sooner fuck a pig than fight with the likes of her. Though I'd wager she's a hellion in the sack." He leaned closer to Jael and smiled, his putrid breath washing over the Prince's face. "I've heard stories."

"Have you?" Jael's lip curled in disgust. He imagined all the ways he could make Matteus pay for what he did to Amarynn.

"Aye. Shame I didn't find out myself before I cut her down." Matteus snickered.

"Ah. I heard there was an incident in the practice yard," he said, his voice a venomous whisper.

Matteus, sensing the change in Jael's voice, straightened. He narrowed his eyes and cocked his head to the side. "Aye," he said. "On the King's orders."

All the breath rushed out of Jael's body as the words took hold. *On the King's orders.*

His father.

There.

No other catalyst was necessary. Jael's magic sparked and danced with a life of its own. He clenched his fists at his sides as a blue glow enveloped them, and a seething energy writhed behind his eyes.

Matteus, mouth opening in surprise, stood frozen in place. No one knew of Jael's magic save the few who had been with them at Athtull Keep. Even the King didn't know his own son's powers had been restored.

The Traveler shrank in fear against the railing, and Jael took a step towards him, his lips pulled back in a snarl.

"You attacked a fellow Traveler, a Legion comrade," Jael hissed. He took another step. "You cut her throat in cold blood."

Matteus was trembling, though he tried to keep his expression unaffected.

Jael raised one hand to Matteus' throat, enveloping the Traveler's upper body in a flickering blue light. The air quivered in the space around them.

"I don't know what my power can do," Jael said softly. He tilted his head, studying Matteus's face. "It might kill you."

Matteus panted nervously and attempted to smirk. "Y-you can't kill me. No one can."

Jael arched one eyebrow and wrapped his fingers tighter around the Traveler's throat, lifting him ever-so-slightly. He inhaled deeply, the pulsating magic welling up inside of him. He did not know what the effect of his magic would be on Matteus, but he didn't care. He wanted to make him pay for what he had done to Amarynn.

"My Lord!"

Bent's sharp tone gave Jael pause. Matteus, still in the Prince's grasp, went slack.

"You'd best get settled in your quarters." The Blademaster stepped up to Jael's side, seeming to ignore the tableau in front of him.

Jael held Matteus another few seconds, then reluctantly released his grasp and shook out his hands. The blue glow dissipated, and as soon as the burly Traveler slumped back against the railing, a blade appeared at his throat. Behind him, Ehrinell's blonde curls whipped in the brisk sea breeze. Two more Travelers stepped from the shadows.

"Don't worry about this one, Lord Prince," she promised. "He'll keep his mouth shut, or we'll be sure he suffers the same insult he delivered to our sister." The other Travelers, Endric and Wake, strode forward and grasped Matteus by the arms.

Wake, a giant of a man with ebony skin and a shaved head, leaned in by Matteus' ear.

"He may suffer, regardless," he growled.

Jael stepped back and turned on his heel, ducking into the shadowy recesses of the forecastle companionway and down the narrow steps.

Bent watched until the Prince was gone before he eyed each Traveler before him.

"You didn't see what you think you saw tonight." Bent grimaced as he fixed his gaze on Matteus. "And—" He spat at the deck, sticky drops of his saliva clinging to Matteus' boots. "Immortal or not, I'll rip your head off myself if you even *think* about what happened here."

Bent watched as Wake and Endric escorted Matteus down the steps toward the quarters below. The aging Blademaster waited for Ehrinell to sheathe her dagger before he sighed deeply.

"Thank you, lass."

"That pig deserves what he's getting," Ehrinell muttered. She nodded toward the ship's bow. The rest of the Legion guard were gathered there, waiting for their orders. "Do you think they saw anything?"

"Let's hope not." He nodded to the dark shadows of the passageway that led to Jael's quarters. "You get our Prince off this ship and ready to ride. I'll speak to the men and let the newcomer know it's time for his act." Bent tugged on his tunic and cleared his throat. His next steps might very well lead to his demise.

"There's a dinghy tied to the starboard side of the ship and a well-paid man waiting for you. You're going to go back to Banmorrow. Now."

"What will happen when you arrive in Vhaleese without me?"

Ehrinell looked toward the porthole and squinted her eyes. "Ah, well. Y'know how the seas are this time of year. Unpredictable weather, rough water..."

"You aren't going to Vhaleese, are you?" Jael's voice was a whisper. The planning that had gone into this ruse was astounding, as were the risks that were being taken.

She tilted her head, her smirk undeniable. "Oh, we'll get there. Eventually." She opened the door, peering quickly in both directions of the passageway. "It's clear. Follow me."

Ehrinell slipped out, and Jael did the same, closing the door behind him silently, and when he turned back, the Traveler had become one with the shadowy recesses, almost difficult to follow. They stepped lightly up to the deck, but Jael paused when he heard Bent's voice.

"Parrick, you'll return to Calliway and deliver a message to King Lasten telling him we are safely on our way. Everyone else, divide into your watches and get some rest when you can. The seas are unpredictable this time of year."

The sound of footsteps, moving in his direction, prompted Jael on, to round the corner and follow Ehrinell over the side of the ship, where a rope ladder was waiting for him.

"Quickly now," Ehrinell whispered from the dinghy below. Jael dropped into the boat where the lithe, blonde Traveler and a hooded figure waited. As soon as he settled onto a crossbench, Ehrinell produced a cloak from under the bench in the dinghy and draped it over his shoulders. She knelt in front of him and pulled the hood up over his face. Her eyes were kind and clear.

"Do not return to the keep at Banmorrow. Head for a tavern called Cliff's Edge. It's west, just outside of the city proper. Rhyssa's there — saddled, provisioned, and ready to ride." She nodded to the hooded figure, who sat in silence in the rocking dinghy. "He'll bring you ashore below the cliffs, near one of the lesser-used climbs."

Jael eyed the stranger. As a Traveler assassin, Ehrinell would have countless nameless contacts at her beck and call. This must be one of them.

"How long do I have to reach Athtull?"

"I'd say no more than two, maybe three days. But if you miss them, they shouldn't be hard to track. Finn's been leaving you signs along the road."

Jael shook his head in gratitude. Bent had gone to great lengths to see this plan through. His resolve surged.

Ehrinell squeezed his shoulder, then stepped back onto the bottom rung of the ladder and pushed the boat away with her foot.

"Safe travels, My Lord," she whispered. "Don't fail her."

CHAPTER 16

Moonlight ebbed and flowed through the passing clouds, giving Jael and his hooded oarsman enough light to find the western-most access to Banmorrow proper, and enough cover to have gotten away undetected. The Prince leapt over the side of the dinghy as soon as he felt the hull scrape against the sand. He didn't speak to the man who sat silently in the boat but gave him a nod and a casual salute before he sprinted toward the wooden steps that crisscrossed the cliffside up to the edge of the city.

Though his legs ached from his sprint across the sandy beach, Jael took the stairs two at a time. With each step, his desire to get on the road and closer to Amarynn grew stronger, but when he reached the top, the outer walls loomed before him. He was ready to run to the inn, but the narrow footpath hugging the stone face was not a path to take lightly, much less in the dark.

He could go through town, instead, he supposed. Access would be a problem, though. If he were lucky, he might find himself close to a guard door, but he'd be at risk of putting Bent's plan in jeopardy. Should one person recognize him, the ruse would be over, and all the careful planning would have been for nothing.

No, he thought. Risk was not an option — not now.

Jael took his time on the climb, one careful footstep after another, until he came to a corner where the wall turned inland. More clouds were moving in, but once the path widened and he was able to increase his pace, he took the opportunity to jog toward a cluster of lights in the distance, just outside the western gate.

The inn was not difficult to locate. Most of the buildings were ramshackle, but not the Cliff's Edge. A chimney billowed smoke while the windows glowed with lamplight, sounds of laughter and voices singing raucous shanties audible even from a relatively long distance. Jael scanned the area, looking for the stable, and when he found it, he crossed the last distance into the shadow of the building.

Only two stable hands were visible as he peered inside, and they were so busy telling wild stories, they didn't notice when Jael silently slipped through the door, scanning the dimly lit building for what he was searching for. A familiar whicker drew his attention to the second stall. Rhyssa flicked her ears forward and dropped her head when Jael opened the stall door and squatted down to reach for the reins dangling in the straw.

"What're ye doin?" a young voice exclaimed. Jael spun on his heel, still in a crouch. From a stall near Rhyssa's, one of the stable hands, a boy of eight or so years, stepped out with a pitchfork in his hands. His eyes went wide, then he whispered. "Wait. Are ye the spy Nelly told us about?"

"Thick-headed fool!" An older boy appeared from inside the stall across from Rhyssa's. "Why would he tell you if he was a spy?"

Jael seized the opportunity.

"Shh," he whispered, holding one finger to his lips. "Nelly told you I was coming?"

The boys exchanged glances and nodded.

"Well then, let me be on my way before someone comes in, yes?" He purposefully lowered his voice, trying to fortify this 'Nelly's story that he was a spy, and not the Prince.

"Aye, sir," the older boy said, stepping back, pulling the younger child with him.

Jael stood. He led his horse out of her stall and swung into the saddle. Nodding to the boys, he urged Rhyssa to go. They were nearly past the stable doors when the older boy called out in an urgent half-whisper.

"Sir!"

Jael stopped his horse and turned to see the younger boy trotting up. He fumbled around in his pocket then handed him a folded piece of paper.

"Nelly said to give this to you."

Jae's brow furrowed. He assumed 'Nelly' was Ehrinell, but why would she leave a note for him with a child?

"Thank you. And..." Jael tucked the paper into his coat pocket, then cast his eyes around the barn to be sure they were still alone. He pulled a coin from his pouch and tossed it in the boy's direction. "I was never here."

He gave a wink, then watched as the boys nodded eagerly and returned to the stalls, returning to their work with their pitchforks. He squeezed his heels and Rhyssa broke into a trot, and then a gallop. He wanted to read the note Ehrinell left for him, but he was still too close to Banmorrow and there was not enough light on this side of the wall. The western road he was on would soon meet a crossroad that led to Calliway; he could stop there. It was peculiar and slightly alarming that she had not told him everything before he left the ship. What would be so secret that the oarsman, obviously paid handsomely for his silence, couldn't be trusted? And why would she have faith that a stable boy would do as she asked without question?

What if she knew something about Amarynn? The King had already tried to end her once before; what would keep him from trying again in Jael's absence? Rhyssa, sensing his urgency, picked up her pace until she was at a full run. Jael let her have her head. Multitudes of scenarios played out in his mind while the fields and forests flew by.

Within an hour Jael pulled Rhyssa to a trot as they neared the road to Calliway.

"Good girl," he murmured, rubbing her neck briskly. It was fitting to read this at a crossroads, he mused as he eagerly pulled the paper from his pocket. The note was brief and written in a nondescript hand.

Be warned.

The island union was a lie.

An aegis spider may be hiding in your home.

Jael read the paper three times, turning it over in the moonlight. Ehrinell had taken care not to leave any obvious clues — if this note fell into the wrong hands, it could be dangerous. And to leave it in the hands of children?

The island union.

Vhaleese.

If he understood her meaning, she was referencing the betrothal. Why would he be on his way to Vhaleese if the marriage was a farce? Caeda was family, of a sort, and Vhaleesians were nothing if they weren't loyal to a fault. Betrayal by one of his mother's people seemed highly unlikely, but it was an undeniable fact that their world had changed. He shook his head and furrowed his brow.

Ehrinell also said an aegis spider — a simple, but deadly creature cleverly disguised as a common house spider — may be hiding in Calliway. Native to Vhaleese, Aegis spiders did not live in this part of the world, and only rarely made their way ashore when hidden in cargo taken off sailing vessels. The aegis spider could be part of Caeda's family's entourage, maybe disguised as a servant, someone who would be unnoticed — undetected.

His father was in danger.

His instinctive urgency immediately turned to anger. His hands shook and, with a clenched jaw, he recalled Matteus's words.

On the King's orders.

His father wasn't worth his protection.

Jael shook his head, torn between vengeance and loyalty. He was ready to ride away from Calliway right now, but if there was an assassin loose in the capital, his mother was at risk, and Queen Feramin did not deserve the same fate as her husband. While Lasten did have some redeeming qualities, all his good deeds combined could not outweigh the murderous directive he'd given to end Amarynn. *His* Amarynn.

His fingers curled against the parchment.

He would ride for Calliway, but not for his father's sake; he had to ensure his mother's safety, but he made no such vow for his father.

Rhyssa broke into a gallop while, behind them, the paper fluttered to the ground.

"I'm sure." Ehrinell stood against the railing of the bow. The ship coursed through waters turned nearly black by the night sky. Sails billowed and snapped against the brisk ocean wind, their sound drowning any traces of her voice from any unwelcome eavesdroppers.

"But Caeda's parents are the Queen's kin!" Bent shook his head, grimacing.

"Aye, they are, but I know what I heard and what I saw. I imagine they mean to remove Lasten while Jael is away."

The long silence that followed was broken only by the wind and the ship as it sliced though the inky ocean water. Finally Bent spoke, his voice rough.

"Does the Queen know?"

Ehrinell shook her head. "No, I don't think she is aware."

"Thank the gods," he muttered. "But if what you're saying is true, this world is getting uglier by the day."

Wake, who had been sitting in the shadows, unfolded his large form as he stood. "Why are you telling us this now? If King Lasten is in danger, why are we here?" He crossed his arms. "You should have said something."

"I did," Ehrinell hissed. "There are still other Travelers in Calliway, you realize." She did nothing to hide her sarcasm. "Wake, if I had alerted everyone, we would have no means to catch the assassin. If Vhaleese is trying to overtake Karth, not only must we stop it, but we must also be able to prove it!"

"Fair point, lass." Bent sighed. "Who did you tell? Who do we have back in Calliway quick and strong enough to keep watch on the King?"

"Arch, for one. And Rell."

"Did you tell any Blademaster Travelers? Or did you only share this with your shadow-walkers?" Bent started pacing. "If there's a fight—"

"I doubt there will be a fight. Vhaleese only left a single person behind. That kind of plan suggests they are more interested in King Lasten's demise than claiming responsibility. Think about it," she said, pushing off the railing. "There's no reason to make a show if it. Vhaleese already has a place in court with Jael's mother."

"And by luring Jael away—" Bent started.

"There would be no other course of action but to hand control of Karth to the Queen," Ehrinell said, nodding.

Bent sighed and rubbed his temples. Queen Feramin was a good and kind woman. To weave her into this plot was treasonous, even if she was innocently implicated. But Ehrinell made sense. Nearly three decades ago, Vhaleese's bid to put Feramin on the Queen's throne was an unexpected alliance and enough time had passed that no one would suspect a Vhaleesian coup — not even her.

"So, do we carry on?" Wake asked, casting glances at the small assembly. Next to him, Endric shrugged.

"We're in the middle of the ocean. What else can we do?"

The group was silent for a long while. In the distance, lightning flashed, and a low rumble of thunder rolled across the waves. Finally, Ehrinell elbowed past the men.

"We can ask Matteus what he knows. I'd bet my life that greall-turd knows something. And I am especially good at making people — even Travelers — talk."

Chapter 17

"I'll be leaving tomorrow afternoon."

Essik looked up from the boot he was mending.

"Hmph," he frowned, then dropped his head to return to work. For a moment, he said nothing; then, he cleared his throat. "And how do you reckon you'll be doing that once it grows dark? You don't know the way to the pass, do ye?"

"No," she said, squatting beside the fire. She held her hands out to warm them over the low, steady flames.

"Magic, then?" Essik continued working on the boot, not looking up. He chuckled to himself. "The wee fairies coming to whisk ye down?"

Amarynn shook her head and smirked. Essik hadn't changed a bit. He couldn't go five minutes without a smart-ass remark. Now that she felt better and her injuries had faded to a manageable ache, he held none of his gruff back.

"Mithras will take me." She stole a glance at her old mentor to gauge his reaction.

"Mithras?" he grunted. "You've named it, and you're fast friends now, hm?"

"Of a sort."

Essik's jaw clenched as he busied his hands, and Amarynn could tell his mental wheels were turning. The wind outside the cave whistled behind her, complimented by the quiet crackling of her mentor's low, rough hearth.

"Mithras," he mumbled again. "You come up with that? Or did the damn thing talk to you?" His voice was quiet, but there was an edge to it.

"I don't know," she shrugged. "It's a name I think I heard once before. It just seemed to fit." She considered telling him more about her experience with the dragon on the ledge but changed her mind. The way Mithras communicated with her was difficult to understand and even more complicated to explain, and Essik was not known to be a deep thinker. The less anyone knew, the better, even if it was Essik. "We've come to an agreement, I think."

"Being carried in the beast's claws as it brought you here, or are you thinkin' of ridin' it?" He still hadn't looked up at her.

"Him." She corrected Essik without thinking. "I was going to talk to you about that." Amarynn stood and rubbed her hands together. "Do you have any spare leather? I'm going to need gloves and something to hold on to."

"Are ye' seriously thinkin' of climbing up on that scaly bastard's back?" She could see his eyebrows furrowing, though, turned away as he was, she still couldn't fully see his face. "Lass, if it's a steed you want, I can get ye' as far as the Suhonne. They have herds of sturdy little ponies well suited for the cold and the snow."

"No." Amarynn pushed past Essik and began to rummage through a pile of furs and leathers. "I'm leaving the mountain the way I came. But on *my* terms."

"Of course ye are." Essik sighed and sat back, finally leveling his gaze at her. "But tell me this. Where'ye headed? Back to Calliway?"

"No. I'm going to get the Gate back from Venalise. I'm going to the Reaches."

"On yer own, I'm guessing."

Amarynn gestured to the cave entrance. "You're welcome to join me. There are several more dragons large enough to carry you."

"Dragons?" Essik barked out a laugh. "I thought ye said the beasts were big, scaly dogs."

"They are most definitely not dogs," Amarynn frowned, surprising herself with her protective tone. "Look at them! They are like the dragons in Regealth's books — the books full of stories and myths."

Essik shook his head. "Never looked at a book. Can't read it, so why would I?"

Amarynn raised her eyebrows in surprise.

"Ah, now, lass. You know the heavy fighters can't. Only the shadow-keepers learnt their letters. That's one thing that made you different. It's one of the reasons so many Travelers gave ye grief. No one likes a favorite."

"A favorite? I wasn't a favorite!" She threw her arms up in frustration. "When I was with Regealth, *like we all were*, I learned the language by reading the books in his chambers. He taught me words that way. Unlike you, I couldn't pick it up just by listening and speaking."

Essik frowned as Amarynn turned and continued to rifle through his scrap materials pile. She heard his footsteps but didn't turn. One brawny arm reached around her and pulled something from the bottom of the pile. Essik lifted a thick piece of greall hide and pushed it into Amarynn's hands.

"Nothing tougher than greall. I've a knife sharp enough to cut it cleanly and a way to cut straps long enough without stitching."

Amarynn grasped the hide. The thick, oily leather was as much skin as it was scale. It was so tough that many soldiers paid extra to add it to their legion armor if they had the coin.

"That should do," she murmured as she turned to face Essik.

"Now, I don't think this is a wise thing yer doin', but the least I can do is make sure your arse doesn't fall off." He returned to his stool by the fire and produced a small but very sharp blade. "Not too sure how a Traveler comes back from having their guts splattered all over the mountain, and I don't intend to find out."

Mithras snorted when Amarynn showed him the makeshift harness Essik helped her craft. She felt it best to let him pass judgment before she attempted to secure it to his heavily muscled neck.

"This was your idea," she muttered to the dragon. Mithras whirled his eyes greenly and gave her a long, slow blink with the thin inner membrane. A rumble emanated from deep in his throat and a wave of impatience invaded her senses. "Stop doing that," Amarynn hissed. "Be patient!"

"How will ye saddle it?" Essik called from the bottom end of the rocky path. He kept a fair amount of distance between himself and Amarynn when they made their way up the mountain where the atranoch roosted. Several smaller beasts huddled along the path, and though she expected them to take flight as she passed, they kept their wings folded, and only ducked a few paces away from her. There was an air of acceptance that she felt unprepared for.

"I'm not saddling him," she called over her shoulder before she turned her attention to the leather she clutched in her hands. She intended to toss one end over his withers and then try and hook the end with her boot. However, a quick study of Mithras, up close, revealed he was far too tall for her foot to reach the end of the strap. She doubted Essik could even reach high enough to toss it to her. Hesitating, she decided to try to gain a better vantage point. Glancing to her right, she saw a rocky outcrop, dangerously near the sheer face of the mountain. It was more than unsafe, but it offered her the best chance of mounting.

As if understanding her intentions, Mithras angled himself toward the outcrop.

Sky?

It was as much a memory as it was a question. A whole other world was slowly surfacing in Amarynn's awareness, connecting her to Mithras through faded flashes of memory intermingled with emotions, the most prominent being exhilaration and bliss. She adjusted the small pack slung across her shoulder. *Like a painting with feelings*, she mused to herself.

"It'll be dark soon, lass! Why won't ye' wait till tomorrow?"

"I don't want to be seen!" Amarynn picked her way across the mountainside toward the outcrop, Mithras keeping a close watch on her movements. The wind whipped her hair, stinging her eyes as she took one careful step after another. Her heart raced each time the stones scattered under her feet and clattered down the mountain's face.

As she climbed nearly to the highest point, the atranoch rubbed against the outcrop beneath her, and she felt the rock shudder, threatening to buckle beneath her feet. She dropped to one knee, balancing herself against the stone with her knuckles as a powerful gust of wind roared over her.

"Stop it," she growled, but the great dragon continued pushing against the stone. Amarynn nearly dropped to her belly as another thrust of the dragon's shoulder rocked the outcrop.

"Don't!" she shouted. It was as if Mithras paid her no attention now that she was out of his line of sight. She turned her head toward the open air, and her stomach heaved at the dizzying height. One more push from the dragon, and she would surely fall.

She squeezed her eyes shut and tried to push her fear toward him, attempting to conjure a wave of the same panic she had felt as she fell from the ledge at Athtull, broadcasting it as intensely as she could in his direction — the way she lost her breath like a kick in the gut, her arms and legs going cold and numb.

The pushing stopped.

A calming thrum enveloped her, slowing her breathing down and relaxing her muscles. Mithras radiated safety, inviting her to trust him.

She heard another snort and a deep sigh as the dragon settled down.

Interesting.

Ice and snow pelted her as another strong gust roared over the mountain, so she ducked her head and held her breath, waiting for it to pass. When the air quieted, she shakily lifted herself from the ground, remaining in a stable crouch. *Moving is moving. This is no different. It's just higher up*, she reasoned with herself. Amarynn's fear gave way to her stubborn anger, and she began to move. Like a cat, she stalked closer to the outcrop's edge, dragging the leather straps behind her.

"It's not gonna work, lass!"

Amarynn frowned. That much was already apparent. She eased her legs beneath herself and twisted to sit with her feet dangling over the outcrop next to Mithras, her back to the heart-stopping drop of the mountain face.

From this vantage point, she could see the dragon's back had ridges, but they were not large enough for her to be able to maintain a solid grip. There was no way she could ride on Mithras's back without being thrown off by the wind unless she had straps to secure her.

She was devising an elaborate scheme to toss the straps over his back when Mithras startled her by raising and turning his head toward her. The dragon cocked his head to one side, his crystalline green eyes swirling in an almost hypnotic pattern. His snout approached, snuffling at the leather gripped in her hands. He sniffed at the straps, then blew out a quick snort before turning away and stretching his neck out. He leaned toward the outcrop again.

"Not again," she groaned, closing her eyes and squeezing her legs against the rock in anticipation of another quake. But it never came.

Daring a peek, she was stunned to see Mithras extending his neck toward her, offering his head. Unsure, she lifted the length of the strap and held it out. He stretched his neck even further.

Help.

She understood: he wanted her to slip the straps over his head.

She pulled her legs back under her and settled on her knees as Mithras took one step past her, allowing Amarynn to pass the straps over his head like a hoop. Frantically, she secured the ends together with a quick square knot.

The dragon's haunches quivered as he sat back, his rear leg muscles bunching in preparation for a launch off the ledge. He swung his head back toward Amarynn as if to tell her to get on his back, much like when he told her to run from the cave as Athtull Keep fell around them. She needed no other encouragement. She jumped, straddled his back, and wrapped the straps around her forearms, gripping them with all her might just as his wings unfurled, and they fell from the ledge. Amarynn squeezed her eyes shut as the mountain fell away and they slipped into the early morning sky.

The dreamworld preview she had been given the day before was nothing compared to the rush of gravity that assaulted her now. Every muscle fiber in her upper body screamed as she gripped the leather straps to keep herself from being blown off the dragon's back. Wind roared in her ears and her hair whipped her face; all the while, she squeezed her legs as hard as she could. Mithras's scales were bumpy, but slick and despite her strength, her knees slipped slowly back. The straps cut into her hands, cutting off all blood flow to her numb, frozen fingers. When she was sure her legs would fly out behind her, he banked, and she was thrown sideways. As he leveled out, she scrambled to center herself.

Amarynn's fight to stay on the dragon's back had kept her fear of heights at bay; however, as his wings settled into a steady beat, she had a moment to consider her situation, and was taken by surprise at how much less afraid she felt astride the giant creature. Her courage rising, she relaxed her thighs enough to slide her feet under the strap, and wrap it around her lower legs for even more security.

Surprisingly, the strap Essik crafted was effective, though she hadn't initially planned on winding her ankles through it, but that maneuver saved her when Mithras dropped out of a thermal. At the first opportunity, she anchored herself to the strap with both her hands and her legs, keeping her body close to the dragon's back, no matter the gravity.

With us.

She was becoming accustomed to this rudimentary form of communication.

"Aye," she whispered, reveling in the sensation of freedom washing over her. She could go. Mithras could fly with her wherever he wished, and Karth, Jael, and duty be damned. It would be so easy to drop the yoke of servitude from around her neck and—

"And nothing," she growled, though the wind took her words before they could make a sound. "Nothing" was what she feared most before Athtull, so why would she want that now?

I'm with you, friend, she thought. She wondered if he felt her thoughts the way she felt his emotions, but there was no way of knowing. The surety she felt in the measured beats of his wings told her she was safe, and the simplicity of the moment subdued the conflicted emotions warring in her heart. That was all she could ask for right now.

CHAPTER 18

The air was heavy when she woke up. Winter was in full bloom, all deep and dark during the nights, crystalline ice crusting the ground, and a bite to the air that hurt but still made her feel alive.

She rolled her head to the side and saw his bag and boots were gone. He left last night, and now possibility seemed to offer itself up to her, but only hesitantly.

She lay there, still and quiet, afraid the peace would dissolve if she disturbed it. Last night, she had been brave. Last night, she claimed what was left of herself and, with the final shout, earned her freedom back. She would take her little boy and start again. He would never need to know what she endured. He would laugh and play and live. The thought made her smile.

For now, all was quiet.

Too quiet.

She sat up, trying to ignore the worry that threatened her reverie.

Something was off.

Sam.

Where was Sam?

Her heartbeat quickened in the way only a mother's would when they knew their child was in danger. She scrambled out of bed, kicking the thin, worn blanket to the floor.

The hallway was longer than she remembered. His door was there, just at the end.

Before she even touched the handle, she knew.

Maybe it was the watery light that crept up from under the door. Maybe it was the stillness in the air like a little drop of life had fled.

The door was locked, but she already knew it.

Her breaths came fast, and her hands began to shake. She'd unlocked the door with a nail or a wire coat hanger before, but she didn't have either.

"Sam!"

He couldn't hear her. She knew it.

"Sam! I'm coming!"

She scanned the walls around her, searching for a nail. There was always some stray nail sticking out to catch her shirt or rip the skin on the back of her shoulder.

There!

Her fingernails tore as she pulled it from the wall. It took three pulls to dislodge it from the old wood paneling.

"Hang on, baby!"

Her stomach was heaving, her legs going numb. The entire world was moving forward around her, but she was stuck in place with a locked door — infinite despair waiting hungrily for her on the other side.

"Sam..." she jammed the nail in the tiny hole and felt the click.

"Sam!"

A circling dragon broke the quiet, its cry reverberating off the mountain peaks. Warm breath caressed the back of her neck. Amarynn lay in the grass, one arm outstretched, the other gripping the dirt. A rough push from behind roused her, but she squeezed her eyes closed. Her breath came in short pants, slowly releasing into longer breaths as the nightmare dissipated.

After leaving Essik's mountain retreat, they had flown all evening, occasionally stopping in a precarious perch along jagged ridges and smaller peaks. When both moons had cleared the mountain tops, Mithras landed in a high valley north of Athtull Keep. Amarynn, exhausted, all but collapsed after she slid off the dragon's back. Her hips and knees were nearly locked, stiff from the cold and her crouched position on Mithra's back. Too tired to make a fire, all she could do was curl up and fall asleep — a tortuous immersion into memories she feared more than any blade, any army. As she woke, bright moonlight broke through the clouds, and reality crept in alongside it.

Another nudge from behind, this time more insistent, and Amarynn released her grip on the ground and pushed herself to a sitting position. She opened her eyes fully, and an image from her nightmare flashed through her mind. Her heart seized, but an unfamiliar calm descended over her, chasing the prickling terror away. She could feel it emanating from behind her. Again, the scent of moist soil and green things filled her nose, and the quiet rustling of the wind in the trees lulled her into a sense of peace.

Mithras.

Amarynn shifted and turned to face him. His eyes were locked on her and a slight angle to how he held his head told her he could sense her unrest. He stepped back and settled himself in a crouch, his eyes never leaving hers.

"Watching over me, are you?" she murmured.

Safe.

The dragon manifested the emotion, not the word, within her. Amarynn's mind translated the meaning.

"I've never been safe," she whispered to herself.

Mithras snorted in disagreement.

Amarynn ran her hands through her hair. Still too short for her braids, it was a tangled mess, full of knots after their first frenzied flight together.

Her fingers, warm and sweaty despite the chill, stuck in the snarled strands.

She turned her attention back to the hillside where they had landed. The moonlight indicated that they were already deep into the cool night, and it would get even colder before morning. Gathering her legs under her, she rose with a groan and began to scavenge for twigs and branches to build a fire. Immortal or not, she despised the feeling of deep, creeping cold, but she stifled as much of her discomfort as she could knowing Mithras had a watchful eye on her.

Another shriek from above startled her as five other dragons circled in the pearly moonlit night sky, weaving in and out of the low-hanging clouds. Mithras answered, and one by one, they dove towards the hillside where she walked. As they landed, each one lumbered towards Mithras. Most were significantly smaller than their leader and of varying dark shades, though they all glistened with the same iridescence. Mithras greeted them with a low, purring rumble and touch of the nose. Much more than just the flying beasts they appeared to be, there was tenderness and respect between them — a bond.

She recalled there had been many more dragons at Athtull. No less than twenty had been in the aerie when she and Jael made their escape before the mountain Keep fell. Even though they were smaller than Mithras, these dragons looked to be the largest of those she remembered. All of them seemed older, like Mithras, with scars and wear on their wings. But *where had the others gone?*

"We'll go to the Keep tomorrow," she said aloud as she arranged the kindling and wood, then scoffed at herself for speaking to the beast as if he were listening. "That is, if you want to. I have a feeling we'll be going wherever you please."

Amarynn pulled a flint from her pouch and struck it several times before it produced enough spark to catch the tinder of old, brown leaves. Soon, a low fire burned and cast enough light and warmth for her to relax.

She pulled the pack Essik made for her from her shoulder, unbuckling the single strap to peer into it. When she reached inside, her hand closed around something metal. He'd given her a small, roughly made throwing knife. She smiled to herself. She hadn't told him she was missing one, but he'd seen that on his own. Even now, after all these years, he was still looking out for her as he had when she was new to the ranks of the Travelers. She slid the blade into the empty hiding spot in her boot, then returned to discover what other surprises she'd find.

The remaining contents were uncomplicated: several hard-tack grain cakes, a bundle of jerky bound with twine, an extra pair of leather gloves, and the thin, soft blanket she'd used in his cave. He'd told her it was from the Suhonne people — made from the fur of an animal he did not recognize. But it was water resistant and twice as warm as the heavy wool blankets she was used to.

Amarynn wrapped the fur around her shoulders, leaned back against the pack, and let her eyes wander across the dark silhouette of the mountain range. The dragons were behind her, their shifting and low whirring noises a comfort, though she wasn't sure why. Like Mithras, they radiated a sense of acceptance — more confirmation that they shared the same experience of being traveled. To her left were the formidable Stone Giants — the gateway to the Reaches and, presumably, Venalise. On her right were the smaller Dark Mountains, where the ruins of Athtull Keep hid in the Ironwood Forest. Aron, Finn, and Stavin would be there, too, unless they had decided to look for her. She chuckled to herself. Finn and Stavin were most likely still arguing about whether to leave camp. And Aron? He remained a mystery. Since her return to the barracks after Athtull, he had shown care for her. Then the night before she snuck way to Athtull, his concern for her kindled feelings she hadn't yet acknowledged. But there was something in the way he held back, despite the obvious attraction that touched her. Realization crept in. Aron, Finn, and Stavin were truly her friends, and she had selfishly gone off on her own, leaving them to worry.

Aside from her relationship with Jael, this was the first time it registered that she might not be alone in the immortal world, after all.

At that thought, an unusual wave of panic washed over her for a fleeting moment, and she fought the urge to stand up and run away, make her way back to camp. But a low rumble from Mithras slowed her racing heartbeat, and she settled back against the pack, pulling the fur tighter around her shoulders. Before she gave herself over to sleep, movement from beyond the flickering firelight caught her eye. The dragons were moving closer. She closed her eyes but kept one open enough to make out their large shapes against the yellow and orange light.

The mist was creeping up from the forest, and the way the moonlight danced through it enthralled her. The damp, green scent returned, enveloping her in that strange feeling of peace. Before too long, her eyes closed, and she fell into a deep, dreamless sleep.

THE STONE REACHES

CHAPTER 19

"I'm going to the tower. Be prepared for my father to send for both of you."

Venalise dropped her eyes and continued to lace up the front of her blouse. It felt good to take off her heavy dress and change into something more manageable, more *her*. She had never been fond of dresses, but they had been necessary for the role she played in the south. Now that she was home, she could shed the finery in favor of Korr warrior garb — a supple leather coat and breeches paired with a woven blouse made of the fine-stranded wool of summer sheep.

She shrugged on the jacket and finished unpacking a few items from her bag. The stable hands' quarters were sparse and unpleasantly musty, but she required no creature comforts, especially since she didn't intend to be there long. It was well-past midday, though the time was impossible to tell from the small, dust-covered windows that let in very little light. The door closed behind Oravae, and Venalise sighed.

"Why can't we stay at the tower?" Sia climbed onto the bed, pushing Venalise's bag aside. Thera clambered up beside the child, mimicking Sia by snorting and huffing. "This place smells."

Venalise paused, then sat on the edge of the bed. She watched as Thera bullied her way into Sia's lap. The little bear had grown so much in just a few weeks — far more quickly than a stone bear cub should. Her kind lived for decades and didn't mature for at least five or six years. Something to watch, she thought to herself.

"Sia, you know we are here because I want to help you learn more about your magic, and this is the safest place on the continent to do that. But Rhymere—"

"The man we are going to see? Oravae's father?"

"Yes," Venalise continued. "I want to talk to you about him before you meet him. He likes to promise things then go back on his word."

"Then why do you want to talk to him?" Sia wrinkled her nose.

Venalise sighed. This explanation was a double-edged sword. No one else would be willing to help her do what she wanted, but Rhymere would desire a role to play, if not complete control, and that could not happen under any circumstances. Sia must be made to understand the level of caution required before being brought anywhere near him.

"He is very knowledgeable about magic, but he can be manipulative. Rhymere taught me how to wield when I felt my magic take hold. He did so secretly."

"Why in secret?" Sia leaned in closer.

"My mother disapproved of the methods used in Lorce."

"I thought you said she wouldn't let you use it at all."

Venalise frowned. She had forgotten their conversation in Athtull's aethertorium when she was attempting to pry information from Sia about her abilities.

"You're a clever girl," Venalise nodded. "I did say that to you." She leaned forward and lowered her voice to a whisper. "I didn't know if I could trust you then, but I know I can now."

"So, she *did* let you use your magic?" Sia asked, her eyes narrowing as she readjusted Thera.

"You are partly correct, Sia," Venalise said. She sat next to Sia, stroking Thera's fur. Though the bear was growing, she still behaved like a little cub. *Spoiled*, Venalise thought. But better spoiled and tame than unruly and wild. "You see, my mother did not disapprove of my learning about magic. In fact, she wanted me to grow my talents, which was good. But she did not want Rhymere and the scholars of Lorce to show me how to use it."

"Why?" Sia crossed her legs beneath her and leaned forward.

"Because it would not serve her purpose," Venalise murmured. She smiled to herself, then stood. "Rhymere taught me to control my magic — to respect it. But my mother wanted me to use it without rules or limitations. She wanted me to wield it like a weapon."

"Seems to me like you chose both."

Venalise whirled around at the sound of Oravae's voice. She stood just inside the now-open door, one arm braced against the frame. Her friend had not been gone long enough to go the tower and back.

"I thought you were going to see Rhymere."

"I was, but I couldn't stop thinking about something." Oravae dropped her arm and took a few steps into the room. She put her hands on her hips and cocked her head to the side. "Come outside with me."

Venalise looked down, trying to hide her aggravation from Sia as she stood and crossed the chamber. Oravae turned and the two women stepped into the common room. Venalise shut the bedroom door and turned back to Oravae.

"Why are you being like this, Ora? At first, you seem like you have appeared from the shadows to usher me into the next great revolution, and now you question me." Venalise put her hands on her hips. Which is it?"

Oravae chewed on her lip, then mirrored Venalise with fists on her own hips. For a brief moment, Venalise was reminded of the two headstrong twelve-year-old girls they were so many years ago; one of them always trying to have the last word. Finally, Oravae spoke.

"Why do you really want to see my father?" she asked in Ceadari, her eyes flashing her fine-tuned intellect as if she were waiting to catch an inconsistency in Venalise's explanation.

"I told you, *isa*." Venalise's clenched jaw was evident in her response, her Ceadari accent making her tone even more harsh. "I need information."

"I think it's the girl."

"You think too much," Venalise bit back.

"Someone must, Vena." Oravae crossed her arms and held her ground. "You seem to think you can ride back here after running away so many years ago and not answer questions. You must admit it seems strange."

"No one is asking questions except you, so no, it does not seem strange to me, Ora."

"No one knows you're here," Oravae retorted, rolling her eyes. "How can anyone ask questions—"

"Tasar isn't asking."

"Tasar won't. He's a Korr warrior and warriors don't question authority."

Oravae paced a slow circle around the edge of the room.

"Whose authority, hmm?" Venalise followed her friend's path. Her face softened. "Ora, why all the questions? I thought you came looking for me. It seems like something has changed your mind."

"It has. I never expected to find you with a child." Oravae, now on the other side of the room, leaned against the wall. "Especially one that isn't yours. And the bear?" she raised her eyebrows.

"I have my reasons." Venalise turned her back on Oravae and opened the door to the bedroom where Sia and Thera still sat on the bed. She gestured to Sia. "Come, child," Venalise said in the language of the lowlands as she held out her hand. "Bring Thera and come with me."

Venalise turned back to the door and pushed past her friend. She didn't need complications, and she certainly did not need to explain herself to anyone. The less she said to anyone now, the better.

They stepped into the side street. The afternoon was still chilly, but the sun-warmed stone of the spires radiated enough heat to keep the streets bearable, even in the shade. Lorce was a quiet place, with few bustling vendors and trades and more sophisticated shops and guilds. This was a city of innovators, scholars, and intellectuals not interested in hawking their wares. Most provisions were brought in from other parts of the Reaches so there was no need for markets.

As Venalise led the way down the cobblestone side alley, Sia lagged behind, struggling to carry her wriggling cub while taking in the sight of the towering spires. She tugged her hand away from Venalise, and hoisted Thera up into both arms.

"Stay with me, child," Venalise snapped as she turned and grabbed the child by the arm. "This city is easy to get lost in, and we don't have time to waste."

Though many years had passed since she had last walked these streets, Venalise knew exactly where she was going. The entrance to the central spire was not far, and when they arrived, she was surprised to find it unguarded. She pushed against the large black stone door; its weight not as heavy as she remembered. Before she could step into the darkness, a woman laden with scrolls and books elbowed her way out the door. Venalise stepped back to let her pass, but not before knocking one of the papers from the stack in her hands.

The woman, older, by the color of her hair, quickly bent down to retrieve the paper. "Watch yourself," she chided as she narrowed her eyes, her lips pursed in annoyance.

Venalise dropped her chin to hide her face while the woman moved on. She peered into the dark entryway and, satisfied there were no more surprises, gripped Sia's hand and slipped through the door.

Thera, still squirming, began to whine.

"Quiet that bear!" Venalise hissed.

"Why are we sneaking?" Sia hissed back, her defiance catching Venalise by surprise. "I thought her father knew you were coming." Sia hefted Thera up over her shoulder and clutched her tightly as they moved into the dimly lit corridor.

"He knows I am in Lorce. He does not know I am here in the Spire at this moment. If I can get into the Library without having to talk to anyone, this will go much faster, and then we can be out of here."

"I think it's too late for that." Sia looked over her shoulder, fixing her gaze in the distance.

Venalise whirled around to see a woman approaching, flanked by two robed men. The woman glided forward, her green robes rustling against the stone floor.

"Wonderful," Venalise muttered. While she had hoped to make her way into the Spire undetected, that seemed to be an impossibility now. *I am the Empress' daughter*, she thought. *I might as well behave like it.* She snatched up Sia's hand and straightened as the trio came closer. When they were only a few steps away, Venalise recognized the woman.

"Talamynne," Venalise said with a curt nod. "Greetings."

Of all the people in the Spire besides Rhymere, Talamynne had the closest ties to her. She had spent most of her evenings in the scholar's quarters. Talamynne had shown her the maternal kindness that her mother did not; in fact, Talamynne was the only reason Venalise had any skill with Sia.

Talamynne was a small woman, but she projected the strength of a Korr warrior. Her steely grey eyes narrowed as she pursed her lips. She lowered her chin, never breaking eye contact. The two men carried themselves with the same confidence, though Venalise did not recognize either of them.

"*Emmina*," she said. Her voice was soft, though Venalise knew better than to let that fool her. "We have been expecting you, but you've kept us waiting." She leaned back to glance down the long entry hallway before leveling her gaze back on Venalise. "Taking in the city? Re-acquainting yourself with Lorce?"

Venalise couldn't help the smirk that crept upon her lips. "Hello Tala. Honestly, I wasn't sure what my reception would be."

"Why would you spare a moment to be concerned?" Talamynne appraised Venalise and Sia. "You are here. *Be here.*"

Be here.

"You are a fiery one, child. But you are not all that you think you are." Talamynne pointed to a pallet on the floor. "You will sleep here."

The blankets were plenty, but they were nestled next to a comfortable bed.

"Why not the bed?" Venalise, just ten years old, crossed her arms, her brow furrowed.

"Don't look at me like that, Emmina. This is not a tour of the Reaches. You are here to learn discipline — and discipline begins within."

Something about the way the woman spoke made Venalise comply, though she roiled inside at the thought that she, the daughter of T'Korr Uhll would be made to sleep on the floor.

"I still don't see how sleeping on the floor teaches me discipline," she grumbled.

"You need to focus and that's why you need to be here."

"I am here." Venalise couldn't help but roll her eyes.

"No, Emmina. You cling to Korr — to your home. But you are no longer there. You are in Lorce now. Be here."

"Your counsel is wise, Scholar Talamynne." Venalise dropped her head and dipped in quick curtsey. "I am here now."

Sia peered from behind Venalise, Thera clutched in her grasp. If any of the three noticed her, they did not indicate it.

"*Emmina* Vena." The man on the right didn't smile, but he did acknowledge her with a nod. "Scholar Rhymere is waiting for you in his chambers. You will follow us."

The two men brushed past Venalise while Talamynne lingered long enough to cast a questioning glance at Sia before gathering her robes and hastily following her counterparts.

Venalise took Sia's hand and followed the three scholars down the dark passageway. She had not planned on encountering Rhymere on his terms; she wanted more control over the situation. But that was no longer an option. Like a snowball gathering snow as it rolled downhill, she was collecting more and more complications with every move she made. The plans she made in her mind were far simpler than this reality.

"Are we going to meet Rhymere?" No longer defiant, Sia's voice had faded into a whisper, which only exasperated Venalise because there was no longer need to try to hide their arrival. They reached a wide staircase. Here the light was brighter, filtering in through tall, slender stained-glass windows. Blues, greens, and soft violet rays cast wavering patterns on the stone.

"It seems we are."

Without ceremony, the trio of scholars pushed open two great double doors of stone and light-colored wood. Sunlight played across the intricate carvings as they swung wide, emerging from the passageway into a bright and airy chamber. Venalise paused and drew a breath, inhaling the old parchment, ink, and aroma of strong jhea, her memories flooding back. She knew the room well. She'd often spent whole days, from sunrise to sunset, in here when she had the opportunity to visit Lorce.

"Oh! Vena!" An older man turned from an expansive window and crossed the many thick rugs carpeting the room, arms outstretched. A smile broke through his grey and white beard and his eyes twinkled. "It is so good to see you again!"

Venalise did not move to greet him. Instead, she offered a half-smile and accepted his embrace with a noticeable amount of hesitation. As her eyes wandered the room, she noted a disapproving frown on Talamynne's face, which planted an ember of anger in her belly. The woman still viewed her as a child. Little did she know that Venalise could break her with no more than a thought. This gave her some pleasure, and she could not hide her smirk.

"Rhymere," she said, straightening. A long silence followed, punctuated by the growls and huffs of Thera. Venalise turned to tell Sia to manage her bear, but before she could, Talamynne was beside the child.

"What a pet you have, little one," she cooed, bending to ruffle the fur between Thera's ears. Surprisingly, the bear allowed the scholar's touch. "Does she have a name?"

"Thera," Venalise snapped before Sia had a chance to respond. Both Talamynne and Sia raised their eyebrows at Venalise's tone. Talamynne stood, straightening her skirts with dignity.

"I will take the child and *Thera* to the Library. You two," she gestured to Venalise and Rhymere, "have much to talk about, I'm sure." Talamynne placed one hand on Sia's back. "Come with me, child."

"No!" Venalise's hand shot out and snatched Sia's hand. She pulled her close. "She stays with me."

"As you wish, *Emmina*." Talamynne took a step back, pursing her lips, with narrowing eyes. She cocked her head to one side. "She looks a bit like you."

Venalise took in a long breath, closing her eyes as she tried to contain her frustration. If she didn't curb her emotions, her intentions would be suspect, and she would not accomplish what she sought. She needed everyone to believe she wanted to control Karth with no interest in the Reaches. But letting Sia out of her sight was out of the question. She faced Talamynne and put a placating smile on her face.

"She has terrors, Tala," she said in Ceadari. "I don't want to frighten her. She is fragile."

Talamynne regarded Sia with a hint of a smile. In the southern tongue, Sia's language, she said "Strange, Vena. What is she afraid of? She certainly doesn't seem fragile."

Sia's head snapped up and she looked at Talamynne, then back at Venalise.

"I'm not fragile." She dropped Thera, who landed with a grunt, and squared her shoulders. "I'm not afraid, either."

"Scholars, you may leave us." Rhymere ushered the group toward the door. "Vena and I have much to talk about — and I'd like to get to know you, little bird." He smiled at Sia.

Sia sucked in a breath and moved closer to Venalise. King Lors had called her a little falcon when she was at Athtull. Her brow furrowed. "I'm not a bird," she mumbled.

"Oh!" Rhymere chuckled. "Of course you aren't. Birds don't have bears as companions. How silly of me."

Venalise watched as Rhymere did what he did best — find subtle ways to endear himself. She kept a close watch on Sia to be sure she did not fall prey. He could turn a rabid stone bear to his favor with nothing more than a side comment and a smile; he was wily and skilled. But Sia was wary, which was to be expected, given her past. She must warn Sia against this, specifically.

"So," he said. "You've returned to us." His smile widened. "Is it time?"

Venalise tilted her head. "Time?"

"You learned the Traveling magic, haven't you? Or have my little spies gotten it wrong?"

"I learned many things in the south, Rhymere."

He turned and gestured to a long table. "Let us sit. I want to hear everything, especially how you came to be with this child."

Venalise debated how much she should share with Rhymere. She needed his expertise, but she didn't want him to have unfettered access to Sia. He had such a way with words, and it was easy to get turned away from the direction you thought you were going. Rhymere pulled out the chair at the head of the table and offered it to her.

"Thank you," she murmured, taking a seat as she snapped her fingers at Sia and pointed to the chair to her right. Sia groaned as she picked up her bear and clambered up onto the overstuffed cushion. Rhymere settled himself to her left, folded his hands on the table, and settled his gaze on the child.

"You have been busy, Vena. Tell me everything."

CHAPTER 20

Mortified that the Empress' daughter had chosen quarters in an old stable, Rhymere had their things sent for at once. In less than an hour after their meeting, Sia settled in with Venalise in an empty bedchamber on the third floor, where dignitaries and esteemed visitors were customarily housed.

Since her conversation with Rhymere, Sia had sensed a shift in Venalise's mood. The mage had always been driven, but now everything she did and said was laced with a heightened urgency. When they began their journey into the Reaches, Venalise had told Sia stories about her own childhood. Often, she gave a reason or some kind of simplification every time she asked something of the child. Now, Venalise explained very little, gave her directives that felt more like orders.

While they were in Rhymere's chamber, he and Venalise had spoken in a language Sia didn't understand, but she could tell when Venalise was lying by her tone and the short, clipped way she spoke. When the two of them had finished, Rhymere had asked Sia a few simple questions that she'd tried to answer, but Venalise's warning gaze made her keep her responses short and vague.

"This room smells much better, Vena."

Venalise stopped unpacking her things for the second time and turned to Sia, who sat on the floor, flipping through pages of a large, colorful book. She unclenched her jaw and cleared her throat. "Vena?"

Sia frowned. "I never know what to call you. That's what Oravae and her father called you, so I thought it would be all right."

In the weeks she had spent with Venalise, Sia had avoided addressing her by name out of fear she would say something wrong. She had also been afraid of asking. Why, she did not know, but there never felt like a good time to broach the subject. Whether she was on a horse for hours at a time, entertaining Thera, or practicing her fire magic, Venalise never seemed to be approachable in such a way that made her feel comfortable. Often, the mage behaved like her mother had before her parents sent her to Master Omman's ship. What if she wanted Sia to call her "aunt," or worse, mother? For that reason alone, Sia had been afraid to ask.

She watched Venalise to gauge her reaction, but the mage seemed unaffected. "Lady Vena will do for now," she said as she turned her back and continued to unpack her bag, though Sia caught an expression on Venalise's face that was a cross between concern and irritation.

She crossed her arms in front of her and rubbed at the skin on her forearms as she studied the page in front of her. It was filled with words she didn't understand, but on the top half of the page was the most fascinating image of a giant, with thick, muscled arms and a bone torc around his neck. The artist had taken great pains to add vibrant detail to his yellow and blue loincloth, even adding the same blue in a diagonal mark across his angular face.

"What is this?" She held the book up to Venalise.

"A dragon," Venalise said. "They do not exist anymore, but when they did, they were magnificent."

"They look like the atranoch."

"I know." Venalise's hands stilled for a moment before she finished folding Sia's heavy cloak. She gathered the stack of garments on the bed and crossed the room to put them in a dresser drawer. "I was inspired by the old stories when Plinus and I Traveled them."

Sia started at the drawing. The dragon stood tall, its massive body covered in silvery scales with flecks of blue and green. Its wedge-shaped head was a collection of horns and teeth, yellow eyes looking as if they were actually staring at Sia from the page. She traced the figure with her finger until Thera started to bat at her hand, threatening to tear the page with her claws.

She snapped the book shut and pushed it beneath the bed, scratching at her scalp. Standing, she wandered around the expansive room, peeking around the large pieces of furniture and peering underneath the thick tapestries that hung along the stone walls. Rhymere's insistence that they move into the Spire was a welcome surprise. Though Venalise had protested, she had finally given in and now Sia was exploring this massive chamber, three flights of stairs up in the tower. Sia wedged herself between an ornate armoire and the wall, half-expecting to find a hidden passage behind the tapestry that hung there, but uncovered only more stone wall.

She scrubbed at her arms, trying to brush away the prickly feeling that had started the minute they stepped inside the Spire for the first time. She hadn't noticed it much at first; she was too overwhelmed by the beauty and size of the spiraling tower and all the carved details in its walls. The other buildings surrounding the Spire were beautiful as well, but they paled in comparison.

As uncomfortable as the sensation in her skin was, she felt like something had come alive inside of her. But it was not unwelcome. Strange, but intriguing, a new awareness had been unlocked, revealing an entirely new world — one of magic that beckoned to her.

She hadn't told Venalise about it.

It seemed wise to keep some things to herself, especially now that Venalise was acting so differently. While she felt she could mostly trust Venalise, she still wasn't completely sure, and that made her hold back. Regealth's warning that people would use her or even hurt her never stopped playing in her head. Even Master Omman had given similar advice, encouraging her to maintain her boyish disguise. Both Regealth and the ship's captain encouraged her to be cautious, and she felt compelled to comply — neither had given her any reason to doubt them.

Thera grunted behind her, and she shimmied around, leaning her back against the wall. The bear could barely fit in the small space. Her withers were wider than before, and she had to twist at an almost unnatural angle to try and fit.

"No, Thera," she said, pushing off the wall and squeezing herself forward while Thera backtracked awkwardly. As she stumbled out, Sia tumbled to her knees, hitting the bare stone floor. "Ouch!"

Thera whined, snuffling around her and licking her legs.

"What happened?" Venalise strode across the room and began to kneel beside her when Thera whirled, positioning herself between Sia and the mage. The bear lifted her muzzle in a low growl.

"Thera!" Sia gasped, reaching for the cub. "Stop it!"

Venalise's expression changed from concern to a dark scowl.

"What is this?" she asked.

"I–I don't know," Sia muttered, gripping the loose skin around her cub's neck as she tried to pull Thera back. "I think she got confused."

"Confused about what?" Venalise eyed her suspiciously.

"I don't know," Sia repeated. Her heart was beating faster, heat threatening to rise from within. But just when the warmth surged, Thera turned and pushed her head into her chest, quelling the wave. The bear huffed and grunted as she sniffed beneath Sia's arms and legs. Then, satisfied, she lay down beside her, keeping her position between Sia and Venalise.

"Control her," Venalise snapped as she straightened and turned away. Thera groaned and rolled on her side, throwing her head back against Sia's leg.

"Stop it!" Sia hissed, but Thera's position was comical and Sia couldn't stop herself from changing her scowl into a resigned smile. She reached down to rub the bear's head between the ears. Thera twisted completely over to face Sia, who pulled her halfway into her lap with a grunt and buried her face in the bear's fur. "You are going to cause more trouble," she murmured, her heart aching with worry.

She lifted her eyes to watch Venalise. The mage continued to rifle through their packs, though, from what Sia could see, she did nothing with the contents except rearrange them from one bag to another. After what seemed like an eternity, she turned to Sia.

"Stay here. Do not leave this room." Her tone was exasperated. Sia glanced down at Thera, hoping her frustrations weren't because of Thera's behavior.

"Where are you going?" Sia asked.

"I have some things to attend to with the scholars. Do not leave this room," she repeated. "Do you understand?"

Sia nodded. Venalise turned and exited the chamber, the door closing with more force than was necessary.

It was hard to imagine that, only a few weeks ago, she had been just a girl masquerading as a boy on a sailing vessel. Now, she had a stone bear cub and powers she'd never known existed, let alone that she possessed, all the while becoming a ward of a powerful mage — it was overwhelming. The enormity of her situation threatened to take her breath away while she contemplated it. So much change in such a small amount of time. Sia tried to remain still, to disappear, but Thera made it difficult with her groaning and wiggling. Finally, she gave up and released the cub.

"Stay out of the way," she whispered as Thera lumbered away. Standing, she turned a watchful eye on the door, half expecting the doorknob to turn. She wanted to escape Venalise's watchful gaze and explore the Spire, but she knew it would never be allowed.

"So I won't ask," she murmured as she padded lightly across the floor and opened the door.

"You are past the need for tutelage. Were you planning to use this little one to help us achieve our aspirations, or would you rather that she uses her gifts to sprout a forest and live happily ever after?" An older man was speaking to someone. Sia slowed her steps as she approached the corner.

"Don't be dramatic." She paused as soon as she recognized Venalise's voice.

"Well? If you will not submit to allowing my scholars to study her, then why are you here?"

"*I* want to study her. I just need access to the Library."

Venalise was talking to Rhymere about her. It made her feel odd, like she wasn't a person, but a doll or an animal in a cage. For a brief second, she thought of Amarynn and how Venalise had wanted to "study" her at Athtull Keep. Thoughts of the warrior surfaced now and then. She had wanted to help her when she was chained in Venalise's chamber, and she still didn't understand why Venalise hated her so much.

"I sense she has potential, Vena, but so much potential that you would have me break a thousand-year rule?"

"Who is here to enforce it but you? Will you upset the pantheon on high if you let your former student and a little girl inside the Library for a few days?" Sia heard Venalise's footsteps come closer to where she had pressed herself against the wall. She tried to hold her breath. "I need to know what she is truly capable of."

Venalise told her over and over that she had potential. She said that summoning a bear like Thera on her very first try was an indication that greatness was hidden inside her, and that Venalise was her best chance of understanding all that she could do. Sia looked down at her hands. Most of Venalise's affirmations felt like words spoken to keep her happy and compliant, but maybe greatness truly *was* inside her.

"Is she willing? Does she know what you intend to use her for?"

Use me? Sia's eyes widened and she covered her mouth to stifle a gasp.

" 'Use her'? Rhymere, with power like hers, simply using her is not an option. Once she realizes what she can do, our best hope is to be sure she feels a strong allegiance to the Reaches and to me."

"This is why I urge you to avoid the Library until she is ready. One misstep, and the cost could be dear." Rhymere's voice had grown louder and more agitated — impatient with Venalise's argument.

"Then take me yourself! We waste time debating!"

"Vena, *Emmina*, have patience. Let me have some time with her before we try to unlock what she holds. There is great benefit in patience."

The voices were moving away from the end of the hallway. Sia's heartbeat thundered in her ears. They were talking about her like she was something to be feared. *One misstep and the cost could be dear.* What did Rhymere mean? How could she be dangerous?

Sia held her hands in front of her and turned them over slowly, studying them in the dim light of the interior hallway. They seemed so small and weak now that the callouses from her days aboard the Blackfly had sloughed away. How could she have enough power inside of her to make grown-ups take such precautions?

Venalise said her best hope was to make sure she felt a strong allegiance to the Reaches and to her. But when Sia thought about allegiance, the face of the Traveler Amarynn flashed in her memory. In the cave under Athtull Keep, she had reached for her, called for her to leave Venalise and go with them.

What magic could she possess that made everyone want her on their side? Venalise had been clear that possessing more than one elemental affinity was unheard of, so that must be why. But even now, all she could do was make water move and fire appear. Of course, she had summoned Thera, but she had help from Venalise. Right now, her magic felt more like parlor tricks, not real power. A few weeks ago, no one wanted her at all, but now it seemed everyone did.

Sia shook her head and squared her shoulders. No one was taking her anywhere she didn't want to go. She peered around the corner and saw a sweeping staircase leading upwards. She'd have to find it, but she was sure that something in Rhymere's Library could help her understand the magic that had awakened inside of her. She needed to know, before Venalise was able to discern her abilities. Besides, the thought of being studied by Venalise made her stomach turn. She had seen what that looked like in Venalise's aethertorium, and it was brutal.

A sudden bleating growl and the sound of claws scratching on wood reverberated down the passageway. Thera! Though Sia had left her in the chamber before slipping out to explore, the bear cub was having none of it.

"Stupid bear!" Sia hissed between clenched teeth. "Be quiet!"

A whimper followed Sia's directive, and then silence. Sia took a step toward the stairway, then hesitated. Without knowing how long Venalise would be gone, looking for the Library would be risky. And Thera was proving to be a challenge, too. The bear would have to come with her when she snuck away to look again.

With a deep sigh and her bravado deflated, Sia decided to return to the bedchamber. She needed more time to plan her adventure and puzzle out the best way to keep her exploits a secret from Rhymere and Venalise if she planned on visiting the Library on her own.

CHAPTER 21

"I am told that you are the reason for your bear cub's existence."

Rhymere settled himself in the chair near where Sia and Thera sat on the woven rug beside the hearth. She briefly looked up at the elderly scholar before returning her attention to Thera, who was gnawing on the large, meaty bone Talamynne had provided earlier at breakfast. Thera seemed to like the older woman, most likely, Sia thought, because she provided her with more than just dried meat and withered berries. Since Thera and Venalise's exchange the day before, Sia had begun to notice how Thera interacted with each person she encountered.

"I am," Sia said. "I guess. I didn't really know what I was doing. She just appeared."

"Summoning a stone bear is an extraordinary accomplishment, especially for one your age." He smiled. Sia knew he was trying to be her friend, and it was hard not to respond to his kind eyes and friendly manner. She had spent so much time with Venalise, it would be easy to get drawn in.

"Don't diminish yourself, child." Venalise came around the largest of the bookshelves in Rhymere's study, a large book in her hands. "You did the heavy work. I only guided your magic. She is a product of your making."

"She's not a *product*. She's my friend."

Sia stole a glance at Rhymere and saw his eyebrows raised in surprise. She lifted her chin and maintained her stern expression.

"Don't be so sensitive, Sia. She *is* a product of your magic." Venalise snapped the book shut and deposited it on the table. She made for a large row of bookshelves on the far side of Rhymere's chamber.

"That doesn't mean she can't be your friend," Rhymere whispered, leaning down closer to Sia. "What do you remember about how it felt?"

Sia thought hard about that moment in Venalise's aethertorium. It had been so soon after she had arrived in Athtull, and everything was so new. The heat and the fire that roiled from her was something she felt often, though she had learned to quell it before it threatened to overtake her. In times of fear or anger, that sensation was the first thing to appear.

"It was hot," she said. "And angry," she added.

"Fire, then?" Rhymere sat back and looked across at Venalise.

"More than that," Venalise replied without turning her attention away from the tomes on the shelf.

"Oh?" Rhymere arched one eyebrow and turned back to Sia.

"It was cold after," she offered, unsure of what he meant. "Freezing."

The older man said nothing. Instead, he leaned back in the chair and kept his eyes fixed on her. In a way, he reminded her of Regealth, though beneath his kind smile lurked something she didn't quite trust. Regealth made her feel the same way Rhymere did, but Regealth had done more than smile and say kind words — he had put himself in harm's way. A faint ache in her chest swelled as she thought of the old mage on the ship. In the silence, Thera grunted and growled around the bone in her mouth. Rhymere took a sip from the dainty cup sitting on the side table beside the chair.

"Have you felt anything else with your magic?" he asked.

Sia hesitated. Venalise knew she had other magic inside of her, but she didn't know if it was wise to offer up that information. Water was the first magic she learned, and it was the one she was most confident in wielding, but she wasn't sure if there was more in her arsenal. A few times during her travels with Venalise, she thought she felt other kinds of magic pulling at her, but she couldn't be sure.

"No," she lied, glancing over her shoulder at the bookshelf where the mage had disappeared. Venalise stepped out of the shadows and back into the room with another book in her clutches. She watched Sia intently. "Just the fire."

"Oh, come now!" Rhymere chuckled. "My lovely Vena wouldn't have brought you all this way of you only channeled fire!"

"She has water, Rhymere." Venalise had wandered closer, and stood directly behind her now. "Fire and water, for certain. Now will you let me into the Library?"

Rhymere kept his eyes fixed on Sia, eyes glittering, a smile still curled on his lips.

"Show me," he whispered.

Sia was taken aback by his request. She twisted around to see Venalise's reaction.

"Go ahead." She nodded.

"I need a cup of water," she said reluctantly, pushing Thera's front paws off her lap. Rhymere had already risen and was pouring from an earthenware jug into a metal goblet. He scurried back and handed it to her, then stood back with an expectant look.

Sia set the cup on the floor. Taking a deep breath, she held both hands over it and closed her eyes, imagining the water streaming towards her like a quiet little brook. That was all it took to feel cool mist caressing her fingers. Calling the mist was easy now, so it took little time to hear Rhymere's excited intake of breath.

"How did you teach her this, Vena?"

"I didn't. The water mage from Karth did." Venalise's tone carried a hint of disgust.

Sia opened her eyes and let the magic drop, and with it, the water. As she wiped her hands on her skirt, Thera nudged them and began licking the water away.

"If she can access both water and fire, that could mean—"

"She has access to all four. I know," Venalise interrupted. Sia kept her eyes down and busied herself blotting at the spilled water droplets from the rug. The conversation she overheard in the hallway still had her on edge. "Now do you see why I want access to the Library?"

Rhymere did not answer, though Sia thought she saw him nod.

"Let me consider your request and consult with my council."

"There's no time for that. And clueing the council in on what she can do is... not ideal. It is best that we keep her and her abilities to ourselves. Don't you agree? Please, let me take her."

"*Emmina*," Rhymere said. "We do not open the Library for just anyone. It is a central point of magic and unless you are prepared and skilled in navigating that kind of energy, it is dangerous. You know this."

"I do, and I have been in there. Or had you forgotten?"

"You had Talamynne and I with you. And you know that as a mage tuned to fire, you cannot single-handedly navigate the power contained in the Library. You must have a minimum of three of the four elements present to keep the power in check. The two of you would risk the balance."

"Why did Lady Vena get to go in the Library?" Sia asked in an attempt to derail their conversation. Both adults turned to look at her. Rhymere tilted his head and narrowed his eyes.

"She was my student, and when she was ready, we took her there to develop her gifts to their full potential. You, my dear, are not ready for that."

"Please," Venalise moved closer to the scholar and gripped his arm. "We don't have time to study her outside of the Library. I need—"

"We need," Rhymere corrected her. Venalise sighed and pursed her lips.

"*We* need to ascertain what we are working with so that plans can be made. Time is a luxury we do not have."

For a long moment, Rhymere stood still. Finally, he cleared his throat and used his free hand to pry Venalise's hand from his arm. When he finally spoke, his voice was soft. "Vena, take the child back to your chambers. I will consult with Talamynne and Ortis — not the full council — to decide how to proceed. In the meantime, I suggest you work with her to see if your little prodigy has other tricks up her sleeve. I sense she has more than fire and water within her, as I think you might suspect as well. Try her with the stone; it is abundant here and should require little effort, should she have the ability. I will send for you when we have discussed the matter."

The old scholar pursed his lips and dismissed them both with an impatient wave of his hand. Sia scrambled to her feet, picking up Thera's bone to lure the bear to follow.

"Don't be too long, Rhymere," she said. Then, as she ushered Sia through the double doors, she glanced back at the scholar and muttered under her breath. "I should have been in that Library the minute I arrived. That waste of time is on you."

Venalise walked at a clipped pace towards their quarters. Sia stumbled to keep up, following behind her with the bone in her hand and Thera following behind her. The mage's hands were balled at her sides as she stopped at the foot of the large staircase in front of them.

"I should just take you there now. We do not need a third."

Sia couldn't decide if that was an exciting or a terrifying possibility. All the talk of her possessing the power to wield multiple elements had her head spinning. She stopped beside Venalise and looked up the stairs and into the darkness where it curved out of sight. The prickles on her skin buzzed and crackled, the sensation emboldening her. If she was something special, she wanted to know for sure. She lifted her chin.

"I'm not afraid." Even as she said the words, her chin trembled. She clenched her jaw to steady it.

"You should be," Venalise said, looking down at her. "You will not be the same once you have entered those doors — for better or for worse."

She twisted and lowered herself to one knee in front of Sia and grabbed her hands, looking her in the eyes with an intensity that was startling.

"The doors will not open for the powerless. They require no less than three elemental wielders for them to open. It's a failsafe, put in place to prevent a catastrophic imbalance, centuries ago. There needs to be three wielders of separate elements to keep the balance, but no one knew there might be a wielder that could hold more than one element. It has never happened."

"Then why don't we go?" Sia challenged her. She was ready to prove herself and stop running and pretending. "What will happen if you are wrong?"

"The Library is infused with latent power from all four disciplines, Sia. I'm certain that you wield fire and water, but I don't know how strong you are yet. This is my dilemma: I could take a chance. I want to, but if I am wrong, you would be consumed, and I would lose you. I won't allow that to happen." Venalise appeared conflicted. In one moment, her expression broadcasted anger and determination, but as she continued her deliberation, that sentiment turned to concern. "You are too special. I can't risk it."

Decision made, Venalise stood up, still holding Sia's hands.

"We will wait, and I will test your skills as Rhymere asked me to. But if he has not relented by sundown tomorrow, I might be willing to take a chance. Are you?"

Sia's mind was spinning. She wanted to go to the Library, but now that she knew more about it, it was a frightening idea and it filled her with an unfamiliar energy. Thera nudged her leg, and she dropped one of Venalise's hands to caress the bear's rounded ears. She had created Thera, pulled her from nothing with magic she didn't know she had and had no knowledge of how to use. If she could do that, she could hardly imagine what else she might be capable of. Possibility fueled her desire to know more, even if Venalise was unsure and afraid.

"Yes," Sia breathed.

Venalise smiled, though her eyes glittered with a darkness Sia had not seen before. She gave Sia's hand a quick squeeze, then dropped them. She turned and started back down the corridor toward their chambers.

"Let's go, Sia. We have work to do."

Chapter 22

S ia pulled the comforter over her shoulder, trying to get comfortable on the over-stuffed mattress. Her arms felt weak and shaky after the hours of work she had done with Venalise. When she had saved Amarynn and the Prince in the bowels of Athtull Keep, she proved she could wield the power of the earth. Stopping the rockfall as they made their escape was proof, but Venalise wanted to be sure it was true earth-wielding and not a byproduct of her confirmed dual powers of water and fire.

Oravae had paid them a visit after dinner was cleared from their room. She didn't stay long, but Sia judged that nothing had changed, by the way she and Venalise bantered back and forth. The child did her best to make herself as scarce as she could, squeezing between furniture or snuggling with Thera near the hearth in the corner. The women's tones were unmistakable, though, and Oravae left with the door closing with a resounding thud behind her. Venalise said little after her friend's departure, except to get them ready for bed.

Sia reached up to rub her eyes, but her fingers were still coated with a fine layer of dust from the stone-shaping she had done. A sneeze threatened to escape, which she stifled with her corner of the blanket. The room was dark and quiet. She didn't want to wake Venalise, but Thera shifted beside her, then raised her head, her rounded ears twitching back and forth.

While Sia had entertained Venalise's wish to confirm her power, her mind had been wholly focused on the Library. The more power she called on to stone-shape, the more convinced she became that she could handle the Library on her own. She was tired of being told what she could and couldn't do, especially if she was as gifted as Venalise said she was. The taste of power she'd felt tonight was fueling her impulse to explore more.

She slipped out from the covers and let her bare feet slide onto the floor. Just the touch of the smooth, cold slate sent thread-thin slivers of earth energy up the backs of her legs. Behind her, the blankets rustled as Thera sat up to see what she was doing.

Rather than say anything out loud, Sia reached out for the bear and rested her hand on the top of her head between her ears. *Quietly*, she mouthed as she tried to will the cub's silence while Thera butted against her hand. A quick glance across the room confirmed that Venalise was asleep, so Sia lifted Thera off the bed and the two of them padded to the door, the only noise the soft clicking of Thera's claws on the floor.

She held her breath as she turned the door handle, wincing at the soft click of the latch. Sia waited several seconds before opening the door, making sure Venalise did not stir. When she was certain the mage remained asleep, Sia shouldered the door open only enough for her and Thera to slip through.

As the door closed behind her, she hesitated. She was ready to start her journey down the dark corridor towards the staircase, but she couldn't dismiss the fear that tugged at her belly. Until now, she had always done as she was told, never pushing back or disobeying Venalise. She had always tried to follow the rules — on The Blackfly with Master Omman, and even at home for her mama. But the pull she felt from the mysterious Library at the top of the stairs was undeniable and unavoidable. She could feel the power welling inside her. The magic inside of her demanded release.

A sharp noise from behind made her jump, her heart hammering inside her chest, and icy cold fear seized her. She froze. The silence that followed allowed her to catch her breath and slowly turn. Where she expected to see Venalise, there was nothing but shadow and the flickering lights of the sconces. Her imagination was running wild as adrenaline coursed through her body.

A few steadying deep breaths later, Sia clucked for Thera to follow and together they rounded the corner of the corridor, scurrying toward the staircase. She didn't slow when they reached the first step, knowing that if they stopped, hesitation would get the better of her. She bounded up the steps and followed the staircase as it curved upward for what seemed to be forever.

More than once, she slowed, but as Thera lumbered past her with a steady pace, she redoubled her efforts and continued. The tug in her belly was growing stronger, and the prickles that danced along her skin moved faster and harder, the energy humming with an excited frenzy, painful, but seductive.

With every step, her timidity sloughed away, replaced by an eager desire to understand who she truly was. No more scrambling on a ship pretending to be a boy. No more staying quiet and frightened behind the skirts of Venalise.

Once she realizes what she can do, my best hope is to be sure she feels a strong allegiance to the Reaches and to me.

Venalise was afraid.

She was afraid that Sia would not want to share her magic once she learned to unleash it. An unexpected rush of confidence rushed through her body just as she cleared the last step. Thera, already at the top, sat on her haunches in front of two simply decorated doors.

Sia furrowed her brow and looked around the landing. This had to be it — she had reached the very top of the Spire, and there was nothing else to see. She didn't know what she had been expecting, but surely the mysterious and fabled Library would be protected by more than two average-sized wooden doors, bound by three bands each of rusted metal. They were set back in a shallow alcove, where two simple sconces sputtered on either side. Carvings, old and worn, revealed themselves in the undulating light of the torches. The wood around the door handles was darkened and shiny from age and use.

Thera padded across the landing and rose up on her hind legs to lean against the doors. She pushed against them, grunting.

"Be careful, Thera," Sia whispered as she approached. "We don't know what's in there."

As if understanding her words, Thera dropped to all fours and backed away. Sia knelt beside her and together they stared at the doors while Rhymere's words came back to her and the gravity of the moment settled in — whatever happened when they entered the Library would change everything. She clutched Thera and buried her face in the cub's fur, thinking. Even if she did nothing tonight but go back to their chambers, the awareness of what was right in front of her had changed them both.

They sat like this for several minutes, Thera's breathing slowing and Sia's quickening. Finally, a low rumble from the bear urged Sia to rise. As she took a step towards the doors, the runic carvings, dark and oily with age, brightened and shimmered. A thrumming started, low at her feet, building and spreading upwards through her body like the fire did when she was afraid. Only she wasn't afraid now — she was ready. With trembling hands, she reached for the handles.

The world exploded.

All the breath left her body, and she was consumed.

Like the moment when she had pulled Thera through with her magic, the Library breathed her in, pulling her from the deepest part of her insides. Her lungs couldn't open against the crush of the freezing void that gripped her, enveloping her. Now, instead of fire, she was alight with crystalline energy that crackled and danced around her like sparks falling from the sky.

Just when she thought she might burst, the magical onslaught weakened its grip. She could feel her feet again, and her hands, still resting on the door handles, prickled and stung like they were covered in coral ants. But she was determined; rather than let go, she twisted both handles and pushed.

As she entered the round chamber, she was surprised to find it much smaller than she imagined. Not much larger than Rhymere's chambers, the Library was a circular room lined with books. A dim blue-green glow filled the room, not bright enough to cast shadows. It almost looked like moonlight, but there were no windows, making the eerie illumination seem all the stranger.

Sia took slow steps to the center of the room, feeling the air around her thick like syrup. Book-laden shelves curved along the entirety of its circumference, broken only by the double doors. Something about it reminded her of being on the Blackfly. A sumptuously plush carpet made each of her footsteps silent as she padded forward until it ended, and her bare feet rested on the cold stone of the Spire. Her breath frosted as she breathed in and out, and a strange moaning from behind turned her attention. Thera appeared beside her, bobbing her head, growling, and whining. She sounded strange, like she was underwater.

The whole of the room undulated in the strange light. In her periphery, flashes of flames and crackles of lightning wavered in and out with no discernible pattern, while an oppressive weight settled on her shoulders and pushed her to her knees. She could feel Thera beside her, but the distressed cub's cries and growls were distant, and she couldn't see her anymore; her vision had completely faded to grey, and then her ears began to ring with a high-pitched keening that sounded like a warning.

Sia panicked and leaned forward to place her hands on the floor, her heart racing as a tiny voice inside her head screamed for her to run away.

Wind whirled around the trunk of her body, so hot she thought she might burn up, as icy needles assaulted her hands and feet. The stone beneath her palms and knees was cold at first, but a warmth spread until she felt like she was aware of the entirety of the Spire. She could feel every flagstone, every wall all the way to the ground, and then even further than that into the depths below the city itself.

Droplets of water, condensing from the air around her, clung to her skin. She began to shake from the cold and the shock of the magical attack. The elements warred with one another for her body, threatening to tear her apart. She couldn't separate one from the other — she could only brace herself through the onslaught.

Her fire, its familiar growing heat in her belly, finally manifested and spread upwards. Airy and flickering, it changed, transforming until it felt like liquid metal coursing through her veins. The chaos quieted as stone merged with fire, fortifying her against what, she did not know. She opened her eyes to see the droplets on her body turning to a fine, rippling mist that encircled her. Ribbons of gauzy haze tightened their loops, growing more and more opaque as they circled her. Lightning flashed in her periphery again, this time from above. She lifted her gaze to the center of the ceiling, where four rounded openings were carved into the stone just below the topmost point of the Spire.

The prickles, which had abated under the new, overwhelming encounters, began again to crawl all over her body. No longer just an annoyance, her skin burned with their intensity. The sensation roiled across, and then snuck inside her body, terrorizing her with pain. She screamed as lightning struck from above.

Sia's unconscious form fell, splayed in the center of the room. Thera remained beside her, unmoving, until the tendrils of energy dissipated, then nosed at Sia gently, whining and pawing at her side.

"Easy, little one," a voice cooed from the shadows. The Library had returned to its less energized state, the only light coming from flickering sconces along the wall. Talamynne emerged, flanked by two men in deep blue robes. Thera took a defensive stance beside Sia, her front paws planted wide and her head down, swinging back and forth. She issued a low, long growl.

"We aren't going to hurt her, Thera," Talamynne said in a low, sweet voice as she continued her slow walk to the center of the room. Thera clearly posed no real threat, but her bond with Sia was evident by her protectiveness. "She needs rest and special attention."

Thera relaxed her stance as the scholar approached. Talamynne signaled to her counterparts, who glided over to Sia. One of them bent low and gathered her up in his arms, while the other reached for Thera, who continued to snarl and snap at both men.

"Let the bear walk." Talamynne stayed the man with a gesture. "We wouldn't want to bloody up the Library, would we?"

Talamynne led the way to the door, the scholar carrying Sia and Thera in tow. The other scholar trailed behind the bear, maintaining a safe distance as they exited the Library and disappeared down the staircase.

Behind them, the Library doors swung shut.

PART TWO

CHAPTER 23

"**I** was beginning to think you wouldn't return, little fox."

Venalise's eyes flew open. At the foot of the bed, an older woman in black leather armor stood with her arms crossed. Wide-shouldered and tall, she narrowed her almond-shaped eyes as she studied Venalise. The woman turned and strode to a chair, dropping into it casually. She lifted her legs and crossed them, resting her heels on a small, round table in front of her, not flinching as a cup teetered and fell, crashing into pieces on the stone floor.

Venalise sat up and swung her legs over the side of the bed. Through the window, streaks of color in the early morning twilight told her it was daybreak. She glanced over at Sia's bed and found it empty. Her breath caught.

"What have you done with her, Mother?"

The older woman smirked, and the thick center lock of her hair, nearly black with overtones of red, fell across her cheek. She ran one hand over one shaved side and scratched the back of her neck.

"I haven't done anything, daughter." She dropped her hand and rested both arms on the chair. "But she's safe. Quite a rare find, eh?"

Venalise inhaled a deep breath. Her mother, Empress T'Korr Uhll, was not a woman to be confronted unless you were ready to be put in your place or see your guts on the floor. She pushed herself to standing, crossed the room, and stood before the Stone Reaches war lord.

"Where is she, *emmisana*?" It took all Venalise's self-control to keep her voice steady and calm. Uhll lifted her chin as she looked her daughter over.

"You have gotten soft, little fox," she said. "Being Below does not suit you."

Venalise didn't respond. This felt eerily like her childhood; true to form, her mother was toying with her to see how much she had changed since leaving the Reaches.

"Let us hope your magic has fared better, hmm?"

The empress stood, another cup clattering to the floor, and gazed down at her daughter from her full height, a handswidth taller, cocking her head to one side.

"My magic is strong, Mother. Very strong."

Her mother laughed and grabbed Venalise by her shoulders, and squeezed. The mage winced.

"Soft! You see?" Uhll shook her head. "Magic can't grow muscle, can it?"

"When did you arrive?" Venalise took a step backward and rubbed her arms, warming them from the early morning chill.

"Late last night. My war band will be here tomorrow." She looked around the room and wrinkled her nose at the flowery decor. Then she turned back to Venalise, eyebrows raised. "Oh! You'll never guess who we picked up last night on our way in." She waited for her daughter to ask, and when she didn't, Uhll shrugged. "Your cousin. Tasar. He was leaving — riding for Korr. I insisted he join me."

Venalise weighed her options: admitting she knew he was in Lorce or pretending she had no idea. Her mother was shrewd. It was best not to hide anything.

"Yes. He was in Suhonne when we arrived."

"I think he has a woman there," Uhll said, nodding her head, her eyes focused on the far wall of the room as if she were lost in thought. "Well, let us hope that's what he was up to, little fox! Now, get dressed and we will see how powerful your little foundling's magic really is." Uhll released Venalise and turned towards a large table near the window where a tray of berries, cheese, and bread had been placed late yesterday evening, kicking the shards of porcelain cup out of her way. She tore off a piece of bread, then selected a wedge of cheese. "Lorce food," she said before taking a bite of both. "How do these people not *starve*!" she said as she chewed.

Venalise maintained her composure with effort, but inside, her mind whirled. Where was Sia? She could only imagine the possibilities and none of them were good. Yes, she had brought Sia here to help her mother take Karth, but it was never her intention to allow the Empress unfettered access to the child. Venalise knew what her mother was like, but she was raised to expect the Empress's behavior. Sia wouldn't be able to handle Uhll's demanding and callous personality alone.

"Mother, please tell me where Sia is," she implored one more time. "She doesn't know you. She frightens easily."

Her mother stopped chewing as her face blossomed into a smile.

"Maybe this girl is not what you think, daughter. I think 'frightened' is not a word one might use to describe her. The Library didn't frighten her, so I do not think I would." Uhll gestured at Venalise with the bread still in her hand. "Maybe she's more powerful than you now, hmm?"

The Library?

Sia was here last night. The Library? All the blood left Venalise's face. Sia had gone to the Library. At that thought, she felt like she might be sick.

As shock registered on Venalise's face, the Empress laughed again. She gathered a handful of cheese and headed for the door. As she entered the hallway, she called over her shoulder.

"Get dressed. And bring that stone with you. We have work to do."

When Sia woke, the world looked different. Framed by the window, the rose and flame glow from the rising sun was as vibrant as fresh roses. She sat up, but reverberations of energy still echoed through her body from the night before, making her dizzy. The room was unfamiliar, though it appeared she was still in the Spire, by the curving stone walls. With one hand, she clutched the soft duvet while she ran the other over its pattern, her fingers noting each imperfection the weave of the fabric. She let her hand rest, closed her eyes, and an image flashed — the Library. For a moment, she panicked. Her heart raced and blood drained from her face as she realized what she had done. But as the sensations that assaulted her last night returned, instead of pain, she felt breathless exhilaration. The prickle on her skin had become a steady, pulsing hum.

"Ah, she wakes." Talamynne, robed again in green, glided into the room with a steaming teacup in her hand. She stopped beside the bed where Sia sat, and held the cup out. "Drink this. All of it."

Dazed, Sia took it and held it to her lips, breathing in an aroma of spices she could not name. She glanced up at Talamynne.

"Go on, child," the scholar prompted. "You'll need your strength."

"Why?" Sia's voice was hoarse, her throat raw.

"Shhh," Talamynne chided, tipping the bottom of the cup to guide the warm liquid past Sia's lips. "Finish this first."

The concoction was sweet, but not syrupy, and it sent a warmth through her that began behind her eyes and spread down through her body and to her limbs. The taste reminded her of something Master Omman would drink on the ship when they crossed into the frigid waters north of Vhaleese.

There wasn't very much in the cup, and when she finished it, she handed it back to Talamynne. "What was that?"

"Something to fortify you," the scholar said as she took the cup. "The changes you are going through will require strength."

"Do you mean what happened to me in the Library?" Sia couldn't stop the memories of fire and ice tearing through her, of light and stone connecting to her. She sucked in a breath as her body stiffened.

"That's exactly what I mean." Talamynne turned away, delicately set the empty cup on the table, and strode towards the door. "Now, you need to get out of bed and get dressed. I will be back soon."

"Where is Venalise?"

Her question was answered with the sound of the closing door.

Sia slipped off the bed. A deep sigh and groan caught her attention, and she turned to find Thera still nestled in the thick, fluffy blankets. She ran her hand along the bear cub's fur, marveling in textures she never noticed before: a mix of silky undercoat and the roughness of the coarse grey fur tufted around her neck. Thera butted her head against her hand and huffed.

"Do you feel strange, too?" she whispered to the cub. Thera answered with a whine and a nip at the air.

At the end of the bed, a change of clothes was laid out for her. Sia pulled on a pair of soft pants and a long, silk tunic. Just as she slipped on the doeskin slippers on her feet, the door opened again and Talamynne returned, followed by the two scholars who had been with her when they entered the Spire two days ago. While the two men stopped just inside the door, Talamynne continued until she stood in front of Sia where she lowered herself to one knee, her expression solemn.

"Sia, you entered the Library alone and without permission. That should not have been survivable, yet here you are. Your curiosity was reckless." She leaned closer to Sia. "You are meant for great things, child."

Everything was happening so quickly. Too quickly. Another wave of dizziness swept over the girl, and she swayed. Talamynne grasped Sia's hands to steady her.

"Where is Venalise?" Sia asked, her voice small. Everything seemed different, and she wanted some sense of familiarity in this room of strangers.

"She will be here soon. We'll leave Thera here to rest," the woman said, standing. She smiled and extended her hand. "Let's go and see what gifts the Library granted you."

Sia and the three scholars wound through the Spire using dark, narrow passageways she had not known existed. Every few minutes, cold dread formed a knot in her belly, then dissipated with a squeeze from Talamynne's hand. Though she did not know her well, Sia was grateful for the scholar's calming presence. The hum across her skin ebbed and pulsed, but as they descended another winding and constricting staircase, it grew steady, so strong she had to stop to catch her breath. The air was thicker here, but cooler and less musty than the rest of the tower. Talamynne stopped with her as the two men continued on, downwards.

"We will go slowly from here. As you near the Spire's aethertorium, your magic will reach for the conduits. Managing one elemental power is strenuous, so I can only imagine what someone like you must endure."

"How many magics are there?" Sia managed to whisper. While she knew water and fire magic existed, the bombardment of energy in the Library had made it difficult to separate one energy from another. Funny, she'd never thought to ask Venalise.

Talamynne was right. Sia felt like her body was not her own as they continued forward. Talamynne held her hand tightly, but the pull to sprint towards the bottom of the stairs was almost unstoppable; it beckoned and whispered to her to let go of her control. Heat in her belly writhed while icy pinpricks danced along her fingers, leaping and diving, the slivers of cold shocking her with each movement. She stopped and stiffened when a crackling electric current sparked at the base of her spine and crawled up her back to her scalp.

"Just breathe, Sia." Talamynne's voice was by her ear, which was a good thing; as the electric energy spread, bright white filled her vision, blinding her momentarily. Sia concentrated on the feel of Talamynne's hand and the sound of her voice. "Feel the breath coming in and out of your body. Do not lose yourself."

It was so hard. Sia tried to focus on the cool air in her throat and the feel of her lungs as they expanded and contracted. Through the onslaught of magic, a tiny fraction of herself swam in its center like a little fish in the middle of the deep, vast ocean. She worked to slow her rapid intake of air to a steady pace. With each focused breath, she felt the magic recede until her vision cleared enough that she could place one foot in front of the other again. Talamynne waited patiently while Sia took small, tentative steps. Then, together they finished the last few steps to the bottom landing.

The scholars that had gone ahead of them waited by two stone doors, pale and stoic.

"Silahn, Ruidel. Open the doors. Do it slowly." The men nodded. As they pulled them open, the stone scraped across the floor with a low rumble. The light from the aethertorium, an unnatural hue of gold and blue, filtered out through the widening doorway. "Remember, do not lose yourself," Talamynne said, stepping forward, tugging Sia's hand. "Though magic does not belong to us, while it resides inside of you, it is yours to command. Do not forget this."

As soon as they crossed the threshold into the chamber, Talamynne released her and drifted away, to the side. Sia stood still for a moment and looked around the room.

Like Venalise's aethertorium in Athtull, it was cavernous. The high ceiling swept upward, so high she could not see where it ended. Four sections of carved symbols and runes lined the walls all the way up into the shadows, each section markedly different from the next. Sia looked to Talamynne for direction; she did not know what was expected of her.

"Let the chamber guide you, child." Talamynne moved behind her, standing back just outside the threshold, and signaled for the men to leave. The huge doors groaned and scraped while Sia watched over her shoulder. Her hands trembled as she watched the doors come closer and closer together with Talamynne on the other side.

I wanted this, she reminded herself. *I wanted to take my power before anyone else had a chance.*

She tried to remember how she felt when she and Thera climbed the stairs and opened the Library door. She was ready then. She would be ready now.

"Does she know what you intend to use her for?"

"Our best hope is to be sure she feels a strong allegiance to the Reaches and to me."

A rush of anger and hurt flooded her senses as Venalise and Rhymere's words replayed in her head. They talked about her as if she were a prize animal to be used, not a magic wielder just like them. *Just like them.*

No. She was not just like them. She was ready to become what they feared. Sia turned her head back to the center of the chamber, and when the doors were pulled to with a groan, Sia felt the world fall away.

The aethertorium was gone, replaced by only a column of energy thrumming like a muted swarm of sea hornets. Again, like in the Library, her hearing dampened as if she were underwater. Instinctively, Sia looked for Thera by her leg, but remembered the cub had stayed behind; while she would feel safer with her here, she didn't want the cub to get hurt. Scanning the room, she searched for anyone, anything she recognized. Then the energy buzzing around her surged and she fell to her knees.

Her eyes locked on the center of the room. There, suspended in the air above intricate patterns carved in the stone floor, was the blue-green crystal Venalise had brought with them from Athtull Keep. The air in the center of the room had been distorted when she entered, but now that she was alone, it stabilized and allowed her to see through it. The stone shimmered and spun, casting the light from its many fractals on the stone walls. Sia breathed in, bathed by the glimmering light while the energy that crackled up her spine changed to a soothing purr.

She stood, this time with steady legs. Sia felt compelled to walk to one carving-filled part of the curved wall, to touch it. The prickling icy shards returned, but as she laid her hands on the stone, she felt magic bleeding from her fingers and into the stone. She nearly jerked her hands away as the freezing cold took hold, but it was replaced by an exhilarating burst less uncomfortable than it was energizing. One by one, the carved symbols and runes began to glow pale blue, brightening all the way up the wall until the very top of the aethertorium was illuminated.

She knew what to do.

The next section ignited the fire in Sia's belly, nearly taking her breath. This time, the familiar rush of heat writhed through body like a tempest before she slammed her palms against the wall to give it release. Again, the carvings glowed red all the way to the top. Where the blue and red glow intermingled at the top of the chamber, they cast an eerie violet hue. She stared as the corners of her mouth turned up. This was what they feared: her power.

She could almost see where the cavern ended, but there were still too many shadows. A surge in the room's energy returned her attention to the next part of the wall. This time, Sia was ready for whatever magic was triggered. She placed her small hand against the carved stone in the third quadrant, and for a moment, doubt took hold when nothing happened. She was about to drop her hand from the wall when her heart began to beat harder and harder, until she thought her chest might explode. Facing the stone, she used both hands to steady herself, leaning her forehead against the wall to try to keep calm. She remembered Talamynne's words. *Don't lose yourself.* When the symbols took on a faint green glow, she was dazed — she did not know what this magic was, but it made her bones ache.

Sia leaned one shoulder against the green-lit wall and looked at the last untouched section. Once again, the chamber's energy surged, pushing her forward, and she used the momentum to carry her across the floor. Stumbling, she lost her footing and tumbled upon the stone, catching herself on her hands and knees just out of the wall's reach.

The magic pushed her, pulled her to stretch out one arm, to touch the bottom row of markings, her fingers barely brushing against the stone. But the minute her skin made contact, a tremendous force yanked her body against the wall. This time she felt as if her insides themselves were rushing out of her fingertips and into the stone. As the carvings began to glow a silvery orange hue, the wall released her, and she sprawled onto her back.

From where she lay, Sia's eyes followed the carvings as they filled with light, climbing up to the very top where all four colors merged into a blinding, pulsating white. The chamber throbbed with a pressure so powerful she couldn't breathe, couldn't move. A deep, thunderous crack sounded, followed by the white light above expanding to fill the chamber. As the light cascaded down, Sia panicked and threw her arm over her eyes.

"Stand up, Sia."

Talamynne's voice whispered in her ear. The child pulled her arm away to find the chamber again looked as it did when she entered. The blue stone still hovered in the center, though now it pulsed with shimmering iridescence and not just the blue-green light from before. She turned her head, muscles screaming from exertion, and saw Talamynne crouched beside her, hands on Sia's shoulders guiding her to sit.

"Wh-what did I do?" Sia murmured.

"Exactly what you should have done," the scholar answered as she coaxed Sia to stand. "But you are not finished." Talamynne gestured to the crystal. "Do you remember when you brought Thera to you? Do you remember what you did?"

A bright keening sound emanated from the crystal. Talamynne took a step away from Sia in the direction of the door. "It is time to do it again."

And then the door closed again, leaving Sia in the room alone once more. The crystal thrummed and whined, as if it wanted release.

Call to the stone.

Venalise had been there the last time, telling her what to do.

Let the world disappear and exist only in the magic of the element.

Regealth's words returned to her as they had at Athtull.

Only the magic.

But which one?

She did not have time to choose. The stone recognized her and began to send out tendrils of energy — a weave of blue, green, red, and silver-laced orange, all crackling with white energy. She remembered Athtull, how she pulled from deep inside herself, like breathing without atmosphere. The magic sought her will then, but she didn't know how to answer. She did now.

"Sia!"

Venalise ran to her when the doors opened. A group of armored soldiers ran past her, to the center of the room. Shouts and orders in Ceadari reverberated off the walls while another sound, a ragged scream, rose above the others. Sia tried to lift her head to see what it was, but Venalise clutched Sia to her chest, hiding her eyes.

"Stop!" Sia cried, her voice muffled against Venalise's shirt. The shouts continued, followed by scuffling and grunting. She had to know what had happened. She needed to know what it was that she called. She squirmed harder, and finally tore herself out of Venalise's arms just as the soldiers passed by with their captive.

A massive man, nearly twice the soldiers' height and wrapped in ropes and chains, stumbled as the soldiers dragged him towards the open door.

His skin, grey as the stone around them, rippled with muscles. He wore a loincloth of vibrant blue and yellow, and a rough torc of bone wrapped around his neck. The man turned his head to look at Sia before the men roughly jerked him forward. He looked dazed. She thought she recognized him, but the blue mark across his face confirmed it. This was the giant she had seen in the picture book in the room she shared with Venalise. She had summoned something that didn't exist.

CHAPTER 24

M orning broke over the peaks of the Dark Mountains with rose gold streamers of light heralding the new day. A dusting of frost encrusted everything in the meadow with glimmering crystals. Amarynn's eyelids fluttered open as the crystals of frost-prisms splintered the light, and her vision was filled with fractals of colors that danced and swirled.

Blue-green facets refracting tiny pinpoints of light, casting thousands of shimmering fractals on the wall.

"Go to the crystal, Amarynn. It's safer there. Better."

Warmth and safety enveloped her in the quiet. She sighed and tucked her hand beneath her chin, but as she did, her fingers grazed frosted blades of grass, and she sucked in her breath and scrambled to sit up. Her eyes were wide now, and her heart raced as she scanned the area to confirm where she was, but all she could see was a wall of tall dark, jewel-encrusted stones. They surrounded her.

Then she was enveloped in warmth and... peace. Her vision sharpened and the sparkling darks stones moved in a slow and rhythmic cadence.

Breathing.

Safe.

The stones were not stones at all. They were the scaled backs of the dragons. During the night, they had formed a circle around her, protecting her.

We.

She turned to find Mithras lying behind her. He lifted his head and offered his snout to Amarynn, who placed her hand on the warm scales and felt her heartbeat slow. Around her, the other dragons stirred and all the tiny ice crystals covering their spines creaked and snapped as they fell to the ground.

Chaos clattered in the back of her mind — a new occurrence. Her mind had been quiet in the waking hours before she fell from the ledge at Athtull, but as soon as her eyes opened in Essik's cave the static hum made its presence known. This morning, in the clear and quiet dawn, her mind was loud; voices mixed with images that made little sense. At least her dreams had a story.

It was strange, though. The waking nightmares that drifted at the back of her consciousness had begun after Mithras saved her from the fall at Athtull's ruins, the night she snuck away from camp. But now, it was only Mithras who could quell them.

He nudged against her hand that still rested on his snout.

"It seems I am at your mercy," she murmured, giving him a soft rub between the eyes. Resisting the urge to press her forehead to his, she pushed back and stood, her muscles stiff in the cold. Mithras rose to his heavily clawed feet and unfurled his wings. The others followed and soon, the meadow was filled with dragons and their outstretched wings. The great creatures lifted their heads toward the rising sun, soaking up the creeping warmth.

Amarynn found herself wanting to do the same, and lifted her chin, closing her eyes against the bright morning rays. The sensation was exhilarating and, as the warmth caressed her skin, she realized she had never allowed herself the space and time to appreciate a quiet moment such as this. Wrapped up in the day to day of Traveler life, it never occurred to her to steal a few moments.

The hollow scraping sound of wings curling onto scales broke her reverie. One by one, the dragons gathered on their haunches and launched into the sky, pumping the air hard and fast with their wings. Mithras stamped the ground behind Amarynn, and she turned in time to see a strip of leather fall from his teeth to the ground.

"How am I supposed to get up there?" she asked, reaching down to snatch up the leather strap. "And how do I get this around your neck?"

The dragon lowered his head and huffed. It took a moment, but she puzzled out what to do. A quick knot in both ends secured the strap in a loop that she draped over his head and slid as far as she could on his neck. Once he stood, the strap would fall back near her perch and she could untie the knot to wrap her arms and feet with each end.

Mithras lifted his head and dropped to one knee, a low rumble emanating from his chest. Amarynn accepted his invitation, shouldering her pack and securing the strap around her neck. She raised one foot up to his thigh and groped for a place to grab to pull herself up.

"I look like an idiot," she growled as she struggled to find purchase with her feet. Finally, she swung one leg over his back and sat up, surveying the meadow around them. All but one of the other dragons had taken flight. She watched as he launched and marveled at how different it looked from this perspective.

Amarynn felt the drop when Mithras sat back, the muscles near his wings bunching together in preparation for takeoff. She leaned forward and wrapped her feet with the leather, then coiled it around her forearms. Pressing herself tightly to his back, she prepared for the rush of air and momentum, but it never came.

Mithras stayed frozen in his crouch; his head tilted to the side. His entire body began to tremble, and the buzzing sensation Amarynn had felt when she first encountered him in the forest surged across her scalp.

Wrong.

The feeling was intense — not like all the others he had shared with her. This one was anger and fear blended, a feeling that sucked the breath from her body, brutal. Gut-punched, and feeling her adrenaline surging, she gripped the straps tighter, but Mithras lowered to his knee and leaned sideways, nearly throwing her from his back. She did not know why, but Mithras needed her to stay behind, so Amarynn vaulted off, tumbling in the grass as his great wings pounded the air. She stayed low, shielding her eyes from the downward gusts from his powerful wingbeats as he took off, but then he issued a call that brought her hands to her ears. The sound was fury and pain laced together, frantic yet resolute.

As the call faded, it was answered by others. Mithras banked and pumped his wings hard, turning in the direction of the Stone Reaches on the north side of the Stone Giants. The other dragons shot past Amarynn's position in a tight group, following Mithras toward the horizon.

"What—" she started, but was cut off by another shriek from Mithras, though this was further in the distance. He was flying fast. Something had spooked him, something he let her know was wrong, but she couldn't fathom what it could have been. He was flying in the direction of the Stone Reaches, and that most likely meant something was happening with Venalise.

Amarynn dropped her hands and looked around, dumbfounded. No longer a resting place for magnificent beasts, the meadow was wide and empty, save for the impressions the dragons had left in the early winter grass. She raised her hands to her head. The stinging electrical buzz that she had grown accustomed to in Mithras's presence was fading, leaving her feeling hollow and alone.

Keeping her eyes fixed on the spot on the horizon where Mithras and the others had disappeared, Amarynn stood and readjusted the pack that had gone askew during her unwieldy dismount. Just as she had settled into the feeling of being watched over, she suddenly felt lost and alone. She watched the skies for several minutes before shaking her head.

"What did I think would happen?" she scoffed. "We would ride off together and be best friends?" She tore her gaze away from the mountains in the distance and started walking in the direction of Athtull Keep.

Aron awoke with a start to the sound of Dax stamping his feet and nickering. They had made camp only a few hours ago, and after struggling to quell his growing concern for Amarynn, Aron was finally drifting off to sleep when the noise jarred him awake. The war horse was obviously anxious about something.

"I've got her! She's close."

Xan clambered through the brush, hands gripping Amarynn's throwing knife as he stumbled into their campsite. Aron staggered to his feet and scrubbed his face with his hands. Dax whinnied at Xan and shook his head, his pale golden mane whipping back and forth.

"I could have told you that," Aron grumbled, nodding towards the horse. "You might as well put that knife away. Dax has a notion where she is, and, let's be honest, he's more reliable." Noticing Xan's frown he added, "No offense."

Xan tucked the knife into his belt, pretending not to be affected by Aron's comment. "I suppose we pack up then?"

"It's not even sunrise! Unless you can use your magic to see in the dark, I'm not keen to stumble around in this forest."

A plume of fire erupted from Xan's hand.

"Or... that." Aron sighed and checked the position of the moons. They were low in the sky, but above the highest of the Dark Mountains' peaks. In the past two days, they had made slow progress through the dense and steep mountain forest, and he wasn't interested in Xan injuring himself. Dax was a concern, too. Amarynn might consider the horse invincible, but one wrong step could lead to a broken bone, and he'd be damned if he would be the one responsible for any harm coming to Amarynn's precious steed. Her bond with Dax was like that of a brother and sister — both of them would kill for one another.

He crossed his arms and eyed the young mage.

"We'll stay put for now. I don't want to chance Dax breaking a leg. We'll move at first light." Aron gestured to Xan's unused bedroll. "No need to try and prove anything tonight. Get some sleep. We'll let Dax find her when the sun rises."

Xan reluctantly knelt by his bedroll and leaned back, closing his eyes, but not after taking a moment to watch Dax. The horse was quivering with anticipation.

"You sure he won't bolt?"

Aron patted Dax's withers, running his hand along his neck.

"He won't. He loves that woman, but he's also a trained war horse and orders are everything. He'll wait. He won't like it, but he'll wait."

Aron let his hand linger in the golden horse's mane. The big gelding swung his neck around, honey brown eyes regarding him with an eagerness, as if he were asking permission to go after Amarynn. Aron could relate to Dax's anticipation: Amarynn was a heady experience, and once you had a taste of her, it was difficult to let her go. She'd been on his mind since the night they met at the outpost where he and Bent found her. It was the first time he had ever laid eyes on the Traveler he had heard so much about. His head had been filled with tales about her desertion, and he expected to find her as some sad, melancholy soul. But the fierce woman he encountered on the other side of the table was no such thing. Defiant and wild, she never strayed too far from his thoughts. Her fierce determination to be free of Traveler servitude resonated with him.

He was the newest of them, called over only shortly before he met her, but he knew he was different from the other Travelers. He had no memories, but awoke with intuition and a sense of what was wrong and right, unlike the others. He was aware that he was not where he should be and he fought like a wild man to escape, but to where, he did not know. Words and phrases tumbled around in his head that felt natural on his tongue, but held no real meaning when he spoke them. After a few days, they faded along with his drive to run away. As his former life faded, his new one blossomed. He acclimated to the Legion quickly, picking up their language and their weapons faster than anyone imagined, he was later told.

So, while Amarynn was off infiltrating Athtull Keep with the Prince, he had started to ask questions. His intrigue and desire to know more about the infamous Traveler got the better of him. While most appreciated her contribution to the safety of Karth, the general assumption was that she was "a loner" and "unstable." Many referenced the mysterious Madness that Essik, the first Traveler, had succumbed to before he deserted, and Amarynn was expected to eventually follow the same path.

But once she returned from the Darklands, the talk quieted. New opinions formed and leaned toward her being instrumental in the return of both Regealth and the Prince. Her image was reborn as a gallant servant of Karth. However, only a trusted handful of people knew that she was a shadow of her former self — tortured by the nightmares and paranoia bought about by Venalise Korr when she forcefully invaded Amarynn's mind.

Night after night, Aron was there when she cried out. He was the one to hold her, stroke her hair, and soothe her out of the terrors that plagued her in her sleep. Not Jael. Not even Bent. Occasionally Finn or Stavin would step in, but he was the one who sat beside her most nights because he understood her pain; he had nightmares, too.

Aron had told no one about the dreams. They had begun just after he and Bent returned from fetching Amarynn, but he was so new to the Legion, he wasn't sure who he could confide in or trust. Most nights, he saw random collections of unfamiliar scenes and a language he didn't know, but more recently, since Amarynn's return from Athtull, the language was starting to make more sense. He did not recognize the scenery, but he got the impression that greatness was expected of him, and he had not risen to the challenge. For days after these nightmares, an overwhelming sense of shame plagued him, and he threw himself into training and learning. Every opportunity he had to learn more about Karth and about the Legion, he took.

"You know, if you're just going to stand there, we might as well try to get moving."

Aron lifted his head to find Xan lying on his side, watching him. The young man let another flame rise from his palm as he arched one eyebrow. "Even though you say we should, it's obvious you don't really want to wait."

Aron sighed. He had allowed his emotions to get the better of him, and Xan obviously saw through his flimsy attempt to appear unaffected. He did want to go; he felt an irresistible urge to find Amarynn, to tell her that he understood how she felt. While his dreams and nightmares had not caused him the same amount of pain as hers seemed to, dread still clung to him like cobwebs. Maybe together they could make sense of what was happening to them both.

"Alright, then." He kicked dirt over the meager fire as he gathered his things. "But if that damn horse breaks a leg, you're telling her. Not me."

Xan stood, pulling Amarynn's throwing knife out from his belt, and as the flames from the campfire sputtered out, another, brighter spark emanated from his outstretched hand. The fire in Xan's palm writhed in an undulating ball, casting strange shadows and flares of orange light through the branches of the dense ironwood trees.

"You first, oh brave one," Aron muttered as he gestured toward the clearest path through the brushy undergrowth. Xan obliged, holding his summoned fire in front of him, the knife clutched in his other hand. He looked back over his shoulder.

"I'll head in the direction the blade leads, but let me know if Dax has other ideas."

"Good plan, lad." He offered Xan a smile and a nod. The young mage was working hard, despite Aron's frequent jabs.

Aron surveyed the sky once more before ducking into the thick forest canopy. The two moons had already set, and the sky was lightening to a deep violet in the north. He hoped the clouds stayed away, even with Xan's magical light source to guide them. The light from the waking sky would make their treacherous expedition less dangerous.

"Be close, she-demon," he whispered before he tugged Dax into the trees, following the dancing ball of fire. Xan was rapidly dwindling to nothing more than a wraith in the shadows. "Don't make me hold my breath for nothing."

CHAPTER 25

Amarynn shielded her eyes as she scanned the horizon for the fourth time, looking without hope for a sight of any of the dragons. She was surprised how much it stung that Mithras had left so suddenly, without warning. Her instincts told her that Mithras had sensed Venalise and her magic, but she couldn't be sure. He and his kin shared grief and rage that was solely directed at the mage, as did Amarynn. They were bent on revenge, and Amarynn wanted to share in that, too.

"He's not a puppy," she scoffed to herself. "He'll return when he wants to. Or... if he wants to." She dropped her hand and surveyed the area. The peaks where Athtull's ruins lay loomed to the west. If the others had waited for her return, it might only be a two-day journey on foot to reach them, by her estimation. The walk would be arduous, but she had no other choice. Amarynn sighed, picked up her pack, and started for the tree line. She had only gone a few footsteps when a snort and then rattling from the underbrush alerted her from the shadows. She felt herself smile as a familiar golden head emerged.

"Dax!"

Amarynn dropped her pack and sprinted toward the warhorse, who had broken into a canter in her direction, reins trailing behind him. She didn't notice the two men that followed, her excitement at seeing Dax overshadowing all else.

As Amarynn and her horse reached one another, she flung her arms around his neck. His scent enveloped her as her hands touched his soft coat, and a lump formed in her throat. She stroked his neck as tears threatened to fall, though she squeezed her eyes shut in denial. Overemotional reactions were not in her wheelhouse, and it was unsettling to feel such a surge of positive emotion like this in her waking hours.

"I told you that horse would find her!"

Amarynn stepped back from Dax, her hand at her short sword, and looked over his back to see Aron and Xan standing just past the trees. At the sight of the other Traveler, her breath caught for a moment. The look on his face — a mix of relief and exasperation — took her aback until she realized her expression must be equally surprising. She dropped her eyes and composed herself before walking towards the forest edge.

"I told young Xan here that your horse would find you!" Aron laughed as she approached, though his mirth couldn't hide the way his eyes searched her body head to toe. It reminded her of the way Jael would check her after they sparred, to be sure she was uninjured — a silly show of his affection. "Where did you go?"

Amarynn ignored his question and turned to Xan.

"You used magic?"

He nodded proudly and produced her throwing knife from his pocket. His eyes sparkled as he held it out to her. "You left this behind when you went to Athtull. I was able to attune to it and locate you."

Staring at the blade in his hand, she kneeled and reached into her boot to confirm; indeed, her knife was missing.

Aron started to speak, but bit back his words as Amarynn rose. Xan appeared to notice as well.

"Not like you, is it?" the young mage asked. Aron shot him a glare.

Amarynn tilted her head, then reached for the blade. "No. It's not," she murmured and met Aron's eyes. His surprise was evident in the way he looked at her, so she changed the subject.

"I estimate a two-day walk back to camp. Yes?"

Both Aron and Xan nodded.

"Well, we better get started before Stavin and Finn decide to leave." Amarynn turned to retrieve the pack she had dropped, with Dax dutifully trailing behind her. She wanted to look behind her to gauge their responses, but she chose to wait. She put the strap over her shoulder, then turned to Dax, running her hand along the saddle on his back.

"Full tack on you, with no one riding?" she said with a frown. Reaching up to unbuckle his bridle, she let it fall into her hands. Dax worked his mouth around and shook his head. Aron should have known that her horse had no need for reins or a lead rope. "We'll make them pay, my boy," she said. As if in understanding, Dax snorted and began to snuffle at her pants pocket.

"No, I don't have any honey brittle," Amarynn chuckled.

"We should start back while we have a full day," Aron called out.

Amarynn ignored him as she searched the ground at her feet. "Ah ha!" she exclaimed, pulling out a small plant by its root. She offered it to Dax, who lipped it away from her fingers. "Sweet vine," she said. "It's not brittle, but it's better than nothing."

She patted his neck and turned back to the men. Dax followed without prompting, and when they reached them, she shoved the bridle into Aron's hands.

"If you didn't ride him, why is he wearing this?" she growled.

Aron laughed. "We are all afraid of that horse, Rynn!"

Amarynn smirked and pushed past him without comment. She scanned the forest floor, found their incoming tracks, and traced them back into the shady undergrowth. Her companions' footsteps behind her confirmed they were following.

She scowled to herself. Aron's regard for her felt different, somehow, and she supposed it could have been from their encounter in her tent before she snuck away, but she did not have the mental energy to engage in a conversation about that. As long as they were following her, no one needed to talk. That would happen soon enough, when they camped for the night, and she needed the time to gather her thoughts.

Dax snorted and shook his head as if to chide her for leaving him behind and in the hands of Aron and Xan. As she rubbed his neck beneath his mane, she frowned. Riding Mithras had made her completely forget about him, and that worried her.

"I'm sorry, my boy. If you could fly, you'd have saved me faster than Mithras did." She patted his neck and ran her hand over his ears as he dropped his head to nip a quick bite from the low bushes. "No one could replace you," Amarynn murmured as she scanned the sky between the trees and hoped she was telling the truth.

Camp, hours later, was simple and rushed. Early in their journey, they passed the previous camp Aron and Xan had made before their nighttime trek and settled near a rocky downward path.

The three of them sat around a roaring fire, easily started by Xan, and ate a silent meal of Essik's jerky and hard tack as well as a handful of nuts from the oshwal tree under which they had set up camp. Amarynn considered sharing what had happened after her fall, but there were too many details she was not ready to talk about. It was easier not to say anything.

She stole a quick glance at Aron as she stretched. She would be lying if she wasn't a little ashamed for playing him the way she had. Aron showed real concern for her the night she left, and when they found her today, his relief was obvious. She knew very little about him, in truth, and she was intrigued as she learned more. She tore off another bite of jerky and chewed on it thoughtfully while she studied both men. Finally, Xan swallowed his last bite, nodded, and excused himself to his bedroll.

The silence continued, ensued, and Amarynn debated going to sleep herself, mostly to avoid an awkward conversation. Telling Aron about Essik would make little impact; he was too new a Traveler to realize the significance, and dispelling the myth of the Traveler Madness most likely meant nothing to him. Even if it did, he might not believe her. With so many thoughts whirling around in her head, she was tired. Her dream from the night she woke with Mithras weighed heavy on her, and she was fearful of another one... She reluctantly cleared her throat.

"Do you still have those sleeping drops from Regealth?"

Aron nodded and produced the vial from the small pack beside him. Amarynn held out her hand, and he started to hand it to her, only to pull it back at the last second.

"Are you alright, she-demon?" Aron's voice was hushed.

Amarynn scoffed and kept her hand out.

"I'm serious, Rynn. None of this," he gestured to their camp, "is like you. You disappeared in the most humiliating way possible—"

"For you," she smirked and stood, wide awake again.

Aron shook his head, his worried expression illuminated by the orange glow of the low fire. "Ah, now. None of that. I am trying to be serious here. Yes, it was fairly humiliating for me, but all this sneaking around nonsense isn't boding well for you either. Finn and Stavin were beside themselves. They are like brothers to you, no?"

Amarynn sighed and dropped her hand. Aron had called her bluff. He was cocky and flirty and the Traveler she knew the least about. But she desperately needed to talk through all that had happened, though she had figured it would be Finn or Stavin she confided in; the weight of her last dream, her interactions with Mithras, and finding Essik was too much for her to contain by herself. Her mind was fractured, and it felt as if she were coming unraveled.

And Aron had noticed.

No one ever noticed things like that in her, except Bent and most recently Jael. But Aron was offering, and she needed to talk. At least they were in the middle of a remote forest with no witnesses.

"Aye, they are, but they're not here right now, are they?" She sat down on the log beside him, unsure of how to begin, even though she felt she could trust him.

"I'm here," Aron said in a low, soothing voice, leaning towards her. His blue eyes glittered in the firelight, exuding empathy. "I think I can understand at least a little of what you need to say."

"How's that?" Amarynn was questioning her decision now. Aron seemed uncharacteristically eager to commiserate with her, and she really knew very little of him. Confiding in him was beginning to feel less than ideal. "What would you know of what I might say?"

"Your bad dreams. I have been having them as well."

Amarynn rolled her eyes and shook her head. Though he had been there most nights when her nightmares tormented her, there was no way he could truly understand the depth of the despair and terror she faced night after night.

"Everyone dreams. Everyone has nightmares. It's not the same," she said as she stood. "I'm going to sleep. Give me the vial."

"Wait, now," Aron started, standing up beside her. He searched her face, his expression earnest. "What about nightmares that make you want to turn yourself inside out? Nightmares that aren't fantasy? Hmm?" His voice was getting louder.

"You know about those kinds of nightmares from *me*, Aron!"

"So you know everything about it, is that right? You're the only one that wakes up terrified? You know what everyone sees when they sleep?" His tone bordered on irritation, and it frustrated her.

"Aron, I took a chance. I thought I could talk to you, but I see what a stupid idea that was. Give me the vial," she said again, holding out her hand. Aron glowered as he thrust it towards her. She turned her back to him, stepped over the log they'd been sitting on and began to unpack her blanket from her pack.

"What about the nightmares you know are real?" Aron's voice had gone quiet again. "The kind that aren't fiction, but memories. Awful memories where people get hurt. Where they die."

Amarynn's hands froze. How could he know? Her heart raced and her breath quickened. The only person she had told was Regealth, and Regealth hadn't had time to talk to anyone in her party before they left Calliway.

"Who told you?" she asked, still facing away. She wasn't sure she wanted to hear his answer.

"Told me what?"

"Who told you about my nightmares? Who told you what happened?" When he didn't answer, she turned to look at him over her shoulder. He looked hurt. Bewildered.

"What are you talking about, woman?"

Amarynn sighed. She looked up at the night sky, indigo with a smattering of twinkling stars peeking through the trees. The crisp night air chilled her lungs as she breathed in deeply and considered the wisdom of the conversation she was about to have. She whispered a quick prayer to Nyra, then waited a long moment before she finally spoke.

"Two nights before we left for Athtull, I had a dream about a child. He was... mine." Amarynn paused, unsure if her voice would remain steady. The wind in the trees seemed to roar for the silence that fell between them. She bit her lip, regret washing over her.

Aron stepped over the log to where she knelt. She could see the sympathy in his eyes, and it disarmed her. She half expected him to make a snarky comment, but she had to admit that he had only ever been tender when he helped her out of a nasty dream. They never interacted then, though; she had never opened up about her trauma and looked him in the eyes like she did now.

"Ah, no," he breathed, reaching for her hand, drawing her up in front of him. His fingers closed over hers and he pressed her palm to his chest. "I'm so sorry. Do you know what happened to him? Where he went after you were pulled across?"

Amarynn dropped her eyes. She was terrified the tears would fall again, and she didn't know how she would recover her dignity if they did. Mithras had helped her recover before, otherwise she might still be curled up in a ball in the middle of a meadow. She had no clue what would happen to her now that he wasn't here.

"Rynn." Aron took her other hand. "What happened?"

Amarynn took her time. Her hand still rested on his chest and the steady rise and fall of his breaths were fortifying. As she drew in a breath, her lower lip trembled, and she silently cursed herself for being weak. She couldn't look Aron in the eye.

"I— I don't know," she mumbled, still looking down. But as the grief crawled up, relentless, from the gaping hole in her heart, she gasped and looked up at Aron, her eyes frantic. "I lost him." Amarynn clenched her jaw in a futile attempt to maintain her composure, but after the onslaught of dreams here in the mountains, the dam had broken. "I– I lost him. I don't know how. I can guess, but I don't want to because my guess is the last thing I want to be true."

There. She had said it out loud. A squeeze of her hands pulled her back into the moment, and she noticed how close Aron stood. The steady pulse of his fingers wrapped in her own and the rise and fall of his chest grounded her.

Aron released her hands and brought his own to her face, cupping her cheeks.

"You are stronger than I thought, she-demon." His voice was raw, as if he, too, was holding back from breaking, and his ice-blue eyes held her captive, searching her face. The forest fell away and all she could see were those eyes and the indigo sky behind him. As his thumbs gently stroked her temples, Amarynn's tears came with a roaring, hollow rush that took her breath away, making her want to double over with the agony of the memory.

But just before her knees buckled, Aron pulled her tightly to his chest. One hand on the back of her head and the other around her waist, he pressed her against his warmth while she shuddered with sobs silenced by his embrace. He lay his head on top of hers, his fingers tangling in her hair.

"Oh, she-demon," he breathed. "What have they done to us?" He held her close, tightening his hold on her. For the first time in what seemed like an eternity, she let herself be held by someone else while she let herself fall apart. His touch was safe, as if he were absorbing some of the worst parts of her pain. It never occurred to her that Aron, or any other Traveler for that matter, might have had the same experiences. She thought the only reason she was facing these memories was because of Venalise. But then she remembered something Bent had said.

King Lasten had him sent to me. Strange, it seemed. He kept babbling on and on in a language no one could understand. He had his wits about him, too, unlike you.

"Do you really think your dreams are memories?" she whispered against his chest.

"I do."

Amarynn pushed herself from Aron, reluctant to leave the security of his embrace. He slid his hands down the length of her arms to steady her, his hands ending in hers. While Aron glanced over his shoulder at Xan, she released her grip and wiped her face and nose on her sleeve. Xan tossed and rolled over, his sleep light.

"Come with me," Aron said. He took her hand again and led her into the shadows of the forest, beyond the reach of the firelight. They picked their way over the rough terrain and didn't stop until a wide opening in the canopy of trees revealed the ever-present moons. The hillside sloped down to another stream that should eventually lead them to Athtull, or what was left of it. But for now, there were only dark, silhouetted hills standing between them and the rest of the night.

Aron stopped and settled himself on the ground, legs splayed out in front of him. He pulled Amarynn down beside him and she stumbled, falling into him before sitting down, following his heavenward gaze. Her willingness to follow Aron surprised her. Though they were both Travelers, and had sparred together frequently since she returned, she hardly knew him. While he held nothing back in the practice yard, he had been quite the opposite behind the closed door of her barracks. Each night he rescued her from her terrors, and he was compassionate and tender, but they never spoke. Embarrassment kept her from acknowledging his kindness face to face.

They stared at the sky for several minutes, silence broken only by the creaking of tree branches in the wind and the occasional hoot of an owl. Finally, Aron spoke.

"Do you still think about leaving Karth?"

She turned to look at him. The question took her by surprise. He hadn't asked her about why she had disappeared for the last two days; it was as if nothing had happened, and he hadn't just spent two days in the mountains looking for her. This question cut to the heart of her unhappiness.

"I hadn't thought about it lately," she lied. It was all she thought about in the recent days since Jael's betrothal.

Aron stared out at the expanse of hills and sky. The moonlight filtered through his dark eyelashes, dancing in the depths of his icy eyes while a smile played on his lips.

"Liar."

"Alright, I do. I just don't know where I would go or what I would do. The last time I deserted, it didn't turn out well for me." Amarynn twisted her body until she sat sideways facing Aron. "What about you? I don't know much about you, except that your crossing was strange."

"Aye, strange it was," he smiled again. Amarynn studied his face, noticing how he looked away when his mouth curled up in amusement. Unintentionally, she compared the Traveler to Jael. The Prince had an endearing and genuine quality to his expressions, no matter what they were. But Aron always looked like he held a secret behind his eyes, like he knew something no one else did.

"I do know that you are annoying, but you are a very good fighter, so... I tolerate you." She offered a half-smile.

Aron laughed out loud at her last remark. "You *tolerate* me, do you?" He turned to face her.

"I guess I do." She looked away, trying to hide her amusement. This man had managed to anger her, disarm her, and make her smile, all in an hour's time.

"You do?" There was that smile again. *Goddess!*

"I do. Especially since I came back from Athtull. What you have done for me..." Amarynn couldn't finish her sentence. *Thank you* was never easy for her to say. Needing help only made her angry, but she felt none of that right now. Quite the opposite, really.

Aron leaned closer, his eyes never straying from hers. Amarynn's heartbeat fluttered wildly in her chest to the point of absurdity. *What was happening?* She wasn't an innocent girl. Twenty years in a Legion full of men taught her not to lose control of herself, and experience made her exceptionally good at maintaining her composure. Though since Athtull, she'd had no desire to be close to anyone except Jael, and that was taken away from her before she had a chance to really experience it.

"Thank you," she whispered and as soon as the words left her mouth, Aron's lips were on hers. Soft and gentle, he teased her, not committing to a full-on kiss.

"Am I still tolerable, even now?" She could feel his breath on her lips. Her body responded, her own breaths shallow and quick. But rather than answer, she leaned forward and grasped the back of his neck, pulling him toward her. She met his lips again, this time with an unbridled urgency that Aron seemed to reciprocate. She pushed him back, forcing him down onto the soft grass as she threw her knee over his torso to straddle him, like she had in the practice yard.

Aron growled. "I remember being in this position, she-demon, and I most definitely won't tolerate it." He grabbed her by the waist and rolled until she was beneath him. He raised himself up on one elbow. "But this, I could tolerate for quite a long time."

His lips took hers again, and this time, his need was apparent. His tongue tasted hers, his teeth nipping at her bottom lip. Aron's hand rested on the soft skin beneath the knotted scar at her throat. He let his fingers wander across the raised flesh to her collarbone, then grazed his palm down over her shirt. Amarynn arched her back as his hand found its way beneath the fabric to skim along her bare torso.

Her mind was reeling. There was no explanation for wanting this as much as she did, but she did. In this moment, just like in flight with Mithras, her sadness and fear had no place to take hold. Aron's touch was both foreign and familiar at the same time — and she needed it like air. She couldn't get close enough.

"Woman." Aron's voice, low and husky on her neck made chills run up her spine. "I told you that the next time you kissed me like that, there'd be no sleeping for either of us, didn't I?"

"Shut up," Amarynn whispered as she grasping the hem of Aron's shirt. She pulled it over his head in one fluid motion, freeing his arms to unlace hers. The chilly bite in the air spread goosebumps across her bare skin as the sides of her top fell open, but the heat from Aron's body drove the cold away.

His hands had free range over her body now, and they roamed from one breast to another, then across her belly, making her squirm reflexively. She let loose a quiet, nervous laugh, prompting him to continue. He grinned as his hand swept lower and lower with each pass until his finger reached the waist of her breeches.

Amarynn's adrenaline had taken over. All the emotional turmoil of the last few days was crying for release, and she would claim it here. Now. Her hands trembled as she grasped Aron's head and pulled his mouth to hers. He tasted like metal and musk and, alongside the heady scent of sweat and forest coming off his skin, the combination was intoxicating.

"Slowly, she-demon," he murmured. He sat back on his heels so he could reach her boots. One by one he pulled them off her feet, then his hands were at her waist again, working her breeches down and off into the grass.

Amarynn's mind had lost control. A wild and unbridled need raged in her belly, had taken over, and she was powerless to stop it. Before he could do it himself, she looped her thumbs in the waist of his breeches and pulled.

"Not slowly," she hissed as she pulled him back to her. He buried his lips at the nape of her neck as she looked to the sky. Nyra had finally answered her.

They joined with fury and anger and release all together. Aron matched her energy —never more than she wanted, but exactly what she needed. And when they were spent, they lay curled against one another, face to face.

Amarynn studied Aron's sweat-beaded face in the blue light of the two moons. He had not taken his eyes off her — they held her as tightly as his arms did now.

"Earlier," she started, but hesitated.

"Aye, earlier...," he prompted.

"Earlier, you said something about nightmares that seemed real, where people got hurt."

"I did." Hie brow furrowed. "I have them, just like you."

Amarynn pulled her hand to curl underneath her chin. She cast her eyes down while she considered her next question, not wanting to break the peace they had found just now. But she needed to know.

"Who died?" She looked back to Aron. "I told you that I lost my son. But you said that someone died in your memories, too. Who was it?"

Aron chewed on his bottom lip before he rolled away and onto his back. Amarynn was sure she had made a mistake asking, but then she heard him take in a breath. Then one word, the softest whisper, escaped his lips.

"Me."

She was sure she misheard him. Amarynn reached for her clothes behind her, then propped herself up on one elbow. She pulled her discarded shirt up to her chest.

"You?"

Aron nodded, his eyes fixed on the night sky.

"They say if you die in your dreams—"

"I know." He sat up and the melancholy in his eyes was unmistakable. He shrugged. "I guess they're wrong."

Amarynn couldn't tear her eyes away from Aron. The man was usually so sharp-witted and sarcastic, making this vulnerability hard to reconcile; it seemed there was no in-between with him. But to hear that he was the victim in his own nightmares was a turn she did not expect. She rested her head in her hand while she watched the moonlight cast shadows on the newest Traveler's face, wondering what secrets the other Travelers had hidden away.

CHAPTER 26

J ael paused at the last crossroad leading to Calliway. He steeled his
resolve and resisted the urge to turn toward the town. He replayed
Matteus's words in his head to reinforce his decision to ignore Ehrinell's
warning and instead, ride for Athtull, for Amarynn. His horse pulled at
the bit, her instinct to make the turn.

"Easy, Rhyssa," he said, patting her neck. He looked over his shoulder
at the silhouette of Calliway on the brightening horizon. They had ridden
hard through the night, and he knew the mare was ready for her stall and
a bucket of oats, but he couldn't face his father. Not after what Matteus
said. The Arnell River was nearby; Jael decided to give Rhyssa a reprieve
and let her rest before pushing on.

He urged his mount across a meadow that led to a wide riverbank
he remembered stopping at on hunts. The early morning sun warmed
the chill in the air enough so that Jael could remove his coat as Rhyssa
picked her way down the gently sloping bank to the yellow, rocky edge
of the slow-moving river lined with oshwal and willow trees. Most of the
leaves had fallen with the approach of winter, the delicate, bare spindles
giving them a hauntingly beautiful appearance. His mother used to tell
him stories about the trees that lost their leaves when he was a child.

Queen Feramin was a Vhaleesian, born and raised in the tall majesty of
the northern island nation's cloud forests. She was a wealth of knowledge
about Vhaleesian culture and folklore, and the stories she told always

captivated him. One in particular, the ghost forest, was a favorite that he liked to pretend was true. It was said in Vhaleese, that some of the wisest trees would drop their leaves in the winter to make room for the souls of all the forest creatures who had died that year. Over the dark months, the souls would find their way into the trees' embrace and, in the spring, their energy would give the tree what it needed to grow new buds. Each leaf was a life reborn in that tree.

Jael shook his head and frowned. If only it were true. He ached to ride into the capital and make sure no harm came to his mother. If what Ehrinell's note said was true, he had to have faith that as skilled a huntress as she was, she would be sharp enough to guard against an assassin. Besides, there were guards everywhere, and Regealth had remained in the castle. No. He couldn't let a childhood story guilt him into returning. Not without Amarynn.

He did not bother dismounting. Instead, he allowed Rhyssa to drop her nose to the water and drink. He looked around. Something seemed off, but the morning was quiet, save for the rushing of water punctuated by birdsong.

There was no warning.

It came as a sudden rush, like he had been hit from behind by a charging bull. The force knocked him from the saddle, and he fell to the ground, gasping for air like a fish on land. Deep in his belly, sharp, icy pain blossomed and enveloped him; tidal waves of energy and pain had their way with him, until he was certain he was dead.

Face down, he clutched at the dirt of the riverbank. The force that hit him was beginning to relax its grip and as it did, he became aware of a familiar sensation coursing through his body.

Sky magic. *His* magic, but it was so much more than what he felt before. This was an ocean of power undulating and writhing inside of him.

Anger.

He rolled to his back to see Rhyssa prancing and snorting, her eyes wide. Another wave of magic rolled over him.

Pain.

As he arched his back, the sky darkened and the tendrils of sky magic wrapped around his arms and legs, squeezing and infiltrating his body. Eyes wide, he saw the wispy clouds thickening and gathering while the wind whipped through the leafless limbs of the trees, branches slapping one another and snapping off from larger limbs.

Loss.

The electric shock of his magic raged, hollowing out his body and leaving nothing in its wake. Opening his mouth in a soundless scream, the Prince thrashed and contracted until he thought his body might break.

Finally, the onslaught slowed, allowing him to catch his breath and assess his situation. He lay as still as he could and listened, sure he would hear some trace of calamity, but there was nothing but the river. The birds had gone eerily quiet.

Jael lay on the ground, his chest heaving in great gulps of air. Rhyssa nickered and took a few tentative steps in his direction until her soft, velvety nose nudged his cheek, and he lifted one hand to stroke his horse's head. What had just happened? Regealth had warned him that his power was unpredictable, but he never expected this.

He sat up, then grasped Rhyssa's bridle to steady him as he pulled himself to his feet. He leaned against her and lay his head on her neck, trying to shake the dizziness that threatened to take him back to the ground.

And then the flood came.

Memories of a happy young boy... gritty determination on the battle-field... fear and pain underneath a dark sky... pride as he looked at the hand of his bride. He lifted her slender hand to his lips then lifted his chin to gaze at her face.

Queen Feramin.

Jael lost his breath. These were not his memories. They were his father's.

The rush of magic, the fear, the pain, the loss... In that instant, he knew his father's fate was sealed.

The aegis spider had struck its prey.

Jael's heart wrenched with the certainty of his father's demise, and even more so for at the thought of the danger his mother was now in, if she hadn't already been targeted. No matter the condemnation he felt his father deserved, with the King's death almost certain, regret was immediate as was fear. When he turned to heave himself into Rhyssa's saddle, every movement felt as if he were carrying triple his weight. His body thrummed with his father's newly infused sky magic.

Drunk with its energy, he turned his horse toward the north and let her have her head. She sensed her rider's condition, gathered her muscles, and launched into a run: ears flat, neck stretched, headed for Amarynn.

Chapter 27

A marynn opened her eyes as the first rays of sunlight streamed through the trees, her eyelashes filtering the golden light. Her sleep had been quiet — no nightmares. Behind her, Aron's warm back pressed against hers. She smiled involuntarily as she thought about their night. But as she did, a pang of guilt surfaced. *Jael.* While she wanted him to move on, she had never thought about what that meant for her. What happened with Aron was unexpected, to say the least, but even with the nagging guilt she felt, there was an equal measure of peace.

They had returned to the warmth of the campfire once the cold became uncomfortable, neither of them speaking as they opened their packs. Amarynn paused; she had no bedroll, but Aron opened his near the fire and lay down on one side, leaving space for her. She pulled the greall skin from her pack and lay next to him, spreading it as much as she could over them both. Even after what had just happened between them, they quietly returned to their Legion ways and lay back-to-back, only sharing their warmth through the rest of the long night.

Now, as morning broke, she could hear both Xan and Dax stirring close by. Amarynn waited another moment before sitting up, hesitant to break the quiet. Waking without panic was not a normal occurrence these days, and she wanted to savor the feeling. She listened to the winter birdsong and the gentle breeze rustling through the trees, and remembered a time when waking up had been simple. Train. Eat. Sleep. Go to war. That was all there was.

Finally, the impatient stamp of Dax's hooves encouraged Amarynn to rise. As she pulled the blanket from her shoulders, Aron groaned and rolled to his back.

"Morning, Rynn," he said. His voice was quiet, and a slight smile settled on his lips.

Amarynn returned the smile but turned away quickly. She didn't know what to say to the man who had cracked her heart wide open. *The man who wasn't Jael.* As she busied herself with buckling her sword belt and kicking dirt on the fire, she could feel Aron's gaze on her.

"Do you think we can get back by nightfall?" Xan had already been bustling around and had finished stuffing his pack. Now he waited with Dax. Aron sat up, then stood, pulling the greall skin from his shoulders.

"Aye," Aron answered before Amarynn could open her mouth. "If the weather holds, we'll be there well before then."

"If they are still there," Amarynn added. She wasn't convinced the Travelers would have stayed. While Finn would have wanted to dig in and build a summer home, Stavin probably tried to reason with him, to convince his partner that they were of no help sitting out in the woods. The Travelers would most likely have packed up and begun the trip home by now, especially knowing Aron and Xan were looking for her.

"Well, there's one way to find out, she-demon," Aron chuckled. Amarynn wanted to glare at him for using his nickname for her, but she found herself smirking instead and shook her head as he continued. "The sooner we move, the sooner we know."

Amarynn was already beside Dax, rubbing his velvety nose. She leaned over to pluck a handful of sweet vines when all the breath left her body and stars exploded in her vision. Amarynn fell to the ground, gasping, her hands clutching her head. She cried out as piercing, icy pain shattered against the back of her eyes. Her fingers clutching the dirt, she clung to consciousness with the same ferocity she displayed in battle.

Behind her, she heard Aron gasp as Dax let loose a high-pitched whinny. Her hands groped their way down to her daggers and she unsheathed them, ready to flay whoever had just attacked, her hands shaking as she tried to control her adrenaline and the pain that continued to assault her. But when she rolled to her back there was no one. Dazzling spots clouded her eyes making everything difficult to see.

"Amarynn!" Xan launched himself across the campsite and slid to her side, but as soon as he was close, she saw shock cross his face.

"Wh-what is i-it?" she growled through gritted teeth. When he didn't answer, the tip of her dagger found his throat and she pressed, the shaking point drawing a thin red line. "Aron!" she called in a hoarse voice, her eyes still locked on Xan.

Eyes wide, the young mage held his hands up. "I'm just trying to help!" he stammered as Aron pushed him aside.

Amarynn's hands shook violently as Aron pried her daggers from her hands. He set them on the ground and gathered her in his arms. "Shh, now. Shh."

Her heart raced erratically, jolts and twitches she was powerless to control taking hold of her muscles. Dax whinnied, frantic, as he pawed at the ground beside her.

"Breathe, Rynn," Aron murmured near her ear. "Breathe."

Every part of her body was on fire. Even the breath that left her lungs felt like flames.

"What," Amarynn panted, "is happening?" She wanted to scream, to claw her way out of whatever hell had just descended upon her. Her heart pounded like she had just led the front line into battle and even her bones thrummed with a foreign energy that stung and writhed through every extremity. Her stomach heaved and she threw herself to the side, emptying her stomach. Once her nausea subsided, Aron pulled her back into his arms, clutching her to his chest.

Xan's worried expression came back into view, through her half-open gaze. She watched his eyes flit over her, then widen, when it appeared he had discerned the nature of her attack.

"Sky magic," he whispered, staring.

"Who is using magic against us?" Aron barked, scanning the edge of the clearing. "There's no one here!"

Xan squinted, ignoring Aron, and continued to focus on Amarynn. Suddenly snapping himself out of his stupor, he clumsily fumbled in his pocket and pulled out a small metal object. He held it over her, his lips moving silently and his eyes closed. Immediately, her twitching eased, and she started to be able to catch her breath. When Xan lowered his arm, Aron helped her to sit.

Amarynn's skin was now crawling with a million little spiders, swarming over every inch of her body, but she stared at her still-trembling hands; there was nothing there. She lifted her gaze to Aron. He had a new color in his cheeks and his eyes seemed different, brighter.

Xan kneeled in front of her.

"Amarynn, look at me."

She did, and the way his eyebrows lifted told her something wasn't right. He tilted his head to the side and reached out, his fingers brushing her cheek. He cast a quick, sideways glance at Aron then looked back at Amarynn.

"I don't know how to explain it," Xan said, his voice hushed.

"Explain what?" Amarynn's response was hoarse and unsteady.

"No one attacked us," Xan explained. He reached out for her hand. "But if I am right, it can only mean one thing."

Amarynn lifted her hand to his and he turned it over to face her palm to the sky, keeping it in his own to steady her.

"Think about holding your sword, but don't move your hand. Try to imagine gripping the hilt."

Confused, Amarynn stared at the mage. "I don't understand. What are you telling me to do?"

"Let's try this. Imagine you just pulled your throwing knife because someone is attacking. Try to capture the energy you feel in your hand."

Amarynn concentrated for a handful of seconds, but then growled in frustration, dropping her hand. Xan looked down and sighed, his lips moving quietly. Then, in a burst of movement, he swung his other hand at her head as if he were going to strike her.

She didn't hesitate. Her reflexes responded and she threw her hand up to block, but instead of her fist, a ball of blue energy exploded from her hand, striking Xan in the forearm. Blue crackles of magic dissipated in tendrils around what looked like a barrier of red-hot energy wrapped around his arm.

Aron fell backward, catching himself on his hands.

"What—" he stammered.

Amarynn lifted both of her hands in front of her, eyes wide. She shifted her focus to Xan, who rubbed his arm as the red energy dissipated, staring at it with awe. "You said this could only mean one thing."

He nodded.

"Well?" Amarynn's breaths were shallow as she tried to control the tremors and twitches that threatened to return. She balled her fists, digging her nails into her palms.

"Just before we left, Regealth told me about your unique connection to the Prince. He felt I needed to know everything if I was going to protect you."

"Unique connection?" Aron sat forward. His brows furrowed. "What's he talking about, Rynn?"

"Jael was the source when Regealth Traveled me here," she murmured.

Xan nodded, turning his attention to Aron. "And unlike his father, Prince Jael is a wielder, so his magic is different. It's much more powerful."

"What does that have to do with now?" Aron rubbed his temples.

The mage hesitated.

"Speak, boy," Aron snapped.

"If I am right, Jael has received his father's sky magic, and some of that magical surge has passed to her."

Amarynn scrambled to her feet, swaying unsteadily as she stood.

"You are telling me I have magic now?" Her mind was racing in a thousand directions while her body was ablaze with sensations from this new energy, whatever it was. "How? Why?"

Xan and Aron stood with her and as he rose, Aron stumbled. He bent forward and braced his hands on his knees.

"What's wrong?" Amarynn reached for his arm. She looked to Xan. "Aron's a Traveler. Did it affect him too?"

"I'm right," the mage breathed.

"Stop mumbling and explain this!" Amarynn barked. Xan took a step back, his hands on his slim hips as he surveyed both Travelers.

"This can only mean the King is dead. Jael has inherited his father's power... and all the Travelers are released from their bond to Lasten."

Xan's words took a moment to register. Dead? Lasten? Immediately, Amarynn's thoughts went to Jael. He was on a ship in the middle of the ocean, unable to do anything. He must be frantic — sick with worry and confusion, especially without Regealth to guide him. Then her stomach twisted. *Matteus was on that ship.*

She locked eyes with the other Traveler.

"We have to get back, Aron."

"Aye," he said straightening, clarity returning to his icy-blue eyes as he recovered himself. "You should ride, Rynn. It's not far. Xan and I will head back on foot." Xan groaned behind them.

A piercing cry rang out about the trees and both Xan and Aron ducked, dropping to a crouch, and looking up to assess the threat. But a smile played on Amarynn's lips as the familiar hum of electricity crept up her spine. She glanced at Dax, whose ears had pricked up at the sound of the dragons, and he shifted back and forth on his front hooves, nudging Amarynn's back to try to get between her and whatever he heard in the sky. Amarynn's heart sank, knowing what she had to do.

Find.

"Oh, I'll ride," she said. "But you two can take Dax." She snatched up her pack and ducked through the brush down the trail, unable to look at Dax before giving him one last pat as she left. Aron and Xan followed her onto the open hillside that descended into the forested valley below. Mithras was preparing to land, his hind legs extended while his wings stretched wide to slow his descent. Amarynn, hearing Xan and Aron's footsteps stop, turned to find them gaping.

"I'll go by the camp first, and if no one is there, I'm heading for the eastern coast."

"Amarynn!" Xan pointed over her shoulder while the wind from Mithras's wingbeats whipped her hair across her face.

Aron drew his sword and started towards her. "Get back!"

"It's alright," she called before turning toward Mithras. Then, over her shoulder, she added, "You two make for Calliway. Protect Regealth and the Queen. I will find Jael."

She didn't bother to look back again as Mithras's massive form descended, landing lower on the hill. She sprinted to his lowered leg and vaulted herself up, grabbing the leather strap that still hung over his massive neck, and scrambled to wrap her feet in the leather before she slid backwards. Before she was even settled, Mithras gathered his haunches and launched himself into the air.

Wrong.

Danger magic.

Cold fly.

More wrong.

Mithras sent a barrage of feelings and images — frantic worry, bright white flashes of light, craggy grey mountains with a city at their base. *Cold fly.* He must have flown into the Reaches, she reasoned. The 'wrong' he emoted had to be a magical surge... but Amarynn had no reason why she would think that. She just did.

Once they were aloft, Amarynn craned her neck to look over his wings. Aron and Xan were standing halfway down the hill, staring open-mouthed as she and Mithras banked and disappeared into the morning sky. They were heading north, Mithras's wings beating hard to gain altitude as the Stone Giant mountains loomed before them. It was the wrong direction, but Amarynn was at a loss as to how to communicate with him.

"No!" she cried. "The other way!"

Mithras hesitated. Amarynn noticed.

"Turn around!" she shouted, this time trying to impress her own thoughts on Mithras again. *South.* She focused on a mental image of the forests south of Athtull where she and Jael encountered the dragon for the first time. A wave of uncomfortable frustration washed over her, but Mithras banked again and put the rising sun on her left. The Stone Giants fell to the side of her view and the Dark Mountains loomed. Athtull would be appearing soon, and with it, their camp. She focused on her memory of Calliway on the horizon to try and give her scaly mount a reference point. From there, they could head northeast toward the Sea of Vhaleese, and if she was lucky, Jael.

CHAPTER 28

What is it?

Sia wiggled her toes. She was sleeping in the snow, and it was so cold. Where was Thera?

How did she know what to call?

Water lapped at her ankles. She dangled her feet off the docks in Banmorrow, and watched long, skinny silverfish dart under the sparkling ripples. Master Omman said to wait here, but she was hungry and wished he would return.

How quickly can she call more?

Unrecognizable voices drifted on the air around her as Sia opened her hand and felt soft fabric beneath her palm. Inhaling deeply, the thick spice of incense filled her lungs. She was on her side, a warm weight shifting against her belly. She moved her other hand to bury it in a thick, familiar coat of fur.

"Leave the room!"

Sia sucked in a breath and sat up, Thera tumbling off her.

Venalise sat beside her, brows knitted together with concern. Sia blinked hard and swallowed, coughing when her parched throat caught. She glimpsed a swirl of colored robes disappearing down the hall as the door closed behind her. She was back in the room she'd been in before Talamynne took her to the aethertorium.

"What is happening?" The words were a ragged whisper. Thera issued a low whine and nosed beneath her arm.

"Here." Venalise pushed a goblet into her hands. "You need to drink."

Though it was the last thing on her mind, Sia found that the moment the cool water touched her lips, she swallowed thirstily, allowing Venalise to fill the vessel two more times.

As she drained the goblet for the third time, a sharp headache formed behind her eyes. It was unusual, though. Sharper, and prickly like the bright energy she felt in the aethertorium. She let the goblet fall from her hands as she reached up to press her hands over her face.

"What is it, Sia?" Venalise sounded uncharacteristically concerned as she rested one hand on Sia's arm.

"My head," she groaned through her hands.

"She'll learn to manage that, daughter."

At the sound of an unfamiliar voice, Sia dropped her hands in surprise and peered over Venalise's shoulder at the older woman sitting in a chair on the far side of the room. Dressed like a soldier, the woman was striking. She sat with her feet propped up on a table near the chair. Her partially shaved head made her cheekbones look even sharper than they already were. The woman narrowed her almond shaped eyes at Sia. She resembled Venalise, though Sia couldn't tell why, exactly.

Venalise leaned over to block Sia's view, taking her by the shoulders and guiding her to lay back on the pillows.

"You know nothing of this kind of recovery, Mother."

Mother?

She suddenly remembered. "Where is he?" Sia grabbed one of Venalise' hands and gripped it hard. "What did I do?" A flash of memory conjured the giant man's face as he was being led away; now Sia recognized his look as one of confusion and, more concerningly, pain.

"He is with the scholars. They are caring for him."

Sia scrambled to sit up again, wincing at the unrelenting headache.

"What did I do?" Sia's heart was racing, its beat throbbing in her ears. "Who is he?"

"We were hoping you could tell us that, little one." The warrior woman stood and approached the bed from behind Venalise, hands on her hips. Tattoos of weapons and angry faces crawled down her arms. Now their resemblance was even more apparent, but the difference in their dress and mannerisms made it hard to reconcile. Where Venalise was elegant — exuding a refined power — this woman was severe with a harsh toughness evident in the military-style clothing and light armor she wore.

"I-I don't know," Sia looked away. She did know, but she hoped no one else would notice. The giant had been in the book she was reading. She had never seen anything like him before, and had been admiring the art and the brilliant colors of the ink. "Maybe the magic just did it," she offered lamely.

"Ha!" The woman barked out a laugh. "*Maybe the magic did it?*" She mimicked Sia in a sing-song voice then leveled a hard stare at her. "Do better."

"Leave her alone, Mother," Venalise grumbled. "Let her rest. Magic like that is draining and she's never done it before."

"Oh, I think she knows," her mother said, her eyes still trained on Sia. "I can tell she's a cunning little falcon."

Sia bristled. The last person to compare her to a falcon was King Lors, and that did not end well; he had proven himself to be a very bad man. Taking a cue from Venalise's resistance to her own mother, she lay back down and feigned exhaustion, even though adrenaline was coursing through her veins. Maybe this warrior woman would go away if she were asleep.

"We have no time for resting, daughter. This army will not Travel itself and now that the King of Karth is dead, we must be ready to strike."

Army? Strike?

"Most likely, she will be ready again in a few hours. Until then, we must study the creature she called." Venalise stood and gestured to the door. "What if it doesn't cooperate? Mother, wha—"

Sia felt cool air rush in as her blankets were lifted off. Her eyes flew open.

"Get up falcon," the warrior woman barked, tossing the heavy blanket aside. It landed on Thera, who growled as she thrashed her body to free herself. "Conquests don't begin after a good nap."

Sia sat up and pushed herself back against the headboard. Venalise tried to stand between Sia and her mother, but the warrior woman pushed past her.

"I am Empress T'Korr Uhll and I control the Stone Reaches. I control everything, even," she jerked her head in Venalise's direction, "my daughter. Now, you will get out of this bed and come with me. I want to know if that thing you Traveled will obey you the way the Karth Travelers follow their King." Uhll folded her arms across her chest and leveled a hard stare at Sia.

"You don't know what you are doing, Mother!"

"Who is Empress, daughter? You?" Uhll whirled on Venalise only a hands width from her frowning face. When the mage didn't answer, her mother let loose a hearty laugh. "That is what I thought. Now, come with me, little falcon."

Sia reluctantly nodded and pushed off the bed, unsure of who was really in charge. She looked to a scowling Venalise, who gave the child enough of a nod to make her feel better about following the Empress's order. It was odd, Sia thought, that Venalise would let her mother talk to her like that. No one talked to her like that — not even King Lors.

Uhll waited only long enough for Sia to hastily pull a long tunic over her clothes and slide her feet into her soft, leather slippers, then ushered her into the hallway. Instead of going toward the aethertorium, Uhll led her and Venalise down another staircase, leading to the first floor.

As they followed, Venalise grabbed Sia's hand.

"Swear you'll tell me if any of this becomes too much. Do not try to be brave," she said in a low voice. "This was always the plan, but I intended to take more time to prepare you." Venalise glared at her mother's back.

Sia kept her eyes forward. None of this felt right; hearing Venalise's admittance of her intent made it worse, even though she overheard her say as much to Rhymere the night before. At least the Empress did not keep secrets. That much she could respect. But both were asking her to do things she didn't want to do, to control things and act like both of them. Somewhere in this place was the giant that she was responsible for Traveling, and she wanted make sure he was all right, not be his master.

When they reached the first floor, they left the Spire through a different entrance than the one they had entered a few days prior. After winding through a lush garden, the small group approached a tall stone building with no windows and what looked like only one guarded and heavily chained entrance. Two guards dressed in light armor, similar to Uhll's, flanked the tall doors. All three bore tattoos down their arms, though theirs weren't as elaborate as their Empress's and only parts of the sides of their heads were shaved. The Empress barked orders in what sounded to Sia like the language Venalise often used, and without a glance at Sia or Venalise, the men quickly began to unlock the chains strung through the handles.

"Empress!" a familiar voice called from the other side of the garden.

Uhll stopped and turned as Rhymere scurried over with Oravae at his side. Sia watched Venalise turn away from her friend, concealing an expression bordering on guilt.

"Empress Uhll, I must ask that you reconsider this endeavor." The elderly scholar seemed flustered. He wrung his hands as he spoke, not stopping until Oravae put her hand on his arm.

"Vena," she said, looking to Venalise's downturned face. "What is happening?"

"As I have always maintained, the scholars at Lorce have their value, but expediency is not one of their strong suits," the Empress answered in her daughter's place.

"*Emmisana*, please. Magic of this child's amplitude cannot be rushed. We have never had a mage touch more than one element, and by tapping into two or even three simultaneously, you risk unimaginable consequences!" Rhymere's face was flushed, his breathing heavy. Sia worried that he might be unwell.

"Scholar Rhymere," Talamynne stepped from behind one of the halfway open doors. Sia watched Rhymere's eyebrows lift in surprise. "That time has passed. The child has touched all five."

Rhymere did not speak as he leaned forward towards Sia, his eyes fixed on her, glittering with awe and wonder. "I should have listened to you, Vena," he whispered, taking a moment to glance in Venalise's direction. "You tried to tell me, and I dismissed you."

All of the talk from Rhymere and Venalise was making Sia's head hurt more. The secrets and the lies complicated an already twisted and chaotic situation. She squeezed her eyes shut and tried to block out the voices.

Venalise lifted her head to face both Rhymere and Oravae, pulling Sia closer to her side. "Leave us," she said in a low voice laced with contempt. "Your presence here is unnecessary."

"Sia," Rhymere was looking back at her now, his brow creased with anxiety. He held out one wrinkled, veiny hand. "I can help you master your gifts, not squander them on beasts and war."

Sia, reacting to his kindness, took a step in his direction but was stayed by Venalise's rigid grip.

"You think too much of your contribution here, Scholar." Empress Uhll stepped close to the old man, looking down her nose at him. "It is time for you to retire. Permanently."

Sia stood between the adults as they argued over her, looking back and forth between them. She still did not fully comprehend what had happened in the aethertorium, what she had done. She was exhausted. Her legs were still wobbly, and her headache had not subsided, but no one seemed to care.

Oravae tugged her father's arm. "Come with me, Father. We should leave before they bring the whole Spire down with their recklessness." She glared at Venalise. "Is that it, Vena? You didn't get what you wanted from my father, so now you and your mother just take it?" Vena met her gaze.

"It is unfortunate we find ourselves in this situation, Ora. My mother and I want what's best for the Stone Reaches."

"He is right, you know."

"Ora," Uhll lifted her chin and looked down at Vena's friend. "Your father has had ambitions for a very long time, namely taking control of *my* empire." At his widened eyes, she laughed. "You think I didn't know that you've been plotting to overthrow me all these years? Using my daughter to gain insight, and plying her with your magical wisdom and guidance to sway her loyalty?"

"Enough, mother," Venalise cut in, still keeping Sia close to her. Sia's head still ached, but it had begun to subside, so she opened her eyes. "We are wasting time."

"You are right, little fox." Uhll gestured behind her and four of her warriors trotted forward from the garden, flanking Rhymere and Oravae. "See these two to their chambers and make sure they stay there until I say otherwise."

Talamynne pushed the door open further and gestured for them to enter. Behind her, the other scholars, Silhan and Ruidel, watched from the shadows.

"He's becoming quite restless, Empress." Talamynne's voice was hushed but laced with urgency.

Sia had heard enough. The giant was only there because of her and he was frightened. She pulled her hand from Venalise's grasp, ducking between the adults to scurry toward Talamynne.

"Sia!" Venalise called after her as she slipped past Talamynne and into the shadows. She didn't look back. Inside the building, the air was still and oppressive, but warm, with a scent somewhere between animal dung and the galley on Master Omman's ship. From ahead, heavy breathing echoed off the walls.

With Venalise and Talamynne's voices behind her, Sia increased her pace down the dimly lit corridor. She ran her fingers along the damp stone walls that glistened in the low torch light as she ran. The breathing was louder now, punctuated by grunts and groans, and an unsettled feeling descended over her as she approached the source of the sound.

A barred doorway loomed before her. Here, the light was still dim, but as she approached, she could make out a hulking figure, standing in the center of the room. He was massive, but, except for his heaving chest, he stood like stone.

Sia gripped the bars, standing on her tiptoes to see the giant man better over the wide crossbar.

"I'm sorry," she whispered, then immediately felt silly because of course he couldn't understand her. But when he looked up with his large, round eyes, her mouth opened in surprise. He seemed so sad. He tilted his head, then took a shuffling step toward her.

"Sia!" Venalise's voice rang out from down the hallway. "Step back!"

Sia frowned; Venalise, Talamynne, and Uhll were rushing toward her. More footsteps sounded as the guards followed. She looked back at the giant. His breaths were still coming in heavy pants and his expression was sad. He was both frightened and menacing at the same time: Sia felt the urge to comfort him, but she wasn't sure if it was safe. A low, keening moan emanated from his throat. Sia assessed the space between the bars that separated him from her, glanced once more at the trio hurrying in her direction, then turned sideways and squeezed through. Without a second thought, she darted past the giant, and into the shadows where he followed.

"Sia!" Venalise cried, reaching the bars just as Sia slipped out of reach. The mage leaned in as far as she could. From the shadows, Sia heard a rumble emanate from the giant as he turned and charged the bars. Venalise snatched her arm away and jumped back, bumping into her mother.

"Oh!" Uhll exclaimed, wonder and excitement unmistakable in her voice. "What have we here?" She pushed her daughter aside roughly and took several slow steps in the giant's direction. Around the giant's bulk, Sia watched one hand drift to a short hunter's axe at her belt, the other held out in front of her as one might with an unbroken horse. "Ho, there. Easy now, you magnificent brute."

The giant growled through clenched teeth as he grabbed the bars, shaking them angrily.

Not taking her eyes off of him, Uhll leaned to the side. Finally, she tore her gaze away to peer behind him into the shadows.

"Little falcon?"

Sia stayed frozen in place and did not reply, but another growl from the giant filled the silence.

"Sia?" Venalise sounded panicked as she elbowed her mother out of the way. She looked nearly frantic, and Sia did not know why it gave her satisfaction.

The giant turned back to the shadows and lumbered away from the barred door toward her. He continued to the back wall of the cell until shadows slipped over his body, concealing him from view. Venalise gripped the bars with both hands.

The giant had reached where she sat against the back wall and as he approached, her headache subsided. He had no scent, but he radiated body heat as he turned and slid down the stone beside her. Though she thought she should be afraid, she wasn't.

"Sia—" Venalise started.

"Come out of there, child." This time, it was Talamynne, her expression severe. "Slowly. Do not make any sudden moves."

A defiant smile curled up on Sia's lips as her arm brushed the giant's. He was trembling. They thought she was in danger, but that was not the case at all. As he turned his face to look at her, it became obvious to her that he had no fear of her, only of this place and those people. She was the only thing he knew in this world. In the darkness, she could not make out his face, but she could *feel* him, and he was confused and angry. But one other emotion stood out above the others.

Protect.

"Leave us alone." Sia's voice was quiet, but resolute.

"Sia," Venalise tried again, pleading as she peered into the shadows. When there was no response, the mage's expression turned dark. She lifted her hands, and the floor began to quiver. The metal bars took on a low, shimmery glow. "If you do not come out of there, I will make you." A small piece of the stone ceiling crashed to the floor just beside Sia and the giant, dust and tiny rock pieces peppering her face and arms.

"Hold, Daughter."

"Mother," Venalise breathed as Uhll brought a dagger to her daughter's throat. It was large, and a dull, pearly white color.

"Let your magic go, little fox," Uhll growled at her daughter. "What happens when you bend those bars, eh? Will your earth magic drop a giant?"

Venalise grimaced and dropped her hands, though Sia recognized the small, swift movements she made with her wrist, just like when the mage had used her power to hurl the knife at her aunt in the Suhonne compound, but nothing happened.

Uhll pulled Venalise closer. "I feel your magic, girl. Did you forget yourself? I know better than use metal against you." The Empress turned away, Venalise still in her grasp. "Are you finished, Scholar?"

"Yes, *emmisana*," Talamynne replied. "You can release her."

Uhll let go of her daughter and backed away as Talamynne, Silahn, and Ruidel surrounded Venalise, who stood, rigid and unmoving. The three scholars held white bone objects, all pointed at her. Talamynne's voice was quiet. "My apologies, *Emmina,* but your mother insisted. You have become too attached to the child and that will not do."

Sia's eyes widened. She had never seen Venalise under anyone else's control. Torn between concern and fascination, she could only stay where she was and watch.

"How long can you hold her?" Uhll studied her daughter.

"As long as you need, *emmisana,*" Talamynne slipped a bone circlet over Venalise's head. "What of the child?"

Uhll leaned down to try to see Sia in the shadows.

"We will let her have her moment here and then we will have a chat. Isn't that right, my little falcon?"

Sia's breath caught. The Empress seemed to be looking right at her.

"My guard will stay here to be sure she is safe. When she is ready, we will see what kind of agreement we can come to and find out how much power and control she wants." Uhll turned away from the cell to face Talamynne and Venalise. She gave her daughter a disapproving scowl and shook her head. "Coerced participation is unreliable, don't you think? We will leave her until she is ready to talk."

The two scholars with Talamynne took Venalise by the arms to lead her away. Her eyes narrowed at her mother, but she made no sound as she went with them.

Uhll gestured to one of her four guardsmen.

"Go fetch the bear." She turned back to the cell. "I will leave you now, little falcon. When you are ready, I will tell you about Korr, and how you will always have a choice there."

CHAPTER 29

Wind and icy droplets battered Amarynn's face as Mithras climbed higher over the mountain ridge before them. She still did not understand the connection she shared with the dragon, but it seemed to be growing stronger. Though she could not impress images of the way Athtull Keep looked from above, she could share the memory of the ledge. She planned to add in a memory of the road back toward Morning Hill, in an attempt to guide him south of the mountains. That would make it easier for them to go east and reach the sea where Jael's ship should be.

To the cold?

Mithras had impressed this thought on her just after they took off. It was evident he had discovered something in the Reaches and wanted show her, but Jael came first.

"Not yet!" she shouted over the roaring wind.

The Keep. She thought about the image of Athtull again, willing it at him though she didn't know if it really worked.

Her hands ached with the cold as they gripped the leather strap. *Gloves,* she thought. *I need gloves.* Icy shivers tore up her arms and chilled her core. The last tall ridge skimmed beneath them, and as they cleared the snowy caps, Mithras took a quick turn and dove lower in the sky where the air had less bite. Amarynn smiled and shook her head. Their communication was getting stronger.

Another Mithras image blossomed in her mind.

Wrong.

A tower between mountains. A bolt of sky magic into its very top.

I know, she thought. *It's all wrong. Venalise is up to something neither of us wants to happen. We'll stop her. I promise.*

Mithras opened his wings wide and glided just above the treetops, following the graceful curve of the mountainside as it became a forested valley. Amarynn squeezed her knees and sat a little higher to see. As she scanned the wide valley, a familiar silhouette came into view. Broken and jagged pieces of the mountainside where Athtull had once been reared from the treetops.

She tore her eyes from the ruins as they flew past. A tendril of smoke rising from the forest confirmed that Finn and Stavin were still at their camp. She smiled to herself. Finn usually acquiesced to his partner, but it amused her to see that the gentle Traveler's concern for her had prevailed. She chuckled and, instead of requesting Mithras to stop, she focused her gaze on the road leading out of the Dark Mountains, into Morning Hill. Amarynn scoured the forest ahead for the break in the dense cover and when she found it, she tried to share her view with the dragon. Mithras pumped his wings in response, taking them higher.

He angled his trajectory and flattened out his ascent, allowing Amarynn a better view, showing scattered breaks in the forest canopy that permitted glimpses of the road. Amarynn was contemplating how they would find Jael's ship, when a flash of blue between the trees caught her attention. She leaned low over her knee for a better look, and her blood came alive, the new-found magic inside her writhing and singing.

"Aaah!" Amarynn felt convulsions rip through her body, and she pulled the leather strap tight to stop from falling. Mithras shrieked as if in response and batted his wings to slow his velocity. He extended his hind legs and dropped into a meadow, hitting the ground with the force of a minor earthquake. Amarynn, still reeling, untangled her frigid arms and legs from the leather loop and slumped from her perch, sliding down the dragon's front leg until she hit the ground with a thud.

Face down, she lay still and waited for the unfamiliar sensation to dissipate, but it only steadied and intensified. Hot breath blew at her neck as Mithras lowered his head over her in a protective gesture, but at the sound of a horse's whinny, Amarynn clenched her hands into white-knuckled fists and looked up over her arm.

The morning sunlight burst from behind the trees, creating a halo around the rider as he pulled his rearing horse back. Spooked by the dragon, no doubt, the horse huffed and pranced in nervous circles. The rider made soothing sounds, and the voice sounded achingly familiar. Still fighting the magic's strange, uncomfortable energy, Amarynn squinted against the sun and caught a better glimpse of the rider's face.

She must be dreaming.

Or dead.

Her breath caught as Jael threw one leg over Rhyssa's saddle and bounded in her direction. The throbbing magic welled and rose inside of her as he approached, threatening to take her breath away again until Mithras' familiar thrum at the back of her head spread and dampened the unchecked power.

"Rynn!" The Prince's voice was breathless. As he neared, a throaty growl rolled over and through Amarynn as the dragon positioned his front feet on either side of her, his head snaking out over her own.

"No, Mithras," she panted through the pain, pushing herself up to sit. "He's not a threat."

Reluctantly, the dragon stepped back, permitting Jael to slide to his knees in front of her, appearing to Amarynn as he had when he saved her from Venalise — a light in the darkness. He cupped her face in his hands and the moment his skin touched hers, the roiling magic evened out, settling into a comfortable hum.

"You— You should be on a sh-ship." Amarynn grimaced at her shaky voice. She hated sounding weak.

"Bent and Ehrinell helped me slip away." The Prince searched her face, lines of worry undeniable. "Are you alright? What happened?"

"Where do I begin?" she muttered between groans, as her head swam and the magic twisted in her belly.

"Here," he growled as he claimed her lips. His fingers curled in her hair, thumbs brushing her temple. The kiss was gentle, but deep.

Amarynn closed her eyes and let it happen. She slipped her arms around to his back and held him close, breathing in his heady scent — leather and spice. It filled her nose, her lungs, and in that moment, it was everything she needed — her heart more than her body. The kiss went on for what felt like forever, only broken by a growl from behind. Jael sat back on his heels and looked up nervously at Mithras.

"An atranoch?" He averted his eyes from the dragon back to Amarynn. "Last time it was a spinning dagger." He tucked a strand of her hair behind her ear and chuckled uncomfortably. "You've upped your game."

"Dragon," Amarynn said with a quick glance behind her. "Venalise called them atranoch as an insult. It means 'dog' in her language."

Jael's gaze returned to Amarynn, and he pulled her to him, wrapping her in his arms and burying his face in her hair. The magic danced between them, connecting them.

"My father is dead," he murmured against her ear.

"I know" she whispered back, tightening her hold. "I think I felt it."

He pulled back again, this time searching her face. "You felt it? What do you mean?"

Amarynn held her hands up. "This morning." She stared as she turned them in the sunlight, feeling the warmth on her palms. After a moment, she looked back up. "It felt like someone hit me with a warhammer in the back. It still feels like it."

"The same happened to me, too." The Prince rubbed the back of his neck, then went to one knee and stood, offering his hand. "I was headed this way from Banmorrow." He pulled Amarynn up, then dropped his head. "I should have gone straight to Calliway."

"Why?"

"Ehrinell gave me a warning after I left the ship. She said there was an aegis spider in Calliway." He looked back at Amarynn with his eyes wide. "What have I done? I've left my mother undefended!"

"There are Travelers in Calliway. And Regealth. She's not alone."

Behind them, Mithras stomped his taloned feet and bellowed.

"Goddess!" Amarynn exclaimed, covering her ears. "Stop it, Mith—"

Several answering shrieks sounded from the air.

Jael's hand went to the hilt of his sword, the magic dancing dangerously in his eyes. Amarynn winced as her own magic tried to do the same, but it couldn't find release. She doubled over, clutching her head.

"Give me your hands," Jael said, grasping them before she could respond. The minute they touched, she felt the pressure ease. "I'm channeling some of it away."

"Just take it," Amarynn panted. As her pain subsided, she straightened, grimacing. "I'm not built for this."

"But you are, Rynn." The Prince looked her up and down. "You are, by your very nature, made for this. It's what makes all of you immortal."

Amarynn squeezed her eyes closed as another round of dragon calls sounded.

"What is happening?" Jael's eyes were wide as he scanned the sky.

Cold. Danger. WRONG.

Amarynn let go of Jael and spun around. Mithras lowered his head just behind her, his eyes whirling and a clicking sound like strikes against hollow wood emanating from his throat, accentuating the intensity in his message.

"Rynn?" Jael's voice was quiet behind her. "Care to explain?"

Amarynn placed one hand on Mithras's ridged snout, and he snorted. The magic inside her thrummed and as she closed her eyes, more images flowed between them. A towering spire rising from a city nestled into tall, jagged mountains. Shadows, then a bolt of lightning. Amarynn's chest heaved as she felt the pull of magic — the same pull she felt at her crossing.

"We have to go," she whispered to herself, trying to catch her breath. "It's already happening." Then, over her shoulder, she called, "Take Rhyssa and follow the road. Finn and Stavin are up ahead. I have to go."

"Go where? What else is happening?" Jael had not stepped closer, but his voice was laced with urgency.

"She's calling Travelers." Amarynn adjusted her sword belt. "There's no time to explain." She winced and swallowed as the magic surged again, but tried to hide her discomfort.

"You aren't going anywhere. Not until you learn how to manage this magic."

"Oh really? Do you think Venalise is going to wait? Are you so skilled now that you will teach me?" Amarynn threw her hands up in exasperation. She gestured to the road. "Follow the road toward Athtull; Aron and Xan should be there soon. Ride for Calliway when they get there." Mithras, close behind her, lowered himself to the ground. The meadow spun, but the Traveler clenched her jaw and planted her feet. Then, as her vertigo subsided, she bound up the dragon's front leg and vaulted over the ridges of his back, ripples of magical energy returning and crawling over her skin. She grimaced, this time unable to hide it. "I'll meet you there after I have dealt with all of this, once and for all."

It was the last thing she said before the magic pulled her under.

CHAPTER 30

"See, Finn, I told you. Dragons."

"Goddess..."

Who was that?

"I've syphoned what I can, but it's like blood from an open wound. She's bleeding magic."

That was Jael beside her. His leather and spice scent was unmistakable.

"Let me try something."

Xan.

Amarynn felt two thin, cool surfaces press against her temples — and then the burning magic quelled.

"She must always keep these with her. In a pocket or a pouch, whatever. Without them, the power will overtake her again." She felt the pouch on her belt being opened, then closed again. There was a shuffle of feet around her and in the distance, she heard the trumpeting calls of the dragons — some from the air and others from the ground.

Amarynn loosened her tightened fists and let her palms lay flat beside her, allowing the softness of the grass and soil to soothe her as the magic inside her subsided. When she tentatively reached out for it, it was there, but it felt like it was behind a thin wall, a membrane within her mind.

Inhaling, she opened her eyes and struggled to push herself up on her elbows. She was unaccustomed to being the focus of so much attention, and she was ready to change that.

"I see we've all found each other," she mumbled as she looked around at the faces, the eyes all fixed on her. "You can stop staring," she added.

Finn and Stavin hovered like anxious parents, while Xan knelt beside her. They were in a clearing beside the road, the edge of the forest not far from where she lay. It appeared that she had not stayed on Mithras long after she lost consciousness, most likely falling before the dragon got airborne. Jael sat at her head, his hands stroking her hair, but Aron stood a few paces away. Arms crossed, his eyes brimmed with worry, but his clenched jaw and quick glances at Jael hinted more at jealousy than concern.

"I'm fine," she said, pushing up even further to sit, locking eyes with Aron. "I'm fine." He looked away, then turned toward the horses. Dax was there, and when he saw his mistress awake, her war horse whinnied and took a step in her direction.

"We'll camp here tonight while you rest," Jael said. "Xan has the magic inside you under control—"

"Temporarily," Xan interrupted. At the distant sound of a dragon's call, the men surrounding her flinched and glanced behind them.

"But I can show you a few tricks, too." Jael finished. He offered her a smile and helped her sit up completely, keeping one hand on her arm.

Amarynn pulled away, tucked her legs beneath herself, and stood, taking a few steps to steady herself. "We don't have time to wait."

"Rynn, it's nearly nightfall." Finn said. Yet another trumpeting call from a dragon flying overhead sounded and the men scattered. She looked up at the sky, at the orange and pink streaks that indicated the sun sat low on the horizon. She turned to Jael.

"How long was I out?"

"Hours."

Amarynn turned in a slow circle, taking stock of their surroundings. The large meadow, alongside which ran the road to Athtull, was rimmed by a forest of oldwood trees. In the distance were the craggy peaks of the

Dark Mountains. Finn, Stavin, Nioll, Aron and Xan and all the horses were here, though Aron kept his eyes averted from her, making himself busy with the horses and trying to keep Dax occupied. The dragons, who had landed at the far end of the meadow, were gathered near Mithras, who kept his head high and turned in her direction, his nostrils flared.

"He took some convincing," Jael said. "But I think your atranoch—"

"Dragon," Amarynn corrected him.

"Ah, your *dragon* understands we pose no threat to you."

Safe?

A half-smile formed on her lips, and she nodded, whispering, "I'm safe."

As the words left her lips, she noticed that Jael exchanged a worried glance with Finn. The Prince quickly glanced back at her, his eyes scanning her face.

Then, she turned her attention towards the rest of the men. "What is the plan?"

Finn spoke first. "Lord Jael, Stavin and I will take this lot," he jerked his head in the direction of the others, "and head back to Calliway tonight. If your father is truly dead, and given what we all felt that seems to be the case, we cannot wait."

Amarynn looked at the Prince. "You are going with them, yes?"

"Absolutely not." His mouth was set in a hard line.

"Well, I'm going into the Reaches, and I don't think Rhyssa can keep up with Mithras," she said, shaking her head. "Unless you plan on flying, you should go home."

"Then I'll fly, too." His answer was swift.

"You think that brute will carry you?" Aron called from near the horses. "He's not particularly tolerant of us."

"He's not tolerant of *you*," Jael countered.

"Ah now, can we be sure of that, My Lord?" The bite in Aron's tone was unmistakable.

"Aron, he nearly took your head off. I think My Lord's fairly sure." Nioll offered, smirking as he reached for his horse's reins.

"What is he talking about?" Amarynn asked Jael under her breath. Jael dismissed her question with a gesture.

"Do what you will," Aron muttered, adjusting the girth on his own horse while Dax nuzzled at his side. He paused to rub the golden horse between the ears. "Ah, I know she's consorting with another mount, but I'll get you home, good man."

"Very good," Amarynn mumbled to herself, finding it difficult to keep from looking in Aron's direction, though his comment stung. "Get Dax home. Yes." She turned back to Jael. "You really should go with them, you know."

"Nice try, Rynn," Jael reached for her hand and when their palms touched, she gasped. The magical current fired to life, but rather than pain, she was filled with exhilaration. Jael pulled her to his chest. "I'm not leaving you. Ever." He added the last word quietly, so close to her ear, it made her shiver.

"That's enough of that," Aron growled as he threw one leg over his horse. "We are losing daylight."

"Aye, he's right." Stavin signaled for the others to mount up before approaching Amarynn and Jael. "We'll see to the Queen, My Lord. Don't worry."

"And Regealth," Amarynn added.

"Aye, Rynn. We'll look after him, too. You just watch yourself and get back as quickly as you can." He grasped both of their shoulders. "Nothing stupid, even for you, right?" He nodded and turned away.

As the riders melted into the lengthening shadows of the forest, Jael wrapped his other arm around her. She lay her head against his chest, eyes closed, listening to the steady beat of his heart. In less than a day's time, her world was laid open, completely bare, and then ripped apart and turned upside down. Amarynn didn't expect to feel deep regret at

Aron's disappointment. She hadn't intended to open herself to him and then walk away, but Lasten's death and finding Jael on the road was an unforeseen circumstance beyond her control.

Never in a million years did she think Jael's betrothal could potentially dissolve. He had the power to make that happen now, as he swore he would even before his father's death. But she had not considered the possibility of him ascending to the throne so soon. In fact, she had never considered what might happen when Jael became King. She drew a breath and pulled back from Jael's embrace.

"What does this mean for the Travelers?"

Jael tilted his head. "What do you mean?"

"They are," she paused. "I mean, they *were* bound to your father. But now that he's gone, does that shift to you or are they... free?"

"I have no idea. I hadn't even begun to think about what it all means."

Amarynn studied his face. He seemed harder, less gentle than the Jael she was used to. A hint of dark circles under his eyes testified to the strain of the last few days. He would need his strength if he planned to fly with her, that is, if Mithras even allowed it. She stepped back and took his hand.

"Come on. We'll need to use the darkness to conceal our flight."

"We don't know if Mith..." The Prince's voice trailed off as he tried to recall the name Amarynn used.

"Mithras."

"Will he let me fly with you?"

Amarynn was walking backwards, tugging Jael along with her.

"I don't know."

The ground trembled as Mithras trudged in their direction.

"But either way, I have to go, and there's only one way to find out."

CHAPTER 31

J ael had no idea what he was doing, and it showed. Initially, when Jael settled in behind Amarynn, the dragon's back twitched and he swung his head around more than once to eye them both. But, much like a horse, he gave a snort and a shake of his head before gathering the muscles in his shoulders and haunches and bursting off the ground into the air.

As the new ruler of Karth, it was probably the last thing he should have done — put himself in such danger — but he refused to let Amarynn out of his sight, not after what he had seen of her pain and struggle in the meadow. Regealth had warned him about her potential for magic and all the danger that accompanied it, but the Prince had thought there would be more time before that became a reality.

"Are you alright?" Though Jael could feel that Amarynn was shouting by the way her chest expanded, her voice was small against the gale force winds produced by the great dragon's speed and wing beats.

Dodging the hilt of the broad sword strapped to her back, he buried his face in her neck near her ear, as much to make himself heard as to warm his ice-cold face.

"I'll be fine!"

They had been flying for hours. When the great beast lifted into the sky and Jael managed to stay seated behind Amarynn, the mountains were of typical mountain height. He had awkwardly clung to Amarynn at first, but he soon learned to use the muscles in his legs to supplement his arms as they sought stability. However, when they cleared the last of the Dark Mountain ridges, his heart plummeted and his muscles screamed as he took in the size of the peaks looming ahead. The Stone Giants were aptly named.

Now as Mithras glided along the backside of what appeared to be the enormous mountain range's end, a vast, open plain stretched before them. Moonlight illuminated the snow, bathing it in a blue-green glow, icy plumes of wind-driven crystals whirling into the air and settling along crevasses and snow-dunes. The whole night had an ethereal, dream-like feel — the moonlight, the snow, dragons peppering the starlit sky.

Jael felt Amarynn's magic give a little hitch, and she tightened her grip against his on the leather strap holding them both in place. Mithras banked to the right, and they continued their flight. Just when Jael thought they might succumb to frostbite, more mountains reared up in the distance, though not nearly as tall as the Dark Mountains or the Stone Giants. A city was nestled in the curve of the range, several graceful towers rising from its center. Golden, warm lights, glowing from the tower windows, were a soft contrast to the harsh chill of the northern air.

The dragon's descent into the low hills at the base of the mountains was sudden. Jael gasped as his stomach flipped before they hit the ground with enough force to nearly unseat him, but Amarynn kept her poise like a seasoned rider. Her arm shot out to keep him from tumbling to the stone below, and for a moment, the fiery, willful Amarynn from before showed a glimpse of herself. That self-assured smirk and the hard glint in her eyes gave Jael some small kernel of hope that the Amarynn he had fallen for was still there.

"Take my arm," she said as she untangled their frozen feet from the leather strap still looped around the dragon's chest. As she did so, she swung her shoulder forward and Jael slid awkwardly over Mithras's side and down one leg to land heavily on the ground. He turned just in time to watch Amarynn do the same, but the way she controlled her body, the way her hand went from one scaled spike to another as she slid down the dragon's side was mesmerizing. How could she be so fragile in one moment, yet so powerful and in control in the next?

Amarynn ducked beneath Mithras's chest and signaled for Jael to follow her up the rise, to where the lights of the city were visible. "Mithras seems to think they Traveled another in there." She gestured to the tallest tower rising from the center of the city.

"How do you know?" The dragon had not made a sound or a gesture that would indicate he communicated with her.

"I don't know, exactly. I just know it." She shrugged, then sighed. "He doesn't tell me, but somehow, I know.

Jael wanted to respond, but he was trembling so violently from the cold, he couldn't open his mouth to speak. He worked the muscles in his jaw to no avail while Amarynn dropped to one knee and pulled a small pack from her shoulder. She pulled a thin animal skin from inside and rose, draping it across his shoulders, pulling it tight across his chest.

"It's a greall skin — warmer than you think," she murmured, tucking the ends under each other.

She was so close, he could smell her: her hair, her skin, the scent of night sky and trees. The memory of her braid laying on the forest floor outside of Athtull Keep resurfaced and along with it, his connection to her... Finally, his body warmed, and his mouth cooperated.

"You don't have to do this."

She had gone back to fumbling with her bag but stopped, glancing at him. "What?"

Jael let his eyes wander across the moonlit landscape. Wind whipped around them, even in the sheltered hollow the dragon had landed in.

"I am King now. The Travelers aren't bonded to me anymore. This is my fight, not yours." His voice still trembled, but he was beginning to regain the feeling in his fingers again though the biting wind still made the end of his nose sting.

Amarynn shook her head, the slightest snarl threatening to form on her lips.

"That is the most ridiculous thing I have ever heard." She took a step towards him, her hazel eyes glinting dangerously. "We are here, in the Stone Reaches, with a *dragon*, and you want to call it off? Are you mad?"

"I said *you* don't have to do this." Jael's voice remained steady.

"I'm the reason we are in this mess, or had you forgotten?"

"I don't want to risk you, Amarynn. I can't lose you."

She chuckled and shook her head. "I am immort—"

"I know you are immortal, Rynn. What scares me is what this magic might have done to you. What if your immortality has been affected? And... you don't know how to use it yet. What if it kills you the way it killed my Aunt Dyaneth?" Jael hugged the greall skin tighter and looked away. "Just promise me that you won't try to use your magic until Regealth can train you."

"Jael, I—"

"Promise!" he growled as he dropped the skin and grasped her arms. He jolted at the rush of new energy radiating from her.

Surprised, she stiffened and then nodded.

"I promise." She pulled herself from his grasp and picked up the greall skin, throwing it back over his shoulders, muttering. "I wouldn't even know what to do with it anyway."

"Good," Jael exhaled. "I can show you a way to try and control it until you can train with Regealth. But promise me you won't try to use it, no matter what happens."

"I won't." Amarynn looked back at the city. Light was just beginning to streak over the peaks surrounding the valley, signaling the sunrise. "Sun's rising. We need to decide what we're doing."

Behind them, Mithras rumbled.

"He's telling me we need to look in that center tower. He says Venalise is there."

"How does he talk to you?" She was staring out at the city and the pre-dawn sky. Wind whipped her hair across her face, though she didn't flinch as it slapped against her face.

Amarynn thought for a moment. "It's hard to describe. He doesn't really talk to me. It's more like he shares his thoughts and feelings. I can understand what he's trying to tell me, and if I don't, well…" She trailed off and let loose a low chuckle. "He makes sure I am corrected."

As if on cue, Mithras snorted, drawing a surprised look from both Amarynn and Jael. She smiled, letting loose a quick chuckle. It was nice to have this moment, Jael thought as he looked back out over the city. They had shared very few quiet moments like this. Their bond materialized under extreme duress, and that friction and strain had been ceaseless since their escape from Athtull. Jael realized he hardly knew her, but at the same time, he felt intrinsically connected to her like no other. They must see this through and make it to the other side. The next few hours could bring any number of outcomes, and he was determined to make sure it was favorable, no matter the cost.

"We should make our way down before the sun rises," Amarynn said, breaking the quiet. "Easier to get in that way."

"Right," Jael pulled the greall skin from his shoulders and laid it on Amarynn's pack. "Did you happen to notice an out-of-the-way entrance, or are we just marching through the main gate?"

"I'm making this up as I go," she said as she hoisted herself up and over a rocky ledge that dropped ten feet down to a gently sloping hillside. "Follow me."

Jael closed his eyes and said a quick prayer to any god or goddess who was listening to see them to the end of the day intact and unscathed. He shook his arms, prompting a few, scattered sparks of magic from his fingertips, then swung his leg over the rocks and dropped down after her.

Sia could tell morning was approaching by the sound of far-off roosters crowing. The light in the cell had not changed; it was still just slightly brighter than twilight, though sleep had been impossible in the drafty chamber. The giant still sat beside her. She knew he was sleeping by the deep rumble of his snoring. Her stomach rumbled in response.

A clanging sound reverberated off the stone walls, causing the giant to twitch, and for a moment, Sia held her breath, frightened he might react. But as his breathing quickened and he began to stir, her fear subsided. She knew he wouldn't hurt her. How she knew, she did not know, but she was sure of it.

Footsteps, sounding far away at first, moved closer. Sia pushed herself to stand. her muscles aching from sitting on the cold stone floor all night. She stretched as she leaned against the wall in the deepest shadows. The smell of warm bread and savory stew overtook her senses, and her stomach heaved, churning and growling around its emptiness.

"You are stubborn, little falcon." It was a voice Sia recognized. "Much like my daughter when she was your age." Empress Uhll stepped from the shadows of the corridor, alone and with a platter of food in her hands. "I know you must be hungry, and maybe we can get your new friend to try something to eat, hmm?"

Sia didn't trust the woman, but she was most definitely in need of food, and the savory aroma was too enticing to ignore. She pushed off the wall and padded forward to stand in between the shadows and the dim light of the chamber. Uhll set the platter down on the floor outside the bars, then stood, arms crossed.

"I know my daughter has not been honest with you. She wanted to see if you could call Travelers more suited to our needs." She stepped closer to the bars and leaned in. "She should have told you from the start. You should have had a choice."

Sia took a step forward. The food was hard to resist, but so were Uhll's words. Choice was a rarity in her life.

"What if you had that, hmm?"

"Had what?" Sia started to take another step, then stopped. What if the Empress was trying to trick her somehow?

"A choice. What if you had a say in what you do and who you do it for?" Uhll looked over her shoulder into the darkened hallway and jerked her head. Sia's head snapped up at the sound of a high-pitched whine from down the hall. "That's right. I've brought your bear."

"Thera!"

Sia heard the claws scrambling on stone, and then Thera bounded from the shadows straight for the bars, which she ducked through easily. The giant behind her grunted and clambered to his feet, but didn't make any other move as the bear cub ran straight into Sia's arms. Thera rubbed her snout against Sia's chest and then butted against her excitedly. It had been less than a day, but the cub seemed even bigger – heavier. She clutched Thera, despite her wiggling, and looked up at Uhll, who gave her a satisfied nod.

"Thank you," Sia said. "For bringing her to me." She looked over at the platter of food still sitting on the floor. "And for the food."

"Well, we can't make the trek back to Korr on empty stomachs, can we?" Uhll drew a key from her pocket and unlocked the door, sliding the tray through. She pulled the door shut, but didn't lock it. "See what you can make of our big, new friend, and eat. Get your strength. Korr warriors are expected to care for themselves." Uhll turned and started walking down the hallway, but before she disappeared into the shadows, she looked back over her shoulder at Sia. "Consider this your first lesson, T'Korr Sia."

The words lingered in the air long after the Empress left.

T'Korr Sia.

She let the words roll over her tongue as she whispered it to herself. She couldn't even remember her own last name.

T'Korr Sia.

Venalise's mother was offering her a place in her world as a person with choices; not a child, but someone who could think for themselves. Someone who possessed power and the right to use it as she saw fit. She could do what she wanted.

Lost in thought with Thera still in her lap, Sia did not hear the giant shuffle to stand behind her, at first not noticing the faint shadow of his hulking form. At Thera's growl, the child gasped in surprise, whirling to find him eyeing the food on the floor, a strand of drool dripping from his lips.

"Are you hungry?"

Sia gently placed Thera on the ground, and, frustrated that her mistress was not paying attention to her, the cub butted her head against her leg. Leaning down, Sia snatched the bread loaf, pulling it into two pieces and holding the larger of the two out to him.

"Eat?" she asked. When it was clear he did not understand, Sia took a bite from the smaller end of the loaf, then lifted the other end closer to him. Thera tugged on Sia's pants leg impatiently, then issued a louder but playful growl.

It happened so fast. In an instant, the giant dropped to a defensive crouch and roared — deep and menacing — at the cub. Thera whined and scurried away, back through the bars, cowering on the other side.

"No! Stop it!" Sia lunged between the giant and Thera. "She's not doing anything wrong!" The giant stayed in his crouch, but his expression slowly changed from anger to confusion. Sia softened her voice and called Thera back to her. "She's a baby. See?" Thera sheepishly padded to Sia's side and snuffled her nose around her ankle. Sia brushed her away but grabbed a piece of cheese, which she offered to the cub, who nipped it from her hand and turned away. The giant tilted his head to try to get a better look at Thera as she gnawed.

"Do you want some?" Sia offered the bread again, this time dunking it into the crock of stew, and this time he reached for it, bringing it to his face and sniffing it before taking a slow, careful bite. Sia took another bite, too. "Good, isn't it?" she asked, her mouth half-full.

He said nothing but grunted as he pushed the last bite of bread into his mouth. As he eased into a sitting position, Sia took another small piece of cheese from the platter, then pushed it in the giant's direction. "You have the rest."

The three of them sat together in silence while they ate. Except for the occasional growl and whine from Thera, the room remained quiet. Occasionally, Sia smiled at the giant. He still seemed sad, like she thought he did when she first saw him in the aethertorium. Now she wanted to make him understand that she was his friend, but didn't know how.

"He trusts you, child."

Sia's head snapped up at the sound of Talamynne's voice. She and two other scholars emerged from the shadowy hallway, their slippered footsteps silent. Talamynne reached for the cell door and to Sia's surprise, pulled it open. So focused on the giant and the Empress's words, Sia had forgotten that Uhll unlocked it. One of the blue-robed scholars carried a bundle, and the other held a large, rolled fur. Sia stood, eyeing them warily as she stepped back a few paces.

"We have brought you warm clothing and a stone bear pelt for your giant." Talamynne gave an apologetic frown in Thera's direction. "Empress Uhll wishes to depart as soon as you are ready." She gestured to her companions on either side of her. "Silahn. Ruidel. Place their things inside the chamber." Talamynne folded her hands together over her green robe and waited while the scholars hastily deposited the items just inside the opened cell door and scurried away, glancing over their shoulders, watchful of the giant behind them.

"We'll be just outside. When you are dressed, bring him, and we will start our journey." Talamynne smiled as she had when they met for the first time, warmly and welcoming.

Sia watched them disappear. Thera rolled and squirmed on her back near the open doorway, while the giant, who had finished the rest of the food, sat cross-legged in front of her. These two beings existed because of her. Thera, a baby, had no mother, and this giant was completely on his own – there existed no others like him anywhere. It made Sia sad, but it also motivated her to do something about it.

"You need a name," Sia said, studying him. With his high cheekbones and flattened nose, he reminded her of the wooly cattle that her parents used to keep. Her father had called the bull Tior after the guardian god of the harvest, though it seemed to be an ill-chosen name, since blight and poor yields had plagued her family since her birth. It was the reason her parents sold her off to Master Omman.

"Tior," she whispered, sizing him up to see if it fit. He was watching Thera's antics, unsure of how to react, it seemed. Just when his mouth began to curl up in a smile, Thera would growl, and his expression would darken. Occasionally, his eyes flicked back to Sia, but when he noticed her watching him, he looked away.

"Tior," she said again, this time louder. He turned toward her, and she pointed at him. "You are Tior."

His hand drifted to his chest.

"Yes, you. You are Tior. Ti—or." Sia sounded the word out slowly for him.

"Ti..." he replied.

"Ti-or.

"...or. Ti-or."

Sia grinned. "Yes! Tior. That's you."

Tior quietly worked the name around in his mouth several times. "Tior," he finally breathed as he pointed to himself. He pointed at Sia. "Tior?"

"No, I'm Sia. See-ah," she said, pointing to herself.

"See-ah," he said, mimicking her higher pitch. "Sia."

She giggled. She couldn't help it. Here she was, sitting in a cell with a giant and a bear she had created with magic, learning to say each other's names. It was strange and ludicrous, but it made her feel surprisingly powerful. Two creatures that others feared were under her protection and control. Sia glanced at the pile of clothing beside the door. The Empress had given her the name of her people and invited her to go with them back to her home, and she had promised Sia something she had very little memory of ever possessing — choice.

The girl stood and started pulling the warm furs on over her other clothes. If it was choice she was being given, she was ready to exercise it. She was choosing to go.

CHAPTER 32

Amarynn and Jael had not had any difficulty slipping past the guards. It was early morning, and the guards were changing posts. Taking their cue from their time at Athtull Keep, they made straight for the wall while the shadows still fell, then followed along it to the gate. They shrank back as a small contingency of what looked to be Stone Reaches soldiers rode out at speed, then Amarynn and Jael used the dusty trail of powdered snow produced as cover to slip inside.

Once past the city gate, their next obstacle was to navigate the winding streets to get to the base of the tallest spire. Amarynn had deftly swiped cloaks from hanging laundry along the way to help them conceal their identity. However, when one merchant seemed overly curious, Jael wrapped one arm around Amarynn's shoulder and pulled her close, nuzzling the side of her head with overt affection. The shopkeep shook his head and continued with his chores, but Jael kept his hold on her.

"Might as well play the part the whole way in, yes?" he whispered beside her ear. "We should keep up the appearance."

Amarynn cast a sideways glance at the Prince and smiled. If only for now, she relished the feeling of being normal. In this moment, she wasn't Legion, she wasn't immortal. She had to admit it felt good to be so close to him again, this time without his betrothal hanging over her head. They could be walking into their certain demise, but it mattered less knowing there were no more barriers to their bond. She slipped one arm thorough his and leaned in, the way she imagined lovers would do, not that she would actually know.

They wandered down streets, lingering at shop windows for several long minutes before Amarynn's impatience got the better of her and they ducked down a smaller side street, which only opened to another wide boulevard.

"Where is this damn tower entrance?" she hissed after the third dead end.

"It can't be far" The Prince kept his leisurely pace until they found another side street and continued their search.

After one more turn, Amarynn stopped, pulling Jael back into the shadow of the closest building. Directly before them, rising from the ground was the center spire. It didn't seem to have been built; instead, the walls rose as a tree might rise from the ground in one, fluid piece.

"This is it," she whispered, pressing back into the wall behind her. "This is where Mithras said we would find her."

Jael peered up into the morning sky.

"It's tall," he murmured.

"Aye," she agreed. "Let's hope she's not at the top."

They watched from the shadow of the building as over the next few minutes several dark-robed men and women entered a wide, covered entrance at its base. Long blue and white banners fluttered in the wind on either side.

"How are we going to do this?" Jael had not taken his eyes off the tower since it came into view.

"Do you see anyone going in that isn't wearing a robe?" Amarynn shielded her eyes against the rising sun and scanned the area.

"Not ye—"

"There!"

Amarynn pointed to the left, where two armed men dressed in leathers strode towards the entrance. As they approached, they pulled their blades from their scabbards and handed them to a robed figure standing beside the doors.

"Well, *that's* not happening," Amarynn growled. Magic or not, she refused to be separated from her weapons. "We'll have to find another way in."

"We can leave Frost and your short sword hidden here, Rynn," Jael suggested, gesturing to a pile of discarded grain sacks and moldy hay. "You have hidden blades, and the daggers are easy to conceal."

"No," she pointed at the robed man. "Watch."

A woman in plain clothing approached the entrance. The robed man at the entrance waved one hand in front of her, pausing near her waist. The woman's shoulders sagged, and she produced a paring knife from under the contents of her basket, gesturing to the bread and cheese she carried.

"They are using magic to disarm people. And before you suggest that you can use yours to counter it, I'll remind you that you are powerful, but you aren't experienced." Amarynn nodded in the tower's direction. "Like they are."

Jael sighed and placed his hands on his hips. "Any ideas?"

"I have an idea."

Amarynn and Jael spun around at the lilting sound of a woman's voice. She was petite, but the fire that flashed in her green eyes made up for her stature. Her simple black leather armor suggested she was one of the warriors they had seen, but the intricate and delicate braid work in her fiery red hair suggested otherwise.

"Who are you?" Amarynn asked, as Jael stepped to the side and scanned the street and ally for others.

"Relax, Traveler. I'm someone who can get you inside the Spire. But I have conditions."

As the last word left the stranger's mouth, Amarynn's dagger was already at her throat. "You are in no position for conditions," Amarynn growled. "I'll only ask once more. Who are you?"

"Call your dog off, Prince Jael," the woman demanded, lifting her chin defiantly as her expression darkened. "I'm the only way you are getting in there. You need me."

"How do you know our names?" Amarynn's voice was low and dangerous.

The woman chuckled. "I've known who you are for years. What kind of spy would I be if I didn't?"

"Rynn." Jael placed his hand on Amarynn's extended arm. Amarynn did not move, her eyes fixed on the woman. This encounter seemed too convenient, but then she remembered that Mithras was the reason they were here. He had known something big was afoot.

"Stubborn," the woman chuckled. "Just like me. In another life we'd be friends," she added under her breath.

"A spy? Tell me who you are, who you work for, and I'll consider listening to you." Amarynn's said, in a cold, harsh tone.

"My name is Oravae. I was a friend of Venalise."

"Definitely not helping," Amarynn hissed, pressing the blade harder against Oravae's throat. At the mention of Venalise's name, the hairs rose on the back of her neck and her gut twisted. If this woman was working with that witch—

"*Was.* I said... was," Oravae gasped as Amarynn pushed her against the building they stood next to, the blade pressing harder against the woman's throat. "She betrayed my father. She's no friend to me anymore."

"Rynn," Jael stepped between Amarynn and Oravae, pushing the dagger off Oravae's throat. "Stand down." Faint lines of magic crackled behind his eyes.

She shifted her stare to Jael. As she glowered, a more pronounced wave of magic than his danced behind her hazel eyes, but it snapped and crackled, making her drop her dagger and clutch at her head.

The Prince leaned down and grasped Amarynn's hands. "You promised," he whispered, his forehead pressed to hers. "You promised not to use it until you trained."

"I didn't try to do it," she panted. The pain in her head ebbed as Jael stayed close to her. "I can't stop it when it wants release." Her breathing was fast, but she worked to control it. Every time Jael's magic made itself known, hers wanted to respond, even with the talisman that Xan slipped into her pocket. She glared back at Jael. "Keep yours in check. It's responding to you."

"Hate to interrupt, but time is short."

Jael syphoned the surge within Amarynn, pulling at the magic from within himself, and stood, offering her his hand, which she ignored. Rising, she brushed past Jael to tower over Oravae, who raised her eyebrows as she tilted her chin to meet the Traveler's stare.

"Take us, girl," she snarled. "But this is the only warning you get. If this is a trick, you'll die before they take either of us."

Oravae, unfazed, rolled her eyes. "Listen to yourself, Traveler. I am fully aware of what you can do." She pushed off the wall. "I'm not stupid. All I ask is that you take Venalise away from here. She is a threat to my father and to the Reaches. Believe me when I say that her mother's rule is enough to try to manage without her reckless and power-hungry daughter creating more havoc. Now, if you want to get inside the Spire, *you'd* be stupid to turn me down."

"Her mother?"

"Yes. Empress Uhll of the Korr House. She's ruled the Stone Reaches since before I was born. My father was planning on challenging Uhll for control of the Reaches. He wanted to stop this warmongering and bring us peace and prosperity. He wanted to let our people focus more on learning, on farming and crafting, and he thought Venalise would help, but she betrayed him." Oravae dropped her eyes, then looked up in disgust. "She betrayed both of us."

"No surprise," Amarynn muttered. "It's what she does. We just need what we came for. I'm not here to exact justice for anyone. You can do that yourself."

"That is my condition, Traveler. I get you inside the Spire so you can get what you came for, and you take Venalise when you leave."

Amarynn glanced over her shoulder at the Spire. Venalise was in there, and she was Amarynn's for the taking. The need for vengeance took hold, wrapping its thorny fingers around her heart.

"She's right, Rynn. We need to get what we came for. Taking Venalise is a price worth paying."

Amarynn spun around to face both Jael and Oravae, though her eyes were locked on the Prince. "Yes, we came after the Gate and the child, but if we do this, Venalise is mine. When we get her back to Karth, *I* decide her fate."

Oravae narrowed her eyes and started to say something but stopped herself before she let the words out of her mouth. Instead, she tossed one of her braids over her shoulder and ducked in front of Amarynn. "You'll both need robes to get past the adepts at the entrance. I know where the laundry is done. Follow me, do as I say, and I will get you in."

An hour later, Amarynn, Jael and Oravae approached an unguarded, private back entrance to the towering Spire. Oravae produced a key from her pocket and opened the door, ushering them inside. No longer early morning, increased activity in and around the tower made it easier for them to slip through unnoticed.

Once they were inside, Amarynn grabbed Oravae's arm. "I'm not going any further until you explain yourself. How did you know who we were? We could have been anyone," she hissed near the red-headed woman's ear.

Oravae spun around, coming nose-to-nose with Amarynn. "Give me a little credit, Traveler. Our spies are everywhere, even in Karth." She relaxed her stance, looking back and forth between Amarynn and the Prince. "I've been keeping an eye on Venalise for years. It was only a matter of time before I came to know who you were." She smirked at Jael. "And you? We've had our eyes on you since the day you were born."

As they wound through staircases and narrow, curving hallways, Amarynn marveled at the flowing stonework which was a stark contrast to the utilitarian architecture she was used to in Calliway. Even these utility hallways were elegant, smelling of incense and greenery, though no plant life was visible. The narrow, twisting passageways reminded Amarynn of the private pathway to Regealth's chambers she had used so many times before. Finally, Oravae stopped them just outside a simple door and gave them directions.

"Stay here for ten minutes. I need to get back into the room with my father without the guards knowing. Then, you can come. No one uses these passages, so you will be safe. When you get to our door, say that you were sent by Talamynne. They'll let you pass."

Jael opened his mouth as if to speak, but Oravae slipped through the door and closed it behind her before he could make a sound. Though Amarynn was wary of the redheaded woman, she admired her mettle.

"What do we when we get in the room?" Jael leaned one shoulder against the wall. "We can't just take the girl and walk out. And what about the Gate? We didn't think this through." Jael ran his hand through his hair and sighed.

"We'll have to improvise. That's what we've been doing all along, isn't it?" Amarynn adjusted her sword belt beneath her robes then lifted Jael's and peered around his side to inspect Frost's position down the middle of his back. She could hear his breathing, see the rise and fall of his chest with each breath, and for a moment, the scent of leather and sandalwood took over her senses.

As she dropped the robes, she let her hand drift to his side. In the frenzy of all that had happened in the past few days, it still had not registered that nothing stood in her way to be with him. No impending marriage, no disapproving father, nothing. Yes, there were innumerable fallen pieces to pick up back in Calliway, but in this quiet space, she could let herself have this moment. Her heart ached with an increasingly familiar need.

Jael leaned into her, slipping one arm around her waist. She rested her head on his chest as her other hand reached around the back of his neck. "Not the way I usually prepare to break into a guarded, foreign stronghold, but..." she whispered as she pulled his head to hers.

She felt the smile on his lips just before they came together. He tasted of summer and wine, and the instant their lips met, she was transported away from all the anxiety, the pain, the confusion — everything. There was only him. A swell in the energy of her new-found magic sought Jael's and she let their togetherness slide over her like a warm blanket. He was gentle, his lips careful as their tongues explored each other. Jael's arm tightened around her, and his free hand slid to her neck as he pulled back.

"Has it been ten minutes?" she murmured as the hum of their shared magic faded.

"Probably," Jael breathed. "We should go."

Amarynn touched her forehead to his. "Don't do anything stupid. I just found you and this time, I intend to keep you."

"I won't if you won't," he replied. He pulled back again to look her in the eyes. "And I meant what I said. Try to forget about your magic. That's the trick. You have to try to just forget it exists. If you try to keep it quiet, you are focusing too much on it."

"That's going to be hard." Amarynn's brow furrowed. "Especially when you channel yours."

"I'll try to make that my last resort. Just because I have it doesn't mean have to use it, I was Legion-trained, remember?" He arched one eyebrow and stepped back. "I can use a blade."

She nodded, still trying to make sense of how she was supposed to forget about the new magic writhing inside of her. If only Regealth were here. But before she could think of some way to distract herself, Jael had opened the door and was halfway into the larger hall. Amarynn sighed, adjusting her robes as she followed. Every instinct told her this was unwise; this was how traps were laid, but Jael's willingness to believe Oravae was enough to convince her it was worth the risk.

Oravae's instructions were easy to follow. The hallway they sought was only a few paces to the left, and the door was easy to find, flanked by two well-armored guards. The style of their heavy, black leather armor was crude and unfamiliar, but their swords were no different than the Legion's, only slightly longer, with a slight curve to the outer edge of the blade.

Jael took the lead with Amarynn following closely behind him. Even though protecting Jael was her instinct, in matters of subterfuge or diplomacy, he was by far the better choice to lead. Together, they approached the guards, who looked at them with skepticism. The smaller of the two spoke in a language neither she nor Jael understood, and Amarynn experienced a moment of panic, quelled as she heard Jael speak.

"Talamynne." Just the name. Nothing else. Oravae had failed to remember that neither of them spoke the language of the Reaches. But Jael had the sense to flavor his voice with some nondescript accent. The guards looked them up and down. Instinct took control and Amarynn stepped closer to Jael, nostrils flaring as she readied a fortifying breath, though she kept her eyes cast on the floor. Just as Amarynn's hands were drifting to her sides, both guards turned and opened the doors, ushering them inside.

Amarynn held her breath as she walked into the room. She kept her head down until she heard the click of the latch, and even then, she only lifted her eyes to survey the space in front of her. It was dark and the air was oppressively stale, the only light coming from two braziers near the door and a narrow window that allowed heavily filtered light into the room. Instinctively, she took two steps forward, to position herself in front of Jael in a readied stance, bouncing back and forth on the balls of her feet. If this was an ambush, she prepared herself to take the first hit.

"I wasn't sure if you'd make it past the guards. I forgot you didn't speak their language." Oravae emerged from the shadows. She nodded in Jael's direction. "Well done."

Amarynn's eyes began to adjust to the dim light, and she could begin to make out sparse furniture lining the walls. Deep shadows still made things difficult to see, so she kept herself near Jael, loose and ready in case of a surprise. As her eyes swept across the room on her left, she noticed an older man sitting in one of the chairs, looking forlorn.

"If you are able to get in and out of here, why aren't you already gone?" The thought had come to Amarynn as they approached the guards outside the door. This seemed to be nothing more than theatrics to access a space so easily escaped.

"*I* can get in and out. My father isn't physically able, and *she*," Oravae jerked her head to the side, "is magically bound and can't move."

Amarynn's eyes trained on the spot where Oravae had gestured. A figure sat against the wall in the darkest corner of the room, still and silent. It was a woman, Amarynn could tell that much, with a pale circlet set around her dark hair. Amarynn reached across her body and pulled the robes off her shoulder, letting them fall to a puddle at her feet, then stepped out of them in the figure's direction. As she approached and her eyes adjusted more, she was overtaken by a tidal wave of rage.

"You," she hissed, a violent shudder wracking her body. There was no way she could forget her magic now. Her dagger was in her hand in a heartbeat.

"There she is. All yours."

Amarynn whirled on Oravae, backing the smaller woman all the way across the room, where she pinned her against the wall with her forearm at her throat.

"You did not tell me she was *here*." Spittle flew from Amarynn's mouth as she snarled through clenched teeth. Dangerous blue energy flitted through her eyes. "Where is the child?"

"My condition to get you into the Spire was that you take Venalise." Oravae grunted as Amarynn leaned in. "And I have delivered her to you. I never said I had the child."

Red fury welled up from Amarynn's core and if it weren't for Jael's grip on her shoulders, Oravae's neck would have snapped.

"The child is with the Empress Uhll, Traveler." The old man's voice was low, but steady. Amarynn glanced over her shoulder at the old man. He was younger than Regealth, but not by much. His light grey robes were thinner and more elegant than any other she had seen, with embroidered symbols running up the sleeves. "My daughter needed to get you in this room to see me because only Venalise knows how you can get the child back. You were deceived, yes, but it was for your own good."

"And who are you?" Jael asked over his shoulder, still struggling to hold Amarynn at bay.

"Prince Jael, I am Rhymere, the Master Scholar of the Spire and leader of Lorce."

"They lock their leaders away in the dark?" Amarynn scoffed, still holding Oravae against the stone. "If that's the case, I'm not entirely sure you are qualified to help us."

"Listen to him, Traveler," Oravae choked out. "You need her. I want her gone. This serves us both."

"I feel that magic of yours rising, Traveler. I also sense you have no way of controlling it. It trails off you like sweat." The last sentence from the old man was laced with an element of distaste.

"Everyone's an expert!" Amarynn pushed off Oravae and shook Jael's grip from her shoulders. She paced around the room, sword drawn, until she stopped in front of Venalise.

"Nothing to add?" Amarynn leaned down to eye level with the bound mage and sneered. "No? You never shut up back at Athtull." The woman responsible for all the pain and terror she had endured was right in front of her. Amarynn adjusted her grip on the short sword hilt. It would be so easy to end her. She imagined the feel of her blade slipping through bone and flesh. She craved the satisfaction of watching the light dim from Venalise's eyes. Her magic surged again, but this time she was prepared.

"Amarynn." Jael's voice was a low warning behind her.

"You are lucky I made a promise," she jeered before straightening and turning away from Venalise to face Jael. Her body vibrated from the hate radiating from her core, the magic threatening to spill over. "Tell me we don't need her. Tell me that you can manage whatever it is they say we need her for. *Please.*"

"Rynn," Jael started. "I don't know what she knows. You know that."

"Uhll is as good as gone by now," Oravae said, rubbing her neck. "There's nothing you can do here. But Vena knows her mother. She has knowledge none of us have. And with Uhll taking the child and her giant, you'll want everything Vena can give you."

"Giant?" Jael kept one hand on Amarynn's shoulder but leaned in to address Oravae. "What giant?"

"How can you have a giant?" Amarynn turned to Rhymere. "They don't exist here, do they?"

"No, they don't," Rhymere said from behind. "It was the child. She wields more than one element. It is why Venalise brought her here."

Amarynn spun around and knelt in front of Venalise. She looked so much smaller than she had at Athtull. Her cheeks were gaunt and though there were dark circles under her eyes, the mage glared at Amarynn, her eyebrows contracting just enough to make her anger clear. Venalise's lack of movement drew Amarynn's attention to the circlet set upon Venalise's head. She ran one finger along its smooth surface. "Like the torc placed on me," she mouthed quietly to herself. Lost in her inspection of Venalise, Amarynn did not notice Jael until he lowered himself beside her.

"The old man says the Empress has already left Lorce. He said he will keep Venalise here, under this dampening spell, until we can collect her. We can go back to Calliway now and send for her."

"You believe them?" Amarynn turned to Jael, her eyebrows raised. Too much had transpired since Athtull for her to blindly accept the word of strangers in a hostile, neighboring land. Moreover, they were willing to offer Venalise as a bargaining chip. They were either very smart, or they were more crooked than the mage herself. "Why?"

"Think about it. They have been betrayed, robbed, and threatened. I don't know all their politics, but this is an opportunity to gain custody of the woman who nearly ruined us both. We are safer with her in our custody. Everyone is."

Rhymere cleared his throat behind them.

Amarynn and Jael rose, turning to face Oravae and her father. But before she tore her gaze from Venalise, her lip curled in a sneer. "Too bad we need you alive. For now."

"My Lord, you are right. I was blind to Vena's intent, but now that my traitor protégée Talamynne has stifled her, you see she can be contained. I do not know in what ways she has wronged you, but I can imagine. I trained her, you know."

"Not helping your case, old man," Amarynn growled, her grip tightening on her dagger.

"I have no interest in you or your kingdom, Traveler. I only want to take back the Stone Reaches from her violent, power-hungry mother and whatever she intends to do with that child. I thought Vena was with me, but sadly, I was wrong."

"We both were, Father." Oravae moved to stand beside Rhymere as he continued.

"I fear Talamynne and her acolytes have fallen prey to Uhll's coercion and are lost to us. A shame." Rhymere shook his head sadly. Then he looked directly at Amarynn. "Help me regain the Spire and I will hold Vena for you. Eventually, you must take her, though. You must take her far away from here."

"Help you regain the Spire?" Amarynn shook her head and grimaced. This was becoming more than she was prepared to do. She did not care to participate in this civil war, but it might be the only way she could get the very thing she came for. "How?"

"Uhll left a small Korr unit here in Lorce," Oravae explained. "Those two outside are part of it. There are those who stand with my father and I, but not enough to subdue all of them. We don't want Uhll to find out, either."

Jael, who had remined quiet, started to interject, but was stayed with a gesture from Amarynn.

"So, you need to rid yourself of them all?" A wicked grin formed on Amarynn's lips. Her growing anxiety-fueled rage needed an outlet. "Besides those two outside, where are the rest of them?"

Oravae met Amarynn's dark expression with one of her own, and a spark of recognition passed between them. "Oh, my," she smiled. "We'd most definitely be friends under different circumstances." She nodded in the direction of the door. "They are in the stables. They've set up their barracks there. All but those two should be there now. Wh—"

But Amarynn had already opened the door, and with practiced efficiency, dispatched both guards with a wide arc of her sword. She wiped her blade on her pants leg and brushed a strand of hair away from her mouth with the back of her hand. She looked back to Oravae as the bodies still jerked on the floor.

"Now, where are the stables?"

Chapter 33

"**A**re you alright, Rynn?"

Jael followed Amarynn's quick pace out of the city gate, jogging to keep up. He couldn't see her face, but the way her shoulders were set and the way she held Frost at the ready told him she was still deep in her battle frenzy. She had not spoken since they left the room with Venalise. The Prince could feel palpable rage in the trail of wild magic she left in her wake. The energy felt like walking behind a hurricane, battering him at the same time it pulled him in.

Amarynn had carved a path of destruction through the barracks in record time, so quickly, it gave Jael pause. He had never witnessed her in her truest form on the front lines — as Crown Prince, his role was to observe so that one day, he could make the battle plans as his father once did. Her skill, combined with the ruthlessness she exhibited, was brutal to watch. Jael's heart broke to see the woman he could not bear to be without lost in so much anguish. With every swing of her sword, her anger, her fear, and her pain delivered deathblow after deathblow. Battle frenzy was etched onto her face and then, like a betting match, it was over. She stood in the middle of the carnage, breaths coming hard and fast, covered in blood spatter from head to toe. He had fully expected to see her magic rise, but oddly, it never did.

"Rynn!" he called as he hurried to catch up with her, reaching out to grab her arm and get her attention. He wasn't prepared for her reaction.

As she spun on him, she grabbed a fistful of his shirt, drawing her towards him. Her eyes were wild, blue magic dancing, as she pressed Frost's heavy edge to his throat.

"Whoa!" Jael threw his hands up and tried to take a step backwards. "Rynn! Wha—"

He remembered that look. At Athtull, after Lors thrust his dagger into her throat, she had remained stoic and focused until the end. Jael would forever remember the moment she lost her control, just before unconsciousness claimed her. Eyes wild, fleeting fear flitted through her eyes just before they closed, and she fell to the floor, inches away from mortality. The memory of her blood spreading on the stone made him sick to his stomach. Now, in those same wild eyes, the fear lingered. Her breaths were fast, her nostrils flaring.

"It's me, Rynn," he whispered with no regard for his own safety. "It's me." Her grip slackened as awareness crept back into her eyes. "That's it," he said, trying to soothe her. "It's done. It's over. We're going home."

Her dagger clattered to the rocky ground as she sagged against him. Her head fell forward to his chest and her body was wracked with sobs. She clutched at his arms, fingers digging into his flesh until she screamed, the sound muffled by Jael's shirt.

"My heart," he breathed, wrapping his arms around her, holding her as the sobs continued. His heart broke again for her, knowing everything she had endured, pretending to be unaffected while she silently crumbled. Seeing Venalise had to have been the last straw.

Amarynn's sobs slowed until she sniffled against his chest.

"I hate what I do," she whispered.

"It can stop," Jael murmured into the auburn curls on top of her head. "You can walk away from all of it."

Amarynn lifted her head and leaned back to look him in the eye. Her watery, red-rimmed eyes and flushed cheeks were a new sight for Jael, and it made his heart break again for her. She ran the back of her hand under her red nose and sniffed as the wind whipped strands of her hair across her face. A throaty call bellowed from the cliffs above.

"Mithras is coming," she rasped, her voice low and rough.

"He can tell you are upset, can't he?" Jael asked, glancing at the sky, then back towards Lorce.

She nodded, wiping her nose again before leaning down to retrieve her dagger and sheath it in the scabbard strapped to her thigh. "He can."

Another call, this time at a different pitch, sounded closer.

"That's different," she said, turning her eyes to the cliffs. "That's not concern. That is anger. He wants to find the child. He wants to destroy her."

"A child?" Jael's brow furrowed.

"If she traveled something, he won't care who she is. His kind remember where they came from, and the kind of magic she is wielding is like poison to them." Amarynn started up the hill, but before she had taken two steps, great wings rose over the rise and Mithras dropped to the ground in front of them. Jael gasped, still dumbfounded by the magnificent beast Amarynn had bonded with.

A looming sense of urgency took hold of him. "Rynn, you can't let him attack this child, and this whole thing depends on Uhll not knowing we were here."

Amarynn bounded up Mithras's leg and held one hand down to Jael. "I will try, but he's not like Dax. I most definitely do not control him."

"Try," Jael grimaced as he pulled himself up beside her. Fleeting memories of the smiling little girl he saw in Athtull Keep drove his sense of urgency higher. "Try hard. She's just a child, and I'll bet she did not have a choice in any of this."

They settled on the dragon's back and he took flight, pumping his wings hard against the chilly air. Jael wrapped his arms around Amarynn and pressed as close as he could to her, willing her all of his strength to try to persuade Mithras to fly towards Karth. He did not dare to anticipate a flight home as Mithras banked to the south, pushing his wings hard to gain altitude, though hope flashed momentarily as their bearing headed directly for the open southern glacial plain.

Amarynn was tense — he could feel it in his chest where she leaned against him — and his concern mounted as Mithras snaked his head to either side, trying to look behind them. The muscles in Amarynn's arms were taught, trembling with strain. Though Jael could not see her face, he knew she was working to convince the dragon not to turn around, but to no avail. Mithras suddenly screamed and banked hard to the right. More calls sounded around them, and half a dozen other dragons appeared in the sky, leveling out near them.

"I can't stop him!" Amarynn yelled over her shoulder. "Hold on!"

Jael tightened his grip and did as she asked as the spires of Lorce slipped past them. The weyr sailed over the low hills in unison, their movements stunningly coordinated. As they glided around the last tall hill protruding from the vast forest of fir trees, Jael spotted the Korr party. There were at least twenty-five horses and no less than fifty soldiers on foot following a small carriage. A tighter contingency of riders near the front signaled the Empress's position. But all of that was made insignificant by the girl on a white pony and what had to be the giant that trailed behind her. A bear cub padded beside the giant, and all three were flanked by soldiers. Jael maintained a tight hold on Amarynn with one hand and pointed toward them with the other.

"There she is!"

Mithras let out a shrill shriek and dove, strafing the party so close that Jael could see their hair whipped by the rush of air as they passed. Shouts and frantic whinnies sounded, then faded into the background as Mithras's wingbeats drowned out the noise, now far below them. Amarynn was hunched forward, her head pressed onto the dragon's back. Jael, one arm wrapped around her waist, leaned to the side to keep his eyes on the girl.

As they turned a slow arc back towards the ground forces, Jael noticed the procession had stopped. Mithras arced around to come at them from the side, then lowered his rear legs and backbeat with his wings to slow his descent. Only three or four dragon-lengths away, he thudded to the ground hard, then dropped low, stalking forward like a cat, his trajectory clearly aimed at Sia and the giant following her.

"No!" Amarynn shouted, sitting upright. "Not the girl, Mithras!"

From the trees, a flock of small birds burst forth, flying directly towards Mithras's head. Jael shielded his eyes and ducked. From beneath his arm, he saw an older, green-robed woman exiting the carriage, arm outstretched. Mithras shook his head against the flock's assault, the ripples down his neck nearly unseating Amarynn and the Prince. Behind them, three other dragons landed, the ground shuddering as their massive forms contacted the hillside.

The robed woman lifted her other arm. Jael braced himself and tightened his grip on Amarynn, but nothing happened for a moment. Then, a dragon behind them screamed, and Jael twisted around to see the tall winter grasses extending and wrapping themselves around its rear legs. The other two dragons found themselves in the same predicament, twisting around to bite and snap at the climbing plants.

"They're wielding with life energy!" Jael slapped Amarynn on the arm and pointed. Flanking the woman, two men stood with their heads bowed, each resting a hand on one of the woman's shoulders. "We can't stay here! I am not strong enough to fight against more than one."

Amarynn twisted around to face him. He knew that glint in her eyes. "Siphon it," she growled.

"I am not taking magic from you, Rynn. You don't know how to meter it yet."

"Why not?" she asked, smirking and narrowing her eyes as she rested one bare hand on his. "Could it kill me?"

Before he could respond, a blast of heat hit them. Mithras stumbled back as Amarynn released Jael's hand and threw her arm up like a shield. He nearly slipped off the dragon's back, but she had hooked her leg around his and the leather strap, squeezing them all in place. Mithras regained his balance and with a cry, rushed forward towards the source of the fire magic. Amarynn leaned low and Jael followed suit; they had no choice at this point but to hang on. Mithras stalked forward, swing his head back and forth, releasing grating screams that sent shockwaves up Jael's spine. More dragons circled in the sky above, answering his call.

A massive black horse bolted from the front of the caravan through the line of soldiers that had formed. An older woman, with a partially shaved head, pointed her spear in their direction. More waves of heated energy assaulted them, forcing Mithras to stop.

"Do something, Jael!" Amarynn shouted.

He didn't know what he could do against multiple wielders, but Amarynn had not thought twice when she burst though the stable doors in Lorce and singlehandedly taken on a room of armed men. This was his fight to win, but Regealth had not taught him how to use the sky magic writhing inside him as a weapon. He had only learned how to keep it under control.

"I can't!" He growled. "We must leave! Tell him! Make him understand!"

Amarynn clenched her jaw and shook her head. She snarled and grabbed his hand again as her eyes flashed with crackling blue energy. As their skin made contact, he felt her burn with cold, stinging energy that coursed through him like a lightning bolt. The Prince did not know what to do with so much power — except to hurl it in the direction of the fire wielder.

Jael heard horses and men scream as bolts of sky magic exploded from his hand. Another blast of heat singed his face, and he responded with even more white-cold bolts, hurling the magic so haphazardly, so frantically, he couldn't even begin to aim. Amarynn was feeding so much into him, he had no choice but to release it however he could.

"Stop!" he screamed at her, but her eyes were closed. Her body, rigid with strain, threatened to fall from the dragon's back, and Jael twisted his free hand through the strap and wrapped his arm around her. The flow of magic was slowing as she depleted herself. Panicked, Jael pried his hand from hers to break the connection, and Amarynn slumped forward against Mithras's neck, completely spent.

"Rynn!" Jael's heart raced as much from the magic as from his fear of what she had done to herself. "Amarynn!" Her head lolled forward, her body slack. As terror threatened to consume him, Mithras let loose a different cry, echoed by all the other dragons. His powerful muscles tensed under the riders, and then they were airborne, his great wings pulling them upward into the sky. Other dragons followed, and as the weyr fell into formation, they all banked to the south. Even as the wind roared past, Jael felt a stillness descend, now that the magic had dissipated. Where they flew, the sky was clear, bright blue with wisps of high clouds.

Jael pulled Amarynn tight to his chest, making sure he felt her breaths. He twisted the strap as tightly as he could, then clung to Amarynn with everything he had left, praying he had enough left in him to hold on, and to get them both home.

CHAPTER 34

I t was the quiet that woke her. Amarynn could never sleep when there was nothing to process in the background; years of Legion service had ingrained that instinct into her. As she opened her eyes, her breath caught when she saw Jael lying next to her. The morning sun's rays fell across his face, highlighting salty streaks running the length of his cheeks. Even in sleep, his face looked tired, his eyes a little sunken and surrounded by faded dark circles.

With considerable effort, she reached out with an arm that felt like lead and traced the line of his jaw. Tears welled in her eyes as she realized this man had never once considered the possibility that they would not be together. He never doubted. Not when he was on his way to another kingdom to meet his bride, not even when his father, the King, commanded him.

But she had.

Amarynn fought the shame that rose up as she remembered her night with Aron. Not shame of being with the other Traveler, but shame for not believing as Jael had. He had been steadfast — she had not. Aron had given her the release she needed, and perhaps being with him let her satisfy the longing for Jael she thought she had tucked away for good. But now, here they were, together.

Jael's eyes fluttered open when she slid her thumb over his cheek, trying to brush away the salt stains. Relief softened his tightly knitted brows and he reached for her, pulling her close.

"You are awake," he breathed. "You're awake," he murmured against her cheek.

"I'm alright," she whispered back, though she felt like she could go back to sleep for days.

Jael leaned back on the rough pillow, one hand still resting on her cheek. "Regealth warned that you might not wake. He went inside your mind and couldn't find you." Jael nearly choked on his last words.

"Hey," Amarynn tried to soothe him "I'm here. Right here, where I should be," she added quietly.

Jael locked eyes with her. "Yes. Where we both should be: by each other's sides."

Amarynn tried to raise up onto one arm, but she didn't have the strength. Jael moved his hand to her shoulder and gently eased her back down.

"He said you will need some time to recover." He slid his hand to the back of her neck, gripping it. His expression darkened. "Never do that again."

"Do what?" She knew exactly what he meant, but admitting it was not her style.

"Try to give me your magic. This isn't war and magic is not one of your blades. You don't know how to manage it, and it nearly took you from me."

"But I'm immort—"

"Your body is immortal, Rynn, not your mind. You could've been lost. Forever."

Amarynn averted her eyes. Her recklessness never had consequences like this before. She rolled to her back and stared at the ceiling, breathing heavily from the effort. It was rough-hewn wood, not the well-crafted rafters of the castle. She let her eyes wander the room and was surprised to find they were in her quarters near the barracks. "I'm—"

Jael seemed to notice her surprise. "I wanted you to feel as comfortable as you could when you woke."

"How long have I been here?" She looked down across her body. When she woke, she hadn't realized she was dressed in a clean shirt that looked like Jael's, the blood and dirt no longer staining her hands.

"It's been a week and a half."

"Goddess," she breathed. Memories brimming with blood and magic, cold and hate flooded back, and she struggled to sit up, but her head spun and she reached for Jael to steady herself. Her heart was racing. "Mithras? Where is he?"

"After we landed here, he took off. I have heard him and the others and seen them a few times. I think he is close."

"Dax?" She was suddenly consumed with need for the smell of her horse and the feel of his soft coat on her cheek.

"Aron did as he said he would. Dax is here and getting fat with the broodmares."

At the mention of Aron's name, Amarynn winced, but tried to hide her reaction.

"What is it?" Jael sat up beside her.

"N-nothing. I'm just dizzy and sore," she lied. "My muscles ache."

"You held a death grip on me for quite a long time. Regealth says you channeled the equivalent of a hundred lightning strikes. It would have killed anyone else."

Amarynn smirked tiredly and tapped her chest. "See? Immortal."

Jael scoffed as he swung his legs over the edge of the bed, shaking his head. He rubbed his face and stood, turning to take her face in his hands. His grey eyes were tired, but the corners relaxed as he smiled. "You are impossible." He leaned down and their lips met with more urgency than the last time. But it was short-lived. "You need food. Lay back down. I'll be right back."

Jael slipped on his boots and left the room, but not before another glance back at her. His relief was palpable. Amarynn pulled her knees up and crossed her arms over them. Only a handful of days ago, she had been running from Calliway and from Jael. The injustices done to her and the other Travelers were beginning to harden her heart and strengthen her resolve to walk away. Even her night with Aron was another giant step she had taken away from this life. But like an unbreakable tether, Jael had reeled her back to him.

Amarynn took her time lifting her legs over the edge of the bed. She wasn't in pain, but her muscles were stiff from inactivity. Carefully, she stood and padded to the single window. The practice yard was quiet.

A pair of soft leather breeches lay across the stool by the door. She pulled them on, then lay her hand on the door handle and turned it, the cool metal feeling odd in her hand. Outside, she walked barefoot across the frosty ground toward the stables. It was cold, but the stables weren't far. With each step, her body began to warm, strength returning to her limbs.

Dax's shrill whinny awakened something inside of her, quickening her pace. She entered the empty stable, opened the door to his stall, and slipped inside. Running her hand over his velvet nose, she breathed out, letting all the tension fall away. Her other hand rubbed his neck, entwining her fingers in his mane. Someone had brushed it, adding tiny braids along the ridge. She smiled; it suited him.

She leaned her head against the soft spot at the top of neck and breathed in. Dax's scent was simple, and it was safe. It was what she remembered from when she first found him in the forest so many years ago. It was what comforted her when she rode away from Karth after Matteus's attack, and now, it was what brought her back to herself. He dropped his head and blew out softly as if to say *I've got you,* and that stirred a well of tremendous guilt. She shuddered. She had abandoned him for Mithras.

"I'm sorry," she whispered.

"He forgave you days ago." A familiar voice came from behind, and her heart dropped.

Amarynn turned. "Thank you for getting him home, Aron." She searched his face.

The Traveler's mouth turned up, but not quite in a smile. "It was nothing. That horse will do anything for honey brittle." His ice-blue eyes held hers for a long moment with a mix of relief and regret that made her look away. When she looked back, she saw that his hands gripped a bridle. Amarynn looked closer. Aron was dressed for travelling, a pack slung over his shoulder.

"Where are you going?"

"I'm leading the party to Lorce to retrieve Venalise." He leaned against the stall's post and crossed his arms. "I'll be taking Finn and Stavin, and the little fire priest with me."

"Xan?"

"No," he shook his head. "Plinus."

"Plinus is *here?*" She thought he had been lost in the fall.

"He is. Survived the fall at Athtull and made it here on foot, apparently." Aron gestured to her bare feet. "Aren't you cold?"

Amarynn followed his gaze and considered his question. They weren't cold at all. Strange.

Aron stepped inside and reached for her. She stiffened, her breath catching, but instead of an embrace, he plucked a piece of straw from her shirt. "You still look fetching in the straw," he murmured, a soft smile playing on his lips. His eyes lingered for a moment, then he adjusted the pack on his shoulder and turned away. Amarynn wanted to say something, but he was gone before the words could form on her lips.

Dax nickered behind her.

"I know," she said to herself. "He's hurt. And it's my fault."

She gave him another pat before leaving the stall and returning to her quarters with a renewed energy. When she opened the door, the Prince was there with a wooden platter of food, and Regealth was with him.

"My girl!" the old mage exclaimed, looking her up and down. "You should not be out of bed."

"She went to see Dax," Jael chuckled. "I'd bet on it."

Amarynn nodded. "I did. I saw Aron, too. He's going to Lorce?

Jael took her arm and guided her back to her bed. "He is. He volunteered."

Of course he did. She sat on the edge.

"He said Plinus was going, too. Is that wise?" Venalise had controlled and used the priest for years until he was able to escape her control with the help of Regealth and Jael.

Regealth eased into the chair beside the bed. He took a moment to rearrange his robes, then stroked his beard in thought. "No one can anticipate her magic better than him. From what I can gather, the magic they're using to stifle her could wane as they leave the Reaches. My duty is to be here with you and help you understand the magic you now possess." He raised his eyebrows. "It seems you are to be my student once again. But for now, you still need rest. We will begin our work after the coronation."

Amarynn shifted her attention to Jael. She had completely forgotten about his father.

"It's true, then. You were right."

He nodded. "Vhaleesian poison. Ehrinell saw it coming. Apparently, she tried to warn him, but his arrogance got the better of him. At least my mother listened." He sighed and shook his head as he sat down beside Amarynn. "She is heartbroken that this was the work of her home kingdom. Her best estimation is they struck while I was gone to gain the advantage of the heir's absence."

"Prince Jael will take the monarch's vows this evening," Regealth said. "We need a show of competency and strength."

Jael took Amarynn's hands. "If you are able, I want you there beside me."

"What about the Travelers? Their bond — is it broken?" She looked to Regealth, then back at Jael. "I wouldn't know. I'm bonded to you."

"No one has mentioned it, but—"

"Everyone here is loyal to Karth, bond or not," Amarynn interrupted. "What about those who aren't?"

"What do you mean?" Jael released Amarynn's hands and stood.

"Was Matteus on that ship with you? Cam, the other traitor Traveler? What about his pathetic *mortal* cronies?" Amarynn rose beside him and reached for her sword belt hanging on the wall.

"Matteus? Yes, they wer..." Jael trailed off as Amarynn's words registered. "Do you think they knew?"

"I don't really care if they knew," Amarynn said. "Think, Jael. They are on the way to Vhaleese — the kingdom responsible for your father's death. Matteus is on that ship, with Travelers that follow him. And now they are no longer loyal to Karth." She slung the scabbard belt around her waist and buckled it, a renewed energy taking hold even as she swayed from lingering dizziness. She crossed the room and snatched up her boots, dropping onto a stool to pull them on. "Good Legion men and women are in the middle of the ocean with a ship full of immortals, Matteus and his cronies being some of them." She made for the door.

"Wait!" Jael blocked the door with his hand. "What are you going to do?"

"Get Mithras and go," she snapped. "I can't just sit here and wait."

"Why?"

Amarynn pushed Jael's hand away and clenched her jaw.

"Because Bent is on that ship."

"Little falcon."

Sia looked up from the table in her room.

"Yes, *emmisana*?"

"Are you ready for your lessons?"

"Yes, *emmisana*, I am." Sia stood and gestured to Thera to follow her. "What will I learn today?" She smiled to herself. Her Ceadari was getting better.

"Today you will practice with Talamynne, not learn from me." Uhll waited for Sia to reach her side before she turned to leave the room. She held out her hand to the child, who took it. "Your Tior seems lonely. I think it is time for him to have a friend. Do you agree?"

"Yes, *emmisana*," Sia smiled. "I do."

Dramatis Personae

Amarynn (Am-uh-rinn) Immortal Traveler of the Legion of Karth

Aron (Air-un) Immortal Traveler of the Legion of Karth

Bent (Bent) Blademaster and mentor to Amarynn

Cam (Kam) Immortal Traveler of the Legion of Karth

Dyaneth (Dye-uh-neth) Sky mage wielder, late sister of King Lasten of Karth

Ehrinell (Air-uh-nell) Immortal Traveler of the Legion of Karth

ENDRIC (IN-DRICK) IMMORTAL TRAVELER OF THE LEGION OF KARTH

ESSIK (ESS-ICK) FIRST TRAVELER OF KARTH AND DEFECTOR FROM THE LEGION

FINN (FINN) IMMORTAL TRAVELER OF THE LEGION OF KARTH

JAEL (JAIL) CROWN PRINCE OF KARTH, FIRST AND ONLY SON OF KING LASTEN AND QUEEN FERAMIN

KING LASTEN (LASS-TIN) RULER OF THE KINGDOM OF KARTH AND FATHER OF JAEL

KING LORS (LORS) SELF-PROCLAIMED KING OF THE DARK-LANDS AND RULER OF ATHTULL KEEP

LUCAS (LU-KUS) RANKING MEMBER OF THE HOUSE SUHONNE OF THE STONE REACHES EMPIRE

MATTEUS (MUH-TAY-US) IMMORTAL TRAVELER OF THE LEGION OF KARTH

NIOLL (NYE-ULL) LEGION MAN

Omman (Oh-mahn) Sea captain of the Blackfly

Oravae (Or-uh-vay) Daughter of Rhymere, child-hood friend of Venalise

Plinus (Ply-nis) Lakrim Pries of the Far Handaals

Queen Feramin (Fair-uh-min) A native of the island nation of Vhaleese, Queen of the Kingdom of Karth, and mother of Jael

Regealth (Reg-elth) Water mage wielder

Rhymere (Rye-meer) Patriarch and Master Scholar of the Spire in Lorce, the former mentor of Venalise

Ruidel (Roo-ih-del) Scholar of the Spire studying under Talamynne

Sia (See-ya) Child sold to Omman as a ship's deckhand stolen by Venalise

Silahn (Cee-lan) Scholar of the Spire studying under Talamynne

STAVIN (STAY-VIN) IMMORTAL TRAVELER OF THE LEGION OF KARTH

T' KORR UHLL (TUH-CORE-UHLL) EMPRESS OF THE STONE REACHES EMPIRE, MATRIARCH OF THE WARRIOR HOUSE KORR

T' SUHONNE SASHTRA (TUH-SOO-HONE SASH-TRUH) RANKING MEMBER OF THE RANGER HOUSE SUHONNE OF THE STONE REACHES EMPIRE

T' SUHONNE STEFFA (TUH-SOO-HONE STEF-UH) MATRIARCH OF THE RANGER HOUSE SUHONNE OF THE STONE REACHES EMPIRE, VENALISE'S AUNT

TALAMYNNE (TAL-A-MINN) SCHOLAR OF THE SPIRE IN LORCE

TASAR (TUH-SAR) KORR WARRIOR, VENALISE'S COUSIN

VENALISE, AKA T'KORR VENA (VEN-UH-LEESE) EARTH MAGE WIELDER, DAUGHTER OF T'KORR UHLL

WAKE (WAKE) IMMORTAL TRAVELER OF THE LEGION OF KARTH

XAN (ZAN) APPRENTICE MAGE TO REGEALTH

THE IMMORTAL TRAVELERS OF KARTH

Ehrinell, second female Traveler – 16th year
Cam, 17th Year
Endric, 18th Year
Dallin, 19th Year
Rell, 20th Year
Garren, 21th Year
Davet, 22st Year
Aron, 23rd Year

Turn the page for exclusive content.

WAR HORSE

An
Immortal Coil Saga
Origin Story

WAR HORSE - THE FALL

The air smelled of blood and churned soil as a group of riders, followed by war-ravaged men on foot, picked their way across the uneven battlefield. A maze of human and equine corpses made their travel painstakingly slow. One horse trailed behind the other riders, the trudging foot soldiers nearly overtaking it.

"Easy, Mallen," the lame horse's rider whispered, rubbing the sorrel's neck. The woman pulled back on the reins to slow him to a stop.

"Oi!" one of the soldiers barked, slapping at the stallion's flank. "Get out of the way!"

The rider vaulted off the horse's back, bloodied boots landing hard in the mud. Her auburn braids whipped against the man's face as she came nose-to-nose with him.

"That horse has more honor and has seen more bloodshed than you will ever hope to—you *puke*!" she growled, pushing the soldier back so that he stumbled and landed hard on the ground. The woman gripped the hilt of the short sword at her side. "Show some respect," she hissed through clenched teeth.

The man said no more but offered a glare and a grunt as his compatriots pulled him back to his feet. The men continued, and as the last of them moved past her, she turned back to her mount. She ran her hand along his heaving side until her fingers curled in his coarse and tangled mane. A paste of thick, dried blood descended from behind his left ear. Mallen had taken a massive blow from an enemy great sword when the Legion of Karth advanced on Ardwyn's forces. The advancing line of horses fought in close quarters with Ardwyn's infantry. An officer, by the looks of his armor, had engaged with her, swinging his sword wildly. The blade had found purchase at the top of the crinet, just where his ears protruded. Now, that ear hung forward, useless.

She let her hand fall as Mallen shifted his weight and sighed, blowing a deep breath as he lowered his head. She brushed away some of the mud and found another wound – this one more grave – gaping across his chest.

"Amarynn!"

She lifted her head toward the voice calling her name. Claas, the newest Traveler, sat atop his mount Korro, her horse's twin. Amarynn was close enough to discern the other Traveler's dark expression and knitted brow.

"Go!" she called back. "I'll catch up."

Another deep sigh pulled her attention back to Mallen. She turned just in time to watch him groan and fall to his front knees. The stallion's hind legs followed until he was on his side, his breaths increasingly shallow.

He was done. She knelt beside his head, her free hand rifling through the stallion's mane. Her fingers traced down his jaw to the buckle on his bridle, and she quickly worked the leather and brass, pulling it away from his head gently enough to let him work his tongue and teeth free of the bit. Amarynn closed her eyes and pulled the dagger from her thigh sheath, her eyes wandering to the battlefield before she shifted to the other side of Mallen's head.

So many fallen.

"And you with them, friend," she whispered as she slipped her blade beneath the soft edge of his ear. With a deep, shaky breath, she thrust the dagger down, wincing at the feel of parting muscle and bone. He stiffened for the slightest second, then went slack. Amarynn withdrew her blade and gripped his forelock. She took a few strands of his dark brown hair with a quick flick of her wrist. "No more war for you, friend. You are free."

Low thunder rumbled where dark clouds gathered in the distance as Amarynn stood and wiped her dagger on her breeches. She tucked the strands of hair into a small pouch on her belt as Bent, her Legion Blademaster, trotted towards her on his horse.

"Was it that bad that he couldn't be saved?" he asked, frowning.

She cast a glance back at Mallen's still form in the mud. Saving him would have been possible. They could have treated him in Calliway, though the journey home would have been excruciating. But why force him to suffer when being on this battlefield wasn't even his choice?

"No," she lied. "The edges were turning. Infection would likely set in before we got back." She took a step to try and block his view of Mallen's wounds.

With a deep sigh and a shake of his head, Bent turned his mount toward the front of the line.

"Don't leave your gear. Since we have to find you another horse, it'll be on me if we have to replace your tack, too," he said over his shoulder before urging his horse into a canter. As he reached the group ahead, she heard him bark orders at the last supply wagon. The group continued moving forward, but the rear wagon stood still. Amarynn rubbed her face in her hands and then removed her tooled leather saddle. The bridle lay in the mud, but she left it there – a symbol marking Mallen's release. One of the men shouted something in her direction, but she wasn't listening. Hoisting the heavy saddle over her shoulder, she began to trudge up the hill. It was going to be a long ride home.

WAR HORSE - THE RISE

The sun rose and set twice while the Legion marched to Calliway. The rain hadn't let up, making a soggy slog of their travel through the foothills of the Dark Mountains. Amarynn sat on the back of the wagon, one leg dangling over the unlatched tongue. Bent, who had kept his distance while she brooded, finally approached.

"We've got two spirited mares broken and ready for training back in Calliway. One's a wee bit on the small side, but the other," he chuckled, "she a big, brute of a thing. She'd suit y-"

"I'm not thinking about horses right now, Bent."

The blademaster cocked his head to the side. "And how will you be advancing with the vanguard the next time? On foot?"

Amarynn sighed and closed her eyes as her mentor continued.

"Lass, war horses are meant for battle. But even the most sure-footed don't live as long as Mallen. He was rare." He leaned low in his saddle, his voice low. "I know he was your first horse, but you'd better get used to this, given your lifespan."

"I'll never get used to it." Her eyes were open now, anger surging. "No matter how long I live. I'll survive it, unfortunately, but I'll never accept it."

She leaned back against the high wagon side, effectively signaling she had finished the conversation. Bent pursed his lips and frowned but turned his mount and spurred it forward around the wagon. When he was out of sight, Amarynn let her head drop. If only she were a supply runner with no other care in the world for a moment. What a life it would be to know that war was temporary if you survived.

The sound of laughter and hoofbeats caught her attention as Claas and Wake trotted towards the wagon.

"Rynn!" red-headed Claas called out. "Save me from Wake's foul mood!"

He clutched at his chest dramatically while the ever-stoic Wake stared straight ahead, unamused by the other Traveler's humor. She offered them a half smile.

"I'm afraid my mood's no better, friend," she replied as the two Travelers passed. Amarynn twisted to let both legs dangle off the back of the wagon. She leaned back on a pile of bedrolls and let her thoughts wander. Memories of Mallen, fresh and untested, flashed in her mind. He had been challenging to train, but the payoff was in his skill and speed. He was the first to charge and quick in the frenzy of swordplay. Finding another horse with the same skill and spirit would be monumentally difficult.

When the caravan pulled to the side of the road, the daylight had faded, and the rain had dissipated, leaving only a fine mist rising off the warm ground.

Her legs ached.

She grabbed her sword belt and slipped off the wagon's tongue. The scraggly tree line tempted her with respite from camp preparations, so she accepted the dark shadows' invitation, slipping into the hedges.

Quiet rustling and birdsong masked the clatter of camp preparations. The air was still, damp, and so thick that it felt like a cool blanket draped over her shoulders. She kept her blades sheathed as she crept further into the trees. Her chest still felt heavy with sorrow for Mallen, but she had finally found solace in her gift to him.

"A gift of peace," she whispered to no one.

She continued with no purpose except to stretch her legs and escape confrontation with her compatriots. The light was rapidly fading, and if it weren't for a biting chill in the air, she would have gladly spent the night amongst the trees. However, as she rounded a thick brace of saplings, a rustling in the deep brush caught her attention. Heavy breaths punctuated the swishing and shaking of limbs and leaves as she neared. She slowed her steps and drew her short sword as a precaution while she pushed past vines and tangled branches.

A loud snort and stamping feet startled her. Whatever it was, it was big. The foliage shook, and then she heard a snort and a whinny.

With her heartbeat quickening at the sounds of a horse, she ducked through the remaining brush, her pace quickening as the animal grunted and squealed. Flashes of pale yellow signaled she was close.

She pushed through the last bit of brush, not expecting to find herself in the presence of the largest horse she had ever seen snared and tangled in the brambles. A half-broken bridle pulled at an awkward angle while vines and brambles wrapped around its legs and tail. Eyes wide and rolling, he pulled back harder when she stepped into view.

"Easy, now," she cooed, easing forward with one hand outstretched. The horse stopped pulling but stamped his front hooves in a warning. As he stood panting and blowing out flared nostrils, she could tell he was a stallion – young and well-muscled, but his golden coat was dirty and covered in lacerations. She took another step closer. "You're safe now, my boy."

She began removing the tangled plants and branches from his golden tail and legs one by one, and as she did, more injuries revealed themselves. Amarynn's breath caught as she saw fresh burns and other scars that became more apparent as she unwrapped the sticky foliage.

"Who did this to you?" Amarynn murmured as she stood and ran her hand along his flank. He quivered and flicked his tail anxiously. She let her eyes wander over his massive form. She moved along his side to his head, and as she ran her hand over his soft white nose, he mouthed the bit in his mouth. He was young by the look of his teeth.

Finally, she reached his head, unraveling the sticks and brush, tugging the leather halter back over his ear. The tack bore the stamp of Ardwyn, the kingdom they left broken on the battlefield the day before. This horse must have been a part of their cavalry and gotten loose in the battle frenzy, though he bore no girth marks, which was odd.

Gripping the halter, she attempted to back him out of the mess of trees, fully expecting him to bolt when he was in the open, but instead, he dropped his head and pushed it into her chest.

"You're welcome," she said, rubbing him between the ears. He raised his head, golden brown eyes fixed on her. It was apparent now that he was trained and was waiting for her directive. Amarynn didn't hesitate. The forces of Ardwynn had claimed her beloved Mallen, so she would claim this horse as recompense. She wrapped her fingers around the halter, and as she did, she noticed lettering stamped into the cheekpiece. Some of it was scorched and unreadable, but three letters were clear.

DAX

"Dax it is," she murmured. Amarynn patted his neck, smoothing his tangled mane while she leaned against him, breathing in his scent. "I'm sorry you found me," she murmured. "I only bring death."

He stamped his front hooves and shook his head, stepping forward.

"Alright," she said, a half-smile on her lips. "But you choose. Follow me, and death may come to you sooner than you would like. Or —" She turned and surveyed the forest surrounding them. "Stay out here and be free."

Amarynn's hand dropped to her side, and she took one step, then another. Her eyes were fixed on the ground as she listened for hoofbeats behind her, but it remained quiet. She took another few steps, then smiled when the rustle of dry leaves indicated he was following.

She turned as he approached, his head up now, ears pricked forward. Amarynn ran her hand over his neck and picked up the dangling reins. He bobbed his head up and down, then snorted. Amarynn looked him over one more time before turning back towards camp.

"Legion life is dark, my boy. Let's you and I be each other's light, shall we?"

ACKNOWLEDGEMENTS

And just like that, there were two. The first book in The Immortal Coil Saga was born in the crucible of my life at its most unpredictable. The Gate was a journey riddled with joy, tragedy, and everything in between. So, to say that my paradigm shifted as I wrote The Mage Crown would be an understatement.

I could write another eighty thousand words and still not adequately thank all the beautiful humans who supported me as I embarked on my quest to complete book two. Scott, your unwavering encouragement to keep pushing and putting words on paper kept me focused and motivated. My parents, children, colleagues, friends, and new-found community of indie authors – you all made this possible with your endless encouragement and support. Even my Jackson Middle School students kept me motivated to finish. Thank you, 5th-period eighth-grade science students!

Thank you to my editor, Karen, and cover artist, Konstance. Karen, you challenge me to be a better writer whenever I sit at the keyboard. You ask the best questions, and you are a champion for bear equality in literature. Konstance, your vision and your ability to read my mind is remarkable. You must keep a secret summer home in Karth because you know it so well.

Finally, I want to thank my snaggle-tooth, fruit bat, bestest boy, Dax. You live forever in the brave and loyal spirit of Amarynn's war horse. May you have all the peanut butter and possums you can handle, and may your rear end never itch again. I will always love you, Daxtacular.

About The Author

Escapism is her drug of choice. As a child, she was angry that her existence was confined to this reality, and she did everything she could to find a way out. Stories made it bearable. Whether it was Thor's Bifrost, Narnia's wardrobe, or the mirror in Stephen R. Donaldson's *Mordant's Need* duology, she was hooked. Now, she tells her own stories of escape. She creates and invites others to find solace, adventure, love, and passion in fantasy realms, outer space, and reinvented parallel realities. This door is always open.

B.G. Vandenberg has always written stories. She works as a middle school science instructional coach in Texas and has three grown children, a loving partner, her dog named Scout, and three exceptionally unusual cats.

She can be found at:
https://www.thebookishberg.com
FB: B.G. Vandenberg, Author
TT: @bgvandenbergauthor
IG: @bgvandenbergauthor